One Shot

A.C. Wonderland

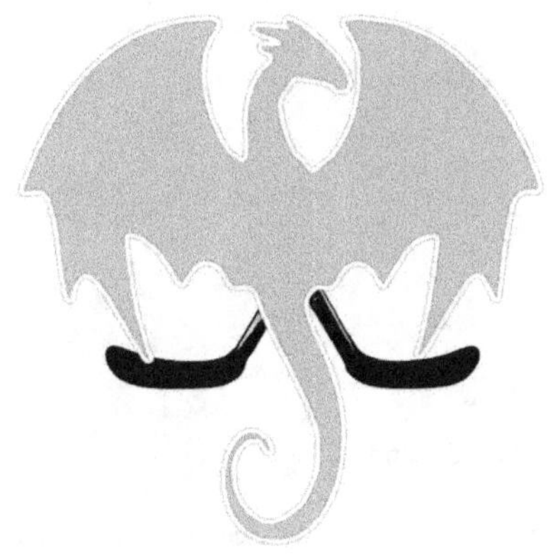

For the girl in the mirror who never put herself first, never felt good enough, and surrounded herself with people who made her feel that way—you have always been more than good enough. You wrote a damn book.

For anyone who has experienced a relationship fueled by toxicity and laced with any type of abuse. You are not alone. You matter. You are more than what that vile person makes you feel. Your story deserves a happy ending. Never forget that.

One Shot

A.C. Wonderland

Playlist

Chapter Thirty-Seven
Fix What You Didn't Break by Nate Smith

Chapter Thirty-Nine
All About It by Dylan Marlowe

Chapter Forty
Show Me Around by Carly Pearce

Chapter Forty-Two
When I Look Back by Dylan Marlowe

Chapters Forty-Five + Forty-Six
Almost by Thomas Rhett

Listen on Spotify

Prologue
Laur

"One shot!" Nick roars in his best douchey jock impression—which not so surprisingly sounds similar to his real voice. I came up to West Michigan University for my brother's first game of the season. As soon as I dropped my bags off at his house, he whisked me off to lunch and some surprise. Mom would be here in a few days with our stepdad, Dominic.

I can't help but question where the hell my brother is taking me as I step out of his F-150 into an empty parking lot of a small building with darkened windows and no signage. He can sense my unease but chuckles and pulls me towards the entrance. If Nick's taking me here, it can't be as seedy as it looks from the outside, right?

My big brother is my best friend. Growing up, people would mistake us for twins but now, our friends joke that we are as weirdly close as twins typically are. I would do anything for Nick, and I know, even though he refuses to let me date any of his friends, I mean the world to him too.

Nick might have a few inches on me and his shaggy light brown hockey flow is lighter in color than my long brown wavy locks, but we both have the famous Bellinger smile. The smile that takes over a room with one grin—or so I've been told. We also both share an obsession beyond love for hockey.

Nick thrusts the door open of the seedy building, which I instantly see is far from sketchy. There's a chic lounge area. Then I notice the trendy tattoo sign. We're at a tattoo shop! I can't help but squeal in excitement.

"NO WAY!"

Nick must have had tattoo appointments booked for the two of us for weeks. He starts to tell me about how this is the top tattoo shop within fifty miles, despite the grim outside appearance. We've talked about getting tattoos for as long as I can remember—matching ones to be exact. We both wanted something to symbolize not only our love for hockey, but for our dad who passed when we were young. Nick had other ideas beyond the one matching tattoo.

"I'm not getting 'one shot' tattooed on me, Nicholas. That's yours and Dad's thing. I'm not a hockey-bro and never will be!" I wince as I hear the tattoo gun turn on. "Aren't you worried about having to play tonight with a sore arm from those tattoos?" I almost screamed the last word as the tattoo gun pierces my skin now. I'm terrified of needles.

"One shot!" Nick replies. He notices me wince, rolling his eyes.

"Toughen up, Chip," he laughs but takes my outstretched hand in his.

He didn't even flinch when he got both of his tattoos done before me. What a showoff.

'One shot' is what Dad would always say to Nick after every hockey game, every practice, every loss, every win. All it takes is one shot to change your entire life. You could be one shot away from your dreams. Why not take it? What's holding you back? You are always one shot away from being your best self, being the best player, or reaching your goal. That's all it takes—just one shot.

I've believed in my big brother more than I've believed in anyone or anything. I knew as soon as he signed on the dotted line of his NHL contract after he graduated West Michigan next school year that I would also get the "one shot" tattoo without any convincing needed. It's the best way I can think of to congratulate him and celebrate his biggest accomplishment and goal since he could skate —playing for the NHL.

Dad passed when I was only six. The memory of feeling the scratch of his stubble when he kissed my cheek goodbye before heading on the road for a hockey game is starting to slip away. It seems like more pieces of him fade the older I get. Sometimes I wonder if the memories I have of him are really mine or just stories that other people have told me. But one thing I am sure of is that Dad was a hockey legend, and Nick is following in his footsteps.

"Done!" the tattoo artist declares five minutes later.

"Wow, that was fast," Nick says.

I'm thinking the opposite. It was the most pain I've ever been in. Well, almost the worst.

I hold my arm out to admire the small tattoo. Nick's forearm gleams with fresh black ink. He holds it out to mine, showing the phrase 'one shot' on his forearm and a wyvern below it. The wyvern above my wrist is almost a perfect replica of his, but in fresh white ink that still looks bright and bold against my fading summer tan. Nick refused to get white ink—his hair wasn't the only thing fairer than mine. He took after our dad's Eastern European side more than I did.

When Dad played college hockey, he played for the West Michigan Wyverns. Nick just so happens to be captain of that team now. Dad was captain his senior year, but Nick made captain his junior year—the only junior captain in Wyverns' history.

"For Dad," Nick says.

"And for the new captain. I hear he's only a junior?!" I tease. "Congrats, Nicky. Dad would be so proud. I am so proud."

His broad, muscular arms pull me in for a tight hug. I squeeze him back tight. I can't wait to watch his first game as captain. I hope that I get to transfer to West Michigan next year to be a part of it all.

Chapter One
Laur

They say that God doesn't give you anything you can't handle, but the two worst moments in my life happened within twenty-four hours of each other, turning me into a shell of a person. Physically, I'm alive. My heart is still beating. My brain is still functioning, but my body and my heart are in excruciating pain. I am bruised, broken, and shattered—just like the pieces of the windshield scattered along the interstate. That windshield used to be attached to my brother's F-150 less than ten seconds ago.

The memory of when Nick got that truck plays like a movie in my head. It was a few months after his fifteenth birthday. The piece of crap was rusted, barely functional. Mom said she had no idea how he even drove it seventeen miles home from the old man's shop. Nick spent every free minute he had between school and hockey working on that truck. Mom and I didn't think he could do it by himself. But he kept at it.

Eight months later, he called me out to the garage. I could hear the excitement in his voice and see the pride in his blue eyes, the same color as mine. The truck didn't have any more rust. Except the ironic paint color he chose was pretty damn close to a rust color. He turned the key in the ignition, and it purred to life. "Runs smoother than silk," he said.

My draw dropped, audibly cracking, as I caught the keys he threw at me.

"Once around the block. Don't tell mom or you'll walk to school every day for the rest of your life," Nick said.

My cheeks hurt from smiling so wide. I can't believe he was going to let me drive his precious car he worked so hard on. I wasn't even fifteen yet, but Mom was away at a conference.

Best big brother ever.

The movie of the memory starts to get fuzzy as if someone smudged the camera lens. The edges of my vision begin to fade. Nick's smiling face as I drive his car down our street is overtaken by small spots. The world seems to be covered in blurry film. Then, everything goes black.

Suddenly, I am an astral projection immersed in a new memory watching the conversation play over and over in my head.

I'm in the passenger seat of Nick's truck. He's fuming with anger even after winning his first game as captain. It's my fault. My heart feels like it is beating in my stomach but is begging to come up my throat.

"How could this happen?"

"I knew I shouldn't have told you. Just forget about it!"

"Like hell I'll forget about it. Of course you should tell me. You should tell the damn police Lauren. You should press charges!"

"I'm sorry, Nick. I'm ruining your big night and your big win. I'm sorry."

"Stop apologizing, Laur. You didn't do anything. I'm glad you told me. You should have told me a long time ago that this was happening."

The sleeve of my sweatshirt is damp from wiping away my tears. My heart is pounding so loudly I am certain Nick can hear it. I close my eyes, swallowing back my raw emotion but the lump in my throat refuses to budge. My mind starts to shut down, wanting to escape the emotional trauma, while my body gives in to crying so hard that my body convulses and it's difficult to breathe. I start coughing, choking on my tears.

Nick takes off his seat belt to pull me in and comfort me. His breath is sharp, quick and intense. His body shakes with rage as he pulls me in. I can feel his heart thumping in his chest. I hear him start to take slow breaths, willing himself to calm down, but it doesn't seem to be working. This is my fault. Nick feels this way because of me.

"I'm going to kill him, Laur."

"Nick, put on your seat belt. Jesus. NICK!"

"Laur. Lauren, look at me. I swear to God and any other higher being in existence, he is going to be—"

"NICK! THAT SEMI IS GOING TO—"

A loud booming sound interrupts me. Then everything goes black again.

I hear commotion. The pain is unbearable. I can't move any part of my body. I remember being in Nick's truck, after his first game as captain. They won. They beat—no—they slaughtered the Eagles. My head is throbbing. It's not black anymore, but my whole world is extremely blurry, as if I am looking through an unfocused camera lens. I can barely make out anything.

Where am I?

I blink, and the world starts to come slowly into focus. I see Nick's F-150 on its side, just feet in front of me. The windshield of Nick's most prized possession is in millions of pieces. I look down and see shards of the glass poking out from my arms. *Is there glass in my legs?!* I'm unsure, but I realize I can't feel my legs. Nausea takes over.

A loud ear-piercing ring fills the air—the kind in movies where the damsel in distress is about to black out. I try to turn my head, but it won't move. I try to focus on moving just my eyes and look to the right. I can make out more glass and pieces of rust colored metal from Nick's car. Wincing in pain, I force my head to turn to the left.

If I could make a sound, my scream would shatter the glass fragments scattered along the highway into pieces so small you wouldn't be able to see them. Goose bumps flood my skin, as I turn ice cold. I couldn't feel my legs before, but now my entire body—my entire being—is numb as shock starts to take over.

A few feet away, I see a figure on the ground with limbs jutting out at odd angles that look inhuman. That can't possibly be a person, can it? I take in the light brown shaggy hair of a boy. Wait. It *is* a person. My eyes almost bulge out of my head as they take in the black wyvern tattoo on the figure's arm. It's Nick. My brother is sprawled across the pavement. He's stiller than I have ever seen him in my life.

I feel the damsel in distress blackout coming fast.

I hear a faint voice. "Don't move. She's alive! Get the medics over here!"

I try to fight the drowsiness that has taken over, but it's quickly pulling me in.

"Nick . . . Nick, my brother." I try to squeak out the words as I am lifted onto a stretcher.

"He's gone," someone eerily whispers. The voice sounds familiar, like what I remember my Dad's voice sounding like.

Everything finally goes completely black as I slip into unconsciousness.

The Next Day

My throat is dry. My eyes are heavy, sticky, hard to open. After what feels like an hour, I finally get my eyes to listen to my brain. I take in the plain white walls and small window. I can see a blue sky outside, but inside it feels like a horrific storm came through. My body won't move. I look down. Bandages cover what appears to be every inch of my body. My left arm is encased in a cast. There's a loud beeping sound coming from the machines that I am hooked up to. They beep louder as my panic sets in. A man in scrubs comes into the room. His eyes grow wide with enthusiasm as he realizes that I'm awake.

"You're awake! Lauren, you've been in a bad accident. You are in the ICU at St. Nicholas Hospital. We are going to make sure you are okay."

He pushes a button on the wall, and the room swarms with what I assume to be nurses. Machines are still loudly beeping.

"How are her vitals?"

"Did you increase her morphine drip line?"

"What's taking the doctor so long? You paged her, right?"

Commotion continues in the room as I am checked over and the doctor comes in. But my mind is elsewhere as the memory comes flooding back. Our conversation. The semi-truck. Nick's F-150. The windshield shattered beyond repair. Nick. My brother shattered beyond repair.

Just like my body, my heart is bruised, broken, and shattered. But I am alive. Why me?

Nick had such a promising future. The golden boy. The legendary hockey player who just made captain as a junior for the West Michigan Wyverns—the first time since the team was founded forty-eight years ago. My idol. My big brother. My best friend. Gone.

Nine Months Later

Chapter Two

Laur

"You got in!" Mom shrieks, opening the curtains in my bedroom.

"What are you talking about," I mumble. I haven't even been awake for a full minute yet.

"Get dressed and come downstairs. Celebration breakfast is waiting!" Mom says, as she turns on the light and closes the door behind me.

How much coffee has she had today? I really need to switch her to decaf. I pull on leggings and an oversize t-shirt from off my floor, brush my teeth, and head downstairs.

Mom and Dominic, her husband of about four years now, are both glowing with joy. Nick and I never understood how she could replace Dad so easily, even though it had been over ten years since dad passed away. Dominic took on the role of stepdad from afar—treading lightly to give Nick and I space. But after the accident, he's tried to be more involved. He's been exactly what Mom needed to get through the loss but far from what I needed.

At first, I needed vodka and endless joints on top of my pain meds, not a new non-blood-related man of the house. We were all finding our own ways to survive the trauma of loss.

For a while, I really stopped living my life. Depression crept in and took over. It gets a little easier every day. I applied to a four-year college like I had always planned to after two years in community college, but I had no intention of really going. I've rarely made time for friends over the last nine months, but recently I have made time to see Bren, my best friend and cousin. I've even dialed back the drinking and smoking significantly. My therapist says I'm making great strides in my coping mechanisms.

I spot an opened envelope next to a stack of chocolate chip pancakes and what appears to be a mimosa. If this is real champagne, then I should be scared. Mom only serves me drinks on special occasions. I take a sip.

Shit.

It's prosecco. She knows I love prosecco more than champagne. Something is up . . .

I sit down and look at her. She has tears in her eyes. I look at Dominic. He's beaming with the biggest, dorkiest smile I've ever seen.

"Mom . . . Dominic . . . what's going on . . ." I ask.

"Read the letter on top!" Mom shrieks shakily, handing me the letter. The tears in her eyes are now streaming down her cheeks, turning into full blown sobs. They must be happy sobs . . . right? If it wasn't good news . . . there wouldn't be chocolate chip pancakes or prosecco . . .

I start to open the letter and see the West Michigan University logo at the top. There's a West Michigan Wyverns hockey logo too.

I start to read:

Dear Lauren Chip Bellinger,

Thank you for your application and portfolio submission for the Wyverns' Student Marketing and Public Relations Program, working on behalf of the Western Michigan Wyverns Men's Hockey Team. We are pleased to inform you that you have been selected as the junior class representative.

What is this? The Wyverns? Junior class marketing and public relations representative?

No, no, no. This must be fake. I didn't apply for this. I haven't thought about this since Nick . . . I've barely thought about my future. I haven't given a single thought to my old hope of being a part of this amazing program. That hope vanished when Nick did.

"Well!? Aren't you excited?!" Mom's gaze is a mix of pride and enthusiasm.

"Did you read this already?"

She nods.

"Let's ignore how that is a felony really quick . . . and focus on how this is entirely fake. I didn't apply to this. It's not real. Someone's fucking around."

"LANGUAGE!" Dominic bellows sternly. He never did get used to how Nick and I cuss like sailors.

"It's not fake," Mom says.

"Yes. It. Is. Annabeth." I call Mom Annabeth when I need her to be a real adult or when I'm mad, annoyed, or frustrated with her. Truthfully, I call her Annabeth often.

"I did not apply to this. You know I haven't even thought about it since the accident. It was my plan to get as many credits as possible at community college to be able to apply for Nick's senior year but . . ." I trail off.

Nick and I always talked about how I would be part of the marketing and PR student team his senior year. I started picturing it. Nick on the ice, me shooting photos like I used to. Forcing him to let me manage his social media. Attempting to do some paid advertising but always getting shot down by him. I mean, he's right. Why would he need to be advertised? His team, on the other hand, could use all the advertising and press it could get—especially with the terrible reputation of some of his teammates.

It was an old dream of mine—an old dream Nick and I shared. I shake my head. He's gone. This isn't a reality anymore. This isn't my dream anymore.

"I didn't apply for this, Mom. Someone is just an asshole," I finish.

Mom doesn't say anything. She looks at Dominic.

"We thought you would have a hard time believing it. Watch this." Dominic slides his phone over to me. I push play on the video.

"Hi!" a girly voice shrieks.

I wince. Who is this wanna-be Barbie? And what does she have to do with the Wyverns?

"I'm Suz! And, of course, you know your cousin, Brenna!"

The blonde Barbie, Suz, pans the video over to a short Latina girl with voluminous curls. Bren comes into view. My heart swells a little. Even though I've seen her a few times the last two months, I don't talk to her almost every day like I used to before. I do really miss her.

"Hi, Chip! Can't wait to have you join us!" Bren chimes in.

"I haven't told her yet."

"Oh. Well get to it! We have shit to do, Suz!"

"Any-who, we have shit to do apparently, so I'll make this quick."

Bren takes the phone and starts talking.

"She can't do anything quickly, and I should be the one telling you anyway. Let me sit down. I miss you so much. I know it's been beyond hard for you. I can't even imagine."

A shaky sigh escapes Bren as she continues.

"But . . . I promised him I wouldn't tell you until we got the news. Because of everything that happened, I needed to keep that promise for him. Your brother. For Nick."

Her big brown eyes swell with sadness, reminiscing about him. Clearing her throat, her mouth starts to curl into a joyful expression.

"He spent weeks putting your application together for you and submitted it before . . . before the accident. He would be so proud of you, Chip. I'm so proud of you.

A Cheshire-like smile is now overtaking Bren's petite face, beaming with pride, just like my Mom. Her words start to speed up with enthusiasm that's almost contagious.

"There is only one new member to the squad this year and it's YOU! I can't wait to see you in a month! Ah, shit. Gotta go set some things up. Call me when you get a chance. Love you, Chip!"

I hand Dominic back his phone.

"See!" Mom exclaims. "You got in!! YOU DID IT! Nicky knew you could. This is so exciting!" She pulls out a notepad from who even knows where and starts to write things down. "We will have to go get you some new things for your apartment. Oh, and find you an apartment."

I drown out Mom's rambling, downing the rest of my mimosa. Then, I grab the bottle of prosecco off the counter and go to my room.

Chip. I should have known Nick submitted it. He was the one to start that stupid nickname. When Nick was three, he started to call me Chip. Mom had no idea where it came from. Maybe *Beauty and the Beast*? Maybe he really loved potato chips that Dad would sneak him? Nick didn't know where it came from either, but it stuck. He went through a phase of calling me Chip until he was about six. He started it again when we got older as an endearing nickname. I actually love it but hated that I never had a good nickname for him.

Nick did this for me—so I could chase my dream of working in sports marketing for a professional team, like he was chasing his NHL dreams.

Is it possible for it to still be my dream? Can I go to a school where my brother should be studying? Can I work for a team that he should be playing on? Can I keep climbing out of my depression and handle the ache of missing him?

I down the bottle of prosecco and pull out a flask of vodka from under my bed. It's way too early for hard alcohol. I know it's not a good way to cope and I swear I have been making a lot of progress — ask my therapist! But sometimes, you just need it. Now buzzed before 10am, I fall back asleep.

"Chippie, Chip."

I stir in bed.

"Chip. Come on." I feel something on my ear, like someone is flicking it to get my attention. Just like Nick used to do.

I swipe at my ear. Something grabs my hand. I turn around, panicked, about to scream.

"Chip. Relax. It's me, your favorite and most handsomest brother."

"My only brother," I mumble.

"You can't live like this anymore, Chip."

He comes fully into focus. There he is. Nick is sitting cross-legged on my bed and wearing a number 88 Wyverns jersey. It seems so real. He looks the same. My eyes sting trying to fight back the tears that threaten to endlessly pour out of my eyes.

"Am I . . . Am I dead?" I whisper, startled with tears in my eyes. "You're not real. Unless I'm dead."

"Drama queen," Nick sings in a high voice. "You're alive loser—just a little drunk and dreaming. Very vividly apparently."

He looks into the mirror "Damn, was I really this hot alive? Poor women everywhere. Not able to get a piece of this now that I'm—"

"Eww. Are you fucking kidding me right now? I'm seeing my brother who has been dead for nine months in my room and he's talking about how attractive everyone finds him?"

"Okay, you have a point. But seriously, Chip." Nick takes hold of my shoulders, and I can faintly feel his hands. My heart aches with an unsettling mix of remorse, distress, and euphoria seeing and feeling my brother after all this time. He looks into my eyes as the tears inevitably come. My body starts to shudder under the weight of my loss hitting me more and more with each tear that falls. I would give anything for this to be real. For him to really be here with me.

He continues, "You can't keep doing this—hiding away at Mom's house and avoiding living your life because I'm gone. I would seriously kick your ass if I was still alive."

"Well, you're not alive, Nick. So, it looks like I can keep doing what I want to do. I've been actually trying a little bit lately."

I somehow have a bottle of prosecco in my hand. I take a big swig. What is happening?

Nick—well, dream Nick—squeezes my cheeks before I down another sip, and I spew liquid all over him. He wipes off his face.

"Laur. Lauren. Please. You're not trying enough. You can't give up on your life and your dreams. You can't isolate yourself from the people closest to you. And you sure as hell can't try to handle it by escaping with alcohol. You witnessed it the night of—"

"Okay, OKAY, STOP," I cut in, not wanting to relive the memories that torment me daily. Nick took his eyes off the road, but the driver of the semi that hit us was above the legal limit. I wonder if the flashbacks and memories will ever stop haunting me.

Nick places his hands on my shoulders again, attempting to calm me. His brows are creased in a serious demeanor.

"You are going to work with the Wyverns. You're going to kick ass. You're going to do this."

Running, his hands through his light brown hair he lets out an exasperated sigh.

"You have to. It's a once in a lifetime opportunity! This is your one shot! To chase your dreams and find yourself again. Stop pretending you'll find it somewhere in a bottle or this small ass town. And go get your one shot back. You know I would if I were you."

I can see the pleading in his bright blue eyes that mirror my own.

"You have to do this, Laur. Please, for me."

I wake up with a jolt and look around my room.

No Nick.

No bottle of prosecco.

Thank goodness.

My head is pounding with a hangover about to set in. I feel my bed—no prosecco on the comforter—so no spit take. It was a dream. Just like he said, and he's right. I can't live like this. I'll do it—for Nick, for Mom so she can stop worrying about me, and for my dad, who would be heartbroken if I gave up being around hockey. Maybe . . . Just maybe, I'll do it a little bit for myself too. Even if it was only dream, Nick's presence made me realize how lonely I am from isolating myself. I miss being social. I miss smiling. I miss laughing. I miss enjoying life.

Walking downstairs, Mom and Dominic are still sitting in the kitchen. I find a glass of water sitting on the table for me.

"Mom, where are those pancakes? Making all these lists, shopping, and packing are going to require some carbs and energy."

I glance between Mom and Dominic before looking Mom in the eyes.

"I'm going to West next month."

Mom squeals. Dominic hands me some aspirin and another glass of water. He can be useful I suppose.

Chapter Three

Laur

After being forced into every store within a twenty-mile radius, I'm finally packed and ready to go to WMU. Mom, Dominic, and I are making the eight-hour drive to Frostburg, Michigan from our home in Illinois. Nick and I could do it in seven and a half hours. We'd only make one stop to pee and get gas and snacks while the tank filled up, and then we'd be right back on the road. I swear with Mom and Dominic it's almost nine hours—they stop a minimum of four times.

I should have done more research on the current team—I haven't been able to bring myself to yet. I still expect to see my brother when I'm anywhere near a hockey rink. I keep holding onto hope that this opportunity with the Wyverns will be healing and bring me closer to him than I expect—at least I'll be doing something with my life again. I'll finish school and hopefully be on track for my dream career if it goes well.

If I'm honest with myself, I know deep down I still want my hockey marketing dream career almost more than anything. I just feel an immense amount of guilt when Nick can't pursue his dreams, but I know he would want this for me too. I try to keep reminding myself of that.

Thankfully, Dominic volunteered to drive the entire way. The drive is very rainy and gloomy, but I snooze on and off in the backseat, attempting to avoid the anxiety creeping in the closer we get to WMU. The rain stopped almost instantly as we arrived. I spot the sun trying to peek through the clouds.

"Are you bouncing your leg again? Or is that the car sputtering?" Dominic asks.

I mumble "sorry" and still my bouncing knee in the backseat.

Dominic pulls into the driveway of a little blue house. Butterflies fill my stomach as I take in my new home. The little blue house is clearly dated but has a charming and comforting appeal. Bren "coincidently" had a room open in the three-bedroom house she lived in. Shocker!

I have no idea how she coordinated this with Nick and kept it a secret all this time. I'm very thankful I didn't have to search for a place to live on my own or have a random roommate that leaves chicken on the counter and then still eats it three days later or something even more bizarre.

As I stand in the driveway and take in my new home, my cousin sprints down the driveway to greet me.

"SHE'S HERE!" Bren shrieks in such a shrill girly tone, which almost makes me cringe.

I am by no means a girly-girl who squeals in shrill tones or gossips about boys and lingerie like it's part of my daily routine. The only time anyone would consider me a woo-girl is when I'm watching hockey. Other than that, I am the farthest thing from girly.

"BRENNIE BEAN!"

I'm giddy with excitement as I turn around, and pull her into a hug. Bren's gorgeous Latina curls bounce as she jumps up and down with excitement in my arms, just like a little jumping bean. I forgot how contagious her bubbly personality is. She's almost an entire foot shorter than me, but with her obsession for heeled shoes you would never be able to tell. I squeeze her petite frame tight. Having someone to hug and something to be excited about was now a foreign concept to me. The realization strikes me that I might have been missing this more than I led myself to believe. I think it's a good sign I made the right decision.

"This is Jaylin, our housemate and a close friend of mine," Bren says, as a girl with light brown hair wearing a flowy bohemian top and denim shorts comes out of the house.

"Hey there. Let me help you all," Jaylin says as she hugs me tight. "We're going to have the best year! And it will be even better if Bren can keep her shrieking to a minimum!"

I can immediately tell I am going to like her. She radiates that 'I don't give a fuck what anyone thinks' energy but somehow with a 'the sun is always shining' attitude. Jaylin seems like a happy-go-lucky hippie, and I smell a hint of the good herb, so I know I'm spot on. Bren and Jaylin are both helping Mom and Domnic unload the car. They are all so chatty and friendly, laughing and smiling while carrying box after box.

"I think this is exactly what you need," Mom whispers to me as we grab the last two boxes.

After we have all the boxes in the house and half unpacked, I start to organize my current disaster of a bedroom. The type-A in me wants to be able to sleep in peace knowing I'm not living in the chaos of boxes in need of unpacking. Within just the short time I've been here, I know it's what I need. I really want—no, I really *need* this to make this feel like a new home for me. A fresh start. A new chance. Everyone else is hanging out in the living room letting me unpack my new life. About an hour and a half later, I hear footsteps and a knock on my open bedroom door.

"Knock, knock," Dominic says—what a dorky "dad" thing to do: say 'knock, knock' and actually knock at the same time. "Your mom's getting hangry, and you know how that will turn out. Are you almost done, need any help?"

I turn to him and smile. "Almost done! Just a few decorations left."

Dominic walks into my room and looks around. "I know it doesn't mean as much coming from me, but I am so proud of you for doing this. Your mom is too. She doesn't say it much, but she is always so worried about you. When Nick . . ." He pauses and sighs loudly. "If she lost you too, I don't think she could make it through that . . . I know you haven't been yourself, and I can't pretend to imagine what you feel. But I think part of her felt like she already lost you. You have given her new happiness and hope and me too. I hope you find some for yourself while you're here. I have a feeling you will."

I look up at him teary-eyed. Dominic is usually a man of few words when it comes to Nick and me. He made it very clear from the start that he wasn't going to try to replace or pretend to be our dad, even though he knew we both felt some resentment toward him after he married Mom.

I hang up a picture on the wall that Dominic took almost six years ago—a picture of me taking a picture of Nick skating on the pond near our house. I'm smiling behind the camera, squatting to get a good angle while Nick is facing me, the puck a blur as he tapped it back and forth for some action shots.

"You still have that photo?" Dominic asks.

"Of course. It's one of my favorite photos of Nick and me. You captured us both in our element perfectly." With tears still in my eyes, I walk over to Dominic and hug him tight. "Thank you," I whisper. "I hope I find some happiness too and maybe even get to know Nick in a different way by being here. I miss him every day."

"I know. Me too," Dominic mutters, hugging me back tighter than he has ever hugged me. I pull away, and he clears his throat a little bit.

"Now," he says, "can we please get your mom some food before she insists we don't eat and just hit the road. You know that will be a drive from hell for me with a hangry Annabeth as the passenger."

"Oh gosh," I joke. "She would literally eat you!" I straighten the photo. "I'm ready. Let's go before she's at the 'chew the waiter a new one' hunger stage. Obviously, we will need appetizers."

Dominic and I walk to the living room. I feel a little bit lighter than I have in the last ten months. It's not anywhere near feeling like my old self, but I can still feel it. I know that Bren and Mom can too because I see them exchange a look, both smiling in acknowledgement.

"Now that I'm officially all unpacked, let's go get some dinner!" I say.

"I know just the place!" Bren responds excitedly.

I hear Mom mumble, "Thank the good Lord. I am about to faint for goodness' sake," under her breath.

Bren and I climb into the back of Mom's car with Dominic riding shotgun. Jaylin went to meet a date for dinner about an hour ago. I don't blame her—I took quite a long time setting up my room. Bren said we will have to grill her tomorrow on the mystery woman she's on a date with.

We walk into a place a few blocks off campus called Haee's. I should have known we would end up at a sports pub. Haee's is packed with college kids in every type of sports jersey you could think of. It's extremely loud with dim lighting and TVs covering the walls.

The hostess lets us know that it will be about ten minutes to be seated. I look around, taking in more of the place. The booths are luscious leather, and the lighting fixtures are sleek modern metal—both classy for a sports pub. It's perfect. I know Haee's will quickly become one of my favorite places.

"I'm so sorry, Laur . . . I should have warned you. This is one of the two hangouts for the hockey team. I don't see them around, so I'm sure they're still at practice," Bren says apologetically. "But I promise this is the best sports bar around and the food is amazing. I come here for pretty much anything and everything. It's my favorite. I'm sure you'll love it soon too!"

A weird feeling forms in the pit of my stomach. I look around the crowded place; no Wyverns jerseys in sight yet. I can prepare myself. I haven't been around anyone wearing a hockey jersey since the night of the accident, the night of Nick's first game as captain. I close my eyes and take a deep breath.

Bren places a consoling hand on my shoulder.

"I'm okay," I say.

For once, I think I might mean it. It would probably be better to meet the team away from the world of hockey instead of on the ice or in the locker room anyway.

"If they do show up," Bren reminds, "we can leave. Honestly, they probably will be here eventually. The full practice schedule starts again soon. The guys have really been taking advantage of having some down time lately." Bren gives my shoulder a reassuring squeeze.

"No. That's okay," I reply. "It might be easier for me to meet them here since I have absolutely no memories here and a hell of a lot at West's hockey rink. I've never been to this place. Nick never took me here."

"It's newer," Bren says. "He wouldn't have . . ." she trails off. "It's a newer place."

"Well then, I can make the Bellinger mark myself." I surprise myself with that response, but I do mean it.

Our table is ready, and the hostess signals for us to follow her. Like the final buzzer at the end of a game, her arrival solidifies my decision. I love Nick so much, but I think I need to make my own mark a bit too if I want to leave here happier and not a haunted, still depressed mess.

We all devour our food—Mom the fastest, of course. I swear I could hear her making little noises of joy as she bit into her burger. Once we finish eating, Mom and Dominic hug Bren and I goodbye. They are going to stay at what Dominic refers to as his "old college buddy's brother's quaint lake house" for the weekend as a getaway. I've met the guy, Cody Stone, whose brother owns the place. I've also seen pictures of this supposedly quaint lake house. I don't consider something with soaring rooflines and more than eight bedrooms quaint. The mansion makes the massive lake look like a puddle, taking up more than half of the shoreline. I'm slightly jealous I can't tag along. Cody's brother must be insanely loaded.

Mom and Dominic both remind me to call anytime and that they will come up to visit. I can tell Mom is worried about me by the look in her eyes.

"I promise I will call. Plus, Mom, you and I both know Bren will be texting you my life story if I don't," I say as I hug her for the second time.

"You know she's right, Auntie Annabeth! She is in good hands with me and Jaylin though! Plus if we ever need it, Liam is a built-in body-guard, especially with any guys," Bren chimes in. LIAM! How could I forget Bren's hockey playing hunk of a boyfriend? I haven't seen him since well before the accident.

"I have sworn off love and dating, so no need to worry about that! Coming here for Nick and Dad." Mom gives me an apprehensive look. "And for my future. Plus, it will help Mom to stop worrying that I won't have one if I stay an inexperienced, depressed homebody at their house the rest of my life. Jokes on you, Mom. Now Dominic is going to know how lush you are without me there drinking your wine!" I hug Dominic, while he quietly chuckles at Mom's annoyed expression.

"Be safe, kiddo. We love you. Find that happiness," Dominic whispers. He slips an envelope into my purse and says, "Here's something to help fund that search for happiness. Don't waste it all on alcohol, please." I look at him shocked. This envelope is full of bills—and she's thiccc as can be with three *c*'s.

"What?!" I say as my jaw almost hits the floor.

Dominic just shrugs. "Remember Cody Stone, my old college buddy?"

I roll my eyes. *That is the only college buddy you ever talk about, Dominic.*

"Well, his brother Ezra is a really great money guy and has made some great investments for me over the years. Now I'm investing in you." I hug him again for good measure.

"Do you want to stick around and hangout?" Bren asks, "I know Liam is on his way so the rest of the team might be too. But Jaylin might head this way too!" I close my eyes and take a deep breath. I'm ready for this. I have to be.

"Yes, I'm in. But first, Mom and Dominic, can you take me back to the house so I can drop this big guy off?" I ask, dramatically pointing to the envelope.

Dominic laughs. "It was maybe not the best decision to give that to you instead of just putting it in your bank account, but it made me feel kind of like a badass to give you a wad of cash in an envelope. We can put some of it in the bank for you."

Mom rolls her eyes at his "badass" comment and mutters, "Yeah. Such a badass, working in accounting and playing video games with his brother and friends when they are over forty-five years old."

Mom puts her arm around me. I let Bren know I'll text her on my way back. On the car ride back to the house—my house now I guess—I take a few more deep breaths and close my eyes. I'm ready to be around people and hockey again. Aren't I?

Coming to West might be one of the hardest things I've had to do. The hardest thing in the last year, but it will be worth it to find myself again. To try to feel like myself again. To be me. It's already starting to feel like something that could actually be possible.

Chapter Four
Laur

"I 've got this," I whisper to myself as I open the door to the sports bar. Bren is pulling me into a hug the second I step in. Thank goodness. I'm lucky to have someone who is watching out for me but will push me outside my comfort zone. I am so thankful for her.

"CHIP!" A deep manly voice that for some reason always makes me think of a brooding, grizzly bear bellows from behind me. I turn to see Liam leaning against a pool table, sipping a nearly empty drink. I practically sprint over to him and wrap him in a tight embrace.

"It's so good to see you! I swear you've gotten even more . . . grizzly somehow?"

I can't help but think of all the memories of watching Liam and Nick messing around playing hockey in our backyard together. They never played on the same team growing up, but college came around and they got to play together here at West.

"Why, thank you," he says with a not-so-subtle hair flip. He has curly locks most girls would be jealous of. "I've been working on it. After all, I am known as Grizzly around here."

"Oh really? Since when?!" I tease him.

Bren chimes in, "Yeah, Grizzly. No one around here is calling you that. If anything, you're a cub."

A cub?! Did she just call her 6-foot, 230-pound boyfriend of six years a cub? I laugh harder than I expected.

"You're so feisty, Bren! I've missed you so much. And you too, Liam!"

"My, my, Miss Lauren, is that a real, genuine, famous Bellinger smile?!" Bren teases using a fake southern drawl for emphasis, "I don't believe I've seen one of those in quite some time. This calls for a celebratory drink!"

I bump into her playfully as we walk to the bar. I'm surprised at the easy feel of the smile despite the memories of Nick circulating in my head from seeing Liam. Maybe, we will both need to get used to me having a genuine smile more often.

Hopefully.

"No, no hard alcohol for me," I say as Liam orders shots. I see him look at Bren, and she gives him a look I can't read.

"Light beer?" Liam asks.

"Perfect. Bud Light, please."

Liam orders our drinks, and someone yells at him from across the bar.

"William Grizzly Welsh. Who the hell do you think you are ordering a Bud Light?! Your ass doesn't have to be in shape yet. Real practice starts next week. Hey, Joe, buddy, give that man an extra shot for me, please."

"See! People call me Grizzly!" Liam boasts to Bren.

I look across the bar to see who harassed Liam over my beer order. It's even more crowded than when we arrived for dinner. I can't figure out who it is, but from the way the mystery man talked to Liam, I'm assuming it's a guy from the team. Then my eyes find them, five of them to be exact, on the other side of the bar.

Their flowy hair, their muscular builds, their cockiness filling the air around them, and of course, a blonde bombshell next to one of them. She looks exactly like she stepped out of a pink Barbie box, outfit and all. Yep, the hockey team, or at least some of the hockey team, has arrived.

I take another calming deep breath and a sip of my beer. Nick played with some of them. I wonder which ones he would warn me about.

"Thanks for the free shot, man. You know, Joe and I go way back; I used to bartend here."

Liam raises the shot to a guy opposite the bar. That must be who made the comment about my Bud Light.

"That goes on Donato's tab, right Joe?" Liam asks Joe.

Joe smiles and gives Liam a thumbs up before placing the rest of our drinks on the bar.

I look across the bar to see a middle finger held up in response to Liam. Of course, it's the guy next to the perfect blonde Barbie. She whispers something in his ear. They clink the glasses together and down a shot in sync. Barbie kisses him on the cheek and walks away.

Someone please explain to me how I can be jealous of Barbie when I'm pretty sure I haven't met this 'Donato' guy? Based on his appearance, I would bet money that he is someone Nick would tell me to stay away from.

I sneak a second look at him.

Okay, I am positive I've never met this guy. I would remember a guy with arms like that. His biceps subtly pop out of his t-shirt, and I do mean subtly. He's not absurdly over muscular with meathead arms. The type of guy who tries to get as much muscle as possible just to show it off to anyone and everyone. That doesn't seem to be his style.

He has strong toned arms you just can't help but notice because you're so curious if your hands would fit around his biceps all the way, even though you know they won't. Unlike the meathead, he would never ask anyone to try and find out. God no, he wouldn't even let you if you asked! Well, not in public at least.

My goodness those arms are so tan too. I mean he's so tan. I can't stop looking at his arms though. Is that tan natural? I swear I try to achieve that sun-kissed to perfection glow but can't keep it for more than a week if I don't lay out every few days in the summer. His t-shirt shows off the rest of his muscles too but with a mysterious air surrounding his body. It's not skintight like Liam's is, which I know Bren loves. It really makes me wonder if the rest of his body matches those sexy arms.

I shake my head. Wow, I've been taking in this stranger, gawking. This delectable Greek God, who is a hockey player, that I will have to see often. That I'll have to work with. Maybe he didn't notice?

Shit.

He noticed. His brown eyes lock onto mine and hold me captive.

His face is flawless, brown stubble that goes along with shaggy brown hair. He's looking at me with an intensity I have never seen before, as though he's staring into my soul. He drinks me in, not afraid to have another glass and find out what more there is to me.

His eyes are the lightest shade of brown I've ever seen, sucking the air from my chest. It's like God ran out of brown to match the dark brown eyes of the rest of the world. Instead, he improvised with a few specks of gold. I wish I could capture the unique color with the lens of my camera, but it would never do justice to the depths of the golds and browns intertwined.

Damn him and damn his eyes. Looking into them makes me wonder—not about him but about myself and what I would let him do if he were next to me and if this wasn't a crowded bar full of people. A crooked smirk spreads across his face. He knows. Is he a mind reader? How can he possibly know by looking into my eyes that I'd be easily tempted to let him sprawl me across this bar without him even saying a single word to me.

"Let's head to a table." Bren's voice pulls me back into reality as I look away from the enticing hockey player. Train of thought over. No being sprawled.

"What? Oh. Yes. Table. Good. After you." I shake my head again and take a deep breath. Who the hell am I? No. No guys. I'm content alone after my last relationship. Content on my own for the rest of my life. No dating and no love, especially not with any hockey players. I take a sip of my beer and follow Bren to our table.

I look to where he, Donato, had been, but he's gone. Sitting down at the table with Bren and Liam, I take a deep breath again, trying to get the thought of that crooked smirk and beautiful, daring eyes out of my head. Did I really think I'd let him sprawl me across the bar? Who the hell am I?

"You okay?" Bren asks me. I take another sip of my watery beer, noticing it's half gone now.

"Yeah, I'm good."

"Well, that's a relief. Because Suz and some of the guys are coming this way." Liam says, beckoning to someone behind me.

Oh, great. Here we go.

Bren stands up and is hugging Barbie like a best friend she hasn't seen in ages. Lovely, so we like Barbie? I was really hoping we wouldn't interact much with her. She seems so—before I even finish my train of thought, Bren is bringing her over to me.

"Laur, this is Suz, PR extraordinaire." Now that she's up close, I recognize her from the video with Bren announcing my surprise acceptance. She is even more flawless in person. How absurd is that?

"Suz got us so much exposure in *USA Hockey Magazine* last year in the 'Big On Campus' section. She's the co-lead for the Wyverns' marketing team with me this year. She happens to have already lined up a job in Seattle's hockey scene after graduation this year!" Bren squeals the last part. Shit, Barbie is impressive . . . I can see why Bren likes her.

"Suz, this is Lauren Bellinger—" Suz cuts her off. "Hi, Lauren, nice to finally meet you." She holds out a hand for me to shake. Stealing a glance at Bren reveals she is rolling her eyes at the formality, but I politely reach out to accept her handshake.

"I have a job *offer* in Seattle. I haven't accepted it yet. Bren stop spreading rumors." She winks at Bren.

"Oh, and speaking of gossip," she continues, turning to face Bren fully. "Don't let me forget to tell you about my date earlier tonight. I need to decide if I should go on a second one."

Barbie isn't dating any of the players? That's surprising.

Then I see him. Fuck, just like Barbie, he's even more attractive up close. Shit. Why does he have to look like an Abercrombie ad? I bet he even has the perfectly chiseled V with his shirt off. He's already looking at me when my eyes meet his. My heartbeat quickens and an ache of longing starts to take over as I try with every fiber of my being not to bite my lip thinking about him shirtless.

"Lauren. These are some of the guys," Suz starts. She rattles off some of the guys' names, their year, and their positions.

I smile and nod politely, but I'm barely paying attention until she says, "Our gorgeous captain Lucas Donato! Lucas, this is Lauren. She's a junior just like you. And Lauren, I'm sure you've heard that Lucas is only the second player in Wyverns' history to make captain as Junior." She stops talking, making the realization that he is second only, because my brother was first. Nick would have had to know who this gorgeous off-limits man is. Did they get along? Were they friends?

They are all staring at me. I down the last of my beer in one gulp. I look at him again, Lucas. He has one eyebrow raised, looking at me post beer chug.

"Laur. Not Lauren," I quickly snap back.

I'm about to start to say that Nick was my brother, but someone cuts me off. Really? This team can't be filled with douchebags! If it is, I will not make it through this season. I turn around to see a familiar face.

"Laur, we are lucky to have you. Bud Light, right? Cheers!" The guy that cut me off hands me a fresh pint glass and clinks his glass to mine.

My entire face lights up. "Ty-Ty!" I screech, sounding like a basic woo-girl for the second time in one night. I jump on him, wrapping my arms around him like a long lost relative I haven't seen in years while spilling a little bit.

A sense of familiarity and home rushes over me. I've known Tyler since we were both eight and Nick was nine. I've chased him around hotels, ice rinks, parking lots, you name it. Nick and Tyler played hockey together a lot as kids. Tyler was like family for a long time. He still is. Having him here is going to make West feel more like a safe space for me —more like home.

"I've missed you too, Chip." Tyler chuckles, wiping the spilled beer off his arm.

I can't believe I forgot Ty is on the team. How could I forget?! How could it have slipped my mind? Did I know? There's no way. Tyler must read my furrowed brow and scrunched lips as confusion

"I transferred last season to play. Nick and I were going to surprise you after the first game but . . ." he trails off not wanting to bring up the accident. "Anyways, then Bren told me the news about you coming here, and I wanted to wait to see you in person . . ." He trails off again and pulls me in for another hug, embracing me as if he is trying to keep me from slipping away too.

I should have remembered him playing that first game with Nick as captain. I must have blocked it out or maybe he didn't play that game. I don't ask questions. I don't want to think more about that day but seeing Tyler Barret has made my night even better.

"I . . . yeah . . . I had no idea, but I should have made the connection, should have realized." I start to defend myself.

Tyler responds, "It's no big deal. You know now! It's so good to see you."

Tyler gestures to a table. "Want to go catch up? You'll be with the guys all the time soon enough. Want to go talk over there and then I'll walk you home?"

I pull Tyler into another hug; it's so great to see him, "Yes, I would love that." Frostburg, Michigan is starting to chip away at the protective shield I've hid behind the last year.

I turn to my cousin and give her a wave. "I'll text you when I get home, Bren. Nice to meet you all."

It'll be nice to talk to someone who knows who I used to be. I'm cautiously optimistic that just being around people like Tyler, Bren, and Liam might ease my depression and help me to find the little sparks of light I've been missing, craving.

I grab Tyler's hand again and start to walk away from the group that's now gathered around the pool table. I feel eyes on me.

Looking back, I see Lucas Donato staring at us, a perplexed look on his face. His eyes briefly meet mine and his expression changes. That yearning for him begins to bloom in me again, wanting to flourish and take root in every inch of my mind and body. That deep ache for him and his eyes—those beautiful brown eyes that inexplicably feel so familiar, like I could find pieces of my old self in them too.

Chapter Five

Lucas

Jealously flares as I watch the brown-haired beauty walking away practically hand-in-hand with my teammate. My heart aches with longing for her to come back so I can get to know everything she hides behind her shielded bright blue eyes and oversized t-shirt.

Ty-Ty? What is that shit?

He's about to be pussy whipped real fast if he's responding to that. But damn, who can blame him? That girl is beyond beautiful. With the fire behind those mesmerizing eyes, she's a beauty with an attitude. I'm not sure what it says about me but that has my blood rushing south.

How does Tyler know her? She is way too good for him. Tyler is a player. A girl as modest and angelic as she seems deserves so much more loyalty. Our stare down takes center ice in my brain again, eliciting a burning desire in my groin.

"Wipe that dirty little smirk off your face, Lucas Donato, before I slap it off. I can smell your filthy thoughts from here," Bren shouts at me and smacks my arm, leaving a stinging behind. "Don't even let yourself think about it. That is my cousin."

"Your cousin?" This should be interesting. "Who cares? You love me. Don't you want to have fun family gatherings?" She rolls her eyes. "Come on, Bren, you know I don't fuck around." My tone is more serious now. I don't sleep around. It's never been my thing and never will be.

Bren's eyes narrow. "Yes. My cousin. As in Lauren Bellinger. As in Nick Bellinger's sister."

Shit. I knew those eyes looked familiar. Now I feel incredibly dirty for what I was just thinking while staring into them. Surprise quickly colors my guilty thoughts. Nick Bellinger's sister? There's no way.

"Wait, hold on. Nick Bellinger's sister? But I thought she didn't go here. What's the—"

Bren cuts me off before I can say anything else, "Have you not been paying attention to any of my emails? You're the captain for fuck's sake, Lucas. She got the only junior spot for the Wyverns' Student Marketing Program. Nick applied for her before . . . before everything."

My mind is racing. Nick Bellinger. He is a legend—was a legend. He was my mentor. Nick was classy, barely got in fights, and levelheaded ninety-eight percent of the time. He was the only guy I've ever shared the ice with who was calm, cool, and collected, yet his skill showed he could kick your ass in seconds. He's one of the best players I've ever watched. He's the best player I've ever played with, even though it was brief.

I idolized—still idolize—him. He was smooth with the ladies and a huge heartthrob but never a man-whore or anything bordering on womanizing. He was someone I aspired to be like from the first time I saw him play for the Wyverns, even before I was on the team. He was my teammate, and he was starting to become my friend too.

But I wanted to do terrible, wonderful things to so, so many beautifully perfect parts of his sister. I had barely even talked to her! Fuck. This season was already going to be hard on me mentally.

I'm the first captain since Nick and a junior—just like him, the second in Wyverns' history. I can't get distracted. I owe it to myself to focus this year and get the team to the finals. While doing that, I'll be making sure scouts everywhere see the success so next year, as a senior, I'm already securing NHL contracts.

I realize I've been quiet for longer than a minute trying to wrap my brain around all of this. Around her. Around her being related to Nick. Bren is still glaring at me. I've never seen her look so concerned.

"I'm not looking for a one-night stand. You've got nothing to worry about, Bren."

"Yeah. That's the thing." Bren pauses. I glare at Bren like she has three heads waiting for her to finish the sentence. Bren glances at Liam, then to me, then back to Liam—clearly telling him to take over.

Liam sighs and chimes in "Bro, I've known you over half my life. And I've never even seen you devour a girl like that."

Throwing her hands dramatically in the air, Bren continues to nag me. "Hooking up isn't the concern, Lucas. She can't have you fuck with her emotions. She says she doesn't want to date anyone, and she's sworn off love. Don't try anything to confuse her. She's been through enough."

My temper starts to bubble up to the surface, ready to start fuming as I grow more and more frustrated with this unnecessary lecture. I wouldn't harm a fly let alone Nick Bellinger's sister. I cut Bren off before she can get another one of her unnecessary concerns in.

"Can you two stop? Nothing happened and nothing is going to happen. I don't even know the girl and you both know I worshipped the ground Bellinger walked on." I sigh, polishing off my drink. "Like you said, Bren, she's not interested in dating. And I sure as hell won't let anything, especially anything with legs like those, distract me this hockey season."

Liam eyes me over his nearly empty drink.

"Why do you say it like that? Or if she didn't have legs, would you?" Liam asks me puzzled polishing off his drink while peering around to order another, which he clearly doesn't need.

He's a damn good friend, and an even better hockey player, but he isn't the brightest bulb in the box. Bren looks like she wants to smack him for the dumb question.

"What the fuck. Dude. It was an expression. I swear on Wayne Gretzky's hockey career that I am not going to fuck around with Lauren Bellinger." I give each of them a long stare reinforcing what I said. "Got it? Good. I'm going home. See you at the gym tomorrow,

Liam. Bren, please get this big guy home before he's at the point where he's too hungover to lift tomorrow."

"With his stupid legs comment, he might be already there," Bren mutters under her breath.

I can't stop thinking about the fire in her piercing, enchanting blue eyes on my walk back to my apartment. Lauren Bellinger and I are going to have a hard time not giving in to each other if twenty minutes in the same bar has me wanting more than just her lips on mine. More than half of those minutes were us on opposite sides of the bar.

Fuck. I'm screwed.

This girl is going to be a distraction and not just one of the sexual variety. I said I wouldn't fuck around with her, and I won't. I wouldn't even without my oath. I don't fuck around. Wayne Gretzky is a hockey God, and I'd never swear against his career and not mean it.

Lauren Bellinger will just have to become my friend or maybe my good luck charm. She'll be at every game anyway and we'll be around each other all the time. That's harmless enough, right?

Chapter Six

Laur

Last night went better than I expected. I didn't have any crying spells. Of course, I thought about Nick on and off, but once I was talking with Tyler, it was easier to just try to be myself and not overthink. Tyler was a wonderful surprise. He was my first crush growing up, but now he's more like a cousin or brother to me. Having him here will remind me of happier days when hockey brought so much joy into my life instead of just heartache.

Bren and Tyler both know the old happy-go-lucky version of me. Mom was right, being around people who bring out that version of me is exactly what I need. Lucas was also quite a surprise, but not the good kind. I bet he's bad news. Any guy that looks like the heartthrob out of the newest pop song music video is bound to be bad news. I know I don't want to date.

I am making a promise to myself: I will not let Lucas Donato derail me in any way, physically or emotionally.

He is part of the team, just like all the other guys. He might be the most enjoyable of them to look at and I might be still wondering what he looks like with his shirt off, but that's it, nothing more.

Eye candy can increase endorphins, right? I need more endorphins.

I finally get out of bed and notice a text from Bren. It says she is grabbing us coffee before we head to the rink at 8am to talk to the coach and the team would be there shortly after. I glance at my clock, it's 7am. Shit. I needed to shower and wash my hair after the day of moving. I rush to get ready.

"Laurrr," sings a cheery Bren dramatically dragging out the syllables at the end of her sentences, "I've come to scoop you up and lift your non-morning human spirits with caffeineee! A caramel macchiato, complete with an extra shot of espressooo. Get moooving!"

I forgot how much of a morning person she is. I come out of my bathroom, towel on with hair and makeup at least done.

"Chop, chop, Chip! We'll be late!" Bren says as she hands me my coffee.

I finally emerge from my room in leggings and a Wyverns t-shirt.

"That's what you're going to wear?" Bren gives me a once over, critiquing my outfit. My face scrunches in confusion. She has on jean shorts and a similar t-shirt.

She giggles. "I forgot how precious your confused face is. I'm kidding. Let's go!"

We're out the door and on our way to the arena. Before passing through the doors, I pause. I haven't been here since last October. Bren raises an eyebrow, tapping her foot as she impatiently waits for me.

My feet finally take me through the door of the hall that eventually leads to the locker rooms. I've never been back here before. This locker room is where Nick thrived, making a name and reputation for himself in college hockey. I just wish he could be here with me.

"Are you coming?" Bren asks.

I didn't realize I'd stopped walking again. I take one of my deep breaths and let it go. I'm going to psych myself out. I need to be in the right frame of mind when I meet the coach and professionally meet the team. I've met Coach Andres before, but he probably doesn't remember me.

We reach the locker room and Barbie—I mean Suz—is waiting for us outside. She is dressed to the nines in fashionable slacks, a bubblegum pink chevron-patterned tank top, and Tori Burch sandals. Should I have dressed up more? Bren is very casual like me, except for the fact that her shorts barely cover her butt. At least I have on leggings!

Suz barges into the locker room without even knocking. To my surprise and relief, it's silent without a trace of the raucous behavior I expected. The guys must not be here yet. Bren starts down a long hallway lined with old jerseys, hockey mementos, and photos. My heart races as panic sets in seeing the photos. I keep myself focused on the end of the hallway, not wanting to see Nick's smiling face in any pictures for fear of a panic attack or worse.

"How is my favorite coach this morning?" Bren says, as she walks into the coach's office and handing him a coffee. I hadn't even noticed she had an extra in her hand for him. I glance around the locker room wondering how much time Nick spent here. Bren looks down the hall, gives me a 'what the hell are you doing look,' and motions for me to come into the coach's office. His office walls are decorated with more photos and Wyverns' memorabilia that I avert my gaze from.

"Coach Andres, this is Lauren Bellinger. She is the junior representative this year for the Wyverns' PR and Marketing team!" Bren attempts to stifle her enthusiasm but bounces back and forth with glee as she pulls me into the room.

"Hi, Coach Andres. It's a pleasure to see you again. I'm not sure if you remember me." I reach my hand out for a handshake.

"Of course I do, Lauren." Coach Andres ignores my hand and pulls me into a quick hug.

"We're lucky to have you. I knew you would be joining us eventually. Your brother always bragged about how you would make the team look the best we have ever looked to fans with your marketing skills. I am glad you joined us."

Coach Andres' eyes are soft as he meets mine, the same color blue as my brother's. The familiar long face of grief appears briefly before he turns to Bren. He tenses, weariness now replacing the grief on his face.

"Apologies for getting into business so quickly, but I need to give you a quick rundown of the key players you are focusing on and any PR nightmares we need to get ahead of."

"Of course, Coach. Suz has a quick print out for you and the details are in your inbox." Suz hands Coach Andres a paper as Bren continues.

"Key player focuses to start off the season will be four seniors and two juniors. All Star Seniors: Jamison Clarke and Micah Lawson. Seniors that are contenders for the NHL: Connor Rizzo and Liam Welsh." She glows when she says Liam's name. "Juniors: Tyler Barret and, of course, Captain Lucas Donato." I catch myself rolling my eyes, hoping Coach Andres doesn't notice. "Problem children: Blaine Mitchell got in a few altercations this summer around campus bars, so he is going to need to be talked to again." Coach Andres looks up at her, shaking his head.

"Look, Coach, you know I won't sugarcoat it. Mitchell is looking to stir up trouble. He tried to get other players in on his antics this summer. Luckily, he hasn't been super successful, but you know that he convinced one other player to join in on a fight this summer. Which brings me to the next problem child, Derrick McAllister. He was almost arrested during one of the incidents this summer for public intoxication. We already talked about that being in the papers and all over the internet. So, this goes without saying but you need to use Mitchell and McAllister as an example that you do not tolerate their behavior or any kind of bullshit," Bren finishes.

Coach Andres runs his hands through his hair with a defeated breath, but nods. Wow, Bren is amazing. I'm surprised that Suz didn't take over and lead. Bren really is in charge and she's a boss bitch!

"They are going to tank the team's good reputation if they aren't reprimanded," Bren adds.

With a big sigh, Coach Andres says, "Thanks, Bren. I know I can count on you girls to focus on the positives and get this team some good press. We have a lot of strong players, so it's going to be a great season. The six you outlined will make for good press, and we truly need it."

"Actually, what about seven? Throw in Keith too. He's a hell of a goalie and was ranked high last year. We'll call them the Sexy Seven. I love it. I'll follow up with details over email and a timeline for the next month or so," Bren rambles more to herself than anyone.

A door slams. Bren is now tilting her head, intently listening to the other side of the locker room. "I hear the boys coming in, so we'll go give them our spiel before you whip them into shape. Can we get fifteen minutes with the boys now?"

Coach nods and asks Bren to close the door behind us. Wow, that was a lot. What did I sign up for? I guess I'm lucky my course load is so light with all the extra community college classes I took the last two years.

Bren gives Suz a thumbs up. It must be the signal she needs because Suz is suddenly strutting down the hall shouting in a singsong, "Boys, it's your favorites. You better be decent for us because we're walking down from Coach's office. Be on your best behavior if you don't want your PR and marketing team to slander your name."

Bren laughs and rolls her eyes at me. We follow Suz to the main part of the team's area. I gaze around the locker room. The numbers above each player's space catch my eye, and my heart sinks into my stomach with despair. How many times did Nick step foot in this locker room? Which locker once bore his number 88? Does someone else use it now? My mind is racing with a million questions as my heart mourns.

Suddenly, I forget all those questions as I unexpectedly take in Liam in a towel. A salacious, eager grin slides across his face as he eyes Bren, who winks in return, mouthing something about losing that towel later.

The players are suited up and decent when we walk in, except one cocky bastard that I've never seen before and now unfortunately am seeing entirely too much of. He's in the back of the locker room, completely naked, just letting it all hang out for anyone to see.

Lucas rounds the corner, naked body also on display, though it's the opposite of unfortunate seeing a glimpse of the captain's glistening muscular body. It takes everything in me not to let my jaw drop in those few seconds.

Droplets of water coat his biceps and stream down his torso. Before I can take in the delectable view and assess the captain's jewels, Liam chucks him a towel. and he turns with his back to us quickly. I notice his sexy back dimples as he hastily ties the towel around his waist.

"Hi, girls." Lucas rubs the back of his neck, flustered as his face turns beet red. Maybe he isn't as bad of a guy as I pegged him to be.

"Sorry didn't know you would be here so early. You know we want to be respectful—" Lucas cuts off his own sentence to turn and look at the still-naked guy in the back. "Mitchell. What the hell is wrong with you?"

Ah, that's Blaine Mitchell, the delinquent trouble child. The pompous smirk on his face is exactly what I was expecting, but he appears boyish with dimples on each of his cheeks and short sun-kissed brown, bordering on blond hair peeking out from under his backwards hat. Naked except for a hat? He really fits the cocky jock role to a tee.

"Donato, always pretending to be a hero. It's nothing they don't want to see, especially the new girl. What's your name, baby?"

Blaine's green eyes scan my body before he gives me a "sup nod." Lucas' brow furrows with outrage. His hands ball into fists and I notice his body tense, showcasing his scrumptious back muscles. Desire stirs deep within me. Drool almost escapes down the side of my mouth as I shake the daydream of massaging those muscles while he lays beneath me.

"I swear to God, Mitchell, if you don't start being respectful and get your shit together—" Lucas starts, fists clenched, but I cut in.

"I'm Laur. Lauren Bellinger." Whispers spread through the locker room when the team hears my last name.

"Thanks, Captain, but it's not a big deal. Next time, Blaine Mitchell, if you want to impress a girl, have something worth showing off. Since you clearly don't—" I say looking him up and down pointedly "—I'd say finding some dignity would do wonders for you."

Lucas' jaw drops along with a few other guys. Mitchell isn't the most attractive on the team—that's clearly Lucas—but he's still hot. He has something worth showing off between his legs, but I don't care in the slightest. I'm not about to let some prick mouth off at me pretending it's flattery. Blaine Mitchell is now on my shit list.

Bren goes through a quick spiel telling the "Sexy Seven" we'll be in touch and that all new players will need to submit a bio by the end of the week if they want any chance at being highlighted on social media or anywhere else.

As I leave the locker room, my heart thumps loudly in my chest thinking about the next time I'll get to see the captain on full display. Bren starts to discuss some next steps for the Sexy Seven, but I've completely tuned her out.

Did Lucas think I was too brash cutting him off and telling off Mitchell? Or did he find it appealing that I can hold my own? Why does he seem to be the only thing on my mind after Bren just went over important assignment details?

Chapter Seven

Lucas

The way she just told Mitchell off while also calling me Captain has me heated. Holy hell. Lauren Bellinger is God damn hot, but she is trouble. Maybe I mislabeled her yesterday as just an angelic looking girl with an attitude. Or maybe she is just showing she's capable of holding her own, which is sexy as hell. I clear my mind of her and then clear my throat to talk to the team.

"Team, listen up." I inhale sharply, unclenching my fists and erasing the image of my dream girl—who's probably just a nightmare dressed as a daydream—out of my head, before addressing my team. As I walk through the locker room, I make sure to meet the eyes of every player.

"We are going to have a hell of a season, and those girls are going to showcase us as the stars or the assholes we are. Don't fuck around and find out what happens if you don't get your shit together before the season starts."

I linger in front of Mitchell and his cronies, ensuring they get the message.

"We need to build an even better reputation. This season is an important one. Not just for some of us, but for all of us."

Someone whispers, "Is she related to Bellinger?"

"Yeah. Don't make it a big deal but, Lauren Bellinger is Nick Bellinger's sister." Chills skitter down my spine as the words leave my mouth, but I'm not sure why.

"If you didn't get to know him, it's your loss."

I find Mitchell again, looking him dead in the eyes before continuing to move through the locker room.

"You treat Lauren with respect. More respect than most of you show your mothers. Because I know Nick would kill any of you who disrespected his sister, especially in his locker room, no matter if you're his best friend or a newbie to this team. Liam and I will do the same."

I intentionally seek out Mitchell to give him a final glare. He knows I am about to take this out on him once we are on the ice, and he'll be in pain the rest of the week.

Being on the ice feels like home to me. The second I step onto it, the only things that matter are the feeling of gliding across the ice, my stick gripped tightly in my hand, and the game I am devoted to. No matter what's going on in the rest of my life, the ice is my escape, my sanctuary. But not today. Lauren Bellinger still lingers in the back of my mind.

I force the team to run skating drills, hoping to quiet my mind. As we start passing drills, Coach calls me over.

"What's going on, Donato?"

"What do you mean Coach?" Can he sense that my mind isn't dedicated to the ice? Am I off my game?

"Just seems like your head might be elsewhere."

"No, Coach, just needing to blow off some steam."

Coach Andres taps the top of my helmet before instructing the team it's time to scrimmage.

Liam skates over to me, offering me a fist bump to check in on me. Exhaling deeply, I signal to him I'm good with my gloved fist bump back before we skate into position and dominate our mock opponents.

After ten minutes into the scrimmage, my mind starts to focus but my emotions linger.

What would Nick Bellinger do?

Fueling my power with anger, I check Mitchell hard against the boards. I'm not someone who fights or antagonizes, but I am a captain who will make sure to teach players a lesson when they need it. Mitchell is a bad seed, and he needs a hell of a lot of lessons.

A minute later, I do it again, only this time I warn him in a low voice, "Get your act together. I won't warn you again, Mitchell. Do not fuck with Lauren Bellinger."

Chapter Eight

Laur

The blaring alarm jolts me awake. Two early days in a row. My warm, cozy bed is calling to me to crawl back in and sleep longer. I am going to have to get used to this whole early morning routine.

After meeting with the coach and the team, Bren told Suz and me we would meet for an early lunch today. She suggested we come to our lunch meeting with fundraiser ideas and story ideas for newbies on the team and our Sexy Seven. She mentioned we'd also discuss divvying up responsibility for articles and content around the seven featured players throughout the season. That means I'm about to be close with two or three of them. I pray Tyler is one, and I pray even harder that Captain Lucas Donato is not.

I'm debating if I want to squeeze a run in before diving into a brainstorming session, so I have something to share during the meeting. Nick would always talk about running in the mornings on campus. Despite my lack of enthusiasm about running more than a mile at a time, I toughen up and decided to give it a go. Maybe it will make me feel closer to Nick. He swore after six miles he always got a runner's high. I never believed him.

I've usually found running the opposite of peaceful. Today is no exception. It didn't take my mind off anything. Instead it gave me time to think about literally all the things I didn't want to think about: Nick not being here; the pressure from being part of the Wyverns' Student Marketing Team; finding myself again; the four classes I need to get books for and one that somehow already has an assignment; the delicious V I got a glimpse of on Lucas' body in the locker room.

I only hit four miles. Maybe I don't run far enough to get a runner's high and escape the world. Or maybe my mind races faster than my feet and I'll never reach that anxiety-free euphoric high no matter how far I go.

After I grab a quick breakfast and shower, I dig through my room to find one of my many planners and notebooks, needing to jot down some ideas to take with me to the WSMP meeting—Wyverns' Student Marketing Program, but Bren usually just calls it "the gals' hockey meeting." I finally find them shoved in a box in my closet. I guess I didn't do as great of a job unpacking and organizing as I thought.

I spot a small, plain black, leather notebook in the box. This notebook is one hundred percent, not mine. If I was going to have a black notebook, it would have shiny gold or silver foiled letters and decals. I open it and slam it shut immediately, throwing the book. On the inside front cover, in the sloppiest male handwriting I have ever seen, it says "Nick Bellinger."

Holy shit. Did I just find my brother's little black book? The oatmeal I had for breakfast threatens to come back up. There is no way. Nick was a good guy! Or at least I thought he was. I'm glad no one else is home right now because I might start screaming profanities at the top of my lungs if I open it again.

Picking up the notebook from the floor, muttering "Please don't be my dead brother's sex adventures," I open it again. The notebook isn't filled all the way. There are some hockey plays, a lot of notes on other teams and other players, what appears to be some notes on his Wyverns teammates, some running routes, and most importantly, nothing about girls or sex. *Thank you, Jesus!*

"Nick, I knew you weren't a perv, but I was worried for a second," I murmur to the sky, well, ceiling.

I thumb through the notebook, stopping on a page with a few sketches. Exhilaration tingles through me, and my eyes widen with delight as I take in the most elaborate of Nick's drawings. An idea for the team's fundraiser literally fell into my lap. I haven't gone through the entire notebook yet, but it dawns on me I haven't found Lucas' name anywhere in the pages so far. I make a mental note to read through it more thoroughly later.

The smell of lattes and pastries fills the air as I walk through Roast & Revelry, the best coffee shop on campus. I spy Bren and Suz huddled together at one of the excessively large community tables that seems to have the entire contents of Bren's backpack frantically scattered across it, clearly hogging the table. They are whispering in hushed tones.

When I sit down, I hear Bren say, "I think it makes the most sense, but she isn't going to like it."

"Am I she? What am I not going to like?" I put my things down next to Suz.

"Well, the Sexy Seven. We are going to need to divide and conquer between the three of us. It makes the most sense to just have players dedicated to each of us. Since you're new, of course, you will only be taking two. We wouldn't put the extra work of a third player on you. We were thinking of just doing it by who's in our year since we would likely have the most similar schedules."

I go through the list on the printout Bren hands me. There are the two seniors who aren't NHL focused: Jamison Clarke and Micah Lawson. Liam Welsh (Bren will of course take him to focus on), and Connor Rizzo are also seniors but are of NHL interest. The goalie, Keith Hall, is technically a senior but he's staying an extra year after switching majors four times. That leaves Tyler Barret, who I of course would love to focus on and—now I see why Bren was concerned. Our glorious captain, Lucas Donato.

"Oh. So, Tyler and Captain Donato." I sigh. "If that's really what you think works best."

"Look, he's one of my best friends. He's a great guy. It shouldn't be a big deal, and we need to be professional! But I'm feeling kind today," Suz says, scribbling down names on seven pieces of paper. "We can draw names. Bren and I will both support the seventh man together. You can pick first, Laur." She scribbles on small torn pieces of paper and throws them in an empty coffee mug.

I looked at Suz, shocked. Barbie is being kind? She's barely spoken a few words to me and has only referred to me as Lauren until now.

"Okay," I say. "Thank you." I carefully select a piece of paper from the coffee cup.

The paper says Captain on it.

"You have got to be kidding me! The universe hates me."

With an excessive sigh, I put my head in my hands in disbelief. Suz laughs almost maniacally before I glare at her.

"Wait. Did you write Captain on all of them?"

"Of course not. Some of them say Luc, Lucas, Lucas Donato. They are all technically different names." Suz laughs.

Bren almost spews her coffee as she cackles, joining Suz. I am clearly the only one not getting a kick out of this. I lunge for the coffee cup containing the paper, thinking Suz will fight to beat me to it to cover up her tracks, but she doesn't budge. Still glaring at her, I slowly uncrumple all the papers inside the cup.

"I was kidding, Lauren. Goodness. You will have to trust and like me eventually," Suz says.

The papers have all seven of the Sexy Seven names. It really is just the universe pushing us to spend time together. Great. I really need to read Nick's little book to find out his opinion of the guy.

"Back to the original plan then. I'll have Liam and Clarke. Suz, Rizzo and Lawson. Sweet little Laur, Tyler and Donato."

Getting to know Lucas more . . . Great! Just what I signed up for!

"Aside from the calendar, and gala dinner we do every year, we need to brainstorm new ideas for fundraising next week. We cannot do another auction of the players. That turned out so badly last year when it got hot and heavy between someone and someone else's stepmom." Bren's face distorts in repugnance like she just smelled a rotten egg.

I very audibly choke on my coffee at the shock of what I just heard.

"Yep, you heard her right." Suz' tone is laced with disgust and discomfort. Her expression is incredibly priceless that I'd almost let out a giggle if I wasn't overly repulsed myself.

"I won't name names. But unrelated, I'm surprised Michael Taylor even graduated, good riddance . . . Anyways, I've got to run. Laur, interview your two players before the end of the week. Juniors will be spotlighted first."

I was extremely distracted finding out about last season's escapades and needing to get buddy-buddy with Lucas all season that I didn't get to bring up the sketches I found in Nick's notebook. I'm going to have to get creative with how I fight my attraction towards him. Maybe I can knock two birds with one stone with both juniors to focus on.

Chapter Nine

Laur

Three days later, I've set up time for interviews with both Tyler and Lucas. I thought it would be easier to meet with both of them on the same day between their workouts. None of us have class today. I just want to rip the band-aid off and get my one-on-one time with Lucas over with.

I haven't interviewed anyone in a while. The last interview I did was with Nick for a class I was taking at community college called Advanced Digital Content Creation. I took classes year-round after graduating high school. The more credits I had to transfer to West meant less classes and more time to focus on the hockey team and building a portfolio. I guess I was pretty successful there. I transferred to West with seventy-six credits. It would have been seventy-nine if my stupid sculpting class I took for fun transferred.

Coming to West and working with this team was a big dream of mine. I wish Nick were here though. I know I sound like a broken record, but at least I feel less like one. Nick would be one of the Sexy Seven if he were here. I wonder whose place he would take. Would I be interviewing and writing articles about him if he were still here?

Near the locker room and gym, there are a few small meeting rooms. I grab a couple bottles of water just in case someone needs them and re-arrange the chairs for a more intimate setting. I'll use my phone as a camera so I can make sure to go back and listen to anything I might have missed while I am taking notes and engaging with Tyler or Lucas. I don't mind interviewing people when it's not live, but I easily get lost in the heart of stories that the interviewees share. Live interviews give me incredibly sweaty palms. I'm a little camera shy and hate the idea of always needing to be "on" in front of an audience, no matter what's happening in real life. I much prefer the writing and digital marketing side of things.

Libby, a sophomore on the Student Marketing team, is sitting in and ready to type out the answers the boys give to the questions I've already prepared. I warned her that I might go off script. I want to make sure we get as much of an authentic story as possible.

I head into the gym and find Tyler lifting with Lucas. How convenient. I greet both of them, and hug Tyler even though he's drenched in sweat. I try to keep my eyes averted from Lucas in his gray sweatpants and cut off tank top that accentuates his undeniably sexy biceps. I know he looks like a Greek God underneath the thin fabric of his clothing. My heartbeat quickens just from my quick glance at him.

"Tyler, you're up first. Lucas, I'll need about twenty minutes after I'm through with Tyler to wrap up notes, and then I'll be ready for you. There will be a camera, just my phone so I can be sure not to miss any details in your answers. Do you consent to being filmed?"

They nod in agreement.

"Great! I doubt it will be good enough footage to use for anything later. Like I said, it's just to ensure I get all the details possible. On the off chance we use the footage, we'll be sure to discuss it with you beforehand."

Both guys nod again. Tyler grabs his water bottle and hoodie then follows me out the gym door. Tyler's interview takes about an hour.

I ask him about his personal life: his family, his relationships, school, where he grew up. I have to ask him about his younger days playing hockey. I knew it would be difficult for us both because he played with Nick. I can sense him trying to hold back and say as little as possible for my benefit.

"Tyler. I need you to give me more than 'yeah, I loved playing hockey growing up. I fell in love with the sport when I was traveling for it.' I need depth."

"Laur." He looks up at me. I haven't seen him look so serious or sad in a long time. "I'm trying to protect you."

"It's okay, Tyler. I love you for that, but the world deserves to hear your story. So, let's start again. Libby,"—I turn to the sophomore helping me—"make sure you take thorough notes on this."

"Tyler Barret, tell us a little bit about growing up playing hockey."

"I started traveling for hockey when I was eight. I didn't think it would last long. Honestly, I thought I would have to quit. My dad was always traveling for work and my mom worked a lot too. I figured a few months on the travel team would be it for me. My mom got promoted and started working more. My best friend's family changed everything for me."

Tyler shifts in his chair, his gaze focused on the floor in front of him avoiding my gaze.

"Let me start by saying, I loved staying at hotels with the team. I didn't have any siblings so getting to hangout all weekend in a hotel with my team felt like I had a giant family. Nick was my best friend. Your mom told my mom that I could come with Nick, you, and your mom, to a tournament one weekend. Mrs. Bellinger overheard my mom telling the coach she wasn't sure if I would be able to join the team for that weekend because she had a work trip."

Tyler looks up, his green eyes locking with mine as his shy smile starts to form.

"I know I said I loved staying at hotels because I felt like I had a giant family, but staying with your family I really felt like I actually had a brother and sister."

Warmth spreads through my body hearing how much we meant to him. Happy tears are tempted to fall before Tyler starts to give more details.

"Nick was a hell of a hockey player, even at nine years old. After that first weekend tournament with you, I went to so many over the years with your family. Nick was slightly older and a better player, so we eventually ended up on different teams when I was about fifteen.

We stayed close but there's nothing like the bond of spending every weekend shooting shots with your best friend. Hockey gave me the siblings I always wanted."

Tyler stops. The story is beautiful. Now, I'm fully teary-eyed, reminiscing about roaming hotel hallways with Nick and Tyler. Tyler clears his throat. He's a little teary-eyed too.

"Tell me about your experience before transferring to West. What made you decide to change schools?"

Tyler starts talking again, but I'm zoned out. My mind is stuck on Nick now. The first time I interviewed Nick takes over my thoughts . . . It was around the time that Nick and Tyler started playing travel hockey together. I was eight and convinced Nick to be my first interviewee. I had to tell him three times to stop making up stories about how he could literally fly across the ice with wings. He was clever and funny, but I wanted it to be a real story I could submit to a paper. I wanted to be a real journalist. Once I told Nick I wanted to submit it to a paper and he realized other people could potentially see it, he got serious.

I took five pages of notes. That's a lot of writing for an eight-year-old. My article was called "Carrying on the Bellinger Legacy." I wrote about how Nick still played hockey after Dad had passed a year ago. Nick was carrying on the Bellinger legacy that he started. Mom was beaming with pride. She helped me submit it to the local paper. I was a published journalist for the first time, and Nick was in the paper for the first time. Nick asked mom to frame the article for his room.

"Laur? Any other questions?" Tyler asks.

"Oh. No, not right now." I wasn't paying much attention the last ten minutes. I'm so glad I video recorded this and have Libby's notes.

"Thank you so much, Tyler." I hug him. "I'll reach out with anything else, but I should be good for the week. Tell your captain you gave me good content, so it'll be closer to thirty minutes before I'll come grab him."

My mind is still swirling with thoughts of Nick as Tyler leaves the room. Diving into my notes about Tyler really focuses me. I got such amazing detail on why he fell in love growing up. It was clear he felt comfortable with me sharing details I didn't know before while we went down memory lane. Jotting down a few key notes, I start to remember how much I enjoy writing about hockey. My content on Tyler is going to have the perfect personal touch to it.

Half an hour later, I finish my notes from Ty's interview and head to the locker room. Lucas is bench pressing a bar loaded with what seems to like every weight plate in the gym. Counting the plates, my eyes widen. He's casually lifting more than twice my weight.

Delicious beads of sweat drip down his bare, hairless chest as he places the bar back down. He was barely wearing a shirt before so why did he need to take it off? He stands up, and his grey sweatpants shift, catching my attention. His bulge is clearly visible, leaving very little to my imagination but, there is absolutely nothing little about it . . .

Lucas Donato, I hate how you take my mind off everything else.

"Hi, Laur." Lucas is a little breathless as he towels off his dripping face and shoulders before walking over to me.

Shit, I'm a little breathless myself as my eyes scan his body. I am getting much more than a glimpse of that glorious V. There is no way in hell all the players look like that. Greek God is a perfect description for him. It's like his torso is made of stone, each ab chiseled to perfection. I notice a little happy trail at the bottom of his V, leading to what I'm sure would be a very, very happy place.

"Ready for me?"

You have no idea how ready and willing I am. My cheeks grow hot as my lady bits start to hum with desire. I want to be the one who sees where that happy trail goes to.

"Laur?"

"Y-yes," I stammer, attempting to reel in my promiscuous thoughts as he pulls his sweatshirt over his head.

What is wrong with me. I'm never this distracted by someone. I can't be distracted by him; I don't want to get involved with anyone. Swearing off love is the right choice for me.

"I'm going to grab some caffeine. I'll meet you there. The room is across the hall, turn right coming out of the gym, second door on the left." I quickly exit the gym before he can say anything else.

I immediately dart into the bathroom, thanking God it's a one-person washroom and look at my reflection in the mirror. My cheeks are flushed. Have I always blushed this much? I swear I didn't use to, but then again, I'm not very used to looking at a man and instantly wanting to jump his bones right then and there. I splash some cold water on my face. That does very little to calm me down. I'm going to have to be around him all season. I need to get through this interview with a clear head and focus.

My chest rises and falls rapidly with my quickened breath fueled by sexual chemistry and longing. It's so out of character for me to even be considering this . . . but my lady bits are now singing with desire and need as my mind revisits the image of the outline of his cock in those thin pants. I tell myself it's just to ensure that I get a great interview and not be distracted by thinking about seeing more of him.

If I sat on his lap fully clothed, straddling him, my leggings and his thin sweats would hardly be a barrier to him hardening against me. There would be no stopping him from feeling my pussy dampen against his growing erection just for me.

This man drives my mind and body into overdrive, just from witnessing him shirtless. Watching the sweat drip down his torso in the weight room sent me into a frenzy wanting to be that bead of sweat, intimately grazing every curve of his sculpted torso continually moving south.

The lust is too much to bear. I willingly succumb to it. Pretending that his rough calloused hands are on me, I insert two fingers into myself.

Chapter Ten

Lucas

She's taking a while to come back to interview me. Is she even still here? She seemed very flustered when she came to the gym to get me. She was frantic and fast with her words, but it seemed like she was barely registering anything I was saying to her. Her mind was clearly elsewhere. Why does Lauren hate me so much? I have to figure out why. I want more time to get to know her. It's a stupid idea but seeing her from behind walking out of the gym today, and the way she holds her own, I just want to know her. I'll have to have someone rig the Beer Olympics for me, so she's forced to be on my team and spend time with me outside of the rink.

A different version of Lauren walks through the door. Her previously frantic manner has turned calm and she's lighter, almost as if she's walking on air. She's almost glowing.

"About time, Bellinger," I say.

She stares at me with a dumbfound, blank expression before it registers with me that she heard Nick's teammates call him Bellinger her entire life.

"Sorry, I mean Laur, Lauren."

If I'm being honest, I'm nervous. It's not about being interviewed. It's because I want to make sure I sound interesting in front of Laur. The last thing I want is for her to think I'm some stereotypical jock without a heart. For some reason, what Laur thinks about me matters to me a lot more than what gets printed in any articles or posted online.

Lauren starts off by asking me what made me want to play hockey and how I got started. I relax into my chair; this is the easiest question she could start off with. Good.

"My family loves hockey. I remember a game always being on TV whenever we had any type of family gathering. My dad and uncles always placed what they called the rivalry bet. All four of them have different NHL and college teams they support. When I was growing up, they were always betting on games against their teams, which meant there was a lot of 'Lucas, put on your earmuffs' from my mom when they got frustrated and swore."

I laugh reminiscing about being seven and hearing my dad cuss out his oldest brother because my dad always rooted for Chicago even though they were terrible back then.

Laur is laughing too. "It seems like you are really close with your family," she says.

"Oh yeah, all of my extended family. I'm the youngest of all my cousins by about six years, so I was the only one who got told to put earmuffs on, even though I usually only did until my mom left the room. Sometimes the men in my family can be sore losers. My dad was losing a lot on those rivalry bets when the Blackhawks were on a losing streak. I grew up watching all twelve of my cousins play hockey. I would beg my mom to go watch them play. It fascinated me, mostly because of the ice-skating aspect. It might sound dumb, but when you think about it, every sport outside of hockey involves running, which anyone can do. Can anyone run fast? No, but everyone can run. Not everyone can skate."

Laur leans in closer to me in her chair, her intoxicating blue eyes eagerly telling me to keep going.

I nervously scratch and crack my knuckles, hoping her interest is on more than just getting the content she needs for articles.

"I think even when I was younger, I liked the challenge of needing to learn more than one core set of skills. When my mom started signing me up for the usual young kid sports like soccer or gymnastics, I refused to go until she signed me up for hockey and skating lessons. I started skating lessons when I was three. When I was four, I asked her to sign me up for skating lessons and hockey. Not the 'learn to skate hockey,' I could already do the basics. I got to do more of an intro to hockey with older kids. I wanted to try to play with my older cousins as soon as possible, even though I couldn't at that age."

Laur asks me about my time freshmen and sophomore years playing. I realize I've never been so comfortable opening up to someone about my life—my past, my future, even things not related to hockey—but with Laur, it comes easily. I can't put my finger on quite on why, but Laur gives me a sense of calm and ease that I have never experienced around anyone. I feel like I can tell this girl almost anything. I reluctantly tell her about my girlfriend freshman year. I try not to tell a lot of people, but she made me choose between her and hockey. She always complained I was too busy to spend time with her and wanted me to just be a college kid.

Laur snorts after I tell her this story. I look at her puzzled.

"What?" Laur says.

"What was that for? I had to put hockey first. I had worked—"

Laur cuts me off. "You don't have to explain yourself, but I'd love to meet this girl so she can. Hockey is clearly more to you than just a sport. I'm going to go out on a limb and guess it was a dream for you to play for the Wyverns. To ask someone to give up their dreams for you is selfish. When you're with someone, you still chase your own dreams, but you support your person's dreams too. They don't compete or envelop each other, but you just start to dream and grow together instead of by yourself."

Laur quickly averts her gaze, shifting in her chair. She's fidgeting with her notebook as her cheeks start to glow with embarrassment. "Sorry, I don't know why I said that. It's none of my business."

Laur gets it. Dreaming and growing together sounds like something I need. I've never met the right person to do that with, but it seems like I might have just met that person.

"Let's move on." Her cheeks are now fully flushed scarlet. Seeing her unintentionally open up pulls on my heart strings. I'm glad I'm not the only one who feels how naturally it comes when the two of us are talking. I don't want to move on from this conversation. I want to pull her chair as close to me as possible. I pull my hand back, running it through my hair instead as I see a girl typing furiously in the corner and suddenly remember we are not the only two people in the room.

She asks me more about my first few years on the team and what it means to be captain now. I leave out one story from freshman year. I don't want to talk about Nick in front of her and make her hate me more. It's a memory I will cherish forever. Someday, when the time is right, I'll tell her the story.

Chapter Eleven

Laur

The interview with Lucas went much smoother than I expected. I'm not sure if it was my self-induced release minutes before or if it is because he's a decent human. I couldn't shake the feeling that Lucas was holding back though. He didn't tell me why he specifically chose to come play at West Michigan and talked minimally about his freshmen year. He surprisingly talked about his sophomore year so much more. I wonder if he's hiding something. Maybe he just really sucked freshman year because of that dumb girlfriend of his telling him hockey wasn't as important as he made it out to be.

I couldn't imagine if someone told my brother that; he would instantly dump them. He wouldn't want to even be friends let alone date someone who didn't support his dreams. I can't imagine someone telling me that, and I don't even play the sport! At least I have nothing to be jealous of when it comes to his ex-girlfriend. Lucas' sour tone showed he didn't have any interest in her anymore.

A few days after my interviews, Bren, Suz, and I attend a practice to watch the team play. I haven't spent much time watching their skills on the ice aside from old footage. The team is only on warmups, but I remember how this is my favorite place to be: the chill in the arena air, the sound of scraping skates on the ice, watching the players smoothly dance across it. Of course, I live for the thrill of being in the arena on game day, but there is nothing like watching a player who is determined, concentrating on honing their skills.

If you look hard enough, you can see the players focused on the attention to detail making small adjustments to improve their shots or passes. You can see the dedication some of the guys have to trying to consistently enhance their game. You can see their commitment to being a better version of themselves. You can also see their love for hockey. Witnessing that when they think no one is noticing is the best part.

"Hey, Bren," I ask, "Can I come to more practices? I'd love to take some rookie photographer shots with my camera and get some raw footage for the socials and articles." I'm far from a professional photographer, but I do love messing around with a camera and pretending I am.

"Of course! Just don't get it into your head that you're going to capture the calendar content. We need a skilled professional with a keen eye to capture the sex appeal so we can sell those babies!"

"No kidding. I would probably instantly be uncomfortable and leave the shoot if I had to do that anyways." I roll my eyes. "I'll come back tomorrow to take some shots."

"Just don't forget to get ready for the Beer Olympics at 6pm tomorrow night! It's the last hurrah every year before the guys really kick it into gear and turn the partying down a notch." She laughs to herself. "Well, most of the guys and most days. They are college guys after all."

Beer Olympics? This is the first I'm hearing of it. What are the Beer Olympics? Shit. I am not athletic enough for this. I am going to make a fool of myself in front of the entire team. Bren must sense my unease.

"I told you, right? I'm sure I did! Don't worry, it will be easy-breezy. Teams are already picked, and you're with me and Liam so you'll be fine! It's mostly just drinking games. You won't have to use those keen athletic abilities of yours. Just don't wear leggings, dress cute for pictures please!"

Bren and Suz get up to leave. Dress cute? I'll have to ask Bren or Jaylin to pick out my outfit tonight, or Amazon Next Day Shipping might have to be my saving grace. What are these teams? It shouldn't be too bad if I'm with Bren and Liam.

Chapter Twelve

Laur

I wake up at the crack of dawn and get ready for a run. I'm slowly getting used to being a morning human. Nick had ten different running routes mapped in his notebook up to twelve miles. I've decided I'll try them all out, gradually working up to the twelve-mile routes. The shortest is five miles so I suppose that's my run for today. Maybe I'll eventually reach that anxiety-free runner's high. But not today. I barely make it the five miles as it is. I doubt I'll be able to make the twelve-mile loop by the end of the year.

After I shower and have breakfast, I head down to the rink an hour and half before the team starts practice. I want to take some practice photos and make sure to adjust the camera settings while no one is watching. I spent three hours last night refreshing my memory with YouTube tutorials. Once I'm alongside the ice, I start to take some shots to adjust the lighting settings.

"Taking photos of ice ghosts?" someone calls from behind me. I whirl around, my feet shooting under me and land flat on my ass. The cool surface of the ice seeps through my leggings. My heart is pounding in my chest. I had no idea someone was in here. The rink was empty when I got in here twenty minutes ago.

"Shit! Are you okay?" the mystery person asks.

I start to get up, but a hand reaches out to me. It's Captain Lucas. Dreamy as ever. I take his hand, and he hauls me up, hard. I slam into his chest, but he seems unfazed. Lucas doesn't even move an inch when my body collides with his. Shit. His body is against mine. I can feel his perfectly muscled torso against me. My brain fixates on the divine V gracing that torso. It's beyond seductive. The warmth coming off his body is so inviting. My body heats in more ways than one. I look up into his brown eyes. They're almost hypnotic this close. The gold specks in the light brown draw me into a trance.

"Laur? Lauren? Are you okay? You look out of it. Shit. I am so sorry. Do you have a medical condition I don't know about? You seem pale. Let me call one of the med staff; someone should be around to come check you out."

"What?" My voice is a hoarse whisper. I blink and shake my head, ridding myself of the trance. "Oh. No." My voice is still quiet. "I'm fine. No, I'm fine. You just startled me! I didn't even hear you come in."

"Are you sure?" Lucas looks at me concerned.

"Yes, yes, I'm sure I was just startled. I'm perfectly fine." *I just have to remind myself I do not want anything from you no matter how gorgeous and fit you are.*

"Okay. You are looking better, I guess . . ." He chuckles. "I'm crazy, and I'm here an hour early two or three times a week to practice more on my own. What are you doing here? You didn't say no to taking photos of ice ghosts."

Look out of it? Oh boy, little do you know how not out of it I was. I was just imagining us out of these clothes with our bodies much closer together. I need to keep my distance from you.

"Oh. Of course you do, Captain. Sorry, I'll leave you to it," I respond instead.

"Trying to stay mysteriously sexy by not telling me?" He raises one eyebrow, looking at me, waiting for an answer. I realize I completely ignored his question. Thinking about the captain is making me act very out of character.

"I just wanted to adjust some settings on my camera so I can take better action shots during practices. It's a hobby of mine. I'm not very good but figured we could use the extra photos for social media, maybe some articles, or whatever." I peer down at the ice, shyly avoiding his dreamy eyes.

"Amateur photographer, huh? Need an amateur model? I'm sure it's easier to adjust the lighting and whatnot with a person in the frame. I don't mind at all. You need to practice and so do I."

"No, that's okay. I'm sure it will be fine." I turn to leave.

"Come on, Laur. You don't have to hate me, you know. We are probably going to spend a lot of time around each other. We might as well be friends." Lucas gazes into my eyes. I can't tell if I see friendship there, but I can't have him thinking I hate him, even if I wouldn't mind hating him.

"Okay." I nod in agreement.

"Let me go gear up. I'll be back soon. Don't get spooked or fall without me!"

Lucas is off to the locker room. Fall without him? I'll just fall for him, and that is not part of my plan for this year. It can't be. This is a bad idea. I shouldn't spend one-on-one time with him. At least during his interview there was another human in the room. It'll be fine. I'll be fine. Plus, I really could use someone so I can get the damn settings right on this camera. Those YouTube tutorials were not as helpful as they seemed last night.

Lucas comes back to the ice in his practice gear. I feel the familiar sensation between my legs as I take in Lucas. How is he somehow even more attractive with more layers on? It must be the appearance of him in full gear with the luscious hockey flow. Damn. I am such a sucker for good hair.

"What do you need me to do?" Lucas asks.

"Just pretend I'm not here and practice like you normally would."

Lucas does a few loops around the rink at various speeds with his stick and puck. After about the third time around, he starts stickhandling drills, moving the puck back and forth rapidly. I start snapping pictures. He looks up, stopping when he notices. He starts again but goes up and down the length of the ice instead and skates backwards every few seconds. I'm done adjusting my camera.

I look at what I've captured so far and notice that he's subtly making faces at me. I giggle at one where he's cross-eyed and his tongue is sticking out just a tiny bit like a little kid does when they concentrate hard.

"Lucas, you're supposed to pretend I'm not here. Stop making faces! I won't be able to use any of these," I reprimand between giggles.

"I thought they were just test photos! Don't use these." He tells me not to use them but keeps going around the ice making ridiculous faces for me to capture.

"Oh, I am going to use them. Especially this one where you look like a constipated seven-year-old trying to wink at a girl for the first time."

I cover my mouth, attempting not to snort with laughter. But the more pictures I take, the more certain I am getting an amazing ab workout in from all my giggling.

Lucas stops right in front of me, spraying me with ice.

"Hey! That's cold. Don't be mean to me, Captain, just because your amateur modeling days will be ending soon with these facial expressions."

Lucas leans over me to catch a glimpse of the photos I've taken, sending my heart racing. My giggles subside as his breath grazes my neck and the longing between my legs is back again. His laughter fills the empty rink, replacing my giggles and pulling me back to reality.

"I hope I'm really not that unattractive when I play. That's so disappointing. I should just put my helmet on so you can barely see my face."

"You couldn't look unattractive. Keep the helmet off. I'll take some real shots if you're up for it." Did I really just admit I find him attractive? Shit. I knew this was a bad idea. I'm too comfortable with him. *I've sworn off love*, I remind myself. I don't want to be invested or interested in anyone.

Lucas has a cocky, crooked grin on his face. That grin makes him look like a model. Anyone would want to jump his bones if they saw that grin. "Deal. Tell me what to do, Photographer Lauren. Make me look good for the fans."

He skates away, giving me a cocky, exaggerated wink.

Lucas and I spend the next half-hour having him skate slowly towards me. He's cracking jokes and making even worse kid-like silly faces now, trying to make me laugh. Boy, does he succeed. I finally convince him to stop goofing around. I sit down on the ice.

"Come at me from the left side. A little slower than normal speed. Keep your eyes about an inch above the camera, look at the top of my head, don't look down at the puck."

"Yes, Photographer Laur." He salutes me and goes to the edge of the ice. "Gimme a thumbs up when you want me to go, please, photographer."

I give him the thumbs up, and he skates to me faster than I expect. Damn, he's got some speed. I can't wait to see him play for the first time. The chilly air gets to me as I sit on the cold ice, asking him to skate toward me a few more times from different directions. The world falls away as I capture him in his element.

Lucas reaches down to help me up, grabbing my forearms. I'm pressed up against his chest again. I pull away quickly, hearing a few players walk into the locker room. Practice must be starting soon. Have we really been taking photos for an hour?

"One more. This time, you stand up, and I'll skate straight towards you from center ice. That perfect booty is probably colder than the ice by now from sitting that long."

My jaw almost drops. Did he really just say that? He is now shamelessly flirting. Lucas Donato thinks my ass is perfect.

"Ready for me?"

Does he always have to ask if I'm ready for him? It's like he's inside my head and knows all the sexual things I think every time I see him shirtless, or his body is close to mine.

"Earth to Lauren!"

I give him a thumbs up, and take ten rapid fire shots. Lucas comes up behind me as I scroll through my camera. My back is almost flush against him. I scoot away a few inches before I stupidly let my desire overtake my brain.

"So why do you come early to practice by yourself?"

I'm curious about Lucas' answer. I know Nick used to do that.

"I like hockey, I guess," Lucas says, making another ridiculous face at the camera. I give him a sassy 'are you kidding me' look.

"I want to be the best I can be. As cheesy as it sounds, I've always felt the most myself and at home on the ice. This game is my heart. Some of the guys last year used to do it, so I started also."

Does he mean Nick? I'm not sure if I want to know. The way he describes his drive and passion for hockey reminds me of my brother. *Nick*. Somehow, I have managed to hold myself together this long. I change the subject as I click through some of the shots.

"These are actually great."

"That was a lot more fun than I thought I would have practicing by myself. I guess we'll be spending a lot of quality time together today. You'll have to send me some of those pictures. Don't post anywhere. Please. I look like I'm learning how to flirt with girls for the first time. Those are for your eyes only."

I stifle a giggle again before my face scrunches in confusion. What is he talking about?

"Quality time?"

"The Beer Olympics. Didn't Bren or Liam tell you the four of us are a team? See you there, Laur!" Lucas skates off to chat with some of the team.

No, Lucas, Bren conveniently left that part out.

I look at my camera to see the last photos of Lucas skating toward me straight on. In all of them, he is looking directly at the camera with that cocky crooked grin of his. He must have purposely looked straight on instead of above the camera, so it seems like he's making eye contact with me when I look at the photos.

Shit. Bren better hope she isn't home when I get there. But now I really need her help picking an outfit since I failed to make her or Jaylin help me last night. At least my Amazon order should be coming in.

Chapter Thirteen

Laur

Lucky for me and unlucky for her, Bren is sitting on the couch when I get home.

"Brenna Marie Martinez!" I wouldn't be surprised if our neighbors could hear me. "Why did you not tell me that the Beer Olympics team is *not* you, me, and Liam?"

"But it is," Bren says.

"*No, no!* It is also Captain Lucas Donato! *That* was conveniently left out."

"Why does it matter?" Suz comes around the corner. Shit. She must have been in the bathroom. I don't need her to know I have a crush on him. She's best friends with the guy and seemingly in love with him.

My lips press together as I fall silent. I can't possibly divulge my lust for the captain to her.

"Do you have a crush on him or something?" Suz asks.

"Not even close," I yell. Suz gives Bren a look.

"She doesn't. Laur is not interested in Lucas. She is guy-free this year and focused on marketing for the team and her future!" Bren chimes in for me. As she turns to look at me, she must instantly sense my infatuation with Lucas oozing from every pore of my skin and can easily see that she is now very wrong. I do have a crush.

Suz looks me up and down. "Look, I know I haven't been the nicest to you, Laur, and I apologize for that. But I'm trying to protect Lucas like Bren is you. The guy is a fucking saint and doesn't even sleep around. Sure, he might look like a cocky player, but he is the furthest thing from it. He can't help that he's attractive. Shit, he can have more than half the girls on campus. I'm not even into him. He's like a brother to me, but even I'm not immune to his good looks and charm."

Barbie isn't in love with Lucas? Thank goodness. I feel like a weight has lifted off my shoulders.

"Oh," is all I manage to reply.

"Do you want to talk about it?" Bren starts.

"No. It can't go anywhere. It's just a schoolgirl crush that will pass. We will just be friends, absolutely nothing more. This stays between the three of us. I will know if it doesn't." I glare at both. "Understood?"

They both hold up a pinky to me, and we promise in a three-way pinky swear.

"Now that we are done acting like high school girls, can someone please pick a cute outfit for me since I will have to be with him all night?" I groan. "I ordered about twenty things from Amazon. And just because Lucas is only my friend doesn't mean I don't need to look hot at the first party I go to."

Bren and Suz look at each other excitedly and stand up.

Suz claps her hands together in typical Barbie fashion, "*Yes*! Bren, grab the wine!"

Chapter Fourteen
Lucas

The Beer Olympics has been an annual tradition for the hockey team before our practice schedule ramps up. It's always been a shit show. I have a blurry memory from last year of Tyler bouncing a quarter so hard it dented the table and profusely apologizing. Nick Bellinger was laughing so hard and said this bonding experience was just "drunk idiots making (not-so-lasting) memories before kicking our asses into shape." His statement will still probably be fitting for this year.

This year, it's in Liam, Connor, and Tyler's backyard. Convenient for me because I live just a block away. I'm in a Hawaiian button-down shirt I ordered four days ago off Amazon. Somehow Hawaiian was our team's theme when other team themes range from solid colors to SpongeBob SquarePants to just straight plaids that just clash. The solid color black team really went for it with all four of them wearing eyeliner and black lipstick.

"Aren't you glad we're black lipstick free?" Liam says as he pats me on the back. "The girls just got here. They're putting their stuff in my room."

"Yes, very glad. I don't think it would be our shade, but a bare nude-rose might look nice with the flowers on your shirt." I chuckle knowing this is part of our typical bit when anyone mentions lipstick around us.

"Bare nude-rose? I tell you one lipstick name, and you use it more than I ever thought you would," Bren chimes in, giving me a hug.

"As much as I do? What are you even talking about? This is probably the third time I've ever said it! But it is very fitting," I tease back.

"You don't think I would look lovely with some bare nude-rose on these lips, babe?" Liam goes along with my stupid joke before kissing her. "Lucas is just looking out for me."

I think Bren responds, but their words fade away as I take in Laur walking into the backyard. I tune them out as soon as I see Laur. Her dark brown hair is down in loose curls framing her face. She's wearing a floral blue and green two-piece outfit that makes it hard to look elsewhere. It's very different than her usual leggings and oversized t-shirt. The top is cropped, showing off her riveting midriff, and very low cut. My eyes linger on her cleavage as I take her in and drag my eyes back up her body. Her body is flawless.

As she makes her way toward our group, our eyes meet. There's electricity and triumph behind her stare from watching me drink her in like I've been lost in the desert for days. It's taking all my focus to fight my hard on while she's looking at me with those baby blues. I could get lost in them for hours, but I'd do almost anything to get lost in that cleavage too.

"Hi. Nice shirt," Lauren says shyly.

"Oh, this old thing? Why thank you. Your outfit is pretty on point. If you dressed like that at practices, the team wouldn't be able to look away. Shit, we'd be out of shape and play terribly. You look beautiful."

That's my line? Seriously. Why do I suck at compliments? I don't need her thinking about what power her beauty might have over anyone else on the team. I just want her to fully understand that she can wield that power over me day and night, while getting to know that I'm far from the bad guy she instantly pegged me for.

"Thanks." A pretty pink creeps over her neck and cheeks, different than the scarlet I've seen the last few days.. "I'll stick to t-shirts then, but Amazon did wonders for my new themed party wardrobe."

"Yeah, when I said this old thing, I meant I got this shirt in the mail three days ago from Amazon. Where else would I get a Hawaiian shirt around here?"

Lauren laughs at my admission. "Good point. I doubt we could find a store that sells them this time of year around West Michigan."

God, the sound of her laugh is melodic, like a song I could listen to on repeat for weeks. I can't hold back my own chuckle.

"So, team," Lauren starts. Liam and Bren are paying attention to us now. "I've never done Beer Olympics before, and you know I am terrible at drinking. Someone give me details on how this works before I make a fool of myself."

I'm sure it's not possible for this beautiful girl to ever look like a fool, but there is no possibility of that happening when she looks like a tropical queen, ready to save her kingdom at a moment's notice. Too bad she doesn't need saving.

Bren starts to explain how the four of us, as couples, will divide and conquer games. Couples. I love hearing Laur and me being referred to as a couple. I swear when the words come out of her mouth, my heart beats faster.

I can't believe I told Bren I wouldn't make any type of move on her. Well, technically I said I wouldn't fuck with her, and I'm not. I think I could be serious about her. Liam tells me to focus as he's explaining the games we'll be playing. There's about ten of them ranging from quarters and beer pong to dizzy bat and flip-cup.

"Wow, that's a lot to keep track of." Lauren is taking it all in. "And a lot to drink."

"Liam didn't even tell you the best game yet. It's called puck and chug. All four of us need to shoot and make a goal after chugging a full beer before all the players on the other team finish." It's my favorite part of the night every single year.

"Why is that the best game?"

"It's not," Bren whines, "half the girls are really terrible, especially drunk. So it takes forever. It's hard! Of course, the guys are great at it, but they play hockey every damn day!"

"Great, I have to be coordinated after drinking for hours too?" Lauren groans. "I'm still processing the other fifty games I'll have to figure out how to play tonight. I am a professional at flip-cup though and great at beer pong. Nick taught me." Laur flips her hair in confidence.

"Well perfect, you and I will dominate the flip-cup table then." I hand her a light beer and hold mine up to her to clink against. "We got this, Laur."

We're about four hours into Beer Olympics now. Our team has won almost every game we've played. Lauren and I are up next at the beer pong table. Then we just have puck and chug left at the very end when all the teams have completed their games.

Lauren wasn't lying. She is pretty good. She's made two of the five shots she's taken. I've only made one. She's making me look bad.

"Not sure if you would have gotten your title as captain if you played basketball instead of hockey." Lauren teases when I miss a shot after she sinks yet another ball in. I love when she teases me. She seems happy, carefree, and almost giddy.

"I swear I'm never this bad. Maybe you're bad luck!"

"You take that back, Lucas Donato! I am the furthest thing from bad luck."

"We'll see, Lauren Bellinger. Right now, it's not looking that way."

"Fine. I'll prove it."

Before I can say anything back, Laur turns towards me with a flirty smile that I haven't seen before. Her bright eyes are brimming with eagerness. Then, she leans in and kisses me. The music and party fade away as I taste the beer that lingers on her lips mixed with her fruity lip balm. Her lips are softer than any mind could dream up, almost like wispy whimsical clouds of pure pink perfection. I know I will never be able to get enough of them. Her skin is soft and heated with passion as I graze her cheek to cup her face and pull her in closer. I brace myself on the table with my other hand to stay upright, stunned that Laur's lips are pressed against mine. She hated me this morning. I have no idea what's happening. But I do know Lauren Bellinger is going to be more than just my good luck charm. Holy hell, I need more of this angel, so much more.

Lauren Bellinger, you are going to be mine.

Chapter Fifteen

Laur

Warning bells and caution signs fill my head as I take in what I just did. Shit. What am I doing? I just kissed him. Why did I do that? I was just coming to terms with wanting to be his friend, then I go and do that? *Stupid alcohol.* I can't let him know I'm spiraling in my head about it. I need to play it cool.

"Now shoot, Captain."

If it wouldn't be obvious, I would pat myself on the back with pride at how I managed to mask the shakiness in my voice. He aims for the island shot—and makes it! A few minutes later, we've won the game.

"Guess you were right, Laur. You are good luck. Good thing you'll be at all our games this season."

While Lucas chats with our opponents, I quickly find a place to sneak off to sit, relax, and hide my now scarlet red face from Lucas. I am getting in way over my head. The last game we have is puck and chug. Lucas saunters over, asking if he can join me as he hands me a solo cup filled to the brim with beer. I definitely should not drink it after having made the stupid decision to kiss him. I didn't even think it through; I just reacted to the flirtatious atmosphere between us. *What was I thinking?* I got swept up in the moment. I need to tell Bren about this stat and hope Lucas never brings it up.

"So," Lucas says, "you kissed me."

That hope lasted less than minute. I just nod dumbly at him. I can't think of anything to say.

"Cool, okay, we don't have to talk about it. We aren't allowed to practice for puck and chug or I'd offer to help you work on your shot,"

Lucas is floundering, grasping at anything to keep the conversation going. "So, tell me something. How's school? How's working with the team and fundraising and whatnot?"

"Actually!" I light up. "Hold on." I chug my beer to ease the nerves. I haven't told anyone about Nick's notebook yet.

"I found a little black book in my things the other week. My mom or Dominic must have put it in my things because it's Nick's." Lucas goes wide-eyed, concern written all over his face at the mention of a possible list of sex-capades. Giggling at his expression, I explain away his concerns.

"Yeah, that's what I thought too, but it's just random thoughts of his: notes on running trails, notes on different teams, notes on Wyverns players, and some random sketches too. There's a page I found that has two different ideas for Wyverns jerseys. What if we created them as an alternative jersey for the team. We could sell them at games?"

Lucas' concern is quickly replaced with vigor.

"Lauren, that's an amazing idea!" I can see the wheels turning in his head while he brainstorms how this idea can come to life even more. "The whole team can wear 'Bellinger 88' jerseys during his jersey retirement ceremony later in the season. Have you told Bren yet?"

I don't respond. Hot tears slide down my face as wrap my arms around myself. I can't blame the alcohol for these tears. I'd still be crying sober. I had no idea that Nick's number would be retired. My heart swells with love for this team and these people more every day I'm here.

"What's wrong? I don't think I said anything to make you upset, but I know I'm not the best with girls even if the entire school thinks I'm a ladies' man. They are dead wrong."

A smile takes over my features. It's adorable how Lucas is distressed over the possibility of upsetting me.

"No, it's not you, but you are a ladies' man, you big flirt. I didn't know that his number was being retired. Bren didn't tell me. That's—I'm speechless. Nick would love that. You know how he always bragged about how he would be the next Gretzky."

Lucas' laughter mixes with mine. "Oh, trust me, the first time I met him he told me." Lucas puts his arm around my shoulder, pulling me into him for a hug. I close my eyes, taking in subtle hints of his woodsy, warm cologne mixed with the fresh smell of clean linens that lingers on his clothes. The blend of these two scents is uniquely him. I cling to his side as I breathe in again, his scent starting to feel too comforting, too familiar, putting me at ease.

"I'm glad I came here—to West Michigan. I almost didn't. But I learn more about Nick every day, and I almost feel like my old self again."

"I'm glad you decided to come too, Laur." I see a glimpse of something on his face like maybe he's going to kiss me, but he hugs me again before standing up and reaching down to offer help up. "Let's go. It looks like everyone is finishing up. I'll go through the puck and chug rules with you."

I shouldn't be sad that he didn't kiss me. *I don't even want him to kiss me, do I?* I don't know. But I can't help wishing we could have shared a real sentimental kiss instead of my quick drunken-stupor kiss. I shake my head. No. No dating. No guys. Especially no hockey players. That was the deal I made with myself. I've sworn off dating. I've sworn off love. I do not want Lucas Donato, and I certainly do not want him to kiss me. We can be friends. That's it.

Lucas shows me three lines marked on the ground that I can shoot from: the closest also known as the newbie line, the rookie line in the middle, and the farthest line, which he says all players must shoot from. He tells me not to worry because I can shoot from the newbie line and Bren has shot from it for the past three years.

Liam goes first. He makes the shot on the second try.

Bren goes next. She scoots an insane amount past the newbie line. She goes through puck after puck attempting to make the goal so the next player can go. After about ten tries, she makes it. We are so close to the team in first place.

Lucas scores flawlessly and hands me the hockey stick. I move to the farthest line back that all the team has shot from. Lucas makes his typical Lucas questioning face—that is to say, he looks sexy and perplexed with one eyebrow raised.

I wink at him and draw in a quick deep breath. Closing my eyes, I picture Nick standing behind me in the crowd fist pumping the air, championing me on. I bring the stick back and hear a scraping clunk when I connect with the puck. My stomach is in knots with nerves as I watch the puck soar slightly above the ground before swishing into the goal.

A collective gasp fills the air. I turn to the crowd, smiling so wide that my mouth instantly hurts.

"Chug your beer!" Lucas screams at me. I almost forgot that's part of the game because I am jumping up and down thrilled with my shot. It's been over a year since I've even used a hockey stick.

I finish the beer and throw down the can. "DONE!" I shriek.

"WE WON!" Liam and Lucas both yell together. Lucas scoops me up into a hug. I notice most of the guys still have shocked faces that I not only made a one timer, but I made it from their designated "player" line.

I turn to Lucas. "See, friend, I didn't need you to help me with my shot. You do remember who my dad and brother are, don't you? I am a Bellinger. There was no way Nico or Nick Bellinger would let me be so in love with hockey and not learn a thing or two."

Chapter Sixteen

Laur

I wake up the next day with a raging headache but find water and aspirin next to my bed. *God Bless Bren, the drunk mom.* I have zero desire to get out of bed, but the enticing smell of bacon fills the house. I pop the aspirin, throw on some shorts with my XXXL Wyverns t-shirt that I claimed from the overflowing box of swag in locker room storage. It's quickly become my favorite sleep shirt.

"Good morning, Chip," Bren says cheerfully from her place at the stove. She looks abnormally put together for the long night of drinking we just had. Plus, she and Liam definitely drank more than Lucas and I did, so I know she should be hurting as bad as I am, if not more.

"How are you so upbeat and lively?" Bren looks like she could run a marathon right now. I have my hair bundled in the world's messiest bun on top of my head.

"Three years of college with Liam and the hockey team builds a strong liver. You'll learn, my dear. Pancakes? Bacon's almost done."

Jaylin comes into the kitchen. I realize I haven't seen her in a while since Bren and I have been so focused on the team.

"Hey, J, what's new with you? Fill us in on your life."

"That bacon smells divine. Laur, did you know that the smell of Bren's bacon is what made me try pork? I wasn't disappointed! She's always cooked a feast when she goes too hard the night before, and I cannot say no to bacon," Jaylin replies.

Bren winks at her. "I have sausage too. You know I crave meat hungover."

"You know I never crave meat." Jaylin laughs. "Speaking of me not craving meat, I did go on a date earlier this week. That's about the only thing new with me."

I almost spew my orange juice at the double entendre. "Oh! Tell us more! We love details."

"Yeah, tell us everything. Laur is a huge gossip." Bren teases. Bren is the biggest gossip I've ever met. Somehow, she can keep a secret, but she lives to hear the drama of everyone else's lives. Her discretion and skillful convincing skills, getting her all the juicy story details, are going to make her an amazing PR manager someday.

"There isn't much to tell just yet. It was only one date. We just went on a walk and got some coffee. It was really sweet. I feel like I got to know her so well in just an hour. But she's not out to the world yet, which I think will be difficult for me. We'll see, I guess. I have plans with her again. I think I'm going to make a little picnic for us to take by the lake before it gets too cold to enjoy being outside."

Jaylin loudly crunches another piece of bacon.

"That's an adorable idea! I want a picnic! Please tell Liam that swoon-worthy date idea."

"So, what about you two? Aside from clearly being hungover from last night, how did the games go?"

"We WON!" Bren dramatically slams the fridge door after putting away the orange juice and is galloping with glee around the kitchen. I swear just watching her is going to make me throw up.

"And Laur shocked all the guys by scoring on the first try at puck and chug, from the player's line!" Bren is shrieking now. My head is pulsing harder.

"Seriously?! That's amazing. I'm sure every single person there was floored and jealous. No one ever shoots from that line except for the team." Jaylin passes me the plate of bacon bowing her head as if to honor me and offer me congratulations in the form of crispy, mouthwatering bacon.

"You've done the Beer Olympics too?" I ask Jaylin.

"Oh yeah, Bren forced me to be their fourth person last year. Lucas is one of the nicest guys I've ever met and beautiful too. I mean clearly, I'm not interested, but I do have eyes." Jaylin shrugs. "Kind of seems like he doesn't bring girls around."

Doesn't bring girls around? Hearing that tugs at the corner of my lips. My head isn't the only thing pulsing now. My heart beats faster thinking about him. Lucas Donato wasn't lying. He plays the part of the ladies' man well but doesn't date.

"What are you smiling about, Laur?" Bren demands. "Spill the tea, now."

I start to feel hot and clammy. Is it the hangover or because I don't want to divulge that I might have more than a crush on Lucas and I made a stupid, drunk mistake last night? Either way, I know I need to stick to my promise to myself. I'm not ready to explore anything outside of friendship with a guy.

"Earth to Chip! You better tell us, or I'll pry it out of you." Bren tries to get my attention.

"IkissedLucaslastnight."

It comes out as one word. I run to the bathroom, hair held back, my head in the toilet. I hate hangovers. I did not have this much fun in community college. I also don't think I've ever drank for more than five hours like I did yesterday. Usually, I was with Bren or Nick. They both were a little wild, so I tried to stay on the tame side.

"Are you okay?" Jaylin enters the bathroom and kneels down next to me.

"What was that?" Bran glares at me from the doorway of the bathroom.

"I drunkenly kissed Lucas last night." I say again. This time with my head in the toilet.

"Holy shit. Finish spewing your guts up so you can have some bacon and share all the details," Bren says.

I come back to the kitchen where Bren has a mound of bacon, sausage and pancakes along with a Diet Coke and more Excedrin for me—the best hangover cure. Even when she's judging me, she's still always taking care of me. Sighing, I pop open the soda before sharing my embarrassing story.

I tell Bren and Jaylin about how flirty Lucas has been and about how adjusting my camera settings somehow led to an amateur photoshoot, and how he keeps getting me to open up to him and keeps sharing pieces of himself with me. I tell them how attracted to him I am, how my slightly tipsy self wanted his lips on mine and just went for it, and how he called me his good luck charm, saying if I was around the team would win more games this year. I tell them about realizing he wasn't the douchey, bad guy I assumed he was after I interviewed him and how I most certainly did not want to be interested in anyone and needed to be focused on marketing and PR for the team, grieving Nick, and finding myself.

"Who knew tipsy Laur was so bold!" Bren teases. "It could be worse, at least you remember everything. Honestly, Chip, it sounds like you might actually like him."

"I don't want to like anyone, let alone Lucas. I came here to focus on my future and get more experience in sports marketing and PR. Maybe to find myself again too. Not to date. I just want to be friends with him."

I finish the last sip of Diet Coke before continuing to pick at my untouched food.

"You can definitely find yourself under him next time," Jaylin blurts out.

"*Shut up!*" I retort back.

"Honestly, I haven't seen Lucas with a girl since his freshman year. He isn't a bad guy at all—people just expect him to be a ladies' man as the captain of the hockey team," Bren explains.

Even though other people have told me this before, it's finally starting to sink in that Lucas is one of the good ones. A sense of relief washes over me, despite knowing I made him off-limits for myself.

"So, you like him, huh, good luck charm?" Jaylin teases.

"Don't call me that! I . . . I don't know. I don't want to, but it's going to be hard just staying friends with him. I don't want to complicate anything. I need to get Tyler's opinion. He's known me so long and would have good advice. I'm going to meet him tomorrow for lunch anyway."

"Oh, so Tyler isn't in love with you?" Jaylin says, "This whole dynamic of the PR girls and team throws me off. Isn't Suz into Lucas?"

"Absolutely not. They are like siblings! Suz would be appalled if she heard you say that. Lucas is wrong for Suz in every way possible," Bren explains.

"And Tyler's like a brother to me. I would never," I respond at the same time.

"Good to know, good to know," Jaylin says laughing.

I go back to bed and sleep on and off most of the day while watching Netflix. Maybe I do like Lucas. Bren claims he's a good guy. I'm not used to good guys. I'm used to seeing a red flag and ignoring it. I apparently love chasing red. But if he is, then what am I afraid of? What would Nick say?

I leap out of bed, remembering his notebook. He wrote notes on all the Wyverns players too. I am desperate to know what he wrote about Lucas. Frantically opening the notebook and almost tearing a page, I thumb through it skimming every single word ensuring I don't miss anything before finally finding Lucas' name in my brother's barely legible handwriting.

Great Guy. Going to go far.
He

Are you kidding me? He didn't finish the notes. He wrote a paragraph about Blaine Mitchell but couldn't finish two lines for Lucas? What the hell? Thanks for the help, Nick.

The next morning, I go to practice and take some pictures. Lucas tries to catch my eye, but I avoid his attempts for eye contact. I know once he looks at me, I'll have a hard time not swooning.

I love watching him play hockey. You can tell by the way he effortlessly seems to dance across the ice, he's in his element. I try focusing on taking pictures of other players before I have an entire memory card filled with just Lucas. Why couldn't he just be a womanizer or a douchey jock? It might make my marketing efforts harder, but at least it would make my feelings disappear.

After about an hour of taking photos, I leave to meet Suz and Bren at Roast & Revelry. I've been waiting to share the idea of the fundraising event with them. Oh, and yell at them for not telling me about Nick's jersey retirement.

Per usual, Bren has a six-person table with little actual table space available. She hands me an iced caramel macchiato, my favorite. We chitchat before getting into business. Suz mentions she went on a cute picnic date recently that went perfectly. That's the second time that someone's mentioned a picnic date recently, are they trendy right now?

I avoid any mention of Lucas, while Bren tries to jump straight to business.

We discuss the stories going out about the Sexy Seven online and hope to get some printed at a discounted price in various college hockey magazines.

"I took some great photos of the guys at practice today and plan to go back again tomorrow. We can use some for the articles if you'd like," I offer.

"You take photos? Can I see some?" Suz asks excitedly.

"Sure. I haven't edited anything yet." I open my laptop to show her some of the photos.

"There are a lot of Lucas on here." Suz notices. I didn't think about how obvious that would be.

"Yeah, he's one of my focuses." I fumble to make an excuse. "Plus, I took some of him before practice the other day when I was just adjusting my camera settings and he was running some drills on his own."

"Well, it's great you are good with a camera. We're going to need you. The photographer we've hired for the last three years for the calendar bailed on us." Suz takes a sip of her drink as she slowly rolls her eyes in the most dramatic way imaginable.

"She did not bail on us, Suzanne. She had a baby!!" Bren turns to me. "Laur, I just found out this morning, and Ms. Big Mouth over here blurted it out before I got to ask, but do you think you could do it? We could pay you a portion of what the photographer was being paid."

Bren eyes are wide with desperation. She clasps her hands together making a begging motion towards me.

"Sure, I'm happy to do it. I don't need the money though. Wait. Can we put the money toward something else? I have an idea that might cost a little bit of money, but it will be worth it," I reply.

"You are an angel, Chip. What's this idea?"

"I've got to jet to my call with *USA Hockey Magazine*," Suz cuts in. "I'm hoping to convince them to get us a discounted rate, if not free placement, for some of these player profiles in the 'Hot on Campus' section. Fill me in later!" Suz gathers up her things and starts typing away on her phone as she leaves the table.

"First of all, you should have told me about Nick's jersey retirement. I shouldn't have had to find out from Lucas."

Bren fidgets in her seat and avoids meeting my eyes.

"I am so sorry. It wasn't intentional. I just wanted to be able to tell you about some amazing elaborate plan I have for it to combine with fundraising in Nick's honor, but of the hundreds of ideas I've come up with, none are worthy of Nick." Bren's slightly slumped over the table, still actively avoiding my gaze.

"I'm not sure if you've heard, but I happen to be a good luck charm. I have an idea for one."

"It must be perfect. You're smiling your famous Bellinger smile." She perks up, finally looking me in the eyes as the lingering guilt in them is replaced with intrigue and thrill.

I go into details on the big reveal of Nick's own designed jerseys from the little black book. She's on the edge of her seat with enthusiasm.

"We can send mockups to the fashion school to design! It will be the perfect way to honor him. Maybe we can even take pre-orders!" I am so glad that Bren is as excited as I am.

"I know Nick would be more than okay with us using them. Hell, he would be telling everyone in the universe about how the coolest custom-made jersey of any college team was designed by him." I laugh picturing him wearing the jersey 24/7.

"Back to Nick's jersey retirement. Do you want to give a speech? Do you want to plan it?" Bren's voice is filled with sympathy as she asks.

"No. No speeches, no planning. This is my contribution. I'll focus on the jersey, if you can send me the design school contacts you have."

"Okay, you can be involved with whatever you want to be. Just know that." Bren grabs my hand and squeezes it.

I only nod and can't find the words to respond.

Bren fills the awkward silence. "What else was in Nick's notebook? Anything worthy of sharing?"

"Not really. Some running trails, some notes on other teams that I should probably share with Lucas. Oh, and some notes on each of the guys. Everyone on the team last year. Nick wrote paragraphs about some people."

"What's in there about Liam and Lucas?"

"You know Liam was one of his best friends. I didn't read it, but I'm sure it's a glowing review. He literally just has 'Great Guy. Will go far' written for Lucas." My eyes dramatically roll instinctively. "Fucking annoying. I could use more intel." I mutter into my coffee as I take a sip.

Giggling, Bren says, "He's a great guy, anyone will tell you that. He's also a great hockey player and captain."

"It looks like he was starting to add more. Every other player has lines and paragraphs. He wrote one line and one word that's clearly an unfinished thought."

"Oh, bizarre. I wonder what he was going to say."

Did Nick have something against Lucas that he didn't want to write down? Or was Lucas just the last team member he was writing about, and he didn't have a chance to complete it? Either way, I need to stop drooling over Lucas.

Chapter Seventeen
Laur

The calendar photoshoot is in a few days. The lingering pit in my stomach has driven me to fiddle with my camera anytime I'm at the house. Bren bought me a new lens with some of the money for the original photographer. I've taken some photos at practice, but they are all in motion shots. I need to practice on the ice with some still shots before the shoot to calm my nerves.

After the team is done practicing, I wait for Tyler outside the locker room. I volun-told him to be my subject, which has the added benefit of getting more pictures of him for social media and articles too.

"Hey, Ty," I call to him. He's walking out of the locker room with Lucas.

"Hey, Laur. Don't be mad at me, but I forgot I have a paper due tomorrow that I haven't even started on yet. I already got an extension on it and can't ask for another one," Tyler sheepishly explains.

Tyler is always so reliable. I frown with disappointment. It's obvious I'm not happy with him, but he can't control that he has schoolwork. I can tell he feels guilty.

"But don't worry! Lucas said he could fill in for me. I'm so sorry! Please don't be mad. I would never bail on you!" Tyler genuinely sounds sorry.

"It's okay. Ty. I get it. Go write your paper."

I give Tyler a hug, and he says bye to Lucas and me, before heading off.

I turn to Lucas. "I'm sure Tyler begged you to do this for me, but don't worry about it. I don't need a test subject. I'll be fine."

In what I've come to realize as a typical Lucas fashion, he raises an eyebrow and looks at me puzzled. "Begged me? I told him I would do it. He was going to ask Liam."

"Oh," is all I manage to say back.

"I had fun the first time," Lucas admits.

"Okay, well this time might be different. You might have to change a few times so I can see what looks good on different backgrounds. You'll probably have to take your shirt off and let me pose you too. It's a lot of pressure on me to do this photoshoot right, and I don't want to disappoint Bren and Suz."

"That's fine, Laur. You can position me however you want."

Did he just make a sex joke? That was definitely a sex joke.

I sigh. I don't really have a choice.

"Okay, Lucas. Get into fresh workout clothes. We'll start in the gym first. I'll meet you there."

I wanted to capture a variety of shots, some in the locker room, some of the guys working out, and then the team on the ice. I needed options for the cover of the calendar and at least one photo for each of the twelve months. I'll be taking photos of everyone on the team, but Bren is working on getting me a list of other players to prioritize outside the Sexy Seven and groups of players to capture too.

Lucas walks into the gym in a Wyverns t-shirt and those thin gray sweatpants again. Damn it. Even with his shirt on, I am about to be distracted.

"Is this okay?" he asks, pulling on his tee.

I am tempted to respond, 'if by okay, you mean I'm going to have a hard time focusing especially when I have to ask you to take your shirt off, then yes.' I just nod instead.

"Cool. Where do you want me, Chip?"

Chip. He's never called me that before. Only my family and close friends have called me that. How does he even know about my nickname? I guess he must have heard Bren, Liam, or Tyler say it.

"Oh." I look at him confused, still thrown off by him calling me Chip. "Let's start just having you do some free weights. You can go much lighter than you would in a typical workout if you want. Pretend like I'm not even here until I give you some direction."

Lucas picks up a heavy weight in each hand and starts to do some dumbbell deadlifts. I'm going to have to ask him to take his shirt off. . I know as soon as that shirt comes over his head, I'll be distraught, but I need to make this as close to the real photo shoot as possible. I'll wait until he's a little bit sweaty and done with his first set. I want his muscles to glisten a little.

"Take your shirt off, please. We'll have baby oil most likely at the actual shoot to mimic sweat and to have those muscles showing off and glowing." I'm almost drooling with hunger for him as he bends at the hip in front of me doing another rep.

"Take a break whenever you need to," I instruct. He just nods, starting up his reps again.

If any guy and any exercise could turn me into a girl that gushes over a man's ass, it would be Lucas Donato and deadlifts. My heartbeat quickens and seems to halt in admiration and longing as I watch him driving his hips forward, his legs and glutes working with each purposeful rep.

Taking pictures of him shirtless, showing off his sexy muscles and alluring V has me a little heated. I can feel my cheeks redden and my breath shorten with each move he makes.

He sets the weights down, bringing my mind back to reality.

"Sorry, I need a quick break. I didn't know this would be a workout. I worked out this morning before practice," Lucas says. I hand him a water bottle. It almost slips out of my grip from how sweaty my palms are. I could use a break too from all this heat.

"We're almost done in the gym. Just three more quick things. Let's have you do some lunges next."

He nods back at me. Directing his workout routine is kind of fun. I wish I could tell him to do push-ups with me on top of him as a weight, but I couldn't take photos laying across him feeling his muscles flex with each repetition.

"You can kind of fake the lunges. Just do one side, up and down slowly for a few reps," I tell him.

He just nods again. Is he annoyed that he's here? He's not as talkative as he usually is. I snap some quick shots. Looking through my camera, I see I've captured at least one perfect shot. He has determination in his eyes and his strong calf muscle pops as it's being worked. Is it possible to be turned on by a guy's leg muscle? That is a first for me.

"Okay. Pull-ups next, please."

He just nods again. He's not a man of many words today. He must be annoyed. I didn't even ask him to do this.

I notice his abs tighten as he pulls himself up, who knew they could look even more toned and chiseled. Again, my cheeks start to tingle with heat every second I take in more and more of his built body. His biceps contract as he pulls his chin over the bar. God was showing off when he created this man. No one was meant to look this delicious while sweating profusely.

"Great! Last thing will be bench presses with a barbell. We won't have to put weights on it since it's just a mock before the real photos are captured. I'm going to have to stand over you somehow—so it might take a little to get my footing right."

He just nods again. What is with him?

"Thanks again for doing this," I mutter before taking any shots. He's doing me a favor by being here.

"Of course, happy to help," he replies.

"Are you sure? You seem pretty unhappy to be here. Sorry, that I am making you work out again."

"Oh. No, it's not that at all. I am happy to be here."

"Then what's up? You're barely even talking to me, Lucas. Is it because I drunkenly kissed you? I'm sorry abou—" He cuts me off.

"No, it's not that at all." He shakes his head no with a slight laugh. "You just seemed to really hate when I called you Chip. I'm sorry. I'm not even sure why I did. I've never called you that before."

"Oh." Well, I guess that makes sense. I was really thrown off by his use of my nickname and didn't realize I was coming off as distant or upset.

"See what I mean?"

"Sorry. I was just surprised. No one calls me that except my family and close friends. I didn't even realize you knew what it meant."

"I don't know what it means. I just . . . Well maybe I wanted to be a close friend."

Lucas locks eyes with me. His brown eyes seem to have extra flecks of gold in them today. Sex jokes and sweetness both from Lucas over the span of an hour? It was going to be harder to resist him than I thought.

"It's really not an exciting story, but if you want to know, I'll make you a deal. After we're done in the locker room, I'll tell you before we do some shots on the ice. Deal?"

His signature crooked grin spreads across his face. "Deal. Bench press time."

Lucas helps me maneuver a soft box, used for jumps and step ups, next to the bench so that I can stand slightly above him while he lays down on the bench to get the right camera angle. I don't love the angle I have just standing to one side of him, so he allows me to have a sliver of the bench to tip toe on. With one foot on the box and one hanging off the bench and Lucas between me, I think I can try to get the angle I want.

"Okay, start lifting," I say.

He gives me a concerned look and mutters "Be careful" under his breath.

I've never seen someone's muscles from this angle before. He really does emit Greek God energy. My mind starts to wander about how the view looks if I was kneeling over him instead of standing.

Head in the clouds, mind in the gutter, I shift and lose my footing on one of the boxes. I try to regain my balance but it's like I'm slipping in slow motion.

Fuck.

Now, I'm straddling him. He racks the barbell and quickly places his hands on my hips. Oh my god, what is he doing?! He sits up and his chest presses to mine. We are chest to chest, nose to nose, lips mere inches from each other's. I take in a sharp inhale as I feel his breath on my skin. My heart is beating so fast I think it might beat right out of my chest. Can he feel it racing? A growing bulge presses against where he sits between my thighs. Those thin gray sweatpants are not hiding much at all. He picks me up effortlessly, pulling me off him as he stands.

"Sorry!" We both say at the same time.

"It's my fault. I shouldn't have stood over you. There wasn't enough room; I was bound to fall. Hopefully I didn't hurt your. . . you."

At least I avoided saying 'hopefully I didn't slam down on your cock when I fell.' Although judging by the slight hard on I can see in his pants, I don't think I did. Whoever designed these pants might be my hero. Or my worst enemy. I've sworn off love and should be focusing on my future.

He clears his throat and says, "Let me build on your idea."

He grabs another box from the other side of the gym and places it on the other side of the bench. Two boxes? Seriously. Why did I not think of that?

"Here, put both feet on the boxes so you're more stable. Try it."

I climb up on the box, this time placing one foot on each box instead of the bench. My feet are perfectly stable, and I have ample room.

"Genius, thank you. I really didn't want to try this again with any of the players in the real photoshoot and end up falling on them. Especially because it will likely be Mitchell. I barely know him."

"You don't want to know him. Stay away from Blaine Mitchell. He's bad news." He growls with angst at the mention of Mitchell.

"I'm taking photos of the entire team. No big deal. But thanks to you I won't have to worry about accidentally straddling him."

His shoulders and back tense. The beautiful gold fades away with his frustration, leaving pure brown in Lucas' eyes. He's not messing around.

"Like I said, Mitchell is bad news."

"I know, I know. I'm not interested, don't worry."

"Good. Glad I could at least help with the setup to make it easier on you." His shoulders shift into a more relaxed position.

Under his breath he mutters, "You can accidentally straddle me anytime, but I will strangle Blaine Mitchell if he touches you."

I'm not sure if I was supposed to hear that. I'm also not sure why I'm so turned on by his possessiveness and protectiveness. Lucas and I are firmly friend-zoned.

I'm still overthinking what he just said when Lucas asks, "Locker room next?"

"Yes, I'm going to grab a Diet Coke from the vending machine first. Want anything?"

"No, thanks."

I'm hoping the Diet Coke will relax my nerves and comfort me a little bit. I head into the locker room. Shit, what if he's changing? I should have announced I was coming in.

He's still in those sweatpants and shirtless, standing next to a locker. All the lockers have the players numbers and names on them. The last time I was in here, he was on the other side of the locker room. Whose locker is he by now if it's not his?

He hears me walking closer and turns his head.

"This was Nick's locker. We never let anyone take over the space."

I'm standing next to him now. The number 88 and Bellinger engraved on a wood plaque are starting to fade above the cubby. I take a deep sigh without even noticing.

"It must be really hard on you to be at West without him." Lucas's voice is low, hushed. It's filled with sympathy and compassion. I've never seen this side of him before.

"It is. Life is hard without him." I fight back tears with each word that comes out of my mouth.

"You're strong. He would be proud of you."

"Oh."

That's a weird thing for him to say. Does he even have the right to say that? Why does him saying Nick would be proud of me upset me so much? How well did he even know Nick? He must sense something in my voice or in my expression. Lucas is answering my questions before I can even start asking them.

"I played with Nick, but not as much as I wanted to. We were on different lines, but I idolized him. I remember the first home game when I was a freshman. Before the game, Nick was so excited and talking about how his biggest fan was coming. I remember seeing a girl taking photos at the game, and it seemed like she was only taking photos of Nick. When he said biggest fan, I assumed it was a girlfriend, but Nick never talked about a girlfriend. It was you."

Lucas' eyes are fixed on me, as I look up to meet his gaze. The pure brown eyes of anguish are gone. Only soft, kind golden eyes meet my teary eyes.

"You were the pretty brunette taking pictures during that game and all the other home games that season. Weren't you?"

Tears start to flow, and I can't seem to speak. I just nod. I was wrong. He did know Nick, and he does have the right to say Nick would be proud of me. I clear my throat and wipe the tears that made their way down my cheeks.

"Nick called me Chip when we were younger. No one knows where it came from. I was probably only one year old when he started it, so I don't really remember much. My mom thought maybe he heard someone else say it, but my dad never called me that. Then she said maybe he just couldn't say Lauren, but he could definitely say Laur so that didn't make any sense. Or maybe that he was trying to say something else, and no one could understand him because he was only two. Like I said, I don't remember much."

"That's cute. I wish you knew why though," Lucas says.

I let out a giggle as I wipe away more tears. "You and me both. Honestly, Nick didn't even know where it came from. He stopped for a while. Then it was Halloween time, and he told mom he wanted to be 'Dip' for Halloween and for me to be 'Chip.' My mom was so confused. My dad asked Nick what he meant. Nick explained; Chip and Dip, the little chipmunks that are friends with Mickey Mouse. My parents laughed so hard. I'm sure I laughed too even though I was only four. Dad said, 'you mean Chip and Dale.' After that, the nickname stuck."

"So, you were Chip and Dale for Halloween then?"

"No." I put my head in my hands, shaking with laughter at the memory. "Nick insisted on wanting to be Chip and Dip. So, Mom handmade us costumes. Nick was a bowl of guacamole, and I was a tortilla chip. We got a lot of weird looks from other kids that year, but it's still my favorite Halloween costume I've ever had."

"I would love to see a picture of that. How original." Lucas chuckles.

"Yeah, it was original that's for sure. But that was Nick for you—original to a tee."

I sigh and run my fingers over his name and number on the locker. Lucas puts a hand on my shoulder and turns me towards him.

"Hey, we can be done if you want to be. Whatever you need, ball's in your court."

Another big sigh escapes me. I swear it's just part of my vocabulary now.

"Thank you. I'm okay. Let's get a few shots on the ice and skip the locker room. The lighting is similar to the gym anyways."

"Sure, okay," Lucas replies. "I'll get my gear on."

"Thank you for showing me Nick's locker. I was wondering where his locker was the first time I came in here."

It still feels surreal being in this locker room knowing my brother will never walk through it. But somehow, each time I come in here it gets a little easier. I learn something new about Nick or think about a memory I've been suppressing. It feels like I am starting to get closer to him, and closer to myself too.

As I head out of the locker room, I can't help but wonder if Lucas is a big part of that.

"Hey, Captain," I yell.

"Yes, Chip?" he replies.

"Ball's in my court? Nice sports reference. But you should probably stick to the sport you're good at," I tease.

I'm craving to share that lighter mood with him again but hopefully less sexual. I'm focused on myself. No matter how charming and sweet ... and sexy ... Lucas Donato is, I will keep reminding myself of that, even if he's bold enough to use my nickname after hearing the story of how Nick came up with it.

His chuckles follow me as the locker room door closes behind me.

Chapter Eighteen

Lucas

I change into my gear and practice jersey. I'll save my real jersey for the actual shoot in a few days. Before I leave the locker room, I go to Nick's locker.

"Hey, man," I whisper, "she's doing great. You would be proud. I promise I'll be careful with her."

I head out to the ice, still smiling. Laur is standing on the ice in her gym shoes. Her smile transforms her entire face into light, she could outshine the stars. Now I understand why Bren calls it the "famous Bellinger smile." When she smiles, it looks like she just walked out of a commercial for a dentist office. It's contagious and makes me smile wider.

"What?" she says to me. I look at her confused why she's asking me that.

"You're chuckling and smiling like an idiot," Laur says back. "Well, that was mean—a happy model-worthy idiot."

"I've leveled up from amateur model, huh?" I laugh. "This is more fun than I thought it would be. I like spending time with you."

She doesn't say anything back, but somehow her smile grows brighter and wider as she turns away from me. Sometimes she's so guarded, but other times she's so free and open. I wonder if it's because of Nick or if it's something else.

I break the silence. "Okay, captain, where do you want me?"

"You're the captain! I'm just the stand-in photographer," she giggles.

God, I love that sound. It should be recorded into a song so I can play it on repeat when I need a mood booster on a rough day.

"Let's just get some snaps of you shooting. Don't pay attention to me at all. Just be in your element."

"Yes, Photographer Lauren."

She snaps some pictures from far away while I shoot pucks into the net. She moves closer and closer. My eyes keep straying back to her.

"You're not supposed to be looking at me, Captain."

Shit. I can't help it. She makes me fall into lust whenever she calls me Captain. Whenever "Captain" rolls off her lips it sounds sultry to me and my groin starts to stir. I start to think about her calling me Captain over and over as I please her, which only makes my blood rush more frantically south.

"Sorry," I mumble back to her, trying to focus.

"Alright. I'm going to stand right in front of you. This time I want you to look right at me. I want to see intensity in your pretty-boy eyes. Just don't hit me with the puck, please. I don't have time to go to the ER today."

Pretty-boy eyes, eh? She admits she's stared into them a time or two—good. I honestly can't tell how she feels half the time.

"I promise I won't hit you. No ER for you today."

She's about three feet in front of me. I close my eyes and take a deep breath to focus. I need to give her that intensity in my eyes. I shoot about ten times.

"Last shot. I mean camera shot. I need you to go against the glass." Laur grabs my arm and pulls me over to the glass. She's pushing me slightly against it and my mind can't help but wander back to thinking about pleasing her.

"Take your practice jersey off," she continues, "and put it over your shoulder and place it so I can see number 98 on the sleeve."

I take off my jersey. Good thing I didn't put any pads on underneath, or I would be much sweatier.

"Hold the hockey stick and turn your body to the left, but only turn your head slightly."

She's directing again, and I don't mind when she tells me what to do. I think I do what she asks, but I'm not entirely sure. I'm far from even being an amateur when it comes to this modeling shit. I hear the click of her camera a few times.

"I'm going to adjust you, is that okay?"

Why is she asking me that? Of course it's okay.

"Yeah," I mumble. She puts the camera around her neck.

"Leave your feet where they are, let me just move your body," she says.

Fuck. I would love for her to move my body. Her hands are cold on my skin. She puts one hand on each shoulder and gently moves me, so I'm angled more to the left. My muscles tense under her soft touch. I'm not sure if she notices. I want her to run her hands all over my body more than I've wanted anything.

She takes my chin in her hand and angles it more toward her. Our eyes lock, and my heart starts to beat faster. This girl has an effect on me that no one has ever had. She smiles that perfect Bellinger smile.

"Okay, don't move. But I want that intensity in your eyes. That hunger like you need to win this game or you'll throw punches."

She's instantly snapping photos, more than she's taken of any other shot. It feels like she takes at least two hundred.

"Perfect. Thank you so much for filling in for Tyler. I know you didn't plan on spending your day like this."

She signals we are done with the mini shoot.

"It's not a problem. I had fun."

She smiles that perfect smile again. Damn. I am not going to be able to get that view out of my head.

"For the record, I would never throw punches. Only if I'm kickboxing or actual boxing. Never against a player."

"You box?"

"When I need to get the frustration out. I want to be the type of leader that is focused, has his shit together, doesn't stir up problems, but will still fight for his team. I've only gotten into one fight playing hockey. Trust me, the guy deserved it. He checked one of my players so hard he had to get checked by a medic. I was eighteen. I'll fight for my team. They are my priority," I explain proudly.

"You sound just like my brother," Laur whispers.

There are a few moments of silence. She knows now that I'm aware of how huge of a compliment being compared to Nick is, especially in relation to hockey.

She breaks the silence. "Anyways, want to see some of the photos?"

I nod eagerly, thrilled she trusts me enough to see the raw photo. We walk off the ice and sit on the team bench. She starts to scroll through the photos. My jaw drops slightly at what I see—my skates spraying ice artfully, my number 98 blurry while I'm in focus, shirtless in the background, and endless photos of me working out that paint me in a much better light than our gym ever will. Most of all, she somehow captured how I actually feel in my element on the ice—peaceful, determined, at home. She has a real talent.

"You're incredible with a camera, Lauren."

"Thank you. It helps to have someone who looks the model part." She blushes with the realization she complimented me again. "And of course who takes direction very well. Look at this one. Your eyes say so much about who you are."

She shows me one of the last photos she's taken.

"What do you mean?"

I'm curious what she sees. She's right that my eyes look intense, but I'm not sure how they say anything about who I am. All I can see is me looking at her longingly.

"I don't know. Now I feel silly for saying that. I guess your eyes are showing your strong will, your love for hockey, and the protectiveness of your team."

All I see a guy reluctantly falling for a girl, but I nod anyway.

"Shoot, I'm late to meet Jaylin, my roommate, for dinner. Thank you so much again, Lucas. It means a lot to me that you did this. You're a good friend."

The word friend hits me like a freight train. She really doesn't see anything more than that with me.

She hugs me swiftly then heads out of the rink. I head to the locker room to change and head home.

She left abruptly, but maybe I'm reading too much into it. It was a wild mix of emotions during the mock photoshoot, but I couldn't be happier Tyler bailed so I could spend time with Laur. Every time I get to know her a little more, my heart aches for her. I don't know what it is about her, but I want to know everything I can about this girl.

Something in the air feels like it changed. I sound like a damn romance novel or one of those Hallmark movies, but I've never felt something like this before. The more time I spend with her, the more obvious it is to me. Laur is always on my mind. I just want to be around her. I want to laugh with her and hold her when she's crying. I want to share memories of Nick with her. I want to know all of her—the good and the bad.

I think it might be time to admit to myself that I can't stay away from her. Maybe it's time to admit it to her too. She can't just think of me as a friend when it's obvious the sparks are there between us, can she?

Chapter Nineteen

Laur

Today is the day. It's the real photoshoot for the calendar. My stomach does somersaults as I enter the arena, but the nerves are nothing compared to a few days ago before my practice shoot with Lucas. I felt guilty that I left so fast. I wasn't lying—I was late to meet Jaylin but I also needed an excuse to leave quickly.

I was starting to feel something for Lucas. We spent the day in close quarters, just the two of us. We shared memories of Nick. I shared memories that I haven't shared since his death. I felt close to Lucas. I trusted him and wanted to share more with him— which is what scares me. I swore off love and I am sticking to that. My heart won't be able to handle any damage from the inevitable agony that comes with relationships.

Bren is at the photoshoot to assist me along with Libby, the sophomore that's helped me with interviews and various tasks. She is easily my favorite of the lowerclassmen on the marketing and PR squad.

Bren gives the team a pep talk and reviews the schedule.

"Alright, team! Do not give Laur attitude today!" Bren's voice booms with authority.

"She is doing us a huge favor by stepping in when our photographer had to back out last week. If you do not listen or if you mess around, I will personally ensure that when Laur and I are editing, we don't do you any favors. Don't forget that we sold thousands of copies last year—even to students at rival schools. You don't want to look bad for this, boys," Bren wraps up.

"Thanks, Bren. Alright, full team locker room shot is first. Act like I'm not here and chat to one another until I give you direction to do something different. Libby, give them the baby oil please."

"Baby oil, you weren't kidding?" Lucas questions with his perplexed look, one eyebrow raised.

I will never get tired of seeing that perplexed look. If I wasn't against relationships, I would purposely make him confused just to see that alluring expression more often. How is it possible that someone could look that enticing when making any type of face?

"Yes, Captain, baby oil. Do you want those sexy muscles glistening for the camera? It's what the people of the calendar want," I reply.

"People of the calendar?" His expression doesn't change as he takes his shirt off before rubbing baby oil all over his abs. I intentionally called this man my friend just days ago, so he knew where I stood, and now it takes every ounce of self-control not to bite my bottom lip. What's wrong with me?

"You know, the lusting girls who want to buy this calendar. Be the thirst trap. Let's go, everyone! Time is ticking."

That thirst trap was already catching me. I had to turn away and start on the other side of the locker room.

I take a few shots of the team and smaller groups of guys. I start with the individual shots making sure to capture every player but knowing we won't use them all. I tell the team to stay so I can capture some group shots on the ice.

Bren lets anyone who is not in the top three lines and defensive pairs or goaltenders go home. I spend about thirty minutes taking shots of the various main line-ups on the ice. I scroll through my camera showing Bren and Libby. They are both giddy with excitement at how great the boys look skating around with their jerseys off.

"Watch out, Chip, if you add these to your portfolio, you'll be hired to do more than one job! You could get a side gig as a photographer. These are amazing," Bren exclaims in awe. "But Libby, give them a little more oil for a few more. Then anyone who is not a feature is good to go."

Libby squeezes baby oil into every player's hands. Of course, douchebag troublemaker Blaine Mitchell and his buddies are living for it. Meanwhile, Lucas dabs a little on his abs then just wipes the rest on Liam. I can't help but giggle. Lucas turns his head in my direction and winks. His body glistens under the lights even with the minimal amount of oil he has on.

Yum. My eyes are eager to take in every muscular inch of him. Lucas has a way of somehow being more enticing each and every time I see him. Liam looks like he could slide across the ice for hours with how much oil is on his body, which makes me giggle even harder pointing it out to Bren.

A look of desire takes over Bren's face as she mumbles, "Yes, that's my slippery man," which just sends me into another fit of laughter.

"Okay," I say, catching my breath from laughing. I've got to pull myself together and be professional. "Tyler Barret, you're the first individual shot of the day, buddy. Let's get you against the glass. Be careful not to get oil everywhere—we want the glass to look clean in the shot."

"Too late," Tyler says. I roll my eyes at him.

"Libby, can you please help?"

"On it!" Libby cleans up the glass quickly making it look even more pristine than before.

"Sorry, can you wipe the oil off Tyler's back? I need him against the glass and don't want it to keep getting smudged." I ask no one in particular, "Can we get another towel?"

There are supposed to be a few other support team members around from PR and marketing. Where are they?

"I've got it!" Libby says cheerfully.

Libby is a gem. She's back in a minute or two. I take the towel from her and wipe the oil off Tyler's back. Without thinking, I put my other hand against his chest, covering my hand in oil. Luckily, Libby is brilliant and brought a whole basket of towels. I have oil all over my hand and forearm from leaning on Tyler.

I turn to get into position to take his photos when I get a glimpse of the look on Lucas' face. It's a look of pure jealousy and disgust. *Do I sense some possessiveness too?* It might have turned me on before, but I don't owe him anything. I made it clear we were just friends. My eyes go cold as they meet Lucas'. He immediately looks away. I'm not enticed anymore.

"What was that?" Tyler mutters under his breath.

"Nothing. Let's focus. I'm going to turn your body a little bit. Then I'll wipe my hands and adjust your face angle if I need to. Is it okay if I touch your chest and shoulders?"

He just looks at me dumbfounded. "Per school policy, I need to ask. I'm aware I was just wiping you off like a Porsche coming out of a car wash okay. Just say yes."

"Yes Lauren." A sly grin spreads across Tyler's face with a chuckle.

I can't help but smile hearing his familiar laugh. I need to be in a more lively, lighthearted mood after that look I just gave Lucas. I angle Tyler's body just like I did with Lucas during our mock photoshoot. Tyler is surprisingly more of a natural than Lucas. I don't even have to adjust his face angle.

"Perfect. You are a born model, Ty. Libby, give him a hockey stick and leave some pucks by my feet, please. Ty, hold the stick behind your head and flex your biceps," I direct. Posing Tyler like this is going to make whoever buys the calendar swoon.

"Work it, work it," I tease Tyler, getting back into my rhythm again. I definitely have the shots I need but now I'm just having fun with my friend. Maybe Bren is right; this could be a side gig for me one day.

"Do something with this." I toss Tyler a puck.

I have no idea what he could do with it. I was just curious. Looking through the viewfinder of my camera, I double over with laughter. Tyler seductively bites the puck. My shoulders are shaking so hard from laughing that I can barely keep the lens in focus.

"Perfect! You are a star. We're more than good here. Stay for the Sexy Seven photos, and then you can head home."

I add, "thanks for the laugh, I needed it," under my breath so no one can hear, and he places a hand on my shoulder.

Tyler is such a great friend. It makes me laugh when people say he's a player; I've never seen that side of him.

I take photos of a few more players individually, rotating between the ice, locker room, and gym. I've just finished up with Connor Rizzo, who blushed the entire time. I'm looking forward to getting to know him better since he's living with Liam and Tyler.

"The Sexy Seven: Clarke, Lawson, Rizzo, Welsh, Barret, Hall, and Donato, I'll take group photos of you. Then every one of you seven is free to go except Welsh and Donato. Blaine Mitchell, you are up after the group shots and before Welsh and the Captain. You can head out after you're done."

The Sexy Seven shots are easily the highlight of my day. Libby, Bren, and I are all drooling with the sex appeal coming from these men. These calendars are going to sell like hotcakes.

"I guess you didn't name them the Sexy Seven for nothing," I mutter to Bren.

"Is the ice melting under them? I swear it is. My goodness. Look at that boyfriend of mine," Bren says back.

"I'd rather not," I tease.

My attention drifts to the captain, even after his stupid jealousy earlier. He's laughing and carefree with his best friends and teammates, flashing smolder after smolder. I never knew someone could have more than one smolder, but he will make any girl's panties wet if I put any of the photos I just took in the calendar. He certainly has me swooning. I can't stay annoyed with him for long.

"Mitchell, let's go. Meet us in the gym."

Libby left for a last-minute study session, so Bren and I will have to finish the shoot.

"Remind me, why do we have to take Blaine Mitchell as a solo shot again?" I ask Bren.

"Because he has a pretty face, girls love the troublemaker, and he's in one of our top lines . . . You know he's actually good on the ice," Bren explains, "Plus his mom donated a lot of money to the team probably to try to make up for her asshole son's behavior."

I roll my eyes. This explains his personality even more now. Mommy leans in whenever needed.

"Right," I mumble under my breath. "Let's get this over with."

I walk into the gym. Mitchell and his lackey McAllister are already in there. Not sure why McAllister joined us since he isn't getting his photo taken, but as long as they don't stir anything up, I don't mind.

"Mitchell, bench press, please. Put weights on the barbell. I'd suggest a little lighter than you usually go since we will be holding it for some shots. Don't worry, you won't be able to see the actual number of plates in the photos anyway," I direct him.

"Lighter? Yeah, right. I'll do my usual weight," Mitchell pretends to mutter but clearly makes it loud enough for anyone to hear.

I spot Lucas and Liam in the corner of the gym now. It seems odd that they would follow us into the gym instead of waiting by the rink.

"McAllister, since you're here, push those boxes all the way up to the bench. One on each side. Thanks."

I don't feel the need to say please. McAllister gives me the creeps.

"Alright, Mitchell, I'm going to stand over you with my feet on the boxes. I need stable footing otherwise the photo will not look good. Got it?"

He nods. Good, no jokes about me being over him.

"I am going to have you hold each rep for about ten seconds so I can get multiple shots in. I'll probably have you do ten reps max."

With a heavy sigh, I climb up on the boxes and stand over him. I tap him a little with my right foot to tell him to scoot over on the bench. He scoots over reluctantly and winks at me. Seriously? I just shake my head, wanting to get this over with.

"Okay, ready? Just start doing reps."

He holds the barbell over his chest seemingly easy for longer than necessary before continuously doing reps. I take a look at the pictures I snapped. Not bad. If I didn't know he was a grade-A asshole, I might find him attractive from these photos, but I want more of his abs included. I climb off the boxes and look through the pictures again.

Still inspecting them, I ask, "Can you scoot the boxes back a little bit please, Libby? And add more oil to Mitchell's abs? I want to get a slightly different angle."

No way in hell did I want to touch Mitchell. I'm still looking at the camera and realize no one's doing anything. Shoot. I forgot Libby already left. Great.

"Here," Bren says, shifting the box back and handing me the oil. I see a smirk start across Mitchell's face. Out of nowhere, a hand smacks my ass.

"You're going to be on top of me anyways, might as well lube me up, baby."

My jaw drops open. I can't believe he just smacked my ass. I can't believe those words came out of his despicable mouth. Before I'm able to say anything, a figure lunges for Mitchell. Chaotic shouts echo through the gym. McAllister pushes Mitchell to the opposite side of the gym. My jaw almost drops open again when my eyes fall to Lucas. His chest rises and falls quickly, with sharp angry breaths as Liam forcibly holds him back. Lucas, who just a few days ago said he is never the guy to get in fights, almost punched Blaine Mitchell.

"Outside. NOW," I shout at Lucas.

Bren and Liam follow. I didn't expect them to. I need to talk to Lucas alone. I pull him away from them, giving Bren and Liam both a warning glare not to follow.

"What the hell was that, Lucas?"

I'm yelling. I meant to keep my voice down, but I am furious. First, he gives off a possessive vibe, oozing jealousy, and now he almost punches a douchebag for hitting on me. Sure, Mitchell deserved it, but at the expense of Lucas going against his moral code? I would rather punch Mitchell myself. Hell, I still might, but that doesn't mean Lucas needs to act like an overprotective boyfriend. We are just friends; do I need to remind him? Would he still act this way if it was anyone else besides me was filling in for the photographer today?

"Well? I'm waiting, Lucas. Any time would be a good time for an explanation." I manage to keep my voice level this time.

"What do you mean an explanation? Did you hear what he—"

I cut Lucas off. "Obviously I heard what he said, Lucas I was standing not even a foot away from him. But you and I are just friends, I don't need you coming to my defense. You also just told me the other day that you're not one to get in fights. That you lead by example. I even compared you to my brother and hi—"

He cuts me off this time. "Nick would have had Mitchell bleeding already for that comment he made. Are you kidding me?"

He's right. Nick almost got into a fight when I told him about my first boyfriend. I was ten. But that doesn't give Lucas the right to pretend he knows anything about my relationship with my brother. I'm now even more heated.

"You are not my brother," I say through clenched teeth. "You are not my boyfriend. Yes, I saw that jealousy when I was taking photos of Tyler, who, by the way, *is* very much like a brother to me. Not that I owe you any explanation. You are my friend. And if you keep acting like a possessive prick, then we won't even be that."

I walk away and grab Bren, telling Liam to stay out of the gym with Lucas until we are done with Mitchell.

About fifteen minutes later, Bren and I come out of the gym laughing hysterically. Lucas and Liam exchange a look. I sigh.

"Liam, you're next. Locker room for you, buddy."

We walk to the locker room, with Lucas sheepishly following a few steps behind. I glance back at him, seeing hurt in his eyes. I can't bring myself to try to make eye contact with him. I'm embarrassed by what I said to him. I was furious with the situation, furious with men like

Blaine Mitchell thinking they can do whatever they want and get away with it, furious with myself for swooning over him earlier. Lucas was trying to protect me, and he was right: Nick would have . . . I'm not even sure what he would have done. Did I want Lucas to protect me?

We get into the locker room to start Liam's session. There is clearly tension between Lucas and me, but I don't want to be the one to break the ice. I only have Lucas left to take photos after Liam. I'm going to have to talk to him at some point.

"I'll get you all good and oiled up," Bren says to Liam with a wink. "Where do you want him, Laur?"

I need to get back into my element. Liam and Lucas are going to be some of the most important photos I take today. They'll probably each have their own month in the calendar. I've been crushing this so far, so I can't let me losing it at Lucas ruin that. Right on cue, an idea comes to me. It will be perfect for Liam.

"Lucas, can you find me something to stand on? Actually, two things, one for either side of the bench in the middle."

He doesn't say a word but disappears somewhere else in the locker room.

"Liam, lay down on the bench close to the end. I have two ideas. Bren, can you grab some hockey sticks and just arrange them under the bench? Make them scattered but not messy."

I can see the vision perfectly in my mind, but I'm not the best at articulating to others how I want it to look. Lucas still isn't back yet, so I decide to go find him. I find him instantly, crashing into him as I turn the corner.

"Sorry!" I blurt out instinctively.

"Lauren." He puts down two chairs he must have grabbed from Coach's office. "I'm so sorry. I didn't mean to—"

"I know. Me too. Can we talk about it after Liam's done? I have an idea and want to keep this energy instead of getting all apologetic."

He doesn't say anything but instead nods and follows me with the chairs.

"Wait, are there two more chairs?"

Lucas and I come back with four chairs to find Bren is straddling Liam on the bench, just casually sitting on top of him. Lucas clears his throat.

"What? I just wanted to make sure the hockey sticks didn't look too out of place! I was following Laur's artsy vision," Bren claims.

"I don't think straddling Liam gives you the best vantage point Bren, you'd have to be standing. But nice try."

She laughs. Liam very visibly grabs her ass with both hands, making exaggerated movements. Bren is now squealing.

"Okay, you two, this is not professional. Would you be doing this if the real photographer was here?!" I ask jokingly.

"Yes," Liam say at the same time Bren replies, "Sorry."

Bren gives him a little teasing slap on the arm, teasing him, "You sexy perv."

Now I'm laughing too. This is the light fun mood I needed.

"Bren, dismount from Liam, please. I need an assistant."

"Dismount?! Oh please, you haven't seen anything!" Bren shrieks when Liam tries to pull her back down while she gets up.

"Let's keep it that way," Lucas mutters.

We are all laughing now.

"Focus. I need an assistant, and it's already 7pm. I'm starving." I glare at Bren.

"What do you need me to do?" She asks.

I explain my idea. Bren and I are going to both stand on the chairs over Liam with one foot on each side of him and the bench. Bren is going to drop four pucks so the pucks are falling in midair while I snap photos. The hockey sticks beneath Liam look great. All he has to do is lay on the bench with his hands behind his head and look pretty.

"I want wallet copies!" Bren shrieks.

I'm sure if these turn out well, she will have them plastered all over. Bren and I get into position.

"On my count, Bren. Three, two, one!"

She drops the pucks. I look at my camera to see what I was able to capture. The pucks moved so fast. It looks amazing, but we need more pucks.

"Lucas, I need your help too. Uhm . . ."

I look around, trying to figure out if there is anything he can move to stand on, knowing we snagged all the chairs from Coach Andres' office. He can't stand on the ground and throw them; it wouldn't have the same effect from that angle. I sigh, realizing the only solution.

"Stand behind me on the chairs, one leg on each side like I have. Both of you drop as many pucks as you can, as high as you can. We'll try it a few times."

I get down off the chairs for Lucas to get up. Once he's on the chairs, he offers me his hand and helps me up. With the minimal space on the chairs, my body is flush against his. The rise and fall of his chest against my back is soothing but my ass is pressed right up against him. If he were wearing those very thin grey sweatpants . . . My mouth starts to salivate at the thought of Lucas' cock growing hard with my ass firmly pressed against him. I can almost feel the bulge from my imagination. Wait. That is not my imagination, but the bulge is oddly shaped . . .

"Don't worry, that's the hockey pucks I shoved in my pockets." He chuckles with a mischievous grin. "You said grab as many as I can to drop."

I let out a giggle. "What a relief! I was going to tell you that you might want to see a doctor with that abnormal shape I was feeling."

He leans closer so only I can hear him whisper, "I promise you it's far from abnormal. Probably the perfect shape for you."

His breath on my ear, while I'm against him, body to body, sends chills down my spine. *Focus, Lauren, focus!*

"Okay." I give my body a shake as Lucas lets out a low chuckle. "Ready? Three, two, one!"

They drop the pucks, and I snap about five pictures.

"Again," I instruct.

They go to get the pucks and end up dropping them two more times. I flip through my camera.

"I'm just not high up enough. But there isn't anything else for me to stand on that would help."

Lucas gives me a crooked smirk. "I have an idea, but you aren't going to like it."

Five minutes later, Lucas and Bren finally persuade me to get on Lucas' shoulders while he's on the chairs. There is no way this turns out well.

Bren is holding my hands for support as I stand on the chairs that Lucas is already on. He picks me up with little effort and puts me on top of his shoulders like we are at a concert.

"Where was this height when I was at Stagecoach?! It would have been useful," I joke. I'm secretly terrified of heights.

"Invite me next time. You are so light I could carry you up there for hours," Lucas replies.

My stomach rumbles.

"Well, we don't have hours. We have two takes at most. Get the pucks ready. Liam, keep doing what you're doing."

He laughs. He's just been laying on the bench, abs oiled up, and arms behind his head, relaxed as can be. We get the first take. I'm about to say, 'that's all,' when Lucas steps off the chairs with me still on his shoulders to get more pucks.

"LUCAS DONATO," I screech, as he squats down to pick up the tossed pucks.

"I got you, Laur, don't sweat it. I'm not going to let you fall without saving you," Lucas says sweetly.

Bren snorts. Lucas and I both look at her, but she just shrugs. I wasn't reading into it, thinking of what Lucas said in a romantic way. But now I am even more eager to get down.

"Lucas," I holler again as he gets back on the chairs effortlessly.

Lucas has a hand on my right thigh, keeping me secure and steady. Thankfully, I barely notice because I am ready to be on the ground.

"Tell us when," Lucas says, patting my left thigh.

Okay, now I notice a little more . . . Heat builds between my legs as he moves his hand slightly higher up my thigh. I hold back a groan, craving for him to go higher until he reaches my center.

Bren makes another barely audible annoyed noise, pulling me out of my lust.

"Three, two, one," I say for the last time. I capture at least ten photos. "We've got to have a winning photo in here after all this."

I scream the last part as Lucas steps off the chairs with me still on his shoulders. He grabs my waist and lifts me over his left shoulder holding me close to him. He sets me down facing him with little more than a sliver of space between us.

"See, I got you, Laur." Lucas says, flashing that crooked smile at me.

"Thanks," I reply in barely a whisper. My stomach growls again, and it's definitely twenty times louder than my whispered gratitude.

"Bren"—I turn toward her—"Can you please do me a favor and pick up some food? I am going to starve if I don't eat soon. By the time you're home with something from Haee's, I'll be done with Lucas and ready to devour the burger, fries, and surprise milkshake you get me."

I hope I'm convincing.

"Are you sure you don't want me to stay for the last shots? Liam can stay if you want," Bren replies.

Does she not want me to be alone with Lucas? Liam wearily looks at Bren, clearly ready to go home.

"Lucas and I will be fine. How about you pick up something for him too? The four of us can eat it back at the house. We shouldn't take more than thirty minutes since we did the mock shoot. I know exactly what I want to capture."

I look at Lucas. "If you want to eat with us, I mean. I should have asked if you had plans first."

"Yeah, that sounds great. Thanks for including me." A shy, half smile forms on his lips as he runs his fingers through his luscious brown hair. I've never seen Lucas look shy before, but it's endearing.

Bren and Liam get their things together while Lucas and I chat about his photos.

"Alright, Captain Donato, I know exactly what I want you to do for me." My cheeks grow hot with embarrassment. That didn't come out how I wanted it to. "I mean how to pose. After the photos I took of you already, I have an idea. Did you happen to bring your jersey with you?"

"Yeah, it's in my bag. Home jersey?"

I nod. Lucas grabs his jersey. I head out to the ice so he can change into his pads and skates. I chuckle to myself, shaking my head with disbelief. I guess I should have told him not to put the jersey on but to stay shirtless. But I certainly won't mind watching him take if off.

"Lose the jersey, Captain. We need these calendar sales and need to give the people what they want."

"Oh? And what is it they want?" Lucas asks, taking off the garment.

I am glad to see nothing underneath it. His perfect Greek God body, with his defined V in all its glory.

"Sexy Wyverns with abs galore. This might be a lot to ask because it's going to be cold. But could you lay on the ice? I put a towel down, but we need to make sure that you can't see it."

He lays down on the small hand towel. I scrunch up some of the towel to hide under him so it's not visible for the camera, brushing his sides with my hands.

"Sorry, is it okay if I adjust things and put some oil on you? It's probably going to be a little cold."

He nods. I squirt some baby oil on him and laugh as it goes on his abs, the ice next to him, and seemingly everywhere.

"Oops, I guess I should have just put it on my hands instead."

"You made a huge mess," he declares.

I squat down next to him on the ice and rub the oil into his body, starting with his arms and chest. I was right when I first saw him in the bar. My two hands together can't fit around his sculpted arms.

The cold radiates off the ice, but I'm so mesmerized and heated from rubbing his muscular body that I don't shiver at all. This is a lot more intimate than I thought it would be. I move down his body, feeling each dip and curve of his abs while I run my hands over each one. They really are as hard as a rock.

"Sorry, I just have to get a little lower."

Why am I making this so uncomfortable and apologizing? I should have just had him do it himself, but I can't change course now. My hands outline the V at the base of his torso. My body betrays me, growing damp with desire in response as I unnecessarily trace his V with my index and middle finger two times. "Really have to rub it in," I mumble. Great. He probably thinks I'm creepy now. I stand up and wipe my hands on one of the extra towels I brought.

"Okay, great, looks great." This is one of those moments I would love to just put my head in my hands. Can this make this anymore awkward?

I grab his jersey and a hockey stick.

"Okay so, hold the hockey stick behind your head, slightly above it. Flex your arm muscles. I'll lay your jersey so we can see your number slightly."

He eagerly follows my instructions.

"Okay, how is this?" Lucas asks.

My body betrays me again, going from damp to lustfully wet between my thighs as I take in the view of Lucas. I know I've said he looks like a Greek God, but he really looks like he just walked out of *Hercules*.

I try to form words, but they don't come out. I end up making a weird noise and just nod. I clear my throat.

"I am going to take some from a slightly left angle and then slightly right. I'll move your jersey to the right side for that. Then I'll take some from above."

"Got it, Chip."

I start snapping photos from the left side.

"Look right at the camera, like you did in the mock photoshoot when you skated towards me. Yes, perfect."

Fire lights up his eyes, burning brown with golden embers. That's the look I want, like he is going to consume me whole if I let him. By the way my body responds to his look, I would certainly let him.

Trying to focus, I go to the other side. After twenty shots with the same fiery, longing look. I need to take the last shots from above, which means standing on my tiptoes with one leg on each side of him. I move the jersey again so his number is slightly visible to the side.

I stand over him, peering down at his deliciously oiled body. I snap a few pictures and can't help but smile. I rise up on my tiptoes to get a higher angle.

I instantly slip.

I forgot I made a mess with the oil. I'm on top of him with my body pressed against his slick, oiled torso. At least he isn't wearing those thin sweatpants.

"Are you okay?" Lucas asks, trying to sit up with me on top of him, but he slips on the oil and lays right back down, leading to me falling on top of him again.

I try to get up, placing a hand on each side of him and pushing back to my feet, but I slip again. The ice is already slick to start off with—obviously, it's ice—and there's baby oil all over it and Lucas, so I can't use him to help me get up either. My eyes meet Lucas' and laughter bubbles up out of me quickly met by his.

"You really did make a huge mess with that oil, huh, Laur?" he jokes.

"Shut up!" I try to get up again and fall. My foot slips and spills what's left of the oil bottle over, causing more chaos.

Lucas' chuckles grow louder echoing off the ice. I can feel his abs contracting beneath me as I use all my strength to sit up. My heart is pounding in my chest, threatening to skip a beat as I'm now straddling him. My hands slip along the smooth oily surface of his torso when I try to push myself up again

"You've got to be kidding me!" I shriek in frustration.

"You are the smoothest of smooth, Laur," Lucas says, taunting me.

I try a new tactic and roll off him onto the ice. I shift over on the ice to get away from the spot where I spilled all the oil. Lucas is almost crying with laughter. "Slick maneuver. Are you really that scared of falling for me, Laur?" he teases.

"Cool it, Captain. I didn't fall for you. I just kept tripping." He grabs my hand and pulls me across the ice to him. I shriek. "Hey! What are you doing?!"

"You're slipping, not tripping," Lucas taunts. His face is a few feet from mine. I'm looking into those eyes I think of so often.

"Stop slipping for me, Laur," he whispers.

I remember how his lips felt against mine at the Beer Olympics, even if I had been tipsy at the time. It's a feeling I can't forget. If I were to break my promise to myself to swear off love, this man would be the one to break it for. There is nothing I am more sure of than that. But I can't think like that, I don't want to be hurt again.

He leans in to kiss me. Even if I want to stick to my promise, it's only fair I let him kiss me right? After all, I did kiss drunkenly kiss him.

My phone rings, snapping me back into the real world. I turn my head, rejecting his kiss. The silence in the rink is eerie until my phone goes off for a second time.

Answering Bren's call, I scoot away from Lucas and finally get to my feet.

No more tripping or slipping or falling over you, Captain. Not today. Not tomorrow. Not ever.

Chapter Twenty

Lucas

Laur refuses to take a shower in the locker room. I tell her I'll stand guard, and Bren has done it plenty of times, but I can't persuade her. She is determined to wait until we get back to her house.

"Hurry, I am about to be hangry, and if we aren't there in ten minutes or less, Bren will call again. She's like the mom of the house, always worrying about everyone," Laur says.

I take the fastest shower of my life or at least I try to. Being half covered in baby oil is tricky. She's on the home team's bench when I get back from my shower ten minutes later, looking through her camera, with a hint of a smile on her face.

"What are you looking at?" I ask.

"Nothing," she replies sheepishly, shutting off her camera. "Let's go. Bren called me once when you were showering already."

I will never be able to get the sound of her laughter out of my mind. And I never want to. I hope it plays on repeat forever. With how the day started, me being a primal douche, being jealous of Tyler, and then almost punching Mitchell, I didn't expect it to end so perfectly. My desire to feel her lips on mine again had me about to explode. Did she only turn away to answer her phone? I have to try to go for it again.

She was going to kiss me back. I could see it in her ocean blue eyes. She longed for that kiss as much as I did. She's avoiding it for some reason. She asks me about my classes and my major. I tell her even if I'm in the business school, it's not relevant; my future is in hockey.

Somehow, we are already at her house. That was the fastest walk of my life. I need to kiss this girl before I miss my chance.

"Laur." I pull her back from putting the key in the door.

Before she can say anything, my lips are on hers. They are just as soft and welcoming as I remember. I feel the immense desire I've had for her for weeks build higher. She grabs my neck, deepening our kiss with a burning desire that is just as strong as mine. The spark between us flourishes into a roaring fire. Before it goes any further, the door opens. Laur jumps away, putting as much distance between us as possible on the small porch.

Laur dashes into the house.

"Hi, Bren! I'm going to go shower and then I'll come eat."

Laur slips away quickly, like nothing happened. Bren's eyes are filled with protectiveness and fury as she glares at me.

Before she can say anything, I say, "I don't want Liam to know. Please let's keep it between the three of us."

Not waiting for a response, I walk into the house to find Liam.

I scarf down my food like it's my last meal, mainly because Bren doesn't relent in giving me death stares, but I also haven't eaten in six hours. I really wish I could stay longer to say bye to Laur, but I do not want to get mauled by Bren, the mama bear, and I am exhausted. I say bye to Bren and Liam, heading towards the door.

"Wait!" Laur's voice calls to me from upstairs. Butterflies fill my stomach. Is she going to finally acknowledge what happened? Better yet, is she going to kiss me again?

She rushes down the hall toward me, reaching her hand out.

"Give me your phone."

Without even questioning why, I reach in my pocket and hand her my phone. She types something in and gives it back to me.

"Goodnight, Captain."

She turns down the hall to the kitchen. No acknowledgement. No kiss. But she can't deny the spark we have much longer. When you ignore a spark, the flames turn into chaos instead of an enchanting fire.

On my walk home, I look through my phone to see what she did. I don't see a text to herself from my phone, and I don't see her name in my contacts. I looked under everything possible I could think of that she might put it under. I have no idea what she did when I gave her my phone.

I'm in a great mood so don't think anything of it. How could I not be after she was touching my abs and my arms, slipping up saying she found me attractive, finally kissing her again? Sure, it ended faster than I would have liked, but at least it happened. Even if she says she isn't falling for me, she is. I can feel it happening just like she can feel it happening for me. I shouldn't be so smitten with this girl, but I can't help it. She's everything. The more time I spend with her the more I *need* her.

As I empty my pockets onto the bathroom counter, my phone buzzes. A text pops up from a number I don't have saved. I'm exhausted from the long day, and I pass out as soon as my head hits the pillow before I can read the message.

An urgent knock on my door stirs me awake. That's odd. It's the middle of the night. I sluggishly get out of bed after hearing a second knock. I answer the door half asleep, but when I see what's waiting for me on the other side, my tiredness vanishes. The sight of her causes my cock wake up too.

Laur is standing there in my doorway with just my hockey jersey on and thigh-high leather boots. Taking her in, I run my hand through my hair. She is by far the sexiest thing I have ever seen. She steps close to me, her body mere centimeters from mine and whispers in my ear.

"Aren't you going to invite me in, Captain?"

I'm so flustered I don't reply, I just open the door wider. She walks right past me and into my apartment. I accidentally slam the door shut from exhilaration.

"Ready to slam something, huh, Captain?"

She winks at me. She's making a sex joke. The girl that I am stupidly falling for is in my apartment, half naked wearing my hockey jersey, and making sex jokes. I might be the luckiest bastard alive right now.

Lauren walks around my kitchen. Hoping up on my counter, she spreads her legs slightly in invitation. She crooks her finger, motioning for me to come to her.

"Come closer. I won't bite unless you do first."

Shit. I want to bite and kiss her. I want to feel soft sweet lips against mine.

"Stop thinking, and just do it already."

She wraps her arm around my neck and pulls me against her, bringing her lips to mine. The sexual chemistry between us is electric. My cock grows hard for her as she wraps her legs around my torso, pulling me flush to her, so there is no space in between my bare chest and my hockey jersey she's wearing. I bite her lower lip softly, and a little moan escapes that beautiful mouth of hers. That beautiful mouth that I want to do very, very naughty things to.

I have waited so long to really kiss her—to kiss her with the desire I have had for her from the moment I saw her next to Liam at the bar. She grips my hair and kisses me hungrily. I push my tongue into her mouth, wanting more of her. My tongue dances with hers wildly. Panting, she pulls away to catch her breath, and I trail kisses down her neck, biting lightly as I go.

"Guess what, Captain," she whispers in my ear again. "I'm completely naked under your jersey."

"Lauren Bellinger, you are a naughty girl."

"Yes, Captain. Tell me what you're going to do about that."

I pick her up off the counter, grabbing her bare ass, and carry her to my bedroom. I throw her on the bed, and she gives a little shriek.

"Take off my boots."

So demanding. I've never had a girl take charge before, but it sends a jolt to my cock. I'm very into it. She holds up her left leg, and I slowly take off her boot, making sure to touch her thigh with every inch I roll them down, teasing her.

I throw the boot across the room.

"Next boot," she commands.

I take this boot off differently. As I roll it down her thigh, I kiss and bite her soft skin until I'm at the bottom of the jersey. I throw the boot across the room.

"My turn to be demanding. Spread your legs for me, pretty girl. Show me how wet you are for me before I devour your sweet pussy," I growl.

She does as she's told. My cock pulses as she spreads her legs and lips open for me, giving me a view of her glorious pink pussy.

"Just like that. Good girl. Now stay still."

Gripping her thighs, I finally taste her with a quick swipe down her center. With that one taste, I know I will never stop craving her. She tastes like the nectar of the Gods. I focus on her clit, swirling the bud delicately as she moans. My tongue goes as deep as it can inside her, slowly in and out, before vigorously devouring her. Her alluring moans fill the room as she runs her hands through my hair.

Climbing back up to her, I playfully nibble at her neck, sending chills down her body before I whisper in her ear.

"Mmm, Laur, I love tasting how wet and ready you are for me."

Then, I slip two fingers into her, making an erotic sound with how wet she is for me. The tightness of her against my fingers causes my cock to twitch in anticipation. Slowly I pull my fingers in and out of her, moving faster and faster. Her warm pussy remains tight as can be, making me moan with desire to feel it around my cock. I trail hurried kisses down her neck to her perky nipples. I want to enjoy every inch of her. Taking the left one in my mouth, I bite and suck hard.

"Mmm, Lucas," she whimpers.

I make a circular motion with my tongue around her nipple. Shifting my attention to her other side, I suck close to her nipple and leave my mark. She writhes and moans at my touch. I slip my hand back down, feeling the wetness dripping down her legs.

Her hands frantically find the waistband of my sleep pants. Slipping inside, her hand is around my cock without hesitation, while I continue to leave my mark along her tits. She's running her hand along the length of my shaft, distracting me. She strokes my cock the exact way I like, causing my hips to buck involuntarily.

"I want you," she whimpers softly.

I quickly remove my pants, her hand lingering on the tip of my cock.

"I want you," she says again with a look of lust in her eyes, begging me to fill her pussy. And to do it *now*.

She shifts up the bed as I hover on top of her. Her hand still grips my cock, guiding me to her drenched pussy and pulling me between her thighs.

"Please," she pleads, "*now*."

I push my cock into her, easing in. She's blissfully tight around my cock, just like I knew she would be from feeling her against my fingers. I have wanted to bury my cock in her perfect pussy for months. I drive into her again, harder. She moans and hungrily pulls my lips to hers, craving me.

"Yes," she moans against my lips. "*Yes*."

Beep. Beep. Beep.

I stir in my sheets. My bed's empty. My sleep pants are on. My cock is hard as a rock.

It was just a dream—the best dream I've ever had. Before getting out of bed, my hand is around my length stroking it the exact way she did in my dream, and I imagine her moaning yes to me over and over again. I come in less than a minute. I have never wanted anything or anyone more than I want Lauren Bellinger.

I grab my phone and open the text message from the random phone number last night. It's from Lauren, she texted herself from my phone but must have deleted the text to herself so I never saw it last night. I know I checked to see if she texted herself my number. I might not date a lot, but I know that's a thing. Girls are always doing that.

The text is a picture of me, up close laying on the ice. It must have been the last picture she snapped when we were both laying on the ice.

I send back a ":)." She quickly responds.

Laur: I shouldn't tell you this. But when you asked me what I was smiling and laughing about when I was on the bench before we left the rink yesterday. It was this picture.
Me: Really? :)
Laur: Yes. Don't gloat about it, Captain.

I have the biggest smile on my face, and my heart feels so full. She is a firecracker. This girl is everything. I hop in the shower, singing to myself. I never sing. I can't carry a tune for shit. I'm tempted to jack off again, thinking about her naked body on my bed, her naked body against mine, my cock in her delicious pussy. How she seems like she craves it too.

It's a longer shower than I had planned to take.

I'm still on a high a few days later. It's been busy as hell getting ready for our first game of the season. I've only seen Lauren in passing. I was worried she was avoiding me, but then I realized I'd barely seen Bren either, which means Liam has barely seen her since I've been with him most of the time. Coach is pushing us harder than ever before for this first game. I'm pushing the team too. This is our season—I can feel it.

For as long as I can remember, I've had first-game-of-the-season nerves. I've always chalked it up to excitement and an adrenaline rush, which both happen every game. It's more than the typical jittery nerves. This will also be the first game that Laur has ever seen me play—at least since we've met.

It's also the first Wyverns game she is watching without Nick on the team. I wish there was something I could do for her.

Chapter Twenty-One
Lauren

Mom let me skip a day of high school for Nick's first game as a Wyvern his freshmen year. I drove up by myself to get there early. I wanted extra time on campus, plus Bren was already part of the Wyverns' student marketing program. She promised to try to save me a seat by her and to sneak me into the arena early before the general public.

Bren, of course, succeeded with both. I instantly spotted Nick on the ice. I had never seen Nick so giddy. He was clearly in his element. He didn't seem nervous at all—he never did.

"Come on," Bren said. "I'm going to interview Nick before the game. You can sit in. I already cleared it with Coach." Now I was giddy! But for some reason, I was nervous for Nick. He had been waiting to play for this team his whole life, just like Dad did.

Bren asked Nick how he was feeling before his first college game especially as the son of the legendary Nico Bellinger.

"My dad instilled a passion for hockey in me as soon as I could walk, but my love, dedication, and drive are all from wanting to be right here after years of playing hockey. I've been dreaming of this day for a very long time. I've never been more ready to take that one shot at my dreams. I know it's just the beginning."

I snapped over a thousand photos of Nick during that game. It was an intense game against the East Michigan Eagles. The teams seemed to go shot for shot. The Wyverns were three to three with the Eagles with two minutes left of the game when the Wyverns stole possession of the puck. Nick was at the front of the net, waiting for a pass. He scored the game-winning goal. The crowd roared for him, louder than I had ever heard a crowd cheer. At that moment, it was crystal clear that Nick was going to be a Wyverns legend.

Walking into the arena today for the first game of the season wasn't going to be easy. But just like Nick said in his first game interview, my love, dedication, and drive all stem from wanting to be exactly where I am right now. Bouncing around my room to get ready, I realize I can't stop moving. The first game has me so antsy—I'm not sure if it's nerves or if it's excitement. I mentally go through the list of everything I need to bring with me. I pick up my planner and see Nick's little black book under it. I can't believe I forgot about it. I throw it in my bag to look through later. Maybe it will give me inspiration for some writing or insights into the other team.

Earlier this week, our hockey girl gang released articles about the season on the Wyverns' website and social media. There's a piece about the team and seven articles about each of the Sexy Seven players. I wrote the two that feature Tyler and Lucas. Those two articles are the first official Wyverns work I put out into the world. Every single photo in the articles is one I've taken. I can't believe I have my name as the photographer on all of them.

The photos from the shoot turned out incredible. The calendar is laid out and in production now. December is easily my favorite month, featuring the last photo I took of Lucas on the ice. Anyone who purchased the calendar was going to wish December was even longer so they can keep ogling over the sexy captain. Liam's shots turned out even better. All the work that went into dropping the pucks paid off. Bren may or may not have swiped an unedited digital photo or two.

She wasn't kidding about making wallet sizes of Liam's photos just for herself.

Campus is buzzing. People are talking about the pieces we released online and showing excitement about the calendar! We've been teasing a lot of calendar content on social media and starting our pre-sale orders at today's game. I've scheduled social media posts to go out an hour before the game starts, at game start, and two throughout the game to drive even more awareness of the calendar and hopefully get more presales. We also shared a mockup of the special edition Nick Bellinger designed jersey! Today is a big day all around.

When I get to the rink, I feel a sense of calm. This is exactly where I am meant to be. I take out Nick's notebook and flip through the pages until I find a page for the Comets—the team we are up against today. In Nick's chicken scratch handwriting, I read:

So-so opponents, historically have a similar record to us
Wyverns won 10 out of 12 games last four years
#12 Donovan—don't let anyone get in a fight with him
#72 Gabriel—weaker on left, avoid right side around glass, hard checks, put someone in hospital last year

I do a quick search on my phone to reveal the record is now twelve out of fourteen games in the last five years. Donovan has since graduated and plays for the San Jose Sharks. Gabriel is a senior. I'd like to avoid anyone on the team going to the hospital. I should tell Lucas what Nick wrote.

I walk into the arena and immediately find Bren. She informs me that I'm interviewing Lucas during the second intermission. I fidget with the hem of my shirt as unease fills my stomach. I had no idea I was going to interview him. She conveniently didn't tell me, but despite my nerves I'm overjoyed at the opportunity. I will have exactly five minutes for the interview. There will be a camera person recording while Libby takes a video from her phone for my reference later and for social media.

I nod with genuine enthusiasm. I'm following my dreams of being a part of the Wyverns' Marketing team. It's the first step towards my future career working for an NHL team. In the words of my brother, I've never been more ready to take that one shot at my dreams. I know it's just the beginning.

I don't have a chance to find Lucas before the game to tell him what I found in Nick's notebook, but I have one of the towel boys put a note in his locker about the interview.

Chapter Twenty-Two

Lucas

I s there a different kind of energy in the arena than there has been in past seasons? Or is it just me being more conscious of my surroundings since Laur is here? I chalk it up to being a mixture of both. The locker room is buzzing with exhilaration; it seems like the other guys can feel it too.

I get my gear on and find a note in my locker. It reads, "Your good luck charm is interviewing you." I know it's only the start of the season, but I can't imagine how it would feel without her here. I'm purposely the last one in the locker room. Liam yells at me from the door to hurry up. I walk over to Nick's locker and tap the number 88.

"She's here because of you, Bellinger. I will spend every second on the ice this season thanking you for that."

I head out of the locker room door, ready for a great game.

The national anthem plays. The puck drops. We win the face off. The game is flying. It's 2-1 at the end of the first period.

We are playing really well, but the Comets aren't playing badly either. I know that we have beaten them more than they have beaten us in the last couple of years. About halfway into the second period, Liam is hot on a breakaway, but the puck is quickly stolen by a defenseman. He turns on the spot to follow back down to our side of the ice.

BOOM!

Number 72 slams him hard against the boards, with a malicious glint in his eye. The sound of the crash amplifies against the ice from the hard hit. Liam doesn't get up right away, which is unlike him. Is he injured? The ref doesn't call a penalty; it was a clean hit. Liam gets up shakily and heads to the bench. Holy hell. I've never seen Liam down for more than a second on the ice. We all need to shake it off. We can't let the brutal hit and anticipation of more get to our heads.

But we can't seem to shake it off. The Comets score two more goals. The period ends 3-2 with the Wyverns down by a goal.

The end of the second period means my interview. I've never been interviewed mid-game before. I pull at the hem of my jersey and take a deep calming breath. I haven't been interviewed by Laur since I realized I was falling for her and falling for her hard. I'm sure she's just as anxious as me, especially with this being her first game since seeing Nick play his last game.

Laur, the camera crew, and a girl with a phone ready to record are all waiting for me when I get to the spot Bren instructed me to go to. Anxious sweat drips down my forehead onto my already drenched jersey. Someone hands me a towel to wipe my face. Laur gives me her famous Bellinger smile, and my nerves ease a little.

"Ready?" she asks.

I nod. She signals to the camera guy, and he counts her down from three.

"I'm here with our beloved Wyverns' Captain, Lucas Donato. Captain, the energy feels wild here today. How would you say that's impacting the team?" Lauren asks.

Her voice is steady and poised—very professional. I'm in awe of her.

"We can definitely feel the support down on the ice. The thrill of fans is incredibly motivating. The team and I are very thankful for the turn out and for our amazing marketing and PR team support pre-season."

She blushes at the mention of her work, but her expression quickly changes. A hint of pain flashes in her beautiful ocean blue eyes as she asks, "How does it feel playing your first game as Captain, especially as a junior?"

I take a sharp breath in. I knew she would have to ask me something like this. I hope she isn't loathing me right now, wishing I was Nick. I couldn't blame her if she did. I wish he was here too. Laur clears her throat, waiting for me to answer.

"I am honored to have the opportunity to lead this incredible, talented group of men. I have big shoes to fill from our previous captain, Nick Bellinger. I know he is here with us today, cheering us on. I hope to make him, the team, Coach Andres, and our fans proud today."

She beams at me, fighting back tears. She does an impressive job staying in focus and remaining composed. Why isn't she considering a career in broadcasting? She's so alluring and captivating. It's a miracle I haven't noticed her while on the ice all game. If I did, I would play like shit with that distraction.

"One more question, Captain. The Wyverns have historically won against the Comets with twelve wins out of fourteen games the last five years, including a winning streak the last three years. Any comments on that?"

Wow, she did her homework. My eyebrows instinctively raise with admiration.

"The team and I intend to keep our winning streak going. Hopefully the fans can bring more of that glorious Wyverns energy to help bring us a first game win!"

My heartbeat quickens as Laur grabs my hand, pulling me to her. She whispers in my ear, "Avoid number 72 on the right side, you saw what he did to Liam. Tell Liam and the rest of the guys. Nick wrote it in his notebook."

I look at her perplexed. Suddenly remembering Laur mentioned Nick had written about each of our opponents in that notebook, I need to ask her if I can look at it. I know it means a lot to her, but if it means learning more about each opponent and helping the team overall, I have to ask. Hockey has to come first.

We're still down by one after five minutes into the third period. The boys are pushing hard and feeding off the crowd's contagious energy. Connor passes to Mitchell, who drives the puck up the ice. He makes a quick pass back to Connor, as number 72 that Nick wrote about approaches to try to steal the puck. Connor takes the puck to the net and scores.

Yes! We're tied with ten minutes left now. The next five minutes are brutal. Both teams are hungry for the win. A Comet player shoots and the shot's deflected by our goaltender. I quickly snatch the rebound and turn to dash up the ice. The Comets don't have their shit together; they didn't expect a rebound off that shot. I easily pass center ice before number 72 comes at me. I pass to Liam. He takes a shot, and the puck soars into the net.

FUCK YES! We are winning with less than five minutes left. We spend those next five minutes fighting for our lives to keep the Comets off the board.

The whistle blows, ending the first game of the season. We won! Hallelujah.

The boys want to celebrate our win by getting rowdy at the bar, but we have an early day tomorrow with another game to win. I inform the team if we win tomorrow against the Comets, we will celebrate, but tonight we need to rest and be ready. It's a marathon of a season, not a sprint.

Bren is waiting with Laur outside the locker room. They must have been waiting over an hour between us showering, my pep talk, and Coach's notes. Laur runs up to me, throwing her arms around my neck in an unexpected hug. My heart aches with longing for her. I squeeze her back, taking in her flowery perfume before picking her up off the ground.

"Congrats on your first win as captain!" she squeals. I put her down, and she hugs me again.

"You would have made him proud. You made me proud," she whispers in my ear.

Knowing that not only is she impressed with me, but that her brother would be too sends a chill down my spine.

"Thank you," I reply. "I must have a good luck charm or something." I wink at her.

We head down the hall and out of the arena as everyone leaves to go home for the night. I'm on cloud nine from the win. The only thing that could make this night better is walking out of here hand in hand with Laur.

"See you tomorrow," Laur calls. "Oh! We have over one hundred pre-orders for the special edition gold jersey that Nick designed already!!! Isn't that amazing?!"

"Wow, congrats! Way to bury the lead and wait to tell me. It must have something to do with the Wyverns' good luck charm we have this year," I say back to her with a sly grin.

She rolls her eyes and links her arm with Bren's as they leave me standing, watching them leave.

On my walk over to the arena the next day, I find Laur by a tree. My heart leaps into my throat. Her hands are covering her face and she's in tears. Rage starts to pulse through me ready to tear about whoever hurt her.

I approach her, and she looks up at me. Her ocean eyes are puffy, red, and swollen, like she has been crying for hours.

"I'm sorry," she garbles between sobs.

"Why are you sorry? What's wrong, Lauren?"

"I don't know why I said that."

She puts her face in her hands again while her shoulders continue to shake with sobs. Sitting down next to her, confused, I put my arm around her shoulder.

"What's wrong, Lauren?" I ask again.

With her hands still covering her face, she confesses to me how she was doing so well with being around the Wyverns and not focusing on how Nick isn't here, but she broke down last night and again this morning.

"I don't know how you didn't break down sooner, Laur. I can't imagine how you feel and how much it hurts. But I can tell you this: you are doing an amazing job. I was blown away by how professional you were interviewing me yesterday. I felt like I was being interviewed by a famous reporter."

"Really?"

Her shoulders stop shaking as she takes her face out of her hands. She looks up at me, tears still falling. Each tear that falls is like an ice pick to my heart.

"Yes. And look at all the pre-sales you've helped to get for the calendar and for the special edition jersey. That jersey was all our idea. You're honoring him every single game by just showing up and soon people will be able to honor him even more by wearing his design."

"You're right. That will be special."

"You have to let yourself hurt sometimes, though. It's the only way to get through it."

She nods, tears starting to clear from her eyes. My hands run down her back soothingly as she leans into me.

"Thank you, Lucas."

"Anytime. Really. I know you have Bren and Liam, but I can be here for you too."

She smiles sheepishly and whispers, "Thanks."

Standing up, I offer her a hand to pull her to her feet. I pull her into a hug. She embraces me like she never wants to let go before stepping back and sighing in relief. Warmth spreads through my body, knowing I can comfort her. We walk together in silence towards the arena for the second game.

Despite number 72's attempts to start fights and play dirty, we easily win.

The team is expecting to celebrate tonight. My body and mind ache with exhaustion but as captain, I have to show my face. We've fought hard the last two games, but we have a long way to go.

The weight of responsibility sets in. I need to ask Laur about Nick's notebook and be up at a decent hour tomorrow to get in a run or workout before cranking out a paper I've been putting off. School still happens even when the season's busy.

Bren and Laur are waiting outside the locker room again. Seeing her eyes bright with exhilaration from the win lifts my spirits. She's gorgeous with her hair curled, up in a ponytail, and decked out in Wyverns gear.

"Suz told me to tell you she'll meet you at the bar," Bren informs me. "You know she never waits."

Typical Suz, she would never be caught waiting around for the team.

"Congrats again, Captain," Laur says, beaming at me. Her eyes are still a little puffy, but there isn't redness in them anymore. Good, she hasn't been crying again.

"Thanks, good luck charm. Are you going to come to the bar for a drink? Everyone is. You have to join in."

She looks at Bren, and Bren confirms she's going. Liam and Tyler are waiting for us, hair wet from post-game showers.

"I guess I have to support my team," she says, flirting as she twirls one of her curls around her finger. "See you there."

She turns to follow Bren, Liam, and Tyler. Does she spend a lot of time with Tyler? I like Tyler. He's a great guy and one of my good friends, but it doesn't mean I'm not jealous of how close they are. I'm jealous of any guy who gets to spend time with her.

"Hey, Rizzo," I say to Connor as he walks out of the locker room, "You driving or you need a ride to Haee's?"

Since Connor moved in with Liam, he's tagged along with us. He's driven and determined just like I am. He's also the only one who likes sushi, so we snag some at least once a month now. He's hoping to make it to the NHL after graduation this year. I owe it to him to be the best captain I can be and push the team harder to show him off to scouts.

Walking into the sports bar, I spot Laur right away. Her dark brown hair cascades in thick waves down her back instead of her usual half up style she had at the rink. She must have stopped home to change before coming to the bar. My eyes linger on her ass longer than they should. She's wearing jeans that hug her curves perfectly. I'm not used to seeing her without yoga pants on.

I start to head over to her but notice she's already talking to someone: Tyler, of course. She throws her hands around, very animated, and enthralled in their conversation. She gasps, giggling and grabbing onto Tyler's arm. I need to know more of the story between the two of them.

She mentioned they grew up together? Did she have a crush on him back then? Is she into him now? I'm getting ahead of myself. She already yelled at me once for my jealousy during the photoshoot. I have to keep a level head; it's a standard I want to always uphold for myself in front of my team. She's a part of that team now.

I notice she doesn't have a drink yet. I meander over to the bar to grab one for her and one for myself too. Suz and a girl I've never seen before come up to me at the bar.

"Hey, you," Suz coos, giving me a hug.

Suz and I have been good friends since my freshman year. She decided to take me under her wing. My ex-girlfriend hated it. I assured her I was not interested in Suz. She's a gorgeous blonde bombshell, but she is not my type at all. I am positive I am not hers either.

"Congrats on your second win this season! This is my friend Shay. I convinced her and a few other friends to come to the game tonight. She was pretty impressed with your skills, Captain. She begged me to introduce you to her," Suz says dramatically.

The shorter girl with hazel eyes, Shay, blushes. What is Suz doing? She knows I'm not interested in dating typically, especially anyone that she's friends with. Plus she has to know I'm interested in Laur. She can't be that blind.

"Nice to meet you," I murmur while taking a sip of my beer.

Suz and Shay keep talking to me, but I'm zoned out of the conversation, scanning the room for Laur. She's still with Tyler, but Connor's joined them too. Her back is to me. I can't help but stare at her scrumptious ass again, the one I grabbed fistfuls of in my dream. She is a dream. I would be lucky to be hers.

I need to stop fucking around and talk to her already. I don't care if she's sworn off love. I don't care if I don't date. She's changed that for me. Maybe I can change her thoughts on dating too.

"Hey," I cut off Shay. "Sorry. Suz, you work with Laur a lot. Do you know why she is so against dating and why she claims she's content being single?" I ask.

Suz snorts. "No, Lucas, I don't, but she seems pretty focused on Tyler anyways."

Does she really? I was hoping I imagined it. I turn my attention to Suz and Shay, trying to distract myself from Lauren.

"Sorry, Shay, that was rude of me to cut you off. What were you saying?"

I'm trying to focus on the conversation now. Suz says she has to leave to meet her date—she seems to mysteriously slip away for dates—which leaves me with her friend, Shay. She's very pretty, tall, with full lips and beautiful hazel eyes. She could have any guy in this room, but she doesn't hold my interest. Shay is telling me about her nursing major stemming from growing up with her dad in the Navy. She seems like a sweet girl.

"Hey, you are beautiful, and any guy would be lucky to have you," I begin. Shay cuts me off.

"Suz said you don't date, but I couldn't help myself. You are dreamy."

Shay looks at me longingly. Even if I had never met Lauren, I wouldn't be interested in this girl or really any girls. I need to focus on my team, this season, and my future playing hockey. Pretty girls were just a distraction I didn't need.

I sigh, "Thank you. I just . . . I need to focus on hockey." She nods her head.

"Actually, I think I'm falling in love with a girl over there, and honestly, I don't want to be. I know she doesn't want to date anyone. She's focused on herself too."

"Do you want to talk about it?" she eagerly invites, her hazel eyes losing the yearning that filled them moments ago.

"You were just hitting on me, and now you're okay with me talking about another girl?" I narrow my eyes suspiciously.

"I get it." She sighs. "I've been there. Plus, I need to move on from someone myself. I was hoping you could distract me." She looks at me like she could peel off my clothes with her eyes. "Talk to me about it. That's a distraction too. I'm sure I'll probably start to spill my guts about my ex and his new girlfriend. So, I'll listen for you, if you listen for me?"

"Deal. Do you like Bud Light?" I hand her the beer I got for Lauren.

Chapter Twenty-Three
Laur

Lucas has yet to come over and talk to me. I'm a little surprised if not slightly upset. If I'm his good luck charm, shouldn't he be interested in talking to me? I have no right to be salty. I've made it very clear to anyone and everyone that I am not interested in any type of relationship, but he's been a great friend.

I spot him at the bar. He is so perfectly brawny but not overly buff. I'm biting my lip thinking about each time I've gotten to see his muscles. All the girls in the bar are probably drooling over him. I certainly am. My body eases with a sigh when he orders two Bud Lights. Could one be for me?

Before I find out, Suz is next to him with another blonde girl. The other girl is practically hanging onto him. My jaw tightens as she touches his arm, leaning more into him. She definitely falls into the 'girls at the bar drooling over him' category.

"What's going on?" Tyler asks, nudging me with his shoulder.

I am not very good at hiding my facial expression. I move so I am no longer facing Lucas and his blonde posse.

"Do you know who that girl is with Lucas? Obviously not Suz."

"Yeah, her name is Shay, and she's obsessed with Lucas," Connor chimes in. "I tried to get her number over the summer, and she was very uninterested."

"Oh."

I feel like my heart is in my stomach, and I am about to throw it up. This is why I shouldn't get even a little bit involved with Lucas or anyone for that matter. It's not going to end well. I swore off love for a reason. But I keep finding myself drawn to Lucas and wanting to spend time with him.

"Do you think he's into her? What else do you know?" I look back and forth between Connor and Tyler with pleading eyes, waiting on an answer.

"Oh no, I'm out of this conversation. Lucas is one of my best friends; I'm not talking about his love life. But for what it's worth Laur, Lucas is rarely into anyone and never has a love life."

Connor walks away to find some of the guys. Tyler laughs lightly at me.

"What?" I say to him, grabbing the beer from his hand and taking a big gulp.

Gross, this beer tastes like grass. It's definitely not a light beer.

"You're into him, aren't you? What happened to no guys and your ridiculous vow to swear off dating?" Tyler teases.

"It's not ridiculous . . . if you knew . . ." I shake my head, not wanting to get into it here. I need to tell him and Bren eventually, but not when I'm insecure over a girl talking to a guy that's not even mine and not when we are supposed to be celebrating.

"Look, Connor is right. Lucas doesn't date. I've seen the way he is with you, he's not like that with anyone. He doesn't take girls home. He doesn't like fangirls. He's focused on hockey, this team and his future in the NHL. He's basically your brother in a different body," Tyler replies.

"Gross. Don't say that he's basically my brother! I kissed him drunkenly and have been insanely flirty with him." Disgust crosses my face before I take a sip of my drink. "I really do need to focus on my future too. I don't know what I'm doing or how he got in my head."

Tyler ignores the kissing Lucas drunk confession, keeping a neutral face. He's a good friend.

"I know you don't want to date anyone, but let me set you up with one of my friends. I have someone in mind. He's pre-med and a great guy. If you're still thinking about Lucas after, maybe it's a sign you should go for it. If you're interested in Brian, maybe it's your way of telling yourself you want to start dating again."

"You're too wise and too good at giving advice. Why can't more men be like you?"

"Let's not tell anyone about how in tune with my emotions I am. Girls will not be into it, and unlike you and Lucas, I love dating. Love it."

Tyler. draws out the O in love for emphasis and laughs at himself. Damn. I was wrong. He is a player, he just pretty much admitted it

"Speaking of Lucas, he's headed toward us by the way."

"Thanks for the warning," I mutter softly.

Lucas grabs my shoulders and gives me a squeeze.

"You looked like you could use a Bud Light. I know you made a face drinking that IPA that Tyler likes."

Lucas hands me a beer. That was thoughtful, but this beer is ice cold, there is no way this is the same beer he bought twenty minutes ago.

"Thanks," I grumble.

"Tyler, what's our good luck charm been whispering in your ear? Did she give you any tips on how we can win this season aside from having her at every game?" Lucas takes a sip of his drink nonchalantly.

"Sadly, no. Laur, give me some of this luck please so I can impress the lady fans and entice scouts to keep an eye on me next year."

"Hey, hey—don't steal my luck, Barret."

Lucas puts his arm around my shoulder. Possessive? Maybe a little, but I don't mind it. I start to settle into him cozily, shifting my feet to be closer to him. It's too easy to relax around him now. Where did the girl who was anti-Lucas Donato go? I look up, and Tyler gives me a "you're doing this to yourself" look. I shrug off Lucas' arm, playing it off as excitement remembering Nick's notebook.

"Actually! I do have something to share with you both. I know I already told you, Lucas, but I found a notebook that Nick had. He wrote about all the different teams over the years, different players from opposing teams, and some other things. He wrote about number

72 on the Comets being brutal on the right side against the boards. I think you guys, Liam, and Connor should take a look at it. I'll text you pictures of the pages."

"Why not just let us have the notebook?" Cold sadness creeps in as I wrap my arms around myself. "Because . . . it's one of the only things I have left of Nick."

Blinking back tears, I look down into my drink avoiding meeting anyone's gaze. I don't need to tell Lucas it has pages of each of the players on his own team in it too. There isn't anything negative, some tips here and there they actually might learn from. Maybe I should give them it. I'll decide later.

"I'll think about it, but in the meantime, I'll send you both a picture of the notes from the next two teams we play. It's not cheating right?"

"Not at all. Nick is part of this team. Plus, it's just his thoughts. It's just like if Tyler shared his thoughts with me from playing with some other guys before he transferred," Lucas says unruffled.

Tension leaves my body with his reassurance. I want the Wyverns to win, but I want us to do it the right way.

"I've got to get going, but, Laur, text me about that thing I mentioned."

That thing he mentioned? Oh. Right. Tyler means going on a date with his friend.

"So ominous with the secrets between you and your boy Ty."

Lucas rolls his eyes. Is he jealous of Tyler again? He's at least not acting like a deranged asshole today. I ignore his comment and instead decide to make a bold move.

"Who's your new friend?"

I hope I don't regret this. What if he says it's his new fling or an ex or something? I shouldn't have said anything, but I can't help it.

"Huh?" Lucas' brows furrow, genuinely seeming unsure of who I'm asking about.

"The girl that was with you and Suz."

"Oh, no idea. She seemed nice though," he says back.

I'm sure there's more to it than he's admitting. He talked to her for at least twenty minutes. If he doesn't want to tell me, that's on him.

"Need a ride home?" Lucas asks.

"No, I'll head back with Bren. See ya." A hint of woefulness lingers underneath my curt reply.

I turn to go find Bren without hugging Lucas goodbye or giving him a moment to respond. Disappointment fills me from how our conversation went to tonight and even though I keep denying it to myself, I would have loved for him to kiss me goodnight while riding shotgun in his truck. Instead, I'm in the backseat of Bren's SUV. I pull out my phone to text Tyler.

Me: I'm in. Set me up, matchmaker.
Me: You can give him my number.

Chapter Twenty-Four

Laur

A few days later, I send Lucas a photo of Nick's notes for our next opponent, the Lions. I hold off on sending him anything on the Jaws. If I wait, I'll have an excuse to text him again. I've always found it odd that there's a college hockey team named after a fictional shark. I look down at my wrist where my Wyvern tattoo is. I guess the Wyverns are fictional too. We should push for a Wyverns movie. I laugh to myself, mentally noting to tell Bren. She'll get a kick out of my stupid joke.

I grab my computer, notebook, and a few other things before heading out the door to meet Bren and Suz in our usual spot.

"Hi," Bren calls cheerfully from a table at Roast and Revelry.

She's sitting by herself, which means Suz hasn't come yet. This could be my chance to ask her about that blonde girl that I'm still thinking about. I can't get the visual of her hanging all over Lucas from my head. I do have my date in a few weeks so that should help.

"Thanks for the caramel macchiato," I say sipping on my hot beverage. "Can I ask you something random?"

Bren nods in response.

"Do you know anything about that girl that was with Suz and Lucas the other night after the game at Haee's?"

"Sorry, Chip, I didn't see her. I was a little . . . preoccupied."

I'm sure she was preoccupied with Liam's face attached to hers. Oh well, it's better for me to know less.

"I can ask Suz?" Bren asks, trying to be helpful.

"NO," I say a little too loudly. I still don't trust her. "No, that's okay."

"Ask me what?" Suz pops up from out of nowhere. How does she manage to always be there when I don't want her to overhear something?

"Oh, nothing important," I reply.

She rolls her perfectly lined eyes.

"Is this about Lucas? I know you have a crush on him, but honestly you are always with Tyler—"

I cut her off quickly, "No, it's not. Tyler is one of my closest friends. I grew up with him. He played hockey with my brother. There's nothing there, don't start that rumor."

I quickly turn the conversation away from talking about Lucas.

"But actually, I was wondering why the Jaws aren't just called the Sharks? Why did they need to have a name with a whole movie about them? Can we have a Wyverns movie?"

I couldn't stop myself. Bren's giggles bubble out of her.

"Are you kidding me? What a weird question." Suz snorts with annoyance.

I just shrug my shoulders. It got the laugh out of Bren I knew it would, so at least it was a funny question too.

"So anyways, this isn't a movie, but I do have some exciting news. I talked to my contact at *USA Hockey Magazine*. I've been sending them the articles we have written so far this season. They love them! And Laur"—she turns to me—"they even love your pictures!" Suz shrieks.

"My pictures? Really?"

"Right? Isn't that amazing! They want an official article written about Liam and Connor!"

She says to Bren, who is beaming with excitement.

"They also want a feature on Lucas and Tyler. Think you can handle it, Laur? They are your assignments, so the opportunities are yours if you want them."

"I—Really? Thank you so much. Will you proof read it?"

I stumble over my words, dumbfounded. Two articles and my photos will be in a national magazine! This is more than I could have dreamed of.

"Of course, I can," Suz replies.

She's being sweet now. Maybe I should give her more of a chance; I feel like I'm constantly saying that.

"Let's make sure snippets are all over our socials too! This is so exciting! Let's wait to tell the boys until after we've submitted all the content, okay? I want to surprise them!"

Bren dives into some details about ticket sales increasing this year with a few ideas on how to keep it going. We go through calendar sale dates, teaser content, pre-sale dates, and the custom jerseys.

I've zoned out a little bit thinking about what content I have that I can use for the articles. I think I have enough on Tyler from his interview, but I want to include more details on why Lucas wanted to be a Wyvern and his journey to captain. That means I'm going to have to sit down with him again. Hopefully Libby is free to come so I don't have to be alone in a room with him.

Bren is talking about her plans for the rest of the day, but I missed the whole conversation preoccupied by the thought of being in close quarters with Lucas.

"I've got to head out. I'll text details on the teaser content to you, Laur. I want these calendar sales to be big."

"What if we do some posters or something cool for giveaways with the larger team shots or the Sexy Seven shots? Have the guys sign them? Enter to win by pre-ordering a calendar?" I'm always trying to think of new marketing ideas for sales and promotion. It's my favorite part of marketing.

"I love that idea!" Suz and Bren respond in unison.

Bren waves bye to us as she bounces out the door.

Suz turns to me. "Listen, I'm sorry about the Tyler comment. I just assumed, which isn't fair of me at all, especially because people used to assume the same of Lucas and me when we became close friends. I didn't mean anything by it."

My eyes widen with surprise at her unexpected apology.

"It's okay," I say. "Thanks for apologizing."

"I really am looking forward to your articles on Tyler and Lucas, Laur. You've been doing such a great job. We are lucky you joined us this year."

She squeezes my arm. Did she wake up on a different side of the bed today? She's being so genuine.

Before Suz stands up to leave, she leans over and says quietly, "Her name is Shay. She's a good friend of mine, but I'm positive he isn't interested."

A wave of relief washes over me.

I text Lucas as soon as she leaves to see when he's free to try to get more out of him for the article. He responds right away. Perfect—I'll see him the day before my date and then decide if I still want to go on the date. That seems logical, right?

Libby isn't free to come help with the interview. I was hoping she would unknowingly play chaperone. I can just record on my camera and go back to take more notes later instead of having someone write them live.

I'm wearing jeans instead of my typical leggings as if they are my armor for the day. I toy with my braid, waiting for Lucas to arrive any minute as unease fills me, which is silly. I've spent a lot of time with Lucas. I enjoy spending time with Lucas so much that I'm thinking of canceling the date with Tyler's friend.

I don't want to be with anyone for the sake of being with someone. I vetoed any type of relationship for a reason. But with Lucas . . . I just can't help it. I want to get to know him. Getting to know him could help me see that some romantic relationships are worth it. I keep saying I'm content being alone, but I won't want that forever, right?

A knock sounds on the door. Lucas struts into the room. He's freshly showered with his brown hair slicked back on his head. He smells like fresh cotton. He's wearing jeans too. Damn it, I was not-so-secretly hoping he would wear his infamous gray sweatpants.

"Hi." He beams at me.

His speckled golden-brown eyes seem like less of a thrill to me today. They feel more comforting and familiar.

"Thanks for meeting with me again. I want to be sure that I get more information from you. We are writing articles for *USA Hockey Magazine* and—"

"Laur! Your articles are going to be published in a big magazine?"

"And my photos." I blush. "But just two articles, one about Tyler, which I've already finished. I just want to ask you for more information to make sure I do you justice."

"I have no doubt in my mind that you will do more than that. Congrats, Laur. That's huge! I'm happy to help. What do you need to know?"

"Well, you didn't tell me much about your first years as a Wyvern before becoming part of the starting lineup and becoming captain. You also didn't tell me why you chose the Wyverns."

A look flashes in his eyes that I can't place.

"I'll tell you why the Wyverns. The other part . . . it sounds dumb, but I want to wait to tell you. Can I tell you why I chose the Wyverns, and if it's not enough for your article, maybe I'll tell you the other part?"

"Oh, sure, I guess."

What is he hiding from me?

"I started going to college games when I was in middle school. Being the youngest cousin by six years, I had a lot of games I could easily go to. I never really thought much about where I wanted to play. I grew up in Illinois, so I thought I would always stay in the area. The best college hockey teams are in Michigan, Minnesota, and North Dakota, if I wanted to stay in the Midwest. Boston was calling my name though."

Lucas' face lights up when he mentions Boston. Does he wish he played there instead?

"It was a lot of pressure to start thinking about it young, but I knew if I wanted to play D1 hockey and have any chance at impressing NHL scouts, I needed to. "

A somber look crosses his face. He sighs as if trying to let go of the weight of growing up with the stress of always thinking about your future.

"When I was twelve, I went to my first D1 game. It was here at West. It was the first time I ever visited. The Wyverns were playing the Boston University Terriers. My cousin played on the third line his sophomore year for them. I know it sounds crazy, but I have such a vivid memory of that game. The Wyverns and Terriers were neck and neck. The Terriers ended up winning. I've never seen my cousin so happy before. I knew I had to chase that type of happiness, so right then I decided I would leave the Midwest and focus on trying to play for the Terriers."

My eyebrows raise with shock. I didn't expect Lucas to talk about playing for one of our three biggest rivals, but it is one of the top NHL recruiting schools in the country. Nick mentioned Boston University and University of Michigan way too often. At least Lucas wasn't talking about playing for East Michigan. He lets out a quiet chuckle.

"I can tell you're surprised by the look on your face—most people are. I was dead set on playing for Boston University. I went to a handful of their games every year after that. I got to know some of the coaches when I was just starting high school because my other cousin started playing there too. It seemed like it could be a cool family dynamic and legacy. Part of me really wanted that since I'm an only child and my dad never played hockey. But my senior year of high school, everything changed."

Lucas scratches his stubble, letting out another quiet chuckle.

"There was talk about this big shot player making a decision on where he went to school. You had to have lived under a rock if you didn't know about him. Anyone who paid attention to D1 hockey prospects and NHL prospects knew about Nick Bellinger for years."

"You came to West because of my brother?" My eyes grow wide with wonder.

"Not exactly."

He didn't say no . . . Lucas being at West has something to do with Nick. I didn't realize Lucas had such a connection with my brother. I assumed he barely knew him even though they played for the same team.

"My senior year of high school I was invited to go to a game at West by Coach Andres. I had already been invited to go to games my junior year from the Terriers and from East Michigan too, but I wasn't interested in East."

Lucas pauses, reaching for a bottle of water on the table, and takes a long gulp.

"Honestly, I'm not sure why I went to the game West invited me to. I was set on going to play for the Terriers. Coach showed me around and introduced me to a few people. Funny enough, I ended up talking to Liam for a while. I had met him a few times before playing travel hockey. He loved playing at West. He told me he could meet up after the game if I wanted to talk about it more."

I frantically take notes as Lucas takes another drink of water.

"The game was amazing. The Wyverns easily won. Liam and Nick both were on the third line as freshmen. Seeing them play together for the first time is ingrained in my brain. Yeah, you could see their impeccable skill, but a lot of guys and teams had something similar."

Lucas closes his eyes briefly, grinning as he replays the memory in his head.

"It was the chemistry and team dynamic that sold me. It might not have been noticeable to anyone else, but I could see the team learn from each other, grow off each other and feed off each other's energy with every movement on the ice. They read and anticipated each other almost flawlessly. I craved being a part of a team like that. I dreamed of being a captain for a team like that. I didn't even bother meeting up with Liam to learn more about the team. I knew in my gut I had to play at West."

My heart flutters hearing Lucas talking about his dream that's now a reality for him.

"The next day, I told my family West was my first choice. My cousin wasn't happy. We could have played for BU together. He was a senior when I was a freshman in college. But I had to go with my gut feeling. I told Coach Andres about a month after that I was all in on being a Wyvern. It was the right choice. I wouldn't be the player or person I am today if I didn't play for the Wyverns. I wouldn't have met you either, Laur."

My mouth goes dry. Does he really think I could be part of the reason fate brought him to him to play for the Wyverns?

"I guess, I just like hockey. My heart's just always been in the game. I'm lucky that I got the opportunity to come here. Is that enough for your article? I can talk more about how I practice without everyone because I'm a pompous douche if you want?" Lucas jokes.

"That's more than enough. You can keep secret stories of freshman year to yourself, I suppose."

I respond teasingly. I'm a little turned on by how much this man loves hockey. His passion and dedication are attractive qualities.

"I'll save it for a rainy day," he says. "Speaking of rainy days, are you free Tuesday?"

"Oh? Is it supposed to rain?"

I haven't checked the weather, but as long as it doesn't start snowing yet, I'll be happy.

"Maybe." He shrugs, chuckling under his breath. "I'm not sure. I just needed a way to ask you if you had plans Tuesday night."

Is he asking me out? I want to spend time with him so badly . . . Then I remember, I have my date that day. I can't use that excuse; he won't like it.

"I do have plans. I'm sorry," I reply, feeling guilty.

It shouldn't matter. I don't owe him anything. I shouldn't feel guilty. This date is supposed to help me figure out what's going on with me and my stupid heart.

Lucas looks at me, perplexed. "Oh, what are you doing?"

A lump starts to form in my throat, and my hands grow clammy. I don't want to give him an answer.

"You're going on a date, aren't you? What happened to swearing off dating, Lauren?" Lucas sneers, "Or is it just me you are swearing off?"

The words stay lodged in my throat beneath the lump I can't seem to swallow.

"Great," he coldly states. "Enjoy your date."

Lucas starts to storm out of the room, fury in each step.

"Wait," I call before he opens the door.

His rage and hurt-filled dark eyes look back at me. Why did I say that? I'm suddenly mute and can't come up with anything to say.

"What?" He launches the word at me like a knife.

"It's just a set up with Tyler's friend, it's not a big deal."

"Not a big d—" Lucas stops mid-sentence frustrated. He opens the door to leave.

Frantically, I grab Nick's notebook and throw it at him. "Here, give it back to me in two weeks. Be careful not to destroy it."

"Destroy it? It's a notebook with incredibly helpful information in it, why would I do that? It's not a heart; I won't destroy it."

I stay quiet but my pulse loudly races like a driver at Daytona.

"I won't destroy it, break it, or ruin it. I take care of the things that mean something to me, Lauren." He releases a heavy breath. "And for the record, I wouldn't break your heart either. Like I said, I take care of the things that mean something to me."

Slamming the door behind him, Lucas leaves a hollowness that wasn't in the air before.

I sink back into my chair. Was that him telling me I destroyed his heart? I didn't even do anything wrong. I wasn't trying to hurt him. I just . . . I'm not ready to be with someone like that again. Now I have to go on this date, he's going to ask about it, or find out through mutual friends.

Chapter Twenty-Five

Lucas

She's going on a date? You've got to be kidding me. This girl that I have been swooning over, who claims she has sworn off dating and sworn off love, is going on a date with someone that's not me? I am going to have to restrain myself from punching my good friend Tyler in the fucking face. He has to know how I feel about her.

Shaking off those thoughts, I start to go through Nick's notebook and find some of his running routes. Perfect, I'll run one of his routes to get my mind right, then focus on these next two games before confronting Tyler. I might have it bad for Laur, but we have a hot winning streak going, and I won't let my anger ruin that.

The first game against the Jaws is smooth sailing. We win 4-1, which is followed by a day off to rest in between games.

The second game isn't as smooth. It's tied 1-1 after the first period. In the second period, the Jaws score on a breakaway. Then Mitchell gets himself put into the penalty box. Fucking prick. He's too much of a hothead. They are now leading 3-1. During the second intermission, I almost let my temper and distress get to me.

"This should be an easy win for us. What's going on? Mitchell, get your shit together, you know better than to start shit. They shouldn't have gotten that second goal," I complain when we get into the locker room.

Liam and Tyler pull me aside.

"Dude," Liam hits me on the back, "What's up?"

"Nothing." I run both hands through my sweaty hair, but I know they see through my laidback façade.

"We all know Mitchell is a fuck up and deserves much worse than what you said," Tyler speaks up, "but that's unlike you. What's going on?"

"Stay out of it, Tyler. You're the reason she's going on a date and my head's all over the place."

"Is this about Laur? Really? Dude, come on. I didn't think you were really interested. She's one of my best friends. I—" Tyler starts.

I cut him off. "Save it. I need to care about this game and not her—not right now. Liam, do you have Nick's notebook? Let's give it another look."

I gave Liam the notebook to look through a day after I got it. I knew he would want the intel on teams and scouts.

#13 Monroe can't shoot from the left side. Push him there and keep him away from the right side of the net
#27 Callihan can't pass for shit, his accuracy is less than 50%
Should be an easy win

I groan. The first game we are down by more than one . . . and this is the one-time Nick writes it should be an easy win. Standing at the sink, I look at my sweat-stained face in the mirror and splash water over my face in an attempt to ease my tension.

"Hey, man, we got this game," Tyler says to me as I walk back toward the rest of the team, holding out a fist to bump. He's showing me he really didn't mean any harm with Laur. I nod and meet his fist bump before we head back out on the ice.

We come back hot, scoring twice in the first five minutes of the third period. We have two minutes left to win the game. Tyler and I lock eyes. He shifts his head to number thirteen for the Jaws and mouths "to the left." Tyler quickly goes to cover Callihan, number twenty-seven. We are banking on Nick's notes being accurate. Tyler gains control of the puck off a weak pass from Callihan. Nick was right about his shitty passing ability. That's a shame for him but incredible for us.

Tyler comes up the ice and passes to Rizzo, who is quickly met by an opponent and passes it off to me to shoot with less than a minute left. There's only one defenseman near the goal. I take a chance and go for a slapshot angle left of the goal.

The shot goes in.

Tyler, Liam, and the guys come rushing toward me, pushing me to the boards in celebration.

"Hey, Luc," Tyler says. "One shot, you took it. Nice job." He hits my helmet and skates away.

They don't score in the seconds remaining of the game. Our winning streak continues.

The team is hyped in the locker room, but my mind is back on Laur instead of the win we pulled off. Celebrating at a bar won't do me any good. Tonight, I don't care if it looks bad that I blow it off and head home. I need a night off from being captain. Bren, Laur, and another girl in their marketing posse are waiting outside the locker room.

"Amazing shot, Captain," Laur congratulates me. Her voice makes my heart ache. I want to forget our argument and just pull her into me.

Before I can even say anything, Liam pipes in, "No drinks tonight. Sorry, ladies, it's boy's night."

He turns to Tyler and me. Tyler looks at me for confirmation, and I nod. I hate to admit it, but I do need to talk to him about Laur before I go insane over this date and over her.

"Babe? Seriously?" Bren says, clearly trying to persuade Liam to spend time with her.

"Sorry, Bren, he's ours tonight." Tyler throws an arm around Liam and kisses him on the cheek. I can't help but chuckle, looking at the expression on the girls' faces. It's priceless.

I drive myself over to Liam, Tyler, and Connor's place. I won't be having more than one drink anyways, so I can easily drive home or crash in their guest bedroom if I'm too tired. I grab a pack of Bud Light at the gas station around the corner from their house. I don't bother knocking and walk right into their house. The three guys are already on the couch with drinks.

"Bud Light? Really, dude? You used to be a Jack and Coke kind of guy. She's really gotten to you," Connor teases.

He's not wrong. I rarely used to drink this stuff before I met Lauren, not that I've drank with her often, but I want to make sure if someone buys a drink for her, it's me. I've gotten used to ordering them, I guess.

"It's bad, bro. I don't want to talk about it." I twist off the cap and take a long swig of my beer.

"Well, you're going to. So that you don't lose it on the ice or in the locker room. It's your turn this year," Tyler declares, looking at me sternly.

We never talk about shit like this. Maybe once a year, if that. We've talked about Connor and Tyler's random flings. We've talked about Liam's rare occasional problem with Bren, but mostly he talks about how he's going to marry her one day. I never talk about girls or anyone. I haven't had a serious relationship since freshman year, and I don't do flings or hookups often.

"I like her," I confess.

"No shit," Connor mutters into his beer.

I throw my beer cap at him. With a long heavy sigh, I admit to my friends that I'm falling for Lauren Bellinger.

"I don't get caught up in girls. You guys know me. I'm focused on hockey twenty-four-seven. But she gets that. She's perfect. I feel more myself around her than I've felt around anyone ever. She kissed me drunkenly at the Beer Olympics, and I've been hooked ever since."

A weight feels lifted off my chest as I finally admit it to someone. I run one hand through my hair before taking a sip of my beer.

"Dude, I didn't know. I wouldn't have tried to set her up. The only reason I did was because she wanted to get you out of her head," Tyler confesses. His expression is guilt-ridden, realizing what he just shared. "Shit. I shouldn't have said that. She's like my sister and best friend. You're one of my best friends too. I don't want to be in the middle."

"I get it. That's why I never said anything to you in the first place. Honestly, I thought she was into you, and I got annoyed at that."

Tyler doubles over with laugher, as if I just made the most absurd comment. "I had a crush on her when I was like ten. She's beautiful, but I could never. Now that blonde that's friends with Suz on the other hand . . ."

"Woah, woah. I call dibs on Shay. I tried to talk to her last year, and she was just drooling over Captain Charming over here," Connor laments.

"Wait, why does she say she is swearing off love or dating or whatever?" I ask Tyler.

"Bro, I don't know. Even if I did, I don't think it would be my place to tell you. But I've been wondering about that too. She's clearly into you."

A small buzz works its way into my system, and it's not from the two 4.2% beers I've had tonight. We could work. Laur and I have chemistry. I felt it from the first night I saw her in the bar. I knew it from the first actual conversation we had.

"Thanks. I swear our traditional once a year serious bro talk was not wasted on me." I start to head to the front of the house to head home. Tyler walks with me to lock up the house.

"Tell me if she goes on that date and is into him at least? I need to know if I have a shot," I ask Tyler on my way out of the front door.

"If she's going to be with anyone, you've got the one shot, Luc," Tyler says.

"Then I'll have to make sure she knows I'm all in on her."

As soon as I get home, I sleep the most peaceful sleep. My mind is finally at ease. I hope my heart will ease soon too. I just have to talk to Laur.

Chapter Twenty-Six
Laur

"How do I look?" I ask Bren and Jaylin. I just finished getting ready for my date with Tyler's friend, Brian. I picked out a black off the shoulder dress paired with my knee-high boots and some fun turquoise earrings to give it a pop of color.

My stomach is in knots. I'm not sure if I can go through with this. I haven't gone on an actual date since before I met my ex-boyfriend, Nathan Kovek. After three years of dating him, I avoid thinking about him as much as possible. Nick was never a big fan of his, but when Nathan went to East Michigan to play hockey, he just pretended Nathan didn't exist. I like to pretend he doesn't exist now too. I was always a bigger supporter of West and Nick's hockey career, which Nathan hated. I guess I don't blame him. What guy wants his girlfriend to care more about if their biggest rival wins?

"You okay, Laur?" Bren's voice dispels my spiraling thoughts.

"Yeah, just anxious. I haven't been on a first date in a long time."

"Well, you look like a dime, Lauren. Flash him that winning Bellinger smile, and he will be putty in your hand," Jaylin declares. "Where is he taking you?"

"I'm not sure. He mentioned some restaurant called Urban Grub or Urban something, I think?"

"Iggy's? Damn, the pre-med boy is showing off. That's the nicest restaurant within thirty minutes of campus! It's delicious. Liam and I have gone on our anniversary every year," Bren remarks in awe.

Good thing I went with a dress instead of jeans. I don't do it often, but I do enjoy dressing up on occasion.

"How fancy? Should I change?" My pulse quickens. I'm panicking even more now.

"Take a deep breath. You look amazing, and you are dressed perfectly. Actually, I am borrowing that dress sometime. It's adorable."

Bren tries to calm my anxiety. It's not working great. Maybe this is a mistake. I should just keep swearing off men, dating, and love. It can't be worth feeling this dread and panic constantly.

Jaylin comes back from the kitchen and hands me a shot glass filled to the brim. It smells like Cinco De Mayo. I didn't even notice her leave the room. Clearly, I am overthinking and way in over my head.

"You are beautiful, and he will love you. If it doesn't go well, then only Tyler has to see him again!" Jaylin jokes. She hands Bren a shot too.

"To you, Laur, to ease the insane anxiety radiating off you right now and to a great night."

Bren holds up her shot glass. Jaylin puts hers to Bren's waiting for me to join. I sigh and cheers them, downing the ice-cold tequila. I'm going to need at least five more of those to feel comfortable going on this date. No one truly understands how difficult it is for me, which is my fault. I haven't told anyone the full story of why I am so adamant about never dating anyone again—except Nick. He knew some parts of the story.

Maybe, if I tell someone else, I won't feel trapped in my own skin any time I'm interested in someone. Maybe it would help me not push away a good thing, like Lucas. I guess it's time for me to find out if I'm truly interested in him or if it's just because he's always around. I feel a pang of shame goes through me for going on a date when Lucas seems to be in my head all the time. I shouldn't have even told him about this date.

I park my car and look at my phone. Brian sent a selfie and a text letting me know he's waiting outside for me. The selfie is a cute touch. I immediately spot him when I walk up to the restaurant. He's even more attractive in person. He has a blue button-down shirt on, which makes his baby blues pop. He's clean cut and seemingly put together—far from any hockey guy I know.

"Hi, Brian, I'm Laur. Nice to meet you!" I try to seem cheerful walking up to him and not still in my head about the date. He pulls me in for a hug.

"Nice to meet you, Laur. Tyler did not do you justice. You are beautiful. Shall we?"

He holds open the door for me. He seems very sweet and kind already. He talks to the hostess, who leads us over to our table. Brian seems very polite and poised as he thanks the hostess.

The conversation moves to our majors, and he asks what brought me to the West. I hesitate. I haven't met a ton of people outside our PR and marketing team, and the hockey team. Because of that, I haven't had to tell my story about Nick, the accident, and how I ended up coming to West. He senses my hesitation.

"It's a long story . . ." I start, "I . . . it's hard to talk about, but my brother went here before he . . .passed away. I wanted to come for the marketing and PR opportunity with the Wyverns. He actually applied for me before he passed. I found out I was accepted, so here I am."

I take a big sip of the wine he ordered.

"I'm sorry for your loss. We don't have to talk about it. Thanks for sharing with me."

He reaches across the table to take my hand in his. Most girls would be swooning at the gesture—he's such a gentleman—but it just causes the knots in my stomach to tighten.

He steers the conversation to talking about future careers, asking me how the program is going so far and telling me why he decided to go pre-med. He's incredibly kindhearted and easy to talk to. We even have a lot in common. He explains pre-med because his mom is a nurse and his dad a neurosurgeon. His sister wanted to go into psychology, which he mentions might have disappointed his parents a little bit even though it's still "brain related." Like me, he seems to be influenced by his family and very close with them too.

Brian is walking me to my car. I somehow made it through the entire thing without bolting. It helps that he's genuine and loves his family. But I know there's only a small spark between us. Guilt washes over me. Am I a bad person? I need to let him know right away so I don't lead him on.

As we stop at my car, Brian leans in to kiss me. Panicking, both fists shove blindly at his chest and with a thud, he hits the sedan next to mine.

"I'm so incredibly sorry!" Hot tears prickle my eyes. My relationship trauma is getting the best of me. I'm not sure I'm ready for someone new, but I know if I am, it can't be with Brian.

"It's okay," he says politely. He seems unfazed that not only did I reject him, but I physically pushed him away.

"I'm really sorry, Brian. You are the nicest guy . . ." I start.

Brian sighs, "But there's someone else?"

"No, that's not it," I reply instantly, which is a slight lie. "Well, I guess I'm not sure. This is the first time I've admitted it, but I have a lot of trauma from a bad three-year relationship. I haven't wanted to date anyone since. I actually swore off dating, but Tyler convinced me to meet you. You are damn near perfect. But yes, you're right. There is someone I can't get out of my head, even if I'm not sure I'm ready for anything real again."

"I get it," Brian sorrowfully says. "I hope it works out for you. If not, you have my number." He kisses my cheek and walks away, leaving a lingering sadness behind. As nice as Brian is, relationships are never that simple.

I could be fine getting to know him, but in the end, I know he isn't truly what I want. I would be content; I wouldn't be happy. I need more than a small spark. I need an ever-burning flame. In a different life, he could have been perfect for me. But in this life, if I am going to go against my no dating rule, I need something that could turn into intense desire and a heart-wrenching love that's terrifying. That's the only way it could be worth it. I need it to be Lucas.

Before I fall asleep, I send a text to Tyler to come over around 7:30 tomorrow morning. I want to talk to him, Bren, and Jaylin at the same time. They are all going to ask about the date, and I don't want to relive the same embarrassing story three different times.

I wake up at 6am to go for a run to clear my mind. I search for Nick's notebook and realize that Lucas still has it. Great. I guess I'll just run a path I already know instead of a new one. I text Bren that Tyler is coming over for breakfast and I'll be back in an hour. I'm out the door, headphones in my ears, with music on full blast. Today would be a great day to hit that runner's high and forget about the world. I hit mile seven, my legs already feeling like Jello. I push myself to keep going, getting lost in my workout playlist.

The playlist ends. I look down at my fitness watch, and it shows mile twelve. How is that possible? I must have finally hit that runner's high and just kept going. My mind feels clear, and my heart feels ready. It's almost 8am, Tyler's probably at the house already. I have two missed calls and ten texts. I quickly type a text to Bren that I'm on my way back home.

"Thank God," Bren exclaims as I walk through the front door.

"We were worried about you, Laur, you told me to be here almost an hour ago! You weren't answering your phone," Tyler says in a panicked voice. Worry lines wrinkle his forehead. His hair is a mess from excessively running his hands through it.

"I'm so sorry! I should have called," I reply, still panting from my run. "I was just getting in the zone running. I finally reached my runner's high!"

"Definitely should have called," Jaylin grumbles under her breath.

"Great, but don't do that again," Tyler sternly response. "You clearly want to talk about something."

"Do you mind if I shower first? I'm all gross from my run. It will give Bren time to make an extra pack of bacon. We are going to need it."

Tyler reluctantly nods, running his hand through his hair again.

Stepping under the shower spray, my thoughts are racing. Am I ready to share this secret?

When I enter the kitchen freshly showered but face still red from my long run, there are three sets of eyes following my every move. I grab a piece of crunchy bacon and start to grab a cup of coffee.

"Laur," Bren demands, "Are you going to just pretend like you didn't ask us to be here to talk about something important?"

I sigh into my piece of bacon and nod. She's right.

"The date was fine. Brian is a perfect gentleman," I start.

"But he's not for you," Tyler acknowledges with a knowing look.

My face betrays my guilt as I confirm with a nod.

"There's nothing wrong with that!" Jaylin chimes in.

"Sure, he's my friend, Laur, but that's okay," Tyler reassures me.

"Yes, he's not for me. But he tried to kiss me, and I pushed him," I continue.

"Like pushed him away or *pushed* him, pushed him?" Bren questions.

I grab another piece of bacon.

"Pushed him, pushed him. I . . . there's something I need to tell you three, but it doesn't leave this room, not yet. It's going to be hard for me to talk about. I will cry. I will need this entire plate of bacon to myself. I will really, really cry. I'm talking snot rockets, losing my voice, dehydration for years. It is going to be ugly, but I need you to let me finish my story before saying anything or trying to comfort me, okay?"

All three of them mutter some type of yes reply with looks of panic and concern on their faces.

"I mean it, I can't have you interrupt, promise you won't." I look at each of them until I hear three yeses.

My hands are trembling as I clench the plate of bacon like it's my lifeline. After over a year of not talking about it with anyone, I start telling them my reason for swearing off love.

"Nathan was a great boyfriend at first. He was so attentive and sweet. He would randomly give me long stem roses, which I love. I was always around most of his friends before dating him, so our lives seemed to integrate easily."

Taking a sip of my coffee, I dig deep in my mind for the memories that I purposely locked away.

"The first year or so we dated, I thought it was pretty great. I didn't notice at the time—but he would gaslight me and make me feel like I was making things up. He was best friends with this girl that would purposely try to get with him and say things to him like 'I wish I could wear your jersey to senior night, but you have a girlfriend.'"

A piece of bacon crumbles in my hand as I think about that dreadful girl.

"I hated her. Nathan made me feel insane. I don't think he ever cheated on me, but he would always say she meant nothing by it, and they were just friends, even when she would flat out say she wished he didn't have a girlfriend. He would call me crazy or insecure. I *was* insecure because he rarely made me feel secure in our relationship."

I spin my coffee mug, staring into it, avoiding their eyes.

"I tried to be as understanding as possible. I had a lot of guy friends growing up with a brother who played hockey. I distinctly remember Nathan even giving me shit about you multiple times," I say the last part to Tyler.

"He would say things like 'you find him attractive, don't you?'"

Tyler grunts his annoyance that he would be used against me like that.

"I mean yeah you're not fucking blind," Bren mutters. I glare at her. "Sorry, no interruptions."

"'You spend so much time with your brother and his friends. They all want you, and you make it easy for them to.' He would just say the most absurd shit to me. Sometimes hammered, sometimes sober. I think he was jealous of Nick. I don't know if he was jealous of my relationship with him, but he was definitely jealous of Nick Bellinger, the star player."

Taking a long drink of coffee, I try to ease the tightness in my throat. It doesn't help one bit.

"When Nick started playing for West, Nathan was more emotionally abusive than ever. But when Nathan started playing for East, that's when the physical abuse started. He would probably strangle me if he knew I told you, but he wanted to play here. West didn't give him any opportunities to even come visit. I don't know if Nick said something to the coaches about him or not, but I do know he wasn't the most skilled player either."

I tug at the collar of my shirt, sweating from the agony of nightmarish memories.

"I won't go into too much detail . . ." My voice gets strangled almost as if Nathan is there silencing me, "it's . . . hard for me to talk about."

"Understandable," Tyler mutters. He takes my hand in his, trying to console me.

"The first time he laid his hands on me was after his first college game. They lost. I don't even remember who they played against, I just know they didn't play West. He had probably about five minutes of ice time, which for a subpar freshman player, that's pretty great. I was staying over at his apartment that night, and he came back hammered. I didn't even know he was going somewhere after the game. I had never seen him that plastered before."

My voice is shaky and barely audible as the dark memories swirl in my head.

"I was on the couch, and all of a sudden, I was being screamed at. He said something about how I barely paid attention at the game, if Nick was playing, I would have paid more attention, and if he was Nick, he would have been on the ice the whole time. As soon as I started to respond back, he dragged me across the floor, and I—" I try to swallow the lump in my throat and tears pour out of my eyes like a hurricane downpour hitting land.

"I woke up with bruises all down my left leg from his fist."

I'm bawling and shaking with each sob.

"Don't say anything, I told you not to interrupt." I clap sternly at Bren, locking eyes with her until she looks uncomfortable. She nods, and I see tears streaking her mascara. Jaylin grabs for Bren's comforting hand to hold as she starts sobbing too. Tyler's eyes are gleaming with tears, but none have escaped yet.

"There were a few more incidents over time. But the worst was the day of the accident. I made the mistake of sleeping at his apartment. I think he woke up drunk. He asked me if I was going to sit with his parents and wear his jersey to the game. Before I could even answer, his jaw tensed. He screamed at me to get out of his apartment. I tried to reason with him, and he pushed me. Hard. The mirror on the dresser shattered. I think my shoulder hit the dresser. I left immediately to meet you for breakfast, Bren.

"After breakfast, I showered at Bren's and got ready for the game. I had one of Nick's Wyverns jerseys to put on. My body hurt so badly. I could barely lift my left arm to put the jersey on. I figured if I was still in pain later, I would go to the ER after the game. I avoided Nathan like he was patient zero. I ignored his texts and calls. I googled what a broken collarbone feels like.

"I went straight to find Nick after the game. Nathan tried to grab my arm, and I screamed in pain. Nick saw it. I knew I would have to tell him something. I could see fear in Nathan's eyes, but at that moment, I didn't care about him or my relationship at all. I just wanted to escape. So, I eagerly went with Nick to celebrate the win with the Wyverns, instead of consoling my boyfriend."

My body trembles as I finish airing out all my trauma. The countertop fills my vision, looking up I finally meet the gazes I've been avoiding. Three grief-stricken faces meet me. The tears Tyler held at bay finally break free from the dam.

"When Nick and I," my words are stilted, and I try to start again.

"When we got in the accident, we were arguing. I told him about Nathan's recent abuse. It's my fault."

My voice cracks with heartache.

"Yes, the other driver was drunk, but if I waited to tell Nick until we got out of the car or if I didn't tell him at all, he wouldn't have taken his eyes off the road trying to comfort me. He would have been paying more attention. He would be alive. It's hard with my brother gone, but knowing it's my fault—it's why I stopped trying to live my life.

Sobbing so hard my entire body shakes, I bury my face in my unsteady hands.

"It's why I never left the house, why I didn't even apply to come to work with the Wyverns. I don't deserve to be happy when it's my fault Nick isn't here."

"Lauren Chip Bellinger, that is just not true." Bren rushes to pull me into a hug, followed by Tyler and Jaylin.

"It is true. If I didn't distract him—"

Jaylin cuts me off, "Stop that right now, Lauren. You don't know what would have or could have happened. The other driver was drunk and probably swerving all over the place. Nothing is your fault. You shouldn't regret telling Nick. You needed to tell someone. You should have told the police or someone else sooner."

"Laur"—Tyler pulls me close to his chest—"I wish you would have told us sooner so we could have helped you. You deserve to be happy and not feel guilty or live with this pain. Not only about the accident but about that dickhead, Nathan."

"You can't say anything to anyone, not about the accident and not about Nathan. I don't want anyone to judge me."

I'm not sure anyone can understand me through my quivering wails.

"Lauren, no one will ever blame you for the accident. It is not your fault," Bren replies, rubbing my back while Tyler still holds me. "And no one will judge you for Nathan, Lauren. That's ridiculous. He is an awful guy and an awful human."

"But it's my fault, if I supported him more and supported Nick and the Wyverns less . . ."

"Are you kidding me, Laur? You can't make excuses for his behavior. YOU did nothing to deserve anything that scumbag did to you. Do you hear me? Absolutely nothing. You should go to the police. You should have tried to—" I cut Tyler off.

"I don't want him kicked off his team," I mumble.

"He deserves to be in fucking jail, Lauren!" Bren screams. "He abused you mentally and physically for years. That is inexcusable."

"And Lucas had a girlfriend that didn't support his hockey career. If he finds out that I supported Nick more than I did Nathan . . ."

"Lauren, that is ridiculous. Lucas will kill that guy in a heartbeat if he ever finds out. Hell, I want to kill him," Bren yells at me.

"Not that it matters, but Lucas' history is nothing like yours. That girl didn't want him to play hockey because she wanted his attention instead," Tyler clarifies.

I pull away from Tyler to go grab some tissues.

"Well, now you know why I swore off dating and love and why I didn't want to be interested in Lucas. I'm too afraid to be in a relationship again after thinking I was so in love and . . . everything he did to me."

"Lauren," Bren says calmly, "Lucas would be the most understanding person. I was very against him and you from the beginning. The first time you met, I told him not to get involved with you."

I give her a death stare and open my mouth.

"Hear me out!" Bren holds a hand up to me before offering me more bacon.

"I knew you swore off dating and that you coming to West after Nick was a huge deal. I had barely seen you, but I knew you weren't in a good place. You needed to focus on you, just like you said. Plus, Lucas doesn't date either for very different reasons. I knew he would fall for you. I didn't want to see either of you hurt."

Bren's gaze is filled with pleas for understanding.

"It's not like he listened anyway. He asked me about your date and admitted he was into you," Tyler says with a shrug.

"What?! When was this?! Why are you just telling me now?" I throw a used tissue at Tyler before grabbing another.

"I don't know how to play middleman between you two. You're both two of my best friends. He was relieved I wasn't into you," Tyler states

"Hold on, back to the serious stuff for a second. Sorry," Jaylin tilts her head. "Does Nathan still play for East?"

My tears start to fall again as I nod knowing where this is headed. "Yes, and I haven't spoken to him or seen him since the day of the accident. I'm not sure I'm ready to see him."

"That's okay, Laur. You don't have to," Bren replies.

"Skip that game. It's not worth your pain. It's okay," Tyler expresses.

"Please keep this between us. I'm not ready to tell anyone else yet. But thank you for being here for me and not judging me."

"There is nothing to judge you for, Laur." Tyler pulls me into a hug again.

"Absolutely not," Jaylin agrees.

"We love you just the same if not more," Bren's voice quakes with sorrow. "We won't say a word."

I sigh in relief, sinking into Tyler's embrace more.

"Thank you. Now I have to decide what to do about Lucas. I like him. I really do. But I don't think I'm ready yet," I say into Tyler's chest.

"It's okay, Laur. You don't have to decide now," Tyler says.

I'm glad I don't. My head and my heart are at war. But with opening up to my friends today and telling them a secret I've held so closely, I think my heart is starting to gain the upper hand.

Chapter Twenty-Seven

Lucas

We're on the bus ride back from a two-game series on the road. The team is still hot on a winning streak with one game going into overtime. I can't blame the girls for saying these games were too far to travel for, but I miss Laur.

Every time I see her, my stomach churns. I hate it. It's been almost a week since I found out about her date. The thought of it makes me feel queasy. It's not a great feeling, but it's especially awful on an almost nine-hour bus ride where I'm left alone with my thoughts. I need to ask her about her date eventually. She's been wrapped up in her articles, and I've been so busy with hockey, but I've just been using that as an excuse.

The team has a home game in a few days. When I see her at the game, I'm going to be in my head wondering how her date went or thinking about her with another guy. I can't let her distract me too much - we are having an amazing season so far. If we keep playing like we have been, I have no doubt we will make it to the semifinals.

My mind swirls with thoughts of Laur and her date, but I'm starting to doze off from the rhythmic motion of the bus. Suddenly I'm in what looks like the Wyverns' stadium, but it's decorated to the nines. The stands are filled, and it seems like there are millions of people all dressed up. Violins start to play—that's odd for a game.

The most beautiful hockey angel fills my vision. Laur is wearing an all-white jersey that seems to sparkle. It hangs well past her knees. She walks past me and smiles. With her back to me, I see the word "BRIDE" in place of a last name on the jersey. She starts walking to the opposite side of the ice down a rolled out white carpet. I try to move to get to her, but I'm stuck. It's like my feet are frozen to the ice. She keeps walking farther and farther away from me. I say her name, but no sound comes out.

At the other end of the ice, I glimpse a figure. Looking up at the jumbotron, I see it's a guy dressed in a white coat like a doctor. It hits me: this is a wedding, HER wedding. Laur is going to marry the doctor right here, right now. This time, I scream her name.

Still, no sound comes out of my mouth. She's now at the other end of the ice. I'm screaming her name and saying "please no" over and over. I can finally hear my own voice, but it seems like no one else can hear me. The violin music stops, and everyone in the stands starts to cheer.

Tears of panic and frustration roll down my cheeks as I try with every fiber of muscle to move my body and put a stop to this wedding. A priest joins Laur and the doctor at the other side of the ice. His voice comes over the loudspeaker, and he starts the nuptials. The echo of "I do" from a male voice fills the arena.

This can't be happening. She isn't supposed to be with him. She's supposed to be with me. Sweat mixes with tears on my face as I keep trying to move with all my might. Finally, I'm free of the invisible force that was holding me back. I'm sprinting down the ice. falling all over the place. I need to get to her before she says I do. I start to scream "I object." I don't hear her say I do on the loudspeakers, but she is leaning in to kiss him.

"NO!"

"Hey, Luc, are you okay?" a voice says from next to me. *Finally*, someone hears my pleas.

I startle awake. My face is covered in sweat, and my eyes are watery. My heart is beating a million miles a minute. A hand rests on my shoulder, grounding me.

"Just breathe, you're good, Luc."

It's Tyler's voice. I rub my eyes and my face with my hands. Tyler's across the aisle from me on the bus. I look across at him. He's breathing in and out dramatically, continually telling me to take deep breaths. Am I having a panic attack?

My heart starts to slow after at least a full minute, and I can feel air in my lungs again. I look at Tyler and nod my head, telling him I'm okay.

"You okay, Lucas?" he asks again.

"I . . . Yeah . . . Bad dream," I mutter to him, pulling on my sweatshirt.

Chills from cold sweat run down my body. It was more than a bad dream; it was my worst nightmare. Truthfully, I think I would rather be rejected from the NHL than witness Lauren marrying someone else. I'm falling in love with her.

"Can I ask you something?" I ask Tyler. He looks at me, making a face that says, 'of course why are you even asking.'

"Sorry to ask you. I don't want you in the middle, but I need to know." Before I can even finish, he responds.

"She went on the date. It was fine, but she isn't interested."

A wave of relief and calm rushes over me. I shudder.

"Thank you," I reply with true gratitude in my eyes. "I just—I needed to know. It's been eating at me."

Tyler nods. I turn away and close my eyes again, hoping for a dreamless, peaceful sleep.

"I found out why she swore off dating," Tyler mutters. "She was . . . overwhelmed after the date. I don't think she even kissed him, but she was . . . I can't tell you, please don't ask me to."

"I understand." Truthfully, I do understand, but my mind spins wondering what it could be. If I know . . . then maybe I can help her through it and show that it's worth working through to be together.

"It's a lot, Lucas. It's not my story to share, but I think she's too afraid to tell you, or anyone."

"I get it. I won't push you. I respect that, and I respect her." I start to turn away again and mutter more to myself than to Tyler, "Nothing she says or has done or has experienced will change anything for me. I'm falling in love with her."

"Good. She deserves someone who will treat her right and won't hurt her."

"Hurting her is the last thing I ever want to do in my life." I truly mean that with every fiber of my being. I hope Tyler can sense the sincerity in my voice.

Tyler pats my shoulder, understanding in voice. "I know. I trust you. Give her time, and I think she will too, Luc."

I close my eyes and drift off into a more peaceful sleep. I'm still restless, but I don't have any dreams or nightmares. I don't wake up until we pull into the parking lot at West.

Chapter Twenty-Eight
Lucas

The next few days, I feel like a weight heavier than an elephant has been lifted off not just my shoulders, but my heart too. I feel lighter, happier, more at ease. I can see it in the way I move on the ice, more fluid and free than ever before. I'm ready to dominate our game in two days. I barely see Laur at our practices this week. She usually comes to at least half of them, even if she's just sitting in the stands and multitasking on her computer.

The scent of freshly ground coffee beans greets me the second I walk in to Roast and Revelry. Suz and I grab a small table in the back. With a sparkle in her eye, she reveals she's been keeping some big news from the team. Articles for *USA Hockey Magazine* will be published soon featuring the Wyverns and highlighting some of our key players.

"Don't let it slip to the team Lucas. I want this to be a secret!"

Rolling my eyes at her need for surprises, I nod my agreement to keep quiet.

"I let Laur do the team write up," Suz confesses to me.

"Wow, really? That's surprising for a diva like you," I tease.

"Don't tell her I told you this," Suz checks to ensure that no one is in earshot, "but she's insanely talented. I'm not sure what it is, but the way she writes about hockey is almost poetic."

"It must be because of her connection to the game, how she's loved and lost around hockey in a different way than anyone else I've known. I won't tell her, but you should, Suz. She's probably terrified of you," I tease her again.

"You're right. Maybe I will tell her. The magazine editor reached out because they want to do a special feature on Nick Bellinger and on the team. I think they'll want to be more involved. As much as I selfishly want to lead the process, it has to be her." Suz checks her phone, before taking a sip of her extra sugary coffee.

"Laur will be thankful for the opportunity. But you're right, it does have to be her," I agree. My last comment has more meaning than Suz probably realizes. It has to be her. "Anyways, how are you? We haven't caught up in a while. Still going on dates with the mystery picnic connoisseur?"

"I am, but the season's in full swing so it's not my focus. It's still hard for me to talk about with a lot of people but it's getting easier. I'm this poised Barbie bitch. People expect me to be interested in the hockey players I work with, not interested in girls." Suz checks her phone again, sighing heavily, putting it face down on the table.

I've known her secret since we met, which is why we probably appear so close to anyone outside looking in. I can't imagine how she feels, not sharing it with the world. Some of the team knows and, of course, Bren. I wonder if Laur knows.

"It seems like you won't be the one people think I'm secretly dating for much longer. You are so in love with Lauren. I can see it written on your face when you talk about her. I can even hear it in your voice. I'm happy for you Lucas; you deserve that."

"I haven't told Laur anything about you. It's your story to share. She's asked, but I've just said that you're not my type and I'm definitely not yours." I can't help but chuckle at the ridiculous notion of people assuming Suz is interested in me. She's the big sister I never had.

I spill my heart out to Suz. I tell her about Laur drunkenly kissing me, the mock photo shoot and the real photoshoot, the date Tyler set her up on, and how Tyler said she wasn't interested. I need to know that it's not in my head, how close Laur and I have gotten over the past few months.

"Do you seriously think it's in your head?" Dramatically rolling her eyes, she finishes the last of her coffee. "Anyone with functioning eyes can see the connection you two have."

"No, I don't think it is. You know I don't like dating. Plus, she claims she swore off love." Anxiety makes itself at home as I wonder if there will ever be a light at the end of the tunnel. Even if it's evident how great we could be together, will it be enough to get Laur to want to jump into dating despite her claims?

"Well, if she's going on dates with Tyler's friends, then I don't think she is really swearing it off." Suz motions for me to finish my coffee, checking her phone again. "Maybe she had an awful past breakup and is protecting herself. Whatever it is, she's interested in you, Lucas."

Butterflies join the anxiety in my stomach hearing someone else validate Laur's interest in me. Smiling into my cup, I take my last sip of coffee.

"Tyler knows why she isn't interested in dating. I understand him not telling me, and you know better than anyone what that's like too. But if she is into me, then why go on a date with Tyler's friend?" I'm hoping Suz has a better perspective on this girl logic than I do.

"Maybe she wanted to see if her spark with you was real or if it was just her heart saying she's ready again and has nothing to do with you. Who knows?" Getting to her feet, Suz signals she is ready to leave.

"Actually, she knows. Talk to her, Lucas. She's the only one who can give you the answers," Clapping my back like she's closing a case with the assertiveness of a judge's gavel, we leave Roast & Revelry.

She's right. It's time for me to just stop talking about her and start talking to her.

Chapter Twenty-Nine
Laur

"**D**ID YOU GET THE MAGAZINE IN THE MAIL?!" I shriek to Mom on the phone. I am officially published in *USA Hockey Magazine* as a writer *and* photographer! My heart swells with pride as I pace around the living room with excited energy pumping through my veins.

"The articles are beautiful Laur; I am so proud of you," Mom replies. "I know it hasn't been easy since your brother passed, but my heart is so happy you are starting to find happiness in life again, Lauren. He would want you to have that. He would be proud of you too."

"But mad that my first published article in a hockey magazine isn't about him." Nick's narrow-eyed peeved expression fills my mind.

"You're not wrong about that." Mom laughs. "It seems like this Donato guy has your interest though. You wrote that he's already the biggest thing in college hockey."

The front door opens. We tend to leave it unlocked when we're home so any of our friends can just walk in. It's Suz. She waves to me, taking off her shoes at the front door. Her energy almost matches mine, delight in her eyes.

I cut Mom off before she asks more about Lucas. I can't divulge anything in front of Suz.

"Hey, Mom, I've got to go. Thank you for always supporting and loving me, even when I don't deserve it. And for not giving up on me. I'll call you later."

"Love you, sweetheart."

"Love you too, Mom," I hang up the phone and look at a very enthusiastic Suz sitting on the opposite end of the sectional coach in the living room. She's almost bouncing up and down on the couch.

"What's going on?" My eyes narrow in suspicion.

"Good morning, Laur!" Suz greets chipperly.

She hands me a piping hot caramel macchiato from a coffee cup tray she's holding. She brought me coffee? Something is definitely going on.

"You're never this nice to me. Did something happen? Do you need something? What's going—"

"Am I actually mean to you?" Concern clouds Suz her impeccably lined eyes.

"No, I guess not. But you aren't really friendly with me."

We haven't gotten to really know each other in the months I've been at West. Neither of us really put in effort. It's not all on her.

"Oh." Suz shoulders sag, her voice hushed with disgrace. "I'm so sorry, Lauren. I swear it's nothing to do with you. You are wonderful." She clears her throat. "Actually, I came over here to tell you that you did such an incredible job on the article!" The disgrace is gone from her voice, and she is chipper again.

"All the articles our team wrote and the pictures—your pictures—were so well received by the magazine team. They think the public is going to eat it up! I couldn't agree more." Suz takes a sip of her coffee before continuing. "They asked me if our team would be interested in supporting them on two additional features."

"Two more?!" I almost spit out my coffee and it has nothing to do with the temperature. I realize I ignored her attempt at opening up, but I'll get back to that when I'm out of shock.

"Yes, two more!" Suz shrieks. She's vibrating with glee. "The editor asked us to partner on these pieces with our team, but you are the right person to take this on."

"Me?"

Am I dreaming? Suz wants me to be the writer and not herself?

"You have a fresh tone and your passion for hockey jumps off the page; those are my words not theirs by the way. One would be on the season so far. The other . . ." She pauses. "The other might be more difficult of a topic. We can certainly tell them no, but I think they will write something regardless of if we are involved. Truthfully, I am surprised they have waited this far along in the season since it's been over a year . . ." Suz trails off.

"The second one is about Nick." My eagerness takes over. A published article about my brother? Tears threaten to come, but I blink them back.

"Yes." Suz nods. After a beat, she continues, "The magazine didn't really confirm what direction they are hoping to take it necessarily or the timing."

"Around his jersey retirement would be the perfect opportunity to release an article," I start.

"Exactly." Suz is beaming at me. "I had the same thought. We have not officially told the public about Nick's jersey retirement. I was hoping you would also write a press release and an article for us to share on the Wyverns' website and social channels after you pitch the idea to the *USA Hockey Magazine* team."

"Can you pitch it to them? I just want to write it. But I don't want to be involved in the business side of things when it comes to Nick. I know that's stupid." Dread fills my stomach thinking about being responsible for the business side of things. But it quickly dissolves as pride and astonishment overfill my heart. I get to share my brother's legacy with the world.

"It's not stupid, Lauren. Of course, I'm happy to do as little or as much as you need me to do for you to feel comfortable. It can't be easy . . ."

I get up off the couch to hug her before she can finish.

"Thank you. For the opportunity and for the support."

"Lauren . . . Laur, you are incredibly talented like I said. You are a big part of Nick's story. You deserve to decide how the world hears it." Suz squeezes me into another hug.

"Thank you," I whisper again with tears in my eyes. Suz sniffles, tears brimming her eyes too.

"Oh no, you got Suz crying? Did you break her?" Bren jokes from down the hallway. I sense she's been there for at least a minute by the way she's trying to lighten the mood.

"Shut up, Brenna. I may seem like I have a rough exterior, but you know I'm a big softie." Suz lobs a pillow from the couch at her.

"Don't tell anyone, Laur. Her reputation will be ruined!" Bren chucks the pillow back in our direction, causing a fit of giggles to escape Suz.

"Thank you for telling me all about the article opportunity in person, but don't think I didn't notice you starting to open up. Truthfully. . . I'm a little terrified of you—well maybe less now that you willingly hugged me," I try to joke to keep the mood light.

"I . . . well . . ." Suz starts, fidgeting with her platinum blonde hair as her wide eyes look to Bren for reassurance before continuing.

"Not a lot of people know this, but I'm gay. I don't like to tell people. Actually, I hate telling people. People used to crack jokes when I was younger about me being a lesbian and playing hockey." Clearing her throat, Suz chokes back tears but remains composed.

"I felt very out of place and judged growing up in a small town, playing what everyone considered to be a 'boy's' sport. It's one of the reasons I stopped playing. But my parents also thankfully moved me after middle school to Michigan. I really didn't miss playing hockey; I was terrible actually." She laughs, but unshed tears glisten in her eyes.

"But I did miss the game . . ." Suz' eyes glaze over as if recalling a memory.

"I decided I still wanted to do something with hockey. I got involved in the school paper to write about sports. No one really knew at my high school that I liked girls. Because of my experience when I was younger, I didn't share it with more than a handful of close friends, which even then was nerve-racking." Suz sniffles before taking another sip of now lukewarm coffee.

"People just assumed I was dating a hockey player. They do the same thing now. They think I'm dating someone on the team or sleeping with multiple of them." Suz curls her lip in disgust. "Ew! No thank you!"

Everything starts to click into place. This is what Lucas meant when he said that he wasn't Suz' type. I had no idea she played hockey. There's so much I don't know about her; I feel guilty for judging her too quickly. Empathy swells in my chest, tempting me to wrap Suz in a comforting embrace. I can't imagine how she felt growing up not feeling like she could be her true self.

"I'm so sorry that people were so cruel. You don't deserve that. You are one of the most brilliant and confident people I know." Her confidence and poised demeanor have been two things I've admired about Suz from the instant I met her.

"Confidence can be faked," she whispers.

"Regardless, who you are romantically interested in doesn't change who you are as a person. I won't tell anyone, but I am glad we are finally starting to get to know each other."

"Me too." Bren pops into the conversation with a beaming smile, watching Suz and I get to know each other.

"It's not a massive secret. People are so much more accepting nowadays. I just don't feel the need to openly share that I date girls. I'm actually a rather private person," Suz adds quietly.

We might have had different experiences, but hearing Suz overcome how people have treated her in the past encourages me to push myself to overcome my past too. This newfound hope fills me and creates a bond between us. A bond that I know will flourish into a close friendship.

"So now, tell me about Lucas." A giggle escapes Suz but is quickly followed by her signature eyeroll. "Because that boy is one of my closest friends, and he is smitten."

"I'm interested. I just . . . don't want to be. That sounds mean." I'm fumbling for words now. "It's not that I don't think he's perfect. He is. There's something about him that I am just drawn to. I just am not sure if I am ready to have a relationship again. I was set on being on my own for the rest of my life."

"For the rest of your life? Is this the whole swearing off dating and love bullshit? I get it; I was afraid to be accepted and loved too. But being content with being alone forever . . . that's just illogical, Laur." Suz' tone is purely fun and jokes as she lobs a pillow at me. The pillow hits me and tears swell. They pour out of my eyes and flood down the sides of my face. I knew I would break down sooner or later.

"Did I throw it hard," she whispers. "I'm so sorry. I—"

"No, no," I manage through sobs. "You wouldn't know. I just . . ." I can't handle sharing it. I'm too emotional with the article about Nick and recently sharing Nathan's abuse with Bren, Tyler, and Jaylin.

"Bren. Can. You." I hope Bren can understand me through my tears. Bren asks if I'm sure and as soon as I nod tells Suz that I won't be going to any games against East Michigan. She shares a very brief version of what I disclosed the other day. Horror, sorrow, and rage all show on Suz' face.

"Lucas will kill that guy if I don't first," Suz mumbles once Bren is finished telling her about my past relationship "I don't have words to say how sorry I am for you going through that experience. I won't tell a soul. Not even Lucas, I promise."

Suz takes my hand in hers, giving it a reassuring squeeze.

"There would never be any expectation for you to come to the games against East, even if you didn't share with us. All you'd ever have to say is you felt uncomfortable." She gives my hand another consoling squeeze.

"Thank you so much for understanding. Suz, you sharing your story, getting through your past, gives me faith I can get through mine," I admit as tears run down my cheeks.

Suz still hasn't let go of my hand. She gives it another squeeze of sympathy, love, and maybe hope too.

"The only person I told before Bren, Tyler, and Jaylin was Nick. It's hard to talk about," I whisper. Suz shifts her eyes around the room at the mention of Jaylin's name.

"I think it will take me a while to be at peace with it, but I do feel lighter than I have felt in a long time just by being at West, by being around the team and having supportive, loving people in my life, like you."

An eerie silence fills the room. It's unlike any of us to be quiet this long . . .

"Can we go get some lunch and stop being sad? It will feel weird not being with you both at the game tomorrow. I could use the distraction."

"Absolutely," Bren agrees. "Let's get some Italian!"

"Let me cancel my date," Suz replies. A faint ringing trickles down the stairs. Suz crinkles her noise in frustration, whoever her date was didn't pick up. "I'll try again. Lunch dates are too comfortable anyways, right? Once you add lunch dates to the mix, it's like you really just want to see each other and jump into a relationship!"

"Suz, why are you calling me when I can hear your voice in my own house?" Jaylin shouts from upstairs.

Jaylin is her lunch date?! She's been dating Jaylin?

The dots start to connect—Jaylin is her lunch date! Has she been dating Jaylin this whole time?!

"Well now I feel dumb for not noticing you were dating Jaylin this whole time," I mutter.

"Why?" Jaylin asks, as Suz says, "We aren't officially dating."

"That's a lie and another conversation topic, Suzanna. We will have the girlfriend talk later." Jaylin comes down the stairs and kisses Suz on the forehead.

They are adorable together—a hippie and her Barbie.

"Because you two both mentioned similar dates, like the picnic date, which by the way was the cutest idea, Jaylin."

"I'll call you later, Jay. Sorry to cancel; we are going to go to lunch," Suz says through a sweet grin.

"I heard. Yes, call me later, non-girlfriend." Jaylin squeezes Suz' arm but doesn't push her and heads to the kitchen.

"She has been so understanding of my situation. It's not like I'm trying to hide who I am; I just still have trauma from growing up," Suz admits. After a beat of silence, Suz quietly adds, "I really am lucky to have met her."

"I knew you would hit it off!" Bren shrieks. Of course, Bren knew!

"Can we have lunch drinks too? It's barely past noon, but this morning has me in a whirlwind already."

I'm not looking for anyone to answer. It was a rhetorical question. A lunch drink is very needed. I'm already over analyzing what Lucas will think once I miss the game against East tomorrow. There is no world in which he doesn't notice I'm not there. Telling him why is going to be harder than any conversations I've had to have in the last few weeks.

Chapter Thirty

Laur

I have a newfound sense of hope knowing I am not the only one who has suffered. Of course, rationally I knew before, but hearing Suz' story gives me strength. I've been progressing so much these past few months. Every day is a battle with depression. Medication and time can't take away the devastating pain that accompanies every memory I have of Nick, but I'm starting to make new memories too. It's impossible for them to replace Nick, but I'm starting to be kind of happy. Moving past my relationship trauma is just another step in the path to finding myself and my happiness. It might take a long time, but I know I can get there.

Bren said bye before she left decked out in her Wyverns gear. My lips press tightly together as I creepily watch her walk down the street out the window. Missing the game is harder on me than I expected it to be. Despair lingers in the now empty house. In my room, I look for Nick's notebook. I want to see what he wrote about East. I start to panic not being able to find it anywhere, but then I remember Lucas still has it. I hastily go through my closet to find my favorite Wyverns sweatshirt. I pull it on and head to the couch.

"This is what's best for me right now," I whisper to myself. Even though my heart aches to be there, I know it would break me to see Nathan's despicable face. I'm not ready. Not yet.

Snuggling into the couch, I pull my fuzzy grey blanket up to my chin and switch my phone to 'do not disturb'—I don't want to get any news about the game. I throw my headphones on and press play on my current audiobook. If anyone has the power to distract me from today's game, it's a morally grey, dark and dreamy fae.

The 'thank you for listening' spiel lets me know that I've reached the end of my audiobook. Already?! It feels like I just hit play. At least the book was a great distraction. I turn my phone off 'do not disturb' mode and mark all my texts as read. I'm feeling weirdly okay, but I don't want any conversations about the game to ruin that. My phone pings with a text from Bren checking up on me and asking if I want her to stay at our house tonight. Her thoughtfulness makes me feel cared for like a warm hug wrapping around me, helping to hold the pieces together. I text her that it's silly to ask, she, of course should stay with Liam. I'll see her soon. I wouldn't mind starting the next book in the series anyways. The outcome of the game doesn't even cross my mind.

It's been a few days since I missed the game against East. I quickly found out that it was the first loss of the season. Rumblings around campus indicate the game was hard to watch. The winning streak is over. Anticipation runs through me knowing Bren, Suz, and I are attending the next away game together, which helps to push the lingering thoughts of the East game out of my mind. I haven't been to any away games yet.

Suz is driving us down to the game in Illinois once she's done with class. Coach Andres would have graciously let us take the bus with the guys, but Bren hinted that it might smell strongly of sweaty equipment. I've had more than enough of my fill experiencing that from growing up with Nick. The three-hour drive seems to breeze by with the three of us screaming 90s boy band hits at the top of our lungs. I missed having carefree fun with friends.

We hit some traffic, so we go straight to the arena for the game and take our seats. Butterflies dust off their wings and flutter in my gut, knowing I'll see Lucas. It's been a while since we talked. I wonder if he knows about the new articles I'm writing or if he's read the article I wrote about him yet. I know Tyler read his article because he sent me a selfie with it. He even said he had to talk his mom out of sending me flowers as a thank you for writing it.

A whistle fills the arena, signaling the start of the game. I truly love watching hockey more than I love most things in life, but I think all hockey lovers would agree when I say not every game is insanely exhilarating. This was one of those games. The Wyverns are crushing the Knights. We are up 5-0 by the end of the second period. I'm thrilled for the impending win at least!

Bren, Suz, and I wait for the team by the visitors' locker rooms. Liam is the first out and wraps Bren in a bear hug. I spot Lucas with Connor and Tyler.

"Hey, good game, guys!" My voice echoes down the hallway.

Lucas looks over at me and instantly looks away. That's a weird response coming from him. I walk over to talk to them more.

"Sorry, your first away game didn't have you on the edge of your seat. We were just too good today," Tyler smirks.

"Watching the team play is always a party! I wouldn't have missed it," I reply back, rolling my eyes at his cockiness.

"But you can miss games a few minutes down the road from you?" Lucas snaps.

My eyes go wide and my jaw drops. I didn't expect anyone to say anything about me missing the game against East. Words escape me.

"Got it." With angry purposeful steps, Lucas starts to walk away.

I grab his arm trying to pull him back. Tyler makes a motion to Connor, and they keep walking. Lucas turns towards me.

"Lucas, I'm sorry I didn't tell you I would miss the . . ." my voice is shaky.

I pause trying to think of what to tell him. I didn't expect him to care so much that I missed a game. He's waiting for me to tell him why I couldn't be there.

Instead of saying anything, I walk away. I was just getting used to the idea of admitting to Lucas I have feelings for him, but I'm not ready to divulge that the reason I missed the game against East was to avoid my abusive ex-boyfriend.

Suz is already at her car and sees the hurt across my face. I get in the car before tears start flowing down my cheeks. Suz pulls me into a tight embrace while she multitasks on her phone. Suz starts the car, turns up the music and starts driving.

"But, Bren." I don't want to leave her behind.

"Texted her. She'll take the bus with Liam."

She grabs my hand and squeezes it just like she did the other night.

"Thank you," I whisper as I let my tears fall to the sound of Jesse McCartney singing 'Beautiful Soul.'

Chapter Thirty-One

Lucas

Waiting for the bus to take off and head back to West, my exhaustion catches up to me. Since the game against East, I haven't felt like myself, and I can't seem to shake off the loss. I've been short with the team. I'm crabby. I'm frustrated. I'm drained. The music blaring through my headphones helps to bring my mind a blissful distraction.

Someone yanks out my earbud, jolting me from my music-induced trance.

"WHAT DID YOU DO?" Bren screams in my face. What is she even talking about? I stare at her blankly, annoyed to be disturbed when all I need to do is relax and get out of my head.

"Well, Lucas Donato, I'm waiting," Bren taps her foot impatiently. She's not going to give me my earpiece back until I say something to get her to go away.

"I just told her it was weird she could come to an away game but not a game a few minutes down the street from her," I reply.

Bren gawks, shaking with repressed fury and a look that very clearly says "you're an idiot Lucas."

Bren's frustration peeves me. Not only did we have a big loss against the Wyverns' biggest rival, but the girl of my dreams who has been to every single home game this season decided it wasn't worth going to the game. If anything, I should be the one fuming.

"What? It is weird. She didn't even tell me. She writes this article about how incredible I am, claiming 'I'm not the next big thing in college hockey, I already am the biggest thing in college hockey' and then the next day doesn't come to my game?"

My tone is whiny and pathetic, but I'm pissed. Bren snorts at me, fuming with aggravation. I've heard her make it plenty of times to a lot of different people. She's amazed at how stupid I'm being.

"What! I can be mad," I try to justify myself.

"Yeah, you can be mad. I think you're just hurt. But news flash, Captain, the world doesn't revolve around you. You know her, don't you think she had a good reason for not going and for not telling you?"

I shrug. She's right; Laur overcommunicates, even when she is denying she likes me, she's usually up-front with me. I didn't really think about her reasoning. I'm just frustrated that she wasn't there, and my head wasn't in the game because of it.

"Get your head out of your ass, Lucas. You are never the douchey conceited guy. Please do the world a favor and don't start being one now." Throwing my earbud at me in frustration, Bren storms down the bus aisle to sit next to Liam.

"She's right," Tyler chimes in from across the aisle. I didn't ask for his opinion, and I certainly don't need it. But if I say that, I'll just be even more of an ass. I can't blame Laur for how the game against East turned out. Her not being there had nothing to do with it. We were running on fumes the last period; there wasn't a chance we would have won.

I need to find her as soon as I'm back on campus.

"Hey, are we going to get this bus moving?" I ask Coach.

Three hours later, I'm knocking on her front door. I know she's home alone—Bren is at Liam's, and I texted Suz to ask her where Laur was at. Even Suz sent me a frustrated, very straightforward "stop acting like a stereotypical douche," which means I really outdid myself. I feel like I've been run over by a Zamboni.

Laur doesn't answer the door. I knock again, patiently waiting. She still doesn't answer the door. I quickly text Suz to ask if she's sure Laur is home, and she responds immediately with a *yes*.

I start to knock out a rhythm on the door, very loudly. I'm leaning into the door making a musical display with my knocking. Maybe this will get her attention, and she'll know it's not some random person trying to sell her something. A smirk forms on my face thinking about Laur stomping down the stairs to answer the door.

She pulls open the door so fast, leaving me off kilter and weightless, just like the first time I spotted her from across the bar. She looks at me with a judgmental look I've never seen her give me before.

"Don't look at me like that."

That's the first thing that comes out of my mouth? Wow. I am off to a great apology.

"I'm not looking at you like anything, Lucas," she replies smoothly and calmly, her words slightly cold.

"You look at Mitchell that way when you are disgusted with him," I start. "I know I was an ass, but come on, I'm not as bad as he is."

"No, Lucas, you're worse. He makes sex jokes and teases me. You pretend you like me, then treat me poorly when you're mad because you lost a game I just happened to not be at."

"You're right. I am worse. I put my feelings and myself first. I didn't think about why you wouldn't be at the game." My hand trembles slightly as I run my fingers through my hair.

"I was just so confused. I *am* so confused—you just wrote this beautiful, almost poetic article about me and then didn't show up. I was hurt you weren't there. It has nothing to do with us losing and everything to do with me being vulnerable to you. I promise I will be better about communicating when something bothers me."

"Thank you for apologizing, but it doesn't change things for me right now."

"I can't walk away from you. I can't let you go. You can't walk away either."

"It just can't happen. We are friends, that's all I can be right now." Her voice is assertive and stern.

"Fuck, Lauren, do you think I want to be in love with the little sister of my old mentor that I looked up to since I was seventeen?! It's not like I'm trying to feel this way."

Her mouth falls open, gaping at me with distress in eyes. The things I want to do with that mouth . . . The thought sends heat southward. This girl has my mind in every direction possible. My heart feels like it will beat out of my chest.

My brain is telling me to shut up, but my words spew out of my mouth faster than I can even think them.

"I didn't plan this. I just feel it. Every time I look at you. Every time I'm around you. I feel more myself than I ever have in my life. It just clicked the first time I hung out with you. This is it. This is the feeling they make movies and write books about. You know I'm right."

She's holding back tears. Her bright blue eyes look like a cloudy, rain-filled sky. I want to hold her in my arms so badly, but she's half hidden behind the door now.

"This is our one shot at something real. It all makes sense—*you* make sense."

I see the tears fall like rain drops from her storm-stricken eyes.

"I'm sorry, Lucas." It's a faint whisper, but it hits like lightning to my heart. She closes the door. Defeat takes over as I crumble to a seat on the porch. What am I missing? What did I do wrong?

Chapter Thirty-Two
Laur

Darkness has started creeping back in, sucking the joy out of my life like a vampire. I thought I'd made incredible progress since I came to West, finding unexpected contentment that finally gave me back pieces of my old self. If I knew it would leave so quickly, I would have clung on to that happiness for dear life. I know I'll keep getting through it, but sometimes a girl just needs her mom. I call her, and she picks up on the second ring.

Her voice is comforting, making me miss home. I try to start with casual niceties and ask how she and Dominic are doing, but I can't help but jump in right away telling her about my feelings for Lucas.

"Oh, sweetheart, did you think I didn't know?"

I roll my eyes. How on earth can I be that obvious to someone I haven't even seen in months?! Not to mention she's never seen us interact.

"Your article about him gave you away, Lauren. I could tell from the first paragraph he was someone special to you," Mom chuckles, and I can hear her wide grin in her voice with every word. "I hope he is a nice boy. You always talked about how nice Nathan was, and he seemed nice when we met him too. But this Lucas seems to have you smitten like I've never seen."

I start crying immediately knowing that grin will fade quickly. What I have to tell her next is going to break her heart. And mine.

"Mom, I lied," Something deep inside me shatters having to tell my mom this. "Nathan was not a nice guy."

Through tears, I tell her about Nathan's mental abuse and jealousy with my support for the Wyverns. I tell her about the physical abuse. I tell her about my argument with Nick the night of the accident.

"Oh honey, I am so sorry you've been coping with this all on your own." Despite Mom's resilience, always staying strong, her voice is shaky with despair. The strain of holding back tears is evident with each word.

"Why did you take so long to tell me?" she asks after a few beats of silence.

"I didn't want you to blame me for Nick's death." The flood gates holding back my sorrow break as my body convulses with each tear that falls.

"Lauren, the car accident happening is the furthest thing from your fault. That man was almost three times the legal limit. It had nothing to do with your argument. It is not your fault in any way, shape, or form." Mom chokes out the words, letting her resilience fall with her tears. "I will tell you a million times over until you feel it in your heart if that's what it takes."

My voice softens to a whisper with the words that I have refused to speak out loud, "I didn't want you to be ashamed of me for staying with Nathan . . . or to judge me."

"My sweet girl, what that boy did to you poisoned your head. You have nothing to be ashamed of. You love with your full heart, even if that person doesn't deserve it. Nathan certainly didn't. I think we should press charges—"

"No." I cut Mom off. "That is the furthest thing from what I want."

"He hurt you, Lauren. And I couldn't protect you from that. We have to do something."

"Please, no."

"Your brother would have gotten arrested beating his ass," Mom says quietly.

"Yeah, he would have."

"But Dominic would have bailed him out of jail."

"With all his mob money?"

"Mob money? What is mob money?"

"It was a joke, Mom. Since he claims to have made good investments with good people."

A small laugh slips through my tears. She always cheers me up somehow.

"Sweetheart, be thankful he's too nerdy to be associated with a mob. Nathan wouldn't stand a chance. I wish I was there to give you a hug."

"I know, me too. I love you, Mom."

"I love you too, Chip. Nothing will ever change that."

We chat a little more about how school has been and about her most recent knitting and reading escapades. She's joined a neighborhood book club apparently. The doorbell rings and I get off the phone with Mom.

"I hope it's Lucas!"

Mom can be ridiculous, but she has me laughing through my tears. It's not Lucas at the door; it's Tyler coming to check on me.

"Hey, Chip. I texted but you didn't answer. I just wanted to see how you were doing," he says as I let him inside.

"I feel . . . okay."

Tyler tilts his head and huffs at my response.

"No really, I do. Talking to my mom was exactly what I needed. I finally told her everything."

"Would ice cream also be exactly what you need?" Tyler asks.

I smile big. Ice cream is always exactly what I need, no matter the reason.

The next home game I try to avoid Lucas, which is not easy to do. Especially since his face is all over posters for our damn calendar. I have to endure his giant face even more because it's my turn to run the merch table with the lower classmen this game. We have pre-orders for Nick's jersey design, new shirts, calendar orders, and sign-ups for our poster giveaway.

"That captain is so delish," I overhear a pretty redheaded girl saying. She looks barely out of middle school. She has to be a freshman.

"I need this poster of him. Excuse me, ma'am?"

Did she seriously just call me 'ma'am?' I'm barely two years older than her!

I plaster on a big smile before asking what she needs.

"Are you going to sell these posters? I need to buy one for my dorm room!" she responds.

"We might be doing some signed giveaways of the posters. Make sure you follow the team on social media!" I hastily reply.

She walks away happily staring at her phone.

"I'm sure my boyfriend will be thrilled to know he could be on your wall!" I call after her. My eyes widen taking in the words that just slipped out of my mouth. Why did I just say that? The girl doesn't turn around or acknowledge my comment. Thank goodness, she must have not heard me.

"You're finally dating Lucas?!" Libby, my favorite underclassman, asks with a goofy grin on her face. The eager sparkle in her eyes beg for me to dish out details.

"Don't tell anyone I said that, please. I'm being petty and jealous, and it's not a good look, especially when it's because of a random freshman that doesn't even know him!" A frustrated groan escapes me. I miss Lucas.

And clearly, I want him all to myself.

"It wouldn't be a bad idea to raffle off signed posters for charitable donations at games." Libby shrugs. "Then that super fan could really have a picture of your boyfriend on her wall."

I roll my eyes and elbow her, but it's a brilliant idea. Nick would have eaten it up. I bet he would have even taken selfies with fans for donations or something ridiculous.

I don't see much of the game at the merch table, but the Wyverns win. Libby and I go to find Bren and Suz to tell them Libby's idea to raffle for donations. I will conveniently omit the part out where I called Lucas my boyfriend, if anyone asks.

Lucas walks out of the locker room. I try not to let out a groan when I see him in my favorite gray sweatpants of his. I lock eyes with Libby, and she pretends to lock her mouth and throw away the key. I roll my eyes and can't help but giggle when I realize Lucas saw her. Libby is redder than a tomato.

"What's this about?" Lucas asks.

"Oh, nothing," I reply. "Just some fangirls want signed posters. So you, Captain Hot Shot, are going to be on some walls in the freshman dorms once we raffle them off at the rest of the home games this season."

"Oh great," Lucas jokes enthusiastically, "just want I've always dreamed of."

"Do I get to be on freshman dorm walls?" Liam asks.

"You're despicable, Liam Welsh," Bren makes a disgusted face and jabs at Liam.

"But you love me." Liam puckers his lips making kissing noises at Bren.

"We'll have a few different prints of the starters, maybe two or three guys featured a game, a full team one, and one of the Sexy Seven every game," I think out loud. "We have enough promo posters to last a few games. I can easily order some more."

"We are pretty much famous," Connor chimes in, throwing an arm around Lucas and the other around Liam as they walk out down the hallway away from Libby and me.

"I wouldn't mind a poster of the captain over my bed," I whisper jokingly to Libby. She makes a high-pitched shrill sound and cackles.

"Hey, Laur," Lucas says, turning around. "You might want to work on those whispering skills."

He winks at me. My heart flutters. I'm positive my face is brighter red than Libby's was five minutes ago. Maybe we still do have our one shot together.

The Wyverns are back on a winning streak with three more wins over the next two weeks. The guys have a little bit of a break, which for me means focusing on my articles I need to write for *USA Hockey Magazine.* Bren tries to convince me we have to go what she, Suz and Libby call "out, out."

"Come on, Laur, I can't go out for the first time without you! Going for one drink or grabbing a drink after dinner doesn't count!" Libby protests. I'm glad that Suz and Bren love her as much as I do. I'm going to need a close girlfriend when they both graduate at the end of the year.

"Fine!" All three of them shriek. I loved spending most of my time with Nick and avoiding the shrieking, but sometimes a girl needs the hype-girl excitement. "But I'm not getting dressed up!"

Thankfully, going "out, out" apparently just meant going to Haee's for some drinks and music. Sure, there would be sports on, but this is a dance floor kind of night.

"I would have agreed instantly if I knew you just meant going to Haee's for some drinks and music," I tell Bren.

"Duh! Where else would I want to go other than Haee's! The atmosphere's amazing, the drinks are cheap, and the eye candy is superb."

She nods her head to the door where a group of the guys just walked in with Lucas, of course, leading the pack. Maybe I should have dressed up a little more. I'll remember that next time that there's a ninety percent chance Lucas will be there. God, I miss being around him. He makes me feel like my old self. I nervously chug the rest of my Bud Light. I rush to the bar to get another one, running into Suz there chatting with some friends.

"You okay?" she asks.

"Is it stupid if a girl buys a guy a beer?" I ask.

"Absolutely not! Fuck gender roles," Suz proclaims.

"I miss him," I whisper, mostly to myself and the dull pain in my heart.

"Talk to him, Laur. He'll understand if you aren't ready to share all your secrets with him. I'm sure he misses you too." Suz throws back a shot. "Now, I'm going to go find Jaylin and tell her I'm ready to hold her hand in public. Wish me luck!" She's off before I can get in another word.

I order two Bud Lights, take a deep breath, and walk toward Lucas with my head held high.

"Hey," I say, walking up to Lucas, Connor, and Tyler. I'm met with three kind, warm pairs of eyes—even Lucas'.

"Connor was just talking about the NHL scouts he's been talking to." Tyler includes me in the conversation.

"That's amazing, Connor! Any team will be lucky to have you!" I reply.

Connor starts to talk about the rep for Anaheim and how much of a sleazeball he is.

"It's one of my dream teams, but I can't stand the guy. He hits on anything over the age of eighteen," Connor explains.

Tyler chimes in with details on a few other scouts, but I pretend to listen, distracted by my close proximity to Lucas. I miss talking to him. He gets me to let my guard down without even trying. His genuine nature makes me want to be around him all the time.

"Here," I say to Lucas, handing him the extra Bud Light I bought.

"You bought me a beer?" he asks, smiling. I nod matter-of-factly and hold up my bottle to his.

He *clinks* his glass with mine and says, "Thank you, pretty girl."

I feel my cheeks heat as I blush. He's never called me that before. I wish he would call me that twenty times a day.

"Don't read too much into it, Captain. I just wanted to show Suz I can break stupid gender norms and stereotypes."

I wink at him playfully.

He chuckles. "She finally told you."

"Yeah, but maybe I just wanted an excuse to buy you a drink and talk to you. After all, at least two girls on this campus have shirtless photos of you laying on a hockey rink. I heard they're even signed."

He almost spits out his drink. "Really? You've already auctioned off two?"

"Yep, and there will be plenty more, Captain Hot Shot!" It's so easy and comfortable falling into this flirty pattern with him. How did it take me so long to realize I feel myself around him? Nick would even like him.

"By the way, Laur, I still have Nick's notebook," Lucas says. I almost forgot he had it.

"So, Luc," Connor butts in, and we are back to talking about NHL potential. "Are you talking to any scouts?"

"Of course. But you know me, Riz, I'm holding my cards close to my chest until next year," Lucas replies smoothly, running his hand through his hair.

"Well, then I assume you know Landon Cox is working for the Blackhawks now, right?" Connor asks.

Does Lucas want to play for the Blackhawks? He's never told me in any of our interviews or conversations which NHL team would be his number one pick if he could choose. But he did mention his dad being a Blackhawks fan a few times.

"Of course," Lucas replies casually.

"And that he will be at the home game in two weeks?" Connor asks.

"So will one of the scouts for Seattle," Tyler adds, "or at least it's rumored that he will be."

"And I heard someone for the Knights will be too," Connor says.

"Sounds like a party," Lucas says, "Laur, will you be at that game? Sounds like everyone is going to be there." Is he playing with fire or is he making an innocent joke? It seemed like we moved past me missing the game and are back to being friends, or pretending to be friends when we are both interested in each other. Maybe he's still mad I rejected him. I can't blame him for that.

"Don't be silly, Lucas; of course I will be," I roll my eyes at him.

"Thank goodness. With my luck charm watching, I'll impress scouts from all thirty-two teams that night. Did you hear? Everyone's coming!"

Okay, so he is innocently joking. Thank God. I know I have a big dorky smile across my face.

"Nah, not anyone from Seattle." Liam interjects, joining the group. Conner seems disappointed with Liam's update. "Sicel for Nashville will be at our last home game in January, the one versus East."

Lucas is laughing now with all the guys spreading conflicting scout rumors. He must have missed the part about the opponent being East, but he does notice I'm not smiling anymore.

"Will you be there?" Lucas asks with a look of plea on his face, like he is asking me to please be there.

"I . . . what?" I'm struggling for words with my nerves.

"The next home game," Lucas asks, finishing his beer, "you'll be there, right?"

"I . . . I'm not sure." My voice is barely a whisper. But he hears me.

"Why wouldn't you be there?" he asks.

"Why does it matter if I'm there?" I try to play it off flirty, but I know he can sense the tension that is creeping into my voice with the thought of the Wyverns playing Nathan again.

"Because." He smiles a crooked grin trying to be flirty and ease the tension.

"I . . ." I feel my walls closing in, and before I can help it, I snap at him out of fear and pain. "It doesn't matter if I'm there."

"You're Lauren Bellinger—my good luck charm, the Wyverns' good luck charm. You have to be there." He grabs my hand, and I quickly yank it away.

My fear and pain push me to snap at him again. "I'm not a good luck charm Lucas. I'm a person, with feelings and emotions. Maybe I don't want to be there. Did you think about that? How maybe I don't want to be there?"

Everyone is staring at me now. He takes my hand again and this time I don't pull away, "Okay. So you won't be there. Thanks for telling me," his voice is genuine and kind, "Do you want to go somewhere away from all these people? You can tell me why and we can—"

"No. I don't want to."

I interrupt him without a second thought. My eyes are starting to swell with tears.

I put my almost full beer down and walk out of Haee's.

I take the long way home, which only adds two minutes to my ten-minute walk. I didn't expect him to ask me why I didn't want to go to the game. He was calm, understanding, kind; all the things he promised he would try to be. But I lost it, I was scared and thrown off guard. Now I was being an ass and reacting badly. I should have just said something like 'not right now' and changed the subject.

Will I always lose it when East comes up? Will I always put Lucas in the line of fire that hides my fear, pain, and shame?

I keep walking past the house for about twenty more minutes trying to clear my head. I don't want to always feel like this. I open my phone and see about twenty text messages from different people, including Bren, Lucas, and Tyler. I even have a missed call and voicemail. It's from Lucas. As soon as I step through my front door, I click my text thread with Lucas.

Lucas: Hey, Laur
Lucas: I just want to know you're safe at home. I promise that's all.
Lucas: I won't push you to tell me anything you don't want to or anything you're not ready to.
Lucas: I'm sorry if it seemed like I did tonight.
Lucas: Please just text Bren.
Lucas: It's late. I just want to know you're home safe.

I'm not sure when my agony-filled tears stopped, but now tears of awe and happiness are threatening to make their way down my cheeks. This man continues to communicate better after the one fight we had, even after I rejected him. I don't deserve someone to be so sweet and amazing to me. He deserves to know.

I call Bren.

"Hi, yes I am home safe. I . . . I can't do it myself," I confess to her. I want him to know. I want Connor and Liam to know. I want them to understand that they are some of the best guys I have had in my life. I want them to know that me skipping games has nothing to do with them and everything to do with one guy they are playing. I need Lucas to know I really want to be there more than he can even imagine.

Chapter Thirty-Three

Lucas

I eye Bren as she whispers into her phone in the corner of Haee's. I know it's Laur on the other end, and I am getting antsy. I wasn't trying to make her sad or mad. I just want to make sure she's okay.

Bren walks towards us, but I can't read the expression on her face.

"Is she—" I start.

"She's at home, yes. She's not mad at you Lucas. She just . . ." Bren's expression changes to disgust and despair. Something's not right.

"What is it?" I plead for an answer. I love this girl. I need to know she's okay.

Bren looks at Tyler, having a brief conversation with just their eyes causing anxiety to sneak up on me.

"Can someone please just tell us what's going on?" Liam asks before I can open my mouth again.

"Let's go to that table over there and sit," Tyler says and motions for Bren and me to follow. "Just Lucas for now. He needs to hear this first."

The seriousness of Tyler and Bren has me concerned. The air is thick with a heaviness that causes my anxiety to make itself at home in my gut.

"She wants to tell you," Bren looks directly into my eyes. "But I honestly think it will break her if she does."

"Okay," I reply patiently, waiting for Bren to continue.

"Lucas, she was abused."

Bren's voice is barely audible, yet each word echoes loudly through my skull.

"By a guy who plays for East," Tyler adds.

I feel a stinging sensation in my hand as Bren shrieks, "Lucas!"

I must have squeezed my beer so tightly without realizing it—the neck of the bottle is shattered in my hand. Blood drips down my palm.

"What . . ." I can't find any words. "What do you mean?"

"Let's get your hand cleaned—"

Bren starts to get up, but I stop her.

"I don't care about my fucking hand. It can wait. Tell me."

Someone abused Lauren. Some guy we play multiple times a season. Some guy whose hand I've shaken after more than one game. Who is he? Because he will be a dead man once I learn who he is.

Bren slowly starts to tell me about Lauren's ex-boyfriend. They dated for three years. He seemed fine, but Nick hated him. Bren and Liam even went on double dates with them. Her mom liked him. She liked his family.

"She just told us recently," Bren says. "Nick was the only one that knew."

Bren tells me how it didn't start until they dated for over a year, but he was always kind of a jerk. The abuse was more making fun of her at first, then turned to mental abuse, and finally physical. Just over a year into their relationship means that she dated him for almost two years, dealing with this shit. Why would she stay? Why would she endure it?

"He hated how supportive she was of the Wyverns and Nick," Tyler spits out with disgust. "Honestly, I think he was jealous of him."

"The more she told us the more I could see it," Bren says. "I can't believe the entire time she was going through this, I was right there, but I didn't know."

It finally all makes sense. Laur is so back and forth. She's flirty but says she doesn't want to be more than friends. She constantly says how she doesn't want a relationship again.

"This is why she says she doesn't want to date anyone. This is why she's sworn off love."

Tyler and Bren both nod.

"What's his name?" Rage starts to bubble inside me.

Bren shakes her head no.

"Don't make me ask again," I snap through clenched teeth. Fury and wrath replace the anxiety in my gut as I slam my hand on the table, causing Bren to flinch. I need to know who could hurt her like this.

"I'll tell you and answer anything I can, but you really should talk to her," Tyler says.

"Tyler. Walk with me outside." It isn't a question, it's a command.

He nods and stands up, ready to leave.

Taking a deep breath, I close my eyes attempting to calm myself, but it does little to settle the outrage pulsing through my veins.

"Are you going to tell Connor and Liam?" I ask Bren before we leave.

"Yes, she asked me to," Bren whispers. Her eyes are overflowing with tears.

"I'll tell them," Tyler offers. "You walk with Lucas." I give him a pat on the back. He knows I am going to need Bren.

I go to the bathroom to clean my hand. It's just a small cut, it looks a lot worse than it is. Bren and I head out the door. I don't think about where we are going, we just walk.

"I don't know what to do," I say and stop walking.

"I don't either." I can't see Bren's face since we are in a dimly lit street, but the distress is evident in her voice. "I love her, Bren. I really do love her. I can't protect her from the loss of Nick. What if I can't protect her from this either?" I don't expect her to answer, so I start walking again.

"You already are, Lucas," she says.

"How?"

"She told us." Bren huffs, trying to keep up with my pace. "Nick was the only person she told and that was just over a year ago. I think she's ready to face the abuse and try to move past it all instead of hiding it."

"Right, but I don't understand how that has anything to do with me?"

"She can't hide behind swearing off love and not working through her trauma . . ." Bren pauses for a beat ". . . not when she wants to be with you."

Her words stop me in my tracks, looking Bren wide-eyed and hopeful.

Bren puts her hand on my shoulder and whispers, "She loves you too, Lucas."

My heart takes over my body, and I sprint the last block to the house. My feet automatically led me where my heart knew I needed to be.

"I'll let you talk to her." Bren is breathless from trying to keep up with me "Liam's already started to walk back to his place. He'll meet me walking there."

"Thank you for taking away a tiny part of her pain by being her voice." I squeeze Bren tight.

"I needed to hear that." She sighs. "I just wish I could do more."

"Me too."

"You take her pain away too, Luc, just by being you."

Bren squeezes my arm as a goodbye. She turns to leave. I'm about to yell at her to remind her to text me or have Liam text me when she meets up with him safely. I hate when any girl is walking alone at night. But then, I see Liam down the block.

Slumping down to the porch, I pull out my phone to send Laur a text.

Lucas: I'm sitting on your front porch

I quickly type another text.

Lucas: If you want to talk. If you don't want to, I completely understand.

I can't help but send another right after.

Lucas: I'm here for you however I can be and however you need me to be.

My train of thought is all over the place. I'm about to send another text to tell her I should have called first and will just leave, but the door of the house slowly opens.

"Hi, Lucas."

Within seconds, I have my arms wrapped tightly around her. I never want to let her go. This beautiful girl who has already hurt so much from the loss of her brother was carrying around more pain than anyone knew before the accident even happened. I want more than anything to take it away.

"I'll be okay," she whispers into my chest through tears. A watery tinge overtakes the world as my tears fall into her hair.

"I wish I could do something. I can't put into words how angry I am, how much pain and disgust are in my heart, and I didn't even experience it. Lauren, I am so sorry."

My embrace tightens around her, as if trying to protect her.

"It's okay." Her voice cracks in agony.

"It's not okay, Lauren." I pull away from her and look into her stormy blue eyes. "What he did to you is the furthest thing from okay. If I knew who he was, I would beat the living daylights out of him until he passes out, then do it all over again when he's conscious. You do not deserve that. No one deserves to be abused. Especially the girl I love."

Her eyes turn from the stormy blue to more of the bright ocean wave color they typically are.

"We don't have to talk about it. You don't have to go to any hockey games ever. I'll quit hockey. Just know I will do everything I possibly can to help you through this. I will show you how much I appreciate you every single day. I will show you how special you are, not just to me and your friends and family, but to the world. I'm here. For whatever you need. I'm yours."

Holding Laur at a distance, I check to see if tears are still running down her angelic face, but her eyes are closed.

"Laur?" I whisper.

"I love you too, Lucas."

All the anger in my heart takes a momentary back seat to a rush of pure bliss hearing her say those words.

Without opening her eyes, she leans in to kiss me. It's not hungry and greedy. Instead the kiss is light, pure, and wholesome, yet the spark between us still brings intensity with it. It's not lust-filled like our first kiss. It's love. I grab the back of her head deepening our kiss as if to show her I'm all in, whatever that means to her. I'm all in.

She pulls away and says, "You are not quitting hockey. Never say that again, Lucas Donato. You love hockey. I love hockey. We love hockey. It's not an option. And I love you."

She doesn't even wait for a response as she leans in to kiss me again.

"I love you too, Lauren Bellinger," I mutter against her lips as my fingers tangle in her hair. She grabs the back of my neck, deepening our kiss further, showing me she needs me. I would let her crawl into my skin to protect her if it was possible. She shivers from the winter chill and lack of jacket. I pick her up, and her legs wrap around me. She breaks the kiss.

"I'm just getting you inside; you're freezing," I say. "I promise I'm not trying to take it further."

"Well, why not?" She croons and starts to giggle. I'm sure she can sense the shock on my face. My eyes widen in unexpected disbelief. My girl is hot as fuck.

I open the door, still holding her. She directs me to the stairs and tells me her room is the second door on the left. She's still shaking, probably from more than just being in the cold air outside. Instead of heading up the stairs, I head to the kitchen.

"What are you doing? My bedroom is upstairs. You do not follow directions well, Captain," she hisses at me, with a mischievous look in her gaze.

God, I love when she calls me Captain when I know she wants me to pleasure her. I put her down and slip off my sweatshirt.

"You're freezing, Lauren. You need tea or something."

"You could probably warm me up much better than tea, Captain."

She winks at me as I go through cabinets, and she pulls on my sweatshirt. My sweatshirt engulfs her, hanging almost past her knees.

I can't help but think about how sexy it would be if she wore only my sweatshirt with nothing underneath.

She moves to the other side of the kitchen and pulls out hot chocolate.

"Fine, if you aren't going to play nice, I suppose you can make me hot chocolate."

She throws three packets at me. I find a pan, fill it with hot water and put it on the stove to boil.

"You have no idea how badly I want to, Laur. I just—We just had a serious conversation, and I don't want it to be because of that . . ." I drift off.

"I know it wouldn't be. But thank you."

"For what?"

"For being such a gentleman. Even when I didn't want you to be." She pouts playfully.

"Trust me, when you call me Captain like that, I don't want to be," I admit. "Why did you give me three packets?"

"I need at least one and a half packets, Captain."

I groan at her use of Captain but try to keep my cool. "That's so much sugar."

"It's exactly what I need. Sweet now, and naughty later."

My eyebrows raise with surprise causing her to giggle. This girl has caught me so off guard with her promiscuous talk. I've easily fallen more in love in the last five minutes.

"Do you have whip cream to go with this?" I wink at her.

She goes to the fridge and laughs. "Actually." She pulls out a can of whip cream followed by a bottle of bourbon from the counter.

"Technically, my special cozy hot chocolate recipe calls for a shot of bourbon too."

My eyebrows arch with skepticism.

"What? It's my comfort drink!"

The hot water is ready for the hot chocolate. I add one and a half packets to both mugs and hand her one. She immediately adds a shot and a mound of whip cream on top of hers.

She puts down the whip cream can and lets out the biggest sad sigh I have ever heard.

"You're right, your signature drink is very cozy." I indulge in more whip cream.

She looks into her mug and whispers, "Are you sure you don't think I'm a bad person?"

Her shoulders sag as if she's defeated. I grab her waist and pull her close, being careful not to spill any of her hot chocolate or whip cream.

"Why would you even say that? You are far from a bad person, Laur."

"Are you sure?" Her voice is quieter than it was a second ago.

"I am positive," I say, squeezing her with one arm as I sip my hot chocolate.

"Even though it's my fault?"

"What do you mean?" I say, "What he did to you is absolutely not you—"

Before I can finish, she says, "Oh. Bren didn't tell you."

I look at her puzzled. She makes that sad, pained sigh again.

"The night Nick and I got in the car accident, we were arguing. I told him about Nathan's abuse. It was the first game of the season and the first with Nick as captain and—"

"—and it was against East," I finish her sentence. She nods.

"Nathan screamed at me for wearing Nick's jersey and going to celebrate with him after the game. Nick saw it happen. I had to tell Nick everything. I wanted to long before . . ." she trails off. I can tell her mind is going a mile a minute.

"Anyways, we were arguing. I can't help but wonder if we weren't arguing in the car if Nick would still be here. If he wasn't trying to comfort me, would we still have gotten hit by the drunk driver?"

I grab her face in my hands, "Lauren Chip Bellinger, do not ever say anything like that again in your entire life. If I hear those words come out of your mouth, I will never speak to you again. There is absolutely no way in heaven or hell or any other realm the accident was your fault."

Tears swell in her eyes again. She tries to blink them back and whispers, "Never speak to me again? That's a bit dramatic."

She leans into me, wraps her arm around my torso and hugs me tight.

"I wouldn't last more than a week. You already know that."

"I'm sorry I made sex jokes about the whip cream and then got all depressed mess again."

"Never apologize for the way you feel. I told you, Lauren, I'm all in."

"Depressed mess and all?" Her round eyes look up at me seeking validation.

"Depressed mess and all, Laur." I kiss her lightly.

"Can we watch *Mystery, Alaska*? Since I already ruined the mood," she asks.

I laugh. No one ever knows that movie, but it's one of my top five favorite movies of all time.

"Is that a yes?"

"Yes, pretty girl. That is one of my favorite movies"

The shadows that plague her eyes seem to have lifted. That bright beautiful blue is my favorite color to exist.

"Nick and I always watched it when one of us was having a hard time. He loved it, but I don't think it's as funny as he does." She shakes her head. "I mean did."

"Well, that's a relief, you can't be too perfect for me." She smiles her perfect Bellinger smile.

I start the movie, and she makes more hot chocolate and popcorn for us. We are about ten minutes in when I notice her staring at me.

"What?" I laugh.

"He would have liked you," Laur says. "Nick. He would have really liked you."

"He did like me." I take another sip of cocoa. "We weren't best friends, but you know I knew him, played with him a little, and looked up to him."

"You idolized him." She's mocking me. "But so did I. So did everyone." She shakes her head to clear her thoughts. "But I meant Nick would have liked you for me. He would have approved."

"Obviously, I'm a catch."

My smile goes from ear to ear. I don't think I've ever smiled so big in my life. She laughs and turns back to the movie.

A minute or so later, she whispers, "He despised Nathan. Nick said he was a whiny, narcissist who will always be a few sticks short of a full set."

"Nathan Kovek? That is exactly what I say about that douche." She ignores me and keeps watching the movie.

"By the way I didn't know it was Kovek until you said Nathan. Bren left that part out. Tyler said he would tell me his name but didn't get to it before I left Haee's to come find you."

Her eyes widen with panic.

"It's okay. I promise I will not do anything except maybe have everyone hit harder on the ice than we would have been already. No one likes that guy."

"Yeah." She snorts. "Nick said that too."

She cozies up into my side, and I put my arm around her. I have waited too long to have her next to me.

"Everyone likes you though," she whispers, not taking her eyes off the movie. "I sure do."

"Nah," I say, picking up a piece of popcorn and throwing it at her. "You said you love me."

Chapter Thirty-Four
Laur

A brawny, muscular body is wrapped around me as I groggily open my eyes, waking up on the couch. Lucas and I must have fallen asleep. I slept so peacefully next to him. I'm glad everything is out in the air now. A blaring phone alarm stirs Lucas awake.

"Shit! I'm going to be late for practice."

"Then get out of here! I'm going back to sleep anyways."

He has very adorable messy bedhead . . . I could get used to waking up next to him. Judging by his enormous grin that radiates happiness, I don't think he would mind that.

"Wait, you told me you loved me. That means you're done swearing off love, right?" I pick up a pillow, ready to launch it in Lucas' direction. "Lucas Donato, get your ass out the door before I throw this pillow at you!"

"I just needed to check! If you are going to be my girlfriend, you can't be going around campus saying you have sworn off dating. People will think I'm crazy!"

"Girlfriend?" A warm sensation fills my chest hearing him say the word.

"Well, yeah. Haven't you heard that girls around campus have me plastered on their walls? If you love me so much, you need to call dibs, Laur."

I can't help but laugh. "Go, you are going to be late, and I am going to be in trouble."

"Okay, okay, I'm leaving."

He opens the door, but I jump off the couch and run to him before he can get a foot outside.

Pulling him into me, my lips hungrily find his before I whisper in his ear, "Bye, Captain."

He grabs his heart and fakes a swooning gesture. I give him a gesture of my own and close the door behind him. Time for me to get a little more sleep.

The week leading up to winter break is insanely busy. Mom and Dominic are visiting for winter break to keep me company with Bren and Jaylin both leaving for a few days. But they'll both be back for New Years. Bren is forcing us all to go to Haee's for their supposedly exclusive NYE party. Suz took some convincing, claiming we always go to the same place, and we should do something different. She's got a point. The team has a game on the 30th. Then, they have to be at practice bright and early on January 1st to be ready for their first game of the new year on the 2nd. I'm a little bummed it's an away game, but I guess the girls can sleep in. We'll see how the night goes!

Lucas is going home for three days on Christmas Eve. Mom is disappointed she won't be able to meet him. She even tried to crash our New Years' Eve plans. I vetoed that quickly. Lucas' cousin just had a baby that he hasn't met yet, so he's really looking forward to going home. Three days without him on campus won't be so bad anyways. I've barely seen Lucas over the last week. He's focused on hockey, and I'm focused on finishing the two articles for *USA Hockey Magazine*.

I have a new spring in my step and an unfamiliar lightness in my heart when I think about Lucas and me. We both are focused on our goals, still supporting each other but knowing that sometimes our dreams need to be put first. It's comforting knowing we both are striving towards our dreams. The flutter in my heart every time his eyes meet mine when I watch the team practice gives me peace—more peace than I've felt in three years.

Mom and Dominic's visit is pretty uneventful. Mom keeps asking if we can FaceTime Lucas. She hasn't even met him, but she's obsessed.

"He's not even my boyfriend, Annabeth," I lie to her. She doesn't need to know all the details of my love life. "We are not going to FaceTime him on Christmas."

I miss him though. I'm excited to see him next week. I'll be done with the Wyverns article by then. I'm still working on my article about Nick.

As December 31st approaches, it seems like Mother Nature has plans that delay my reunion with Lucas. The team is stuck in Illinois, but at least they won their game.

"I knew I should have gone to the game," Bren groans. "Who am I going to kiss at midnight tomorrow without my grizzly man there?"

"We will still have the best time and get all dolled up." A pillow leaves my hand, and flies landing next to Bren. "You're supposed to be the hype girl, not me! What have you done to me?"

"Haee's will never see anything look as good as us after we walk in," Suz adds. "But I am most excited for Bren's New Year's Day Breakfast. Last year, she made crepes!"

"You have a promising PR career, but you could definitely open your own restaurant!"

"I just hope the guys make it for some part of New Year's Eve and for breakfast before they are off to practice and their first game of the year," Bren says.

"Thank goodness it's not the first this year!" Suz chimes in, laughing. "Liam still ate his weight at breakfast. I remember him looking like he was going to be sick on the ice."

"I should have done a light breakfast . . ." Disdain crosses Bren's face at the memory.

After a few hours of bumming around, Bren declares we should start getting 'glam worthy' for the night. She's trying to make the most of it, but she's less bubbly than normal. I can tell she's disappointed that Liam hasn't provided any updates on when they'll be back in town.

I just finished putting on a lacy, somewhat modest black dress when Bren saunters into my room.

"No," she immediately says as she takes in my outfit.

I stare at her puzzled. She tells me to grab my makeup and come into her room to get ready and I will be changing into a more New Year's appropriate dress. I sigh. Knowing that I probably won't see Lucas, I've put very minimal effort into my appearance and outfit.

Bren's bed looks like sequins and glitter threw up on it. My facial expression must be saying it all.

"Courtesy of my closet." Suz beams at me, giddy with excitement. "Help yourself to whatever you'd like!"

"Wow, that's a lot of . . . a lot."

I spend about fifteen minutes sifting through the mounds of dresses. Suz watches me intently, waiting for me to pick an outfit in the sea of sequins she brought over. None of these options seem very me.

"If I pick the perfect dress for you, can I do your makeup?" Suz asks.

I laugh. It's going to be hard for her to pick the perfect dress for me with these options. But, I'll be a good friend and entertain her.

"Sure," I reply. "Good luck."

"I don't need luck," she responds confidently.

She goes to one of the three bags she brought over and pulls out the most stunning black dress. It's the Wyverns' team colors. It's my style, and it's perfect. The dress is black velvet with a sweetheart neckline and a subtle gold sparkly design.

"See, I knew it was perfect for you when I was going through my closet. I've actually never even worn it. Not enough color for me." Suz tosses the dress my way.

"Let me do your makeup first!" she shrieks. "Come sit."

While I'm sitting trying my hardest not to squirm from the tickles of the makeup brush, I realize I've never really had girl's nights like this. Bren and I would have girl's nights here and there, but they would always end with Nick joining. I haven't had genuine time with girl friends since before the accident. I'm sure Nick would make fun of me for it, but I don't even care. It's exactly what I've needed in my life. Close girl friends to distract me when life is hard, to lift me up when I need it, laugh with, cry with, and to apparently spread sparkly goop across my eyelids for New Year's Eve.

"Thank you," I say to Suz as she shows me her handiwork in the mirror. "It's perfect for me."

"Oh, I know," she beams and gives me a hug.

Revealing our emotional wounds from the past created a tight bond between Suz and I. I never would have thought that I would consider the blonde Barbie I spied across the bar when I first met Lucas a close friend of mine.

"Thanks for letting me do it. Jaylin refused," she snorts. "I can do subtle makeup or tweak it to fit different personalities! Not everyone loves the sparkle glam."

"I didn't even have a choice!" Brens shrieks.

I start to laugh. This interaction between them is exactly what I love. I feel like I'm finally starting to find myself again, despite the hard conversations about Nathan lately. I have these amazing people in my life to help me through it.

"You were never going to get one, bestie," Suz laughs. "Let's pop some champagne before we go and have it downstairs. That way Jaylin will join us and not be afraid I'll attack her face with a makeup brush."

I put on the dress and go to my room to pick out shoes. The doorbell rings. Butterflies start to flutter in my stomach, and my heartbeat rushes. Is it the guys?

"Libby is here," Suz calls from downstairs.

The butterflies abruptly stop, replaced by emptiness. I didn't realize how much I wanted to spend tonight with Lucas. New Year's Eve is always an overhyped disappointment. But with four of my best friends, I have no doubt that I'll have a magical night.

"I'm coming!" I call back.

I rush over to hug Libby hello. We talk about the success of the calendar sales and jersey sales for the team. Then Jaylin steers the conversation away from the hockey team a little bit.

"We're late!" Bren rushes us out the door. "And I mean later than we planned to be late, it's almost 11pm. Let's go!"

We call an Uber for once. It's December 31st, and we live in Michigan—none of us would dare walk even half a mile in a dress and heels. Luckily, we've become friends with even more of the staff at Haee's that Libby had no issues joining us. They rarely check our IDs, but on the off chance they do ask, her ID claiming she's Eden Ward will work just fine.

The bar is more crowded than I've ever seen it. The amount of glitter and sequins in Bren's room is a hiccup compared to the explosion of sparkle at Haee's. Bren drags us to the bar before we saunter over to our reserved booth. By reserved, I mean the hockey team comes here so often that Joe, our favorite bartender, just booked one for ten, free of charge.

Bren hands me a Bud Light before we find our booth to put our stuff down. Suz demands we dance and grabs Jaylin's hand. I can't help but smile at how adorable they are. Suz has really come around in the last few weeks to being more public with Jaylin. They seem so happy together. A longing for Lucas to be here overcomes me. I think Libby can tell.

"I know you hate to, but do you want to take a shot?" Libby asks.

"Yes!" I don't even hesitate with my answer. "We'll meet you on the dance floor," I say to the rest of the girls.

I want to have a good buzz going. I take a big swig of my beer, while Libby orders cinnamon whiskey, and it's not terrible. It goes down smoothly.

"Try this instead of that shitty beer," Libby says, handing me a pint glass that is clearly not a light beer. "It's an IPA. Maybe not your style, but it's mango and delicious. Plus, it's free technically so just give it a try."

It is free since we technically paid for the unlimited package. Setting my Bud Light on the bar, I slowly take a sip. The beer hits my taste buds, and I don't cringe. It's not bad! I flash Libby a thumbs up. Libby quickly drags me onto the dance floor, leaving my unfinished drinks at the bar.

The music claims us on the dance floor. Gyrating bodies of strangers bump against me, but I don't mind. Beads of sweat drip down my spine. If Suz didn't put so much setting powder and spray on my face, my makeup would be one hundred percent sweat off. Maybe I should have her buy me makeup, I have no idea what I'm doing half the time. A small panic runs through me as I look around at my friends realizing that Bren has disappeared. We squeeze our way out of the crowd to find her and get another drink.

After a few minutes of waiting in line, I see him across from the bar, just like the very first time I saw him. I instantly know where Bren has gone. I see her with Liam next to Lucas, Tyler, and Connor. They're surrounded by a group of people I've not met.

"Hey, Joe, can you deliver a Bud Light to that guy over there?" A veil of despair that I didn't realize was there lifts at the sight of Lucas.

"Lucas? Yeah, no problem, Laur," he says.

Exhilaration clouds my head more than I thought, I should have just said to Lucas. Joe knows the entire team. We are the definition of regulars. I watch as Joe delivers the beer to Lucas and motions over to me. Lucas' eyes lock with mine as he holds up his beer to toast to me. With a slight buzz, I raise my glass back to him, giving him a flirty wink before chugging my drink. This IPA is a lot harder to chug than the Bud Light. He's chuckling as he chugs his too. Even after we both finish our beers, we don't break eye contact.

"Stop eye-fucking him from across the bar before one of you starts drooling or moaning. We have an image to uphold here. Just go sit on his lap and call him puck daddy already," Suz says with an undercurrent of amusement in her voice.

"I think we have different ideas of what our image should be," I bite my lip as my eyes drift back to Lucas waiting gaze. She's so damn right. And his lap looks way too inviting.

"We don't want bitches thinking they can take our captain, your man! That is the image. You want it. He wants it. God damn. You see those girls around them? Yeah. That's what we don't want. And I don't even like men, goodness." She sighs, kissing Jaylin on the cheek.

"Okay. Yes. You're right," I sigh into my drink. "Joe! Eight shots of Jack Fire, please! To the Captain, we are heading that way!"

"THAT'S MY GIRL!" Libby buzzes with excitement.

I grab her hand, and we start to make our way to the other side of the bar. Haee's is brimming with people now, but I push through the crowd quickly weaving with determination to get to Lucas.

"Hi," Lucas greets me with a warm smile. "You ordered these shots?"

I nod. He's sitting on a barstool. I pick up two shots and hand one to Libby. Lucas disperses the rest and turns back to me.

"Cheers, Laur," he says to me.

"Cheers, Captain," I reply.

I down the shot and move between him and the bar. Sitting myself right between his legs, staking my claim. Bren mouths 'yes' and gives me a thumbs up from next to Liam who's sitting right next to Lucas.

"You look beautiful. You are beautiful," he whispers in my ear.

His whisper tickles my ear, causing heat to my cheeks. We all get to chatting and Joe comes around to take orders. I order another Bud Light. Lucas chuckles, and I turn to look at him, "Didn't like that IPA?" he says to me.

"Hey, Captain Judgy. I did like it. But I had two and two shots. They feel me, and I feel them."

"Let's dance!" Bren says pulling on my hand, dragging Libby and I both to the dance floor.

We are in our groove. The guys don't join for the first few songs. I don't care. After a few songs, I do care. Every part of me wants Lucas on the dance floor, hands on my hips and body pressed against mine. I look at Bren and try to ask where the guys disappeared to but feel a hand around my waist before I can ask.

I start to grind against him dancing. I feel him grow hard against me as I dance on him. The midnight countdown begins, Lucas spins me around, so we are face-to-face.

"Happy New Year, Laur," Lucas says, grabbing the back of my neck, ready to pull me in for a kiss.

"Happy New Year, Captain Boyfriend."

Being here in this moment with him feels like exactly where I belong.

Chapter Thirty-Five

Lucas

Hearing her call me Captain has always been a huge turn on. But I never knew that one word—boyfriend—after it could make me feel this way. As cheesy as it sounds, I have known since the first time I met her, that this is where we would end up. I could feel it in my gut that we would be more to each other than either of us anticipated.

Her hands wrap around my neck, pulling my body against hers. A soft moan escapes her mouth as my tongue meets hers, sending a raging inferno of desire coursing through my veins. My heartbeat accelerates, as my hand slides up her thigh, caressing her soft skin until I find the edge of her dress. Her tongue hungrily tangles with mine, showing me she wants me just as badly as I want her.

I'm not one for PDA, but I have wanted this since the very moment I laid eyes on her in this very spot. With one hand still on her thigh, my other hand slips to her back side grabbing a luscious handful of her ass. I break our kiss to subtly bite her neck.

She kisses my cheek, then whispers in my ear, "Want to know something, Captain Boyfriend? I'm not wearing anything under this dress."

The rest of the world falls away. Every other thought stutters to a halt and disappears, my mind fixating on one thing only.

"I dare you to find out," she whispers against my lips before they are pressed against mine.

My girl is daring. I slide the hand already on her thigh farther up until it slips under the hem of her dress, the sight as erotic as it is forbidden in this bar. The tips of my fingers graze her soft, smooth pussy. Absolutely no fabric blocks my path. I instantly grow hard as I part her. Fuck. She's already incredibly damp for me. Her teeth nip at my ear, playfully begging me to keep going.

Her wet heat beckons to me like an open goal, begging to be taken. The tip of my finger dips barely into her pussy, eager to finally have the opportunity to please her. My mind instantly focuses on what her silky, velvet pussy would feel like wrapped around my cock. A commotion breaks through our bubble, tearing my attention from where my finger teases her entrance. I slip my hand out from under her dress. Bren barges through the crowd, crying and grabs Laur out of my arms. Libby, Suz, and Jaylin aren't far behind. Laur mouths 'sorry' to me.

Making sure her eyes are still locked on mine, I put my finger that was just inside her pussy in my mouth and eagerly suck off her wetness before winking at her. Her sweet taste explodes over my tongue, making me crave even more of her. The surprise on her face at my kinky gesture makes every second that I'm apart from her tonight worth it.

Liam storms over, stomping like a toddler having a tantrum. I should have known this was coming. I guess it's time for the guys to get a few more rounds before the New Year's night ends. A shot of whiskey is thrust into my hands. My mind drifts to thoughts of thrusting into her instead, but I'm a team player so I down the shot.

Laur must have really hoped I would make it here tonight. She was ready and waiting pantiless for me, wet with anticipation. My phone vibrates in my pocket. It's her.

Laur: I'm dripping wet for you.
Laur: I'll call you.

Fuck. I am about to be the luckiest man on campus. I text her back.

Lucas: You taste so sweet on my fingers, pretty girl. I can't wait to taste more.

Someone hands me a beer and another shot. The smell reveals it's tequila this time. I put it back on the bar without taking it and sip my beer instead. It seems we are going to be here for a while. Liam has taken five shots that I've seen in the last hour. He's a big dude, but that's a lot of shots in a short amount of time. Beer stains the front of Liam's shirt. He's wrapped around Tyler, telling him how much he loves him slurring each word.

"Donato, finally get what you've been wanting?"

Someone behind me croons. It's Blaine Mitchell. I ignore him and focus on trying to get Liam to leave the bar.

"I wouldn't be such a good friend if I were you. I would be at Lauren Bellinger's house railing her sweet pus—"

I turn around to punch Mitchell square in the face, but Liam beats me to it. Blaine stumbles back and then swings, hitting Liam on the side of the jaw. It's not that hard of a hit, but it's enough to bruise more than just Mitchell's ego. Mitchell's fists are at the ready still trying to go for Liam, but Joe drags him toward the door before a bouncer steps in, yanking Mitchell to the entrance before shoving him out the door.

Liam wrenches against Tyler and Connor, who each grip onto him, holding him back while he sputters and slurs nonsense at Blaine.

"We are leaving. *Now*," I bellow.

Liam doesn't try to challenge me this time. He knows he fucked up, but at the same time, I'm glad Mitchell got what he deserved for even thinking about any part of Laur naked. I fucking hate that guy.

My head clears on the frigid, cold walk back to Liam's place. This is not good. This is going to get back to Coach Andres. Even if Mitchell started shit, Liam is going to have repercussions too. Shit, I'd rather deal with the headache from a hangover than the headache dealing with what this is going to cause tomorrow. We can't afford to bench Liam and Mitchell while we have another guy out on injury too. I might hate the guy, but he's a good defenseman on our third shift, and we need to keep up our winning streak.

Chapter Thirty-Six
Laur

I can't be too mad at Bren for pulling me away from my night with Lucas, but disappointed doesn't feel adequate enough to describe how I'm feeling either. I finally admitted I wanted to be his. I was very keen on him making me his tonight—so much so in fact that if he had asked me to meet him in the bathroom, I would have bent over the sink right then and there. But Haee's would not have been the most ideal place for Lucas and me to finally be together . . . so I guess I have Bren to thank for that.

Bren is hysterically crying over Liam mentioning talking to scouts from Seattle and L.A. Her drunken state is too emotional, thinking about the possibility of him playing far away and not rationalizing that he was just mentioning two scouts he recently talked to. Bren hasn't talked much about what her future with Liam looks like after the two of them graduate this year. Liam is NHL bound. Bren wants to work for a team in PR, but they could end up on opposite sides of the country or even different countries.

Libby and I try to soothe her on the couch while Suz and Jaylin are out getting some good old electrolyte drinks to try to ease her massive hangover that's about to come tomorrow morning. I swear she's been hysterical for over an hour. I squint to see the oven clock. It looks like it reads 3am.

We must have fallen asleep because I wake up scrunched on the couch next to Bren with Libby on the loveseat. I check the oven clock again; this time it reads 5am. Disappointment fills me realizing I missed my opportunity to see Lucas. I don't even bother to check my text from him. I know I'll just be disappointed I was asleep. I quietly tiptoe upstairs, heading to my bedroom to sleep some more. I don't set an alarm. I doubt there will be a New Year's Day breakfast, but even if there is, I'm not waking up until I'm good and ready.

A loud ringing pulls me from my sleep. I blearily answer the phone after seeing Lucas' name.

"What time is it?" I groan into my phone.

"Noon," the soothing sound of Lucas' voice causes my system to wake up. "Guess you didn't get much sleep last night?"

"Not at all. Bren was hysterical until at least 3am," I groan again.

"Liam insisted we shut the bar down." He sighs with a sense of defeat. "It's a miracle I'm not hungover."

"I'm sorry you didn't get to come over last night and I know you can't tonight. . . "

"It might be the first time in my life I wish I didn't have a game."

We're both silent for a few beats.

"How about I stop by on my way to practice in an hour and bring you coffee and a bagel?"

"That's really sweet but you don't have to."

"I want to. Leave the door unlocked for me? I don't want to get chewed out if I wake Bren or anyone else up."

My gut fills with the well-known feelings of butterflies, knowing I will get to see Lucas, even if it's brief. "Deal. See you soon."

Hanging up the phone, my stomach feels some type of way, and it's not from the alcohol last night. My heart flutters along with the butterflies in my stomach from Lucas' thoughtful gesture to deliver me breakfast before he goes to practice. I'm not used to such sweet gestures from a boyfriend. I sluggishly trek downstairs. Bren and Libby are still fast asleep in the living room. I unlock the door for Lucas and tiptoe back to my room.

I wake up to a kiss on my cheek. I must have dozed off again. Lucas is standing in my bedroom with a latte in hand.

"Hi, pretty girl," he croons, pressing another delicate kiss to my cheek.

I want to pull him into me and kiss him deeply before straddling him on my bed, but I quickly remember I haven't brushed my teeth.

"Bren's awake, bagels are downstairs." He hands me my coffee and sits on my bed. "I wish I could stay, but Coach asked me to come in and talk to him before practice. Assuming it has to do with Mitchell last night."

Mitchell? I have no idea what he's talking about. What happened with Blaine Mitchell? Knowing that guy, it can't be anything good.

"Swing by practice, and I'll fill you in after?" he asks.

"I've got to finish my article about Nick for *USA Hockey Magazine.*" Truthfully, writer's block has taken over anytime I try to write, so I've been putting it off.

"What better place to write about hockey than watching hockey?"

He kisses my forehead and heads out the door. My stomach grumbles. Looks like I'll have to catch up on sleep later. I pull on one of Nick's old hockey sweatshirts and head downstairs.

The scent of fresh bacon leads me to the kitchen. Bren and Libby are up. Libby is sporting last night's clothes, hair wild with racoon eyes. But Bren is fresh faced and showered.

"I'm so sorry about last night," Bren starts.

"Hey, it happens. No big deal," I respond, brushing away Bren's concern.

"I don't want to worry about it at all though," Bren explains. "Liam and I will talk about it when we need to. We are fine though, just a one-night hiccup."

I nod and bite into my freshly toasted bagel. I can't imagine how it feels knowing your boyfriend of over six years might move across the country without you. If Lucas and I get serious, will I be as distraught as Bren, or will my focus still be on my own career?

Chapter Thirty-Seven

Lucas

Anxiety hangs over me like a storm cloud knowing I have to talk to Coach about last night's bar incident with Mitchell and Liam. I have to be levelheaded and unbiased when it comes to being captain. As Captain Donato, I don't want to bench either of them; we need them to play our best. As Lucas, I want to bench Mitchell as long as possible for talking about Laur like she's a prize to win. As the leader of the team, I need to recommend benching them both, likely Mitchell a little longer since he had to be pulled out by security and caused the scene in the first place.

Coach Andres agrees. He benches Liam for four games. Liam never gets into fights, never causes trouble, and has helped give the team a better reputation over the years. Mitchell is benched for six games. I would push for more if I didn't need him to help us keep our winning streak going.

Both of them will be out for the home game against East now. I groan. That game is going to be rough enough now that I know about Kovek physically and mentally abusing my girl. It's going to take every ounce of willpower I have not to slam him against the boards or punch him until the ice below him is bloody. I'm trying not to think about it, but I don't understand how a man can do that to someone he claims to love. I don't understand how anyone can do that.

Before practice starts, I tell Liam the news. His shoulder slump with defeat and he hangs his head in shame. I go over to Mitchell and give him the news too. Mitchell clenches his fist at the news. He very clearly wants to punch me. Before he can get too hot-headed, Coach comes over, telling him if he does anything to retaliate he has no problem making it the rest of the season instead of just a few games. That's the difference between a man and a boy. Liam understands his actions have consequences and is disappointed in himself. Blaine Mitchell lets his frustration fuel him instead. Guess that Nathan Kovek is probably a similar but much, much shittier of a human being. Mitchell stirs up trouble and likes to instigate shit for no reason, but I know deep down he isn't an awful human. Nathan Kovek I wouldn't even qualify as human.

Practice goes by so slowly. I look for Laur, knowing the sight of her will lift my spirits. My heart sinks realizing she's not at practice, but my eyes are drawn to the spot she usually is every few minutes to see if she shows up. Maybe she got distracted by her article. Deciding to stay on the ice after everyone leaves, I blow off some steam. Being on the ice by myself is one of the most calming places to be. It's usually where I can get out of my head and just hone my skill and game. I could use the distraction before I'm the one who hits something. I can't believe two of our players on our main lines are going to be out during the game against East. We are screwed.

I'm practicing some slapshots when I hear a noise on the home bench. Laur's sitting down starting to pull out her laptop.

"Don't mind me!" her cheery voice resonates in the empty arena. I skate over to her. Just the sight of her fills me with some relief. I've never experienced that before. It's nice that just being around someone can turn your day around and distract you from the rest of the world.

"I'm sorry! I didn't mean to interrupt. I ended up having breakfast with the girls and got sidetracked. Why are you out here by yourself?"

"I needed to blow off steam and get out of my head, but seeing you definitely helps."

She smiles shyly and twirls her hair around her finger. Laur is rarely shy, but it's adorable. Her voice is timid.

"Can I write while you blow off steam? I'm still stuck on finishing the article about Nick and hoping the rink will give me some inspiration."

I nod and go back to the ice.

I can't help but steal glances at her every couple of minutes. She's so fucking cute when she's immersed her writing. Her face shows a mixture of emotions: excitement, glee, a little bit of stress, and a lot of thought and concentration. I imagine it's what I look like when I'm focused on the ice, but not nearly as adorable.

She eventually catches me staring, and I skate over to her.

"How are the articles coming along? You said you've already finished the full team one, right?"

"I'll have to do some adjustments after editing, but yes that one is done. Thank goodness. I've got a lot to go on this other one, but I could use a five-minute break."

The heaviness in my heart continues to lift as I sit down next to her on the bench. I pull her in close to me, her floral scent comforting me.

"Thanks for the breakfast. It was really sweet of you," she mumbles into my chest. "How did your talk with Coach Andres go?"

I fill Laur in on what happened once the girls left the bar. I tell her about Mitchell's crude comment, Liam's drunkenness, and their fight. I tell her how Liam is benched for four games and Mitchell benched for six.

"Oh . . . they'll both be benched for the game versus East," she says quietly.

I nod.

"I'm sorry, Lucas. It's my fault."

"How is that even possible?" My eyebrow raises, perplexed by her feeling like any of this could be her fault.

"If I wasn't all over you . . ." she starts before I butt in.

"Are you kidding? Please never apologize for being all over me. Ever." I kiss her softly, pulling her onto my lap so she's straddling me on the bench.

"It isn't your fault that Mitchell is a prick. I guarantee he saw nothing and was just being his usual delinquent self. Liam was hammered. It's no one's fault but theirs."

"I'm sorry you won't have them for the game against East," she whispers, placing her forehead to mine and wrapping her arms around my neck.

"It's going to be a harder game now, but we will figure it out and change our strategy. It's nothing that you have to worry about at all."

I desperately want to know if she is planning to attend the game. Most of me wants her to stay as far away from Nathan Kovek as possible. But a small selfish part of me wants to be able to spot her in the crowd for reassurance during what's likely to be the hardest game of the regular season. I know it will be best for her to skip the game, and I am more than willing to always put what's best for her first. I'll wait until she brings up attending the game.

She sighs and kisses my lips very lightly. Before I can pull her into a deeper kiss, she slides off my lap and pulling her laptop onto hers.

"I've got to finish this article today, Captain Distraction."

"Are you always going to make new pet names for me with Captain in them now?" I ask with a laugh.

She winks at me before focusing on her computer and starting to type away.

I head back to the ice. My stress level is still high, so I decide to do puck handling drills up and down the ice. It will tire me out and get me laser focused. I need to be on my A-game for the next few games.

"Hey, Captain Distraction," Laur beckons from the bench. "I could use a five-minute break whenever you want to come skate on by."

She's very flirty today, and I am all about it. I do one drill to the opposite end of the ice and then halfway down the ice to get to the home team bench. Sweat clings to my skin from the drills, but she doesn't seem to mind since she moves herself to sit on me again, straddling me with her legs behind me on the bench the second I sit down.

"Well, hello," I say to her playfully.

"Hi, Captain," she responds.

I lean in to kiss her. She hooks a finger into the collar of my jersey, eagerly bringing our bodies closer.

"Is this the type of distraction you want?" I whisper against her lips.

"Yes," she whispers back, biting my lip fiercely. I want her so badly, but if she doesn't stop, she isn't going to finish her article.

"Finish your article first," I pick her up off my lap as I stand up.

"It hasn't been five minutes yet!" She explains.

"Laur . . . you know a stopwatch wouldn't work. When it comes to you, I won't be able to stop. Honestly, I don't know how I've had self-control this long with you," I reply, walking back to the ice.

She lets out a very loud exaggerated sigh to make sure I can hear her as she mutters, "Fine, Lucas."

I laugh at her sass. I guess I'm only Captain "something" when she is happy with me.

I'll spend some time shooting drills until she finishes what she needs to. Setting up and re-setting up the targets will take time since I'm on my own, so that should give her plenty of time. At least Tyler won't be benched for any games, he's one of our best shooters. My attention is wholly on my drills because I don't hear Laur tip-toe over to me on the ice. She's holding a Diet Coke. I must have been focused since I didn't hear her get up to go to the vending machines either.

"How's it going, Captain Focus?"

She jokes as she slides slowly across the ice in her tennis shoes. I finish shooting at the two targets I have left, and then skate over to her.

"Sorry, I needed to clear my mind," I say, hooking my arms around her waist to help steady her on the ice but mostly because I just want to.

"Don't apologize, I get it. I've been there," she replies, leaning into my chest with a quiet sigh.

"Did you finish the article?"

Laur makes a frustrated groaning noise before saying, "No, my brain is broken for today. I'll have to come back to it."

We stand on the ice, holding each other for another minute before Laur mutters into my chest, "I don't know if I can do it, Lucas."

"The article on Nick? I can show you my speech for the jersey retirement if you really want me to. I've been trying to save it but . . ."

She interrupts me. "No, not the article. Yes, it's difficult to think about Nick. I wish he was here, literally here, on the team every day. But I know I'll do him justice in the article, and it gets a little easier every day."

"Good, because I am not telling a soul what's in my speech. I was just trying to be helpful. But what are you talking about then?"

She tries to bury her head further into my chest. She says something I can't understand because her words are muffled against me.

"Laur, I can't understand you when you talk into my chest, but we don't have to talk about it if you don't want to."

I want to keep my promise to her that I will continue to work on my communication with her and not make her feel forced to share anything.

"You are too nice to me," she groans, pulling her head from my chest. I laugh at her dramatics and silliness.

She doesn't meet my eyes but says quietly and clearly, "I want to go to the game versus East. But I'm too scared."

My hand delicately lifts her chin, forcing her blue eyes to meet mine, hoping she sees the sincerity in them. "It's okay Lauren. I don't expect you to go at all."

"But you need me there," she begins.

"Lauren, I can't imagine how you feel around him. I will do everything I can to never put you in a position where you feel threatened, in danger, or hurt. It's okay, really," I reply.

"You don't want me there?" she questions, her voice raising in pitch.

Her hands flail in the air before folding her arms across her chest. She is starting to be a tad dramatic now. I know it's probably out of fear, so I am trying not to read much into it. Instead, a brilliant idea hits me. Snatching her up, I toss her over my shoulder. Her shrieks and giggles echo off the ice as I skate us both off the ice to the home bench.

"Sorry, I'm being ridiculous. I just—I want to be there for you, but I don't know if I can be," she sighs.

"I have two ideas. Do you trust me?"

She nods as I take off my skates.

"*If* you decide to come, I'll give you my jersey to wear. That's only if you decide to come. You have no obligation. I promise you I will not be hurt or mad."

She whispers "okay" softly. I grab her hand, cross the small patch of ice between the home team and opposing team benches, and sit her down on the opposing team's bench.

"Lucas, what are we doing?" she asks, confused.

"Do you trust me?" I ask her again, pulling her to the edge of the bench and spinning her around to face me standing at the end. She nods with certainty.

"Good," I reply, taking off her shoes and kneeling in front of her. "Because I am going to finally taste you and not just on my finger."

I flash her a crooked smile as I take off my skates. Slowly, I roll down her leggings, kissing her stomach, and her inner thighs as I go. I keep her black lace thong on but pull it to the side to expose her perfect, pink pussy. She smells like my undoing—delicious and damp, already craving me. I'm so fucking glad I have the same effect on her that she has on me.

I kiss her right inner thigh and trail my tongue across her until I am at her clit. Slowly, I circle it, teasing her before taking her bud into my mouth. A moan escapes her as I ravish her sensitive spot. I drive two fingers deep inside her. Her pussy grips me, seemingly pulling my finger in greedily as she lets out another whimper of pleasure. I pull my fingers out of her dripping heat, circling her clit with my tongue again before moving back to her entrance, thrusting my fingers into her. Nothing has ever turned me on as much as the taste of her pussy does. I am growing harder with every lick and suck of her clit. I crave more of her. I need more of her. My cock strains against my pants, already rock hard with precum trickling out.

I pull my mouth from her pussy to take off her panties, my thumb going to her clit to ensure she doesn't go without a second of pleasure. She's moaning my name, making my throbbing cock twitch with anticipation of what her tight pussy will feel like wrapped around me. My mouth is back on her deliciously soaked pussy. I replace my fingers with my tongue so I can get a better taste of how ready my girl is for me.

"Look at me, Lauren," I say against her pussy. A moan escapes her from the vibrations against her sensitive skin.

Her blue eyes are the brightest I've seen them. She's biting her lip.

"Whenever you see any team on this opposing bench, all you will be able to think about is how you fucked my tongue so good, you came on it right before I bent you over this bench. Finally gave you my cock and made you come again. Understood?" My words are a harsh growl, each one rumbling against her making her writhe against my lips even as she stares at me with unapologetic hunger and desire.

"Yes," she whimpers. "Please."

"What was that?" I ask, teasing her, my voice low and husky.

"Yes, Captain."

At the sound of her calling me Captain, I plunge my tongue into her opening, moving it in and out of that sweet pussy. My fingers grip her hip steadily, while I continue lavishing her clit with my other hand. She thrusts into my tongue, fucking it, taking control. She runs her hand through my hair, pinning me to her as she drives her hips forward moaning with pleasure.

She's crying out loudly in pleasure. Her muscles lock under my touch, as she trembles on the edge of coming, I quickly slide my fingers into her, hitting her g-spot, and move my mouth to her clit. She cries out, coming for me, riding my fingers to heighten her release while I suck and lick her delicious clit. I lap at her entrance, tasting her cum as it slowly drips down her leg. God, she is the sweetest thing I have ever tasted.

"Holy fuck," Lauren breaths heavily. As soon as her eyes are on mine, I suck her delectable cum off my fingers.

"You taste divine," I wink at her.

She pulls me to her, parting my lips instantly with her eager tongue, claiming my mouth. Her aggressiveness is unexpected and so damn hot.

"Mmm," she whispers against my lips. "I like how I taste in your mouth."

That sends me over the edge.

"I need to bury my cock deep in you."

"Yes, please," she replies, sticking her perfectly round ass out teasingly. I squeeze it tightly, eager to bend her over the bench.

"Don't make me beg for your cock, Captain," she purrs, shaking her delectable ass at me.

I grip it with both hands, groaning with desire for her.

"I have to go to the locker room to grab a condom."

I run my hands through my hair, frustrated at my stupidity. I didn't plan for this at all. She turns around facing me.

"I'm on birth control, and I'm clean. I haven't had sex since . . ."

"I'm clean too, it's been more than a while. But are you sure?"

Instead of answering, she drops to the ground before me, pulling my pants and boxers down to my knees, releasing my cock.

"I'm sure I want your massive cock, between my thighs, before you fill me with every single drop of your cum."

She looks up at me with burning desire in her eyes before the tip of my cock disappears into her mouth. A shudder runs through me as she eagerly sucks just the tip, teasing me. The tip of her tongue flicks over the crown of my cock before I'm deep in her throat. She moans against my cock, playing with herself as I hit the back of her throat again. I can't wait any longer to have her.

"Bend over, pretty girl." Yanking her up, I seal my mouth to hers before bending her over.

Putting her pretty pussy on display for me again, she bends over the edge of the bench. I slide my fingers back into her, anticipating that I should get her soaked again only to find she's dripping more than before. Lining up my cock with the entrance of her pussy, I slide into her effortlessly.

We both moan at how perfectly my shaft glides into her. I pull out all the way, teasing her, and thrust back into her waiting entrance with gradual force.

"Fuck, yes," she moans.

Pulling almost all the way out, I grip her hips tightly enjoying the view before I slam into her over and over again. Her wet heat pulsing around my cock. A groan of satisfaction escapes me.

"Yes, Captain. More," she begs.

That sets me off.

"Harder, Captain. Please."

She moans for me to fuck her harder. Whatever my girl wants, my girl gets. Sounds of pleasure escaping her as my balls hit her clit with each hard thrust.

"Don't stop Captain," she moans. "I'm going to come for you again."

I move one hand from her hips around her to her clit, sending her into whimpers of delight. My hips move faster and faster, pumping in and out of her. A pressure builds behind my cock, begging for release. I bite and kiss her shoulder feeling her pussy tighten and spasm in ecstasy around my cock as she comes again making me find my release, filling her sweet pussy with every drop of my cum.

"Holy fuck," she screams.

"I agree," I say breathlessly.

"That was . . ." she pants.

"I know," I reply.

She's confirmed exactly what I felt. This sex is pure ecstasy.

"Best."

"Ever," I finish, shaking my head in disbelief at the intensity of what just happened, then let out a low chuckle.

She smiles and kisses me passionately, sighing with delight. She's still half naked. My cum, probably mixed with hers, drips down her leg, stirring something primal in me.

"Shit. I should have brought a towel."

I take my shirt off for her to use.

"Thanks for your sweaty shirt," she winks at me.

Why would I offer her my shirt I just practiced in? I'm an idiot.

"But even if you did have a towel . . ."

She stops and looks at me. I raise one eyebrow at her telling, puzzled and signaling for her to keep going.

"Okay, well, it's probably a bit taboo. But I wouldn't use the towel anyways. I want to feel your cum dripping slowly out of me reminding me that you . . ." She looks into my eyes. "You just claimed my pussy as yours."

I just claimed her pussy as mine. Did she just say that?

"How the fuck are you so kinky and hot?" I ask, giving her another heated kiss. "Does that mean you don't want to take a shower with me?"

"It means you are going to go take a shower in a gross jock locker room, while I type up some emails and avoid writing my article with your cum seeping out of me."

"I am so damn lucky," I stammer, shocked at the words that just came out of her mouth and turn to go to the locker room.

"Hey, Captain, I hope you remember that your cum was dripping out of my pussy when you read the article about the team."

I chuckle a little. This girl is kinky, eccentric, and all mine.

But no more play for today. She doesn't interrupt me in the shower—not with her deadlines and the distraction I already created. Once I'm out of the shower, I find she's still writing on her laptop.

"Walk me home?" she asks. "I'd love for you to stay over tonight . . ."

"But you have a lot to do, and I have an away game early tomorrow," I finish. "I'm not going anywhere. Laur. We have all the time for all the things."

She smiles her famous Bellinger smile, and there's a twinkle and hint of mischief in her bright baby blues.

"I can't wait to look at the opposing teams sitting on this bench all season. Knowing they are about to get pounded but not in the best way possible like I just was," her eyes go wide as she clamps her hand over her mouth. "I can't believe I just said that."

I let out a laugh and grab her hand, walking to the arena exit. "God, you are perfect, Lauren. I love you."

"I love you too, Captain Boyfriend."

That is definitely my favorite Captain "whatever" to be.

Chapter Thirty-Eight
Lucas

Without Liam and Mitchell and without our second line forward who's out on injury, we lose our away game. I have a feeling we will be losing the next three games too. Laur reminds me that she has Nick's notebook if I want to take a look at it. I eagerly agree to swing by to pick it up.

I text her when I'm on her front porch. She opens the door within seconds, and her lips are pressed against mine. I take her face in my hands and mutter 'Hi' against her lips, before kissing her again. Each kiss seems to chip at the weight on my shoulders that quickly appeared with the stress of the next few games.

"I might have missed you a little," she whispers as she pulls away.

"I missed you. It's going to be a long next few weeks."

"I know. I just got the Wyverns article back to edit this morning; I have a little bit of time to submit the article about Nick, create a mock PR plan for class, do some website updates and social media posts, announce some new contests . . ." she drifts off thinking about the long list.

"At least we are both chasing our dreams," I say pulling her into me. If I had my way, I would never let her go.

"Chasing our dreams together but apart," Laur replies. "I haven't read much more on the other teams. I haven't taken a look at what it says about East. I don't want to know."

I nod my understanding as she hands me Nick's notebook.

"I have something for you too."

I hand her a sealed envelope and a lumpy brown package. Both have DO NOT OPEN UNTIL JAN 27th scrawled across them in sloppy handwriting.

"What's this?" she asks curiously.

A cheeky grin spreads across my face. "Looks like you'll find out on the 27th. I've got to get to the gym."

I press my lips against her temple saying goodbye but wishing I didn't have to.

The second game without Liam or Blaine we lose by one. It's not as bad as the first game where we lost 3-0.

Game three without Liam and Mitchell, we somehow pulled off a win in overtime. I wish I could down beers to celebrate and relieve some stress, but we aren't out of the woods yet. There's still one more game left without Liam and two more without Mitchell.

The knots in my stomach tighten with each breath I take. My heart races with anxiety knowing the next game is against East. West Michigan and East Michigan have always had a big rivalry. They made it to the Frozen Four last year, but the Wyverns did not. We already have a 0-1 record against them this season.

I get to the arena early on game day. I don't want to have to see that fuckhead Kovek before we are on the ice. I'm about an hour earlier than everyone else. Putting my headphones in, I pace up and down the locker room, then start to punch the air. Right jab, left jab, cross. Left jab, right jab, cross. Doing this little boxing combo is helping to work my nerves out. I have never felt this uneasy before any game.

A tap on my shoulder some time later spooks me. Whirling around, I almost punch Tyler. Tyler and Connor are standing before me. I didn't expect anyone here.

"Dude, I would have punched you."

"Doubtful," Tyler teases walking over to his locker. "Why are you here so early?"

"I'm assuming the same reason you two are. I didn't want to get kicked out of the game by killing Kovek before it started."

A long, weary breath escapes me.

"I've never seen you this worked up before," Connor states, "but it makes sense. I wish we could just kick the guy out."

"Me too," Tyler and I both exclaim.

"How am I supposed to make it through this game without punching the guy?" I ask my friends.

"You think about her any time you want to," Connor replies.

"He's not worth it," Tyler pauses, unpacking his gear to look me square in the face. "Luc, Laur, and your future in hockey aren't worth losing,"

"He will get what's coming to him eventually," Connor says, reassuringly patting me on the shoulder. "Is she coming to the game?"

"I'm not sure. I want her to do whatever is best for her, and that's exactly what I told her."

They both nod and silently continue to unpack their bags into their lockers. We don't say much else until the full team is here.

"That scout for Nashville is here," Jamison Clarke says to no one in particular.

Great, now I really can't fuck up with Kovek or my future will be on the line. I haven't told anyone yet, but right now Nashville would be my number two choice if I could pick from all the NHL teams. Chicago is my number one. My dad would probably have a heart attack if I signed with the Blackhawks. I feel a pang of guilt knowing Liam was very interested in talking with Nashville scout. I wonder how badly four games on the bench is going to impact his career opportunities.

It's time to go out on the ice. I avoid any glances toward the opposing team's bench and side of the ice as we warm up. I don't even remember what Nathan Kovek looks like, but I know he's number twenty-two. I see the number on the back of his jersey out of the corner of my eye. I am filled with an overwhelming dark anger. If I'm not careful, it's going to consume me during this game.

The National Anthem starts, and I take a few deep breaths, trying to focus on the game, making Laur proud, and thinking about how he is sitting right where I made my beautiful girlfriend come in ecstasy.

"You good?" Connor asks, noticing the smirk that slid across my face while thinking about what Laur and I were up to on the opposing team's bench.

"As good as I can be," I respond through clenched teeth.

"Well, we all knew he wasn't good enough to make first shift this year," Tyler jokes, attempting to ease some tension.

I laugh, noticing that Kovek is on the bench. He was second or third shift I think earlier this year, looks like he's not improving his game. Meanwhile, I've been vigorously improving mine.

I manage to go eighteen minutes of the first period without encountering Kovek on the ice. Now, he's suddenly behind me as I bring the puck up the ice. I pass it off to Tyler. He shoots, but his shot's blocked. Fuck.

Kovek has control of the puck now. I feel the unhinged rage filling every inch of my body. This pathetic excuse for a human bruised my girlfriend. He broke her inside and out. Without hesitation, I check him hard against the boards, throwing my entire weight into it and tripping him in the process. The whistle blows.

"What the fuck, Donato," Kovek says to me.

"You ever speak to me again Kovek and I swear to God—" Tyler is at my side before I go at him. I have never started any fights my entire life of playing hockey. I have tried my best to stay out of it.

"Shake it off in the box," Connor says.

Fuck. I couldn't tell you the last time I even got a penalty I deserved.

"You got this; we got this," Tyler says, skating by me.

I skate to the penalty box only wishing I hit Kovek harder. There's less than a minute left of the period, so my penalty will go into the second period. The score is still 0-0 at least.

I know I am going to get a talking to from Coach in the locker room, so I go to him first.

"Listen, that guy, he's not a good person. I have issues with him. Coach, you know me. I swear I am trying," I plead.

"Nick Bellinger had issues with that Kovek bloke too and told me the same thing." He keeps his voice low. "Just watch yourself Donato. There are reps here you want to impress and a team that needs you levelheaded."

And a girl that won't forgive me if I fuck this up and go after him, I think to myself.

"I know. Thanks, Coach."

I head back to the locker room. I was so flustered about playing East today that I completely forgot I had Nick's notebook until Coach mentioned his name. I motion for Tyler and Liam to take a look at the page against East.

#30 Victor Penn - great goalie, but can't save a puck if it's in the top left or right corner, send 'em high
#8 Richard Harris - best player on their team, keep the puck away from him as much as possible. One of the fastest skaters I've ever seen.
#22 Nathan Kovek - decent player, fucking horrible human. biggest scum of the earth, weakest man alive. Not a fast skater at all, but decently strong and can hold his own. Biggest weakness - he gets flustered if you say her name.

Nick wrote this before he knew anything about Laur and Kovek's relationship. He really did hate the guy before even knowing about his abuse. At least I know even without that factor in play, Nick Bellinger would think I am a much better choice for his sister.

We get back on the ice for the second period. I have a little over a minute left in the penalty box. Harris gets the puck instantly for East and scores.

Fuck. It's now 0-1.

I skate out of the penalty box and over to the bench. I need to focus.

No less than ten minutes later, I'm sharing the ice with fuckhead again. I'm trying to keep my rage in check, so I decide to test out his biggest weakness according to Nick. Kovek has the puck, and I engage him to steal it.

"You would have never been good enough for Lauren," I whisper quietly and steal the puck.

I'm not sure I was loud enough for him to hear me. Saying that to Kovek motivated me and gave me a tiny sense of relief I needed to make the steal. I'm on a breakaway. Nick said shoot into the top corners. Good thing I've practiced target shooting a lot of recently. I aim for the top left corner.

GOAL.

The score is 1-1.

The arena is filled with rowdy roars from the crowd. I expect my team to rush in and celebrate with me, but instead I'm thrown to the ground by Kovek. I guess I was loud enough for him to hear me.

"What did you say to me, prick?" Kovek says.

"I said you were never going to be good enough for Lauren," I reply, getting up off the ice.

He rushes towards me and starts to throw punches. I throw them right back.

Tyler and Connor are pushing me back as refs separate Kovek and me, then try to separate the small fights that broke out around us.

"He's right," Tyler says. "You're pathetic."

He goes for Kovek this time and gets a good punch or two in before the refs break Tyler and Kovek apart.

Tyler and I each get a two-minute penalty. Kovek gets four minutes. I try to avoid looking at the bench. I don't want to see the disappointment and frustration in Coach's eyes. But at least we are tied now. I glance at the bench, and that's when I see her, sitting behind it on the far side, away from the opposing team's bench.

Lauren's here. My heart jumps in my chest at the sight of her in my jersey. I didn't expect to see her until after the game.

She must have read the letter and opened the package with the jersey I got for her with my name on it. I can't tell if she's upset, mad, disappointed, or all three. I'm too far away on the other side of the ice.

These are the longest two minutes of my life. Once I'm out of the penalty box and onto the bench, I'll be able to see her face. I can't believe she's here. I also can't believe she just witnessed her boyfriend and best guy friend fight with her ex.

The two minutes are up, the score is still 1-1. I rush over to the bench and find Laur against the glass. Her eyes are damp, but she doesn't look angry.

"I have no regrets. He deserved much more than he got," I shout so she can hear me.

"I know. Thank you for defending me. I love you," she shouts with teary eyes.

"I love you. And I love your jersey."

She laughs and mouths "me too."

I scramble to the bench before Coach can yell at me. Kovek's penalty is over, and the game is still a tie. We have two minutes left of the second period. It seems like we are going to go into the third tied. We can easily get a win off a tie. But then, Harris gets the puck and scores again.

Fuck.

We can still get a win, but it won't be as easy. We need to dominate the third period.

I splash cold water on my face in the locker room as Coach comes over to me.

"Donato, try not to get another damn penalty this last period?" he grumbles.

"Going to try my best, Coach!"

I do mean it. I want to win this game. Not for the team anymore, but for Laur.

The team seems worn out. We've been playing hard but so has East.

"Exhaustion can wait twenty more minutes boys. Let's win this game," I roar before we exit the locker room.

The third period is uneventful. East must be worn out too. I say a silent prayer, we need at least one goal, come on please let us win this game for her.

Tyler answers that prayer with a shot to the top left of the net, using Nick's advice.

"YES! We are tied with seven minutes left. We can do this, Wyverns," I shout as we celebrate Tyler's goal.

The next four minutes are the most intense of the game. Both teams have newfound energy with the game tied and bragging rights at stake, but for me there is much more at stake than that. Lauren deserves to see this win.

I force myself to stay levelheaded. I look to find Laur again. She gives me a thumbs up and nods in encouragement. With two minutes left, Connor passes me the puck. I have a shot in sight, but I get slammed hard against the boards. It's Kovek, of course.

"She used to wear my jersey," he sneers at me. My hands curl instinctively into fists.

He must have seen Laur with my last name on her back. The refs are calling it a clean hit, no penalty. I'm shaken but keep fighting for the puck.

"Actually, that's a lie. She's always been a Wyvern," I smugly reply as I take control of the puck and pass it up the ice.

No one is there so it's up to me to skate to keep control of the puck. Kovek starts for it too, heated and riled up from my reply.

Nick's notebook was right. He is not a fast skater; meanwhile I always have been, and I've been putting in the time to improve even more. I easily get to the puck before him. Connor is wide open close to the net. I pass it to him. He shoots.

The shot's deflected by East's goalie. I get the rebound and take a chance with a slapshot. It's not into one of the corners of the net, but I wasn't positioned right for that. A ting of panic goes through me, thinking it's not going to go in.

The goalie dives for the puck but misses it by an inch.

It slides into the net and over the goal line.

Wyverns win. We beat East.

I almost fall to my knees in gratitude. All the heaviness I've carried the past few games lifts.

The entire team is on the ice celebrating. It feels like we just won a championship game. The refs usher us off the ice. Something about "being good sportsmen," but none of us care, not even Coach Andres. I find Laur at the end of the ice by the locker room and pull her into my arms.

"Congrats, Captain! You did it!" Laur squeals.

"I can't believe you're here," I cup her face in my hands.

"It's easier to face my battles when I have you," she squeezes me tighter, clinging to me like her life depends on it.

"I will always try my best to win for you. Not for the team, not to impress scouts, but for you, Lauren."

I kiss her hard, not caring who is watching. She quietly moans into my mouth as I deepen our kiss and part her lips with my tongue. I've missed her. I've missed her lips. I've missed her tongue. I've missed just being around her. Someone taps my back. I groan and break the kiss.

"What?" I turn around. It's a sophomore on the team.

"Sorry to interrupt but someone named Sicel is looking for you," he says.

"Sicel is the scout for Nashville," I tell Lauren.

"Go! That's amazing!" Lauren says excitedly. She doesn't hesitate to tell me to pursue my future; she supports it wholeheartedly.

"Are you sure? I don't want to leave you," I start.

"Lucas, don't be ridiculous. Get out of here! Now! Text me or call me later," she replies

"I will, I will. I promise."

I kiss her quickly and head off the ice into the locker room to change quickly so I can go talk to the scout. Tyler and Connor assure me they will walk her and Bren home once East leaves our arena. No one is willing to risk Laur potentially coming face to face with Nathan. Any one of the players on the team would more than willingly put him on his back without a second thought, no questions asked.

Chapter Thirty-Nine
Laur

I am on a buzz from the electricity of the team and the crowd with the win against East. I wasn't planning to come at all. But Lucas' letter and package changed everything. That man has a way with words.

Lauren Chip Bellinger -

You amaze me every single day in more ways than I can count. You are fiercely loyal, can hold your own ground, and speak your own mind. I could write a novel about all the incredible qualities you have.

It hurts not just my heart but my soul to know how you were treated by someone you willingly, selflessly gave your heart to. No one deserves to experience that. It hurts me more than you know that it's something I couldn't protect you from and something I still can't protect you from.

But I can promise you that I will never lay a hand on you. I promise you I will always remind you of your goodness, how brilliant you are, and all your amazing qualities on days when you need to hear it and on days when you don't. I promise to be here to help you through anything that life throws your way. I promise to help you through this however you need me to. I promise to protect you in every way I can from anyone who dulls the brightness in your beautiful blue eyes.

I love you, Lauren Bellinger.

P.S. I ordered one of the special edition jerseys for you a while ago with my name and number. Libby promised not to tell. I might have my face on random girls' walls around campus and jerseys in random closets or worn to games. But seeing you in my jersey won't compare to any of that. I will be honored, humbled, and proud whenever you decide to wear it.

Reading Lucas' letter made me cry. I knew he had a big heart, but this is the most selfless and romantic thing anyone has done for me. He is consistently proving that he will put me first and understands when I have to do the same. I changed out of my pajamas right away to put on the jersey and a little make up before I went to the game.

Bren was saving me a seat in case I came to the game. Seeing Nathan for the first time in over a year was heart wrenching. My body tensed. On instinct, I wanted to run. I wanted to hide. I wanted to curl up into a ball and cry until I was so dehydrated no more tears would fall.

Then Lucas' eyes met mine and all of those fears took a back seat. I made it through the game squeezing Bren and Suz's hands on and off. I didn't even have to close my eyes when Nathan was on the ice or came close to us. I avoided eye contact easily. I focused on being at the game not just for Lucas but for myself.

I've come a long way from the depressed shell of a human I was months ago. I owe it to myself not to let some asshole have control over my feelings or my actions. I am surrounded by amazing friends who have become family and people who will clearly protect me (Lucas in the penalty box twice? Really?).

Nick would be proud of me for facing my demons today.

I'm proud of me.

Connor and Tyler walk me home. Bren is staying at Liam's. I don't even have to ask them if we can wait until the opposing team leaves the building. They purposely take their time showering and packing up. I might have come to the game and seen Nathan for the first time since the accident, but I was not ready to interact with him up close and personal. He's a narcissistic asshole, and I have no doubt that he would try to talk to me. I'm not sure what I ever saw in him.

On our walk back, Tyler mentions Nick's notebook coming in to save the day again. I'm glad I remembered to give it back to Lucas.

I hesitate to ask but I'm eager to know if it said anything about Nathan.

"What did it say?" I ask curiously.

"About everyone, or about Nathan?" Tyler asks. I shrug in response.

"It said he's a slow skater," Connor responds.

I let out a laugh. Lucas did easily leave him in the dust.

"And that he's a decent player. Lots of name calling too."

"Nick did have a way with words, especially insults." A giggle escapes, thinking of Nick's creative insults. My favorite he used was 'you're slower than a Zamboni on a Monday morning.'

I'm not sure how I ever saw any good in Nathan. Nick really didn't like Nathan at all, even before he knew anything about our relationship

"It said the biggest weakness he knew of was bringing you up," Tyler whispers.

That surprises me. I didn't know I got under Nathan's skin.

"Is it wrong of me that I kind of like I can get in his head?" I ask quietly.

"Not at all," Connor responds reassuringly.

I tell them both thank you and goodnight. I take a quick shower and crawl into bed. Today has been an emotional rollercoaster. Lucas still hasn't called or texted. I'm sure he's busy with the scout. I send him a good night text and quickly drift off.

I wake up with a text from Lucas mentioning he was meeting with the Nashville scout for breakfast but asking if I was free later today. I have a test tomorrow and I still have my damn article to finish. The Wyverns specific one is finalized, edited, and will be printed soon. I'm up against a tight deadline with the article about Nick and his jersey retirement in just a few weeks. I've gotten an extension, but I really need to lock myself in a room and finish. I tell Lucas as much as I'd love to see him, I have to submit the article in two days by 5pm and study for my exam. He, of course, is incredibly understanding.

The next day, I still haven't made much progress. I aced my test but it's 10pm, and I have less than twenty-four hours to turn in my article. The more time I spend with it, the more I'm sure I want to go into marketing and avoid PR.

My phone lights up with a text from Lucas.

Lucas: How's the article?
Me: ...
Lucas: That good?
Me: I am just...drawing a blank. I never have before.
Me: And I don't have a lot of time
Lucas: I wish I could help
Me: Distract me for a little bit? Tell me about your meeting with the scout
Lucas: Are you sure you need a distraction?
Me: Yes.
Me: Just not in person or I will really never get anything done, Captain Enticing ;)

My phone lights up and I answer on the first ring.

"Hi!"

"Hi, pretty girl," Lucas' voice is playful and cheery.

I somehow miss him even though it's only been a day since I saw him. He'll be on the road for another away game tomorrow.

"What's got you stuck on the article?" he asks.

"I don't know. I've gotten so used to sharing stories about Nick and coming to terms with everything. I just can't find the words to piece together. I guess I'm worried I won't do him justice."

"You know that is a lie. Anything you say or anything you write will come from a place of love."

He's right. He's always right. But this is just the first time I've had to truly write about Nick being gone. It will be seen by more people than I will ever meet in my life. It's a lot of pressure.

"Tell me something about Nick that I don't know," Lucas says, trying to spark some ideas for me.

"He wanted a truck so that he never had to have his car reek of hockey equipment," I blurt out. I'm not sure why that's the first thing that comes to mind for me. He would throw it in a large storage box attached to the truck bed so nothing would fly freely around the back of his truck. That box was nasty, but inside the car always smelled fresh and sweat-free.

My heart melts at the sound of Lucas' husky laugh. "That's very smart of him."

"I told you Lucas, I'm stuck. I have one paragraph. Distract me, tell me about the meeting with Nashville."

Lucas lets out a big sigh. Does he not want to tell me? Before I can say anything, he starts talking.

"It was great. Incredible actually. Sicel told me about what they are envisioning for a four-year plan, changing their practice schedule, revamping their community engagement in the general community and the hockey community. Honestly, it sounded almost too good to be true."

"What do you mean in the hockey community?"

"I'm not supposed to really talk about it since it's all under an NDA, but it's exactly what it sounds like. They struggle with being considered a real hockey town being in the south. They want to build more programs and opportunities for youth hockey, high school hockey, and even college hockey programs down the road. For me, it sets them apart from being just another NHL team to play for. It goes beyond me playing hockey. It's spreading the joy and love hockey can bring."

"Nick always talked about that too. Did you know he volunteered at youth hockey camps at least twice a year? I swear he started reaching out to them on his own when he was ten to figure out how he could get involved. What ten-year-old wants to volunteer at youth hockey camps when they are the freaking youth?"

"Sounds like you might have your article, Laur," Lucas claims.

"How did you do that? I've been sitting here writing down every memory and idea I can think of for the past week."

I am amazed at how talking to him for five minutes brought out the exact memories I needed to write this article about my brother. Nick Bellinger—beyond the hockey player. I am giddy with excitement to finish writing it now.

"Thank you, Lucas."

"I didn't do anything, Laur. I just was here to talk to, and I always will be."

He might be the sweetest man I have ever met.

"You really want to play for Nashville? It's far from Michigan . . ."

Not that I will be in Michigan most likely after graduation anyways.

"And from my family in Illinois. But I knew if I wanted to play for the NHL, it could and would take me anywhere without much being in my control."

He pauses, thinking about what to say next.

"I'm not committing or making any decisions until I have to. I still have an entire year. I promise I'll tell you all of my options and where my head is at."

"No!" I shout back at him through the phone. "It's just that . . . I am hopefully going to work for a team, and I don't want either of us to determine the others' decision. I love that we both have big dreams and we can chase them together, but I never want to dictate those dreams. Promise me you will make the decision that's best for you?"

"I don't want to fight like Liam and Bren are," Lucas says quietly.

"We won't. Not if we make the decision up front to wait to tell each other until we have both decided,"

I'm hopeful it could work for us.

"Are you sure?" Lucas asks with deep concern in his voice.

"Yes. I'm positive. It's going to be difficult, but we will figure it out."

"We will figure it out when we have to."

"Exactly, when we have to. But right now, I'm going to finally finish this article about Nick."

"Want to do it at the rink?" Lucas asks. "I was going to go let myself in and practice more shooting drills. The conference championship is going to start right after the jersey retirement. I need to be ready."

"Sure, that sounds great. Leave the side door closest to the locker rooms open for me?"

I love writing near the ice. It makes me feel even more connected to the game and players I am writing about. It will be the perfect place to finish Nick's article.

Thirty minutes later, I can hear Lucas' hockey stick against the ice with each shot while I walk into the arena. A wide smile automatically appears on my face hearing him firing shot after shot. A blade intimately scraping the ice with the intent for the puck sailing into the net is weirdly one of my favorite sounds to hear. I don't want to disturb him, so I try to stay as quiet as possible. I set my things down on the home team bench and start writing. I already finished a quick outline of points for the article so I should be done in an hour to send it off for review.

A few minutes later, Lucas skates over to the bench and kisses my cheek.

"I didn't hear you come in, you should have yelled at me," Lucas says.

He's drenched in sweat from working his ass off, and I find it incredibly sexy. I bite my lip before responding, "I didn't want to interrupt you, Captain Focus."

"You're biting your lip, Laur. You are about to be a distraction for us both," he replies with as a smirk slowly spreads across his face. "Are you thinking about the last time the two of us were here on the opposing team bench?"

"I wasn't, but now I am!"

I blush instantly. I can't say I've been the most reserved girl, but Lucas definitely brings something out of me.

"That penalty box bench is probably jealous," Lucas whispers, leaning in as close as he can to me while still on the ice. "We should probably help it out."

"I have to finish this article, Lucas! And we can't make you happy about going to the penalty box, if anything, you need to witness me with someone else on that bench, so you stay out of it unlike last game," I tease.

Although Lucas does not find it funny at all. His shoulders tense, and his jaw subtly clenches.

"I don't ever want to think about someone else in you." His chest heaves with frustration.

"I'm yours, Lucas, it was just a joke."

"It wasn't funny."

He skates away before I can say anything else. I honestly didn't think he would care about the joke. My heart sinks into my stomach in despair. I didn't mean to hurt him. Note to self: Lucas Donato is possessive of his girl. I'm not going to lie, now that we are together, I find it very hot. Heat swells between my legs thinking about it. I shake my head. I need to focus on this article first.

I'm not sure how long it's been—maybe an hour or so since I arrived. Lucas skates back over to the bench. He's now dripping with sweat. I can see beads along his jawline and neck. I'm tempted to lick them off. He is just so effortlessly sexy.

"Almost done?" he asks me.

"Yes, almost" I reply, trying to focus on my screen.

"I'm going to shower then I'll be back in ten."

Lucas skates off the ice and heads to the locker room.

I frantically finish typing my email to the *USA Hockey Magazine* editor. I finished my article about ten minutes ago and have been patiently waiting for Lucas to get off the ice and into the shower.

I pull out his jersey from my bag and slip off my leggings and sweatshirt. Luckily, I thought ahead and I'm wearing a very enticing black lace bra and panty set. I slip on my sneakers, grab my thigh high boots from my backpack and slowly fumble my way across the ice to the opposing team's penalty box. I toss my sneakers into the home team penalty box and slip on my thigh high boots.

Sounds of Lucas coming out of the locker room float into the rink, he showered much faster than ten minutes. I lean up against the open door when I hear him coming out of the locker room.

"You never asked me about the opposing team's box, Captain," I say to him in a sultry voice. His eyes take me in and widen with thrill. It's evident I have very minimal on under this jersey.

He makes his way across the ice quickly and so smoothly without skates on. He takes hold of my face and kisses me without a word. It's deep, desperate, and passionate. We haven't had each other in weeks because of our stupid busy schedules. Lucas leans my head back as he playfully bites my bottom lip.

"Show me that I am only yours, Captain," I whisper as he trails kisses and nibbles down my neck. He pulls away and smirks at me. His hands slide up underneath the jersey to my panties. Slowly pulling them aside, Lucas slides two fingers in between my folds. A soft whimper escapes me.

"You're already so wet for me," he whispers against my lips before passionately pressing his lips against mine with a new eagerness.

"As much as I love you in my jersey, I want to see what's underneath."

He lifts the jersey over my head.

"Holy fuck. This is just like my dream . . ." Lucas groans.

I watch his cock harden in his black sweatpants as he takes in the sight of me—thigh high suede boots, black lace thong and bra that leaves little to the imagination as my breasts spill out of the top of it. My hard nipples strain against the lace. Lucas traces the edges of the lace along my breasts lightly with his finger then skates his finger along the fabric to my nipple. He traces circles around my nipple before pinching hard.

Chills run down my spine, and it's not because I'm in a bra and panties in a hockey rink.

Above the lace, his tongue replaces his finger, tracing circles smoothly before giving me a soft nip with his teeth. I bite my lower lip as he does the same to my other nipple, sliding his hand teasingly up my thigh.

Lucas pulls down my bra for easier access, while his thumb finds my clit. I feel a heat pool low and deep in me, wanting his touch everywhere and anywhere.

Another sound escapes me as he again takes my nipple in his mouth. I grab for the waistband of his sweatpants and feel his length in my hands.

"Wait," I moan louder as he slides his fingers in and out of me. He stops abruptly.

"I want to show you how much I want you, and only you."

I pull away from him and push him against the wall, dropping to my knees. I pull his sweatpants down to his knees, his erection springing free of its constraints. I can feel myself grow wetter just seeing how hard he is for me. I take the tip of his cock into my mouth, licking every inch before I stroke his length entirely. He grabs my hair, letting out a moan as I take his full length to the back of my throat. Flattening my tongue, I lick from the bottom of his shaft to the tip, taking him into my mouth.

His breaths are ragged and heavy as a moan escapes me, vibrating against his cock. Giving him head is turning me on. I gently and rhythmically lick and suck the head of his cock. I look into his eyes as I sensually pull the tip of his cock out of my mouth, spit dripping down my chin.

"Fuck." Lucas pants as he watches me take his full length in my hand again. Our eyes lock as I hollow my throat and suck him deep, running my tongue along the sensitive bundle of nerves under the head. Sounds of his pleasure echo around us. This time, I don't tease him. I take him to the back of my throat following with my hand, over and over and over until he's panting loudly with both hands twisted into my hair.

"Laur, I'm going to come if you don't stop," Lucas pants, gently tugging me backward as if he wants me to stop.

Putting my hand on his thigh, I pull him flush to my mouth. He takes the hint, moaning and thrusting forward, driving his cock further into my throat. His cum quickly shoots into the back of my throat and fills my mouth.

"Shit, sorry," he mumbles as I pull back with cum dripping down the left side of my mouth.

"Why are you sorry? Your cum is too delicious to waste."

I wink at him. His eyes are glazed with delight and disbelief for my sexual appetite for him. I can't wait to keep surprising him.

"Take me across the ice to shower?" I ask him as he pulls up his sweatpants. I'm willing to brave the showers if it means he's buried deep inside me,

"Oh no, Laur, we are not done here," he says to me, eyeing my boobs half out of my bra.

"You in me. In the shower."

"Damn. I thought I was the captain making the calls?"

He grabs the jersey, my tennis shoes, and then me, carrying me delicately over his shoulder across the ice.

"Not today. Today, I make the calls," I smirk.

That earns me a hard slap on the ass, but he sets me down gently next to the bench where the rest of my things sit. He sits me down on the bench and slowly takes off my boots, trailing kisses up each leg to the apex of my thighs. He pulls my thong to the side and teases me by licking my clit. A moan escapes my lips, and I want him here and now.

Before I can say anything, he grabs my hand and leads me into the locker room.

He strips off his clothes quickly and then takes off my lacy set. He turns on the shower head farthest away from the entrance of the showers. I'm sure he wants to be able to make sure anyone coming in will have a hard time seeing. He pulls me into a hungry kiss as the warm water hits us softly. Lucas puts his hand between my legs. I widen my stance allowing him more access as he slides his fingers into me. I moan against his lips as mine meet them.

"Hello?" A voice calls.

Shit.

Panic courses over me as if the water's turned cold. Someone's here.

I can't tell who it is but Lucas' body tenses. He must know who it is.

"Ask them to grab us towels," I hiss to Lucas, realizing he forgot them.

"I'm not asking him that," Lucas growls at me.

"Hello?" the voice calls again.

"Lucas, it's obvious that we or at least someone is here. Just say something," I hiss at him again.

"Mitchell. It's Donato."

"And someone else by the looks of it unless you've taken up a new taste for thongs," Mitchell snickers. Out of all people. It had to be Blaine fucking Mitchell.

"Don't make me come out there and punch you," Lucas responds.

I playfully slap him on the chest. "Be nice! He is going to come back here if you don't."

"Can you just . . . leave?" Lucas complains.

"Please," I say loud enough for Mitchell to hear.

"Please, Mitchell," Lucas sounds like he's in pain asking for Mitchell's help.

"Yeah, sure bro," Mitchell sounds like he's listening.

"Wait. Can you grab some towels from the closet and put them by my locker?" Lucas asks, holding his breath. "I'll owe you."

"Yeah, Donato. You owe me."

The door to the locker room closes. We both sigh with relief before breaking out laughing.

"Out of all people . . ." Lucas starts.

"I know!" I retort. "Anyone would have killed the mood, but Mitchell . . ."

"Yep, he murdered it." Lucas sighs with disappointment. I expect him to turn off the water and walk out of the shower. But instead, he grabs some body wash and starts washing my body and his.

"Can I wash your hair?" he mutters. "Sorry, that's weird."

"No, it's not," I lean in to kiss him. "I would love that."

I turn my back to him. He lathers my hair with shampoo before running his fingers through it. It's intimate—I think the most intimate moment we've had together. He even puts conditioner in my hair, something I didn't expect this locker room to have. I wash his hair next. It's just as sensual and oddly romantic.

His hand caresses my cheek as his lips press against mine longingly before shutting off the shower. It's not a hot, desperate kiss craving pleasure but a delicate, lush kiss filled with love and compassion.

"Let me make sure Mitchell isn't lingering around," he growls.

The disdain in his voice lingers in the air. He really doesn't like that guy. But it's a good call. After a minute, he calls to me that the coast is clear.

"Who knew the hockey locker room shower could be so romantic?" I croon as I dry myself off with one of the towels Mitchell left.

"Are you kidding me? You should see it after a hard win. It's definitely very romantic," he laughs.

"Do I smell like lavender?" I ask as I dry my arms and legs more after slipping at least my undergarments on.

He laughs. "Yeah. It's lavender body wash. I told you it can get romantic."

Chapter Forty

Lucas

Today is the day the Wyverns retire number 88. I've never been nervous to speak in front of people. Usually, I am damn good at it. Today's different. It's important to Laur, to her family, to the team, and to this community. I can't mess this up. Laur's asked me about twenty times today what I am going to say. All I've told her is that I am going to talk about a story I left out in the interview I did with her back before the season started—the one story I purposely left out.

I put on my special edition Bellinger Wyverns jersey. This one has Nick's number on it. The whole team will be wearing them, and we are raffling some of them off too.

A few hours later, Coach is wrapping up his short intro, and it's time for my speech. I walk out to the podium on the ice and clear my throat.

"Nick Bellinger was more than just a hockey player. He was a son, a brother, a friend to so many. To me, he was a friend and great mentor. We all know Nick Bellinger was a legendary player on the West Michigan Wyverns. He would have made it to the NHL. He would have broken countless records. We all know that ...

But not everyone knows what an incredible person Nick was. He was always lifting up anyone around him, supporting them, and just being a genuine guy. He loved hockey, but he loved helping other people find that same love for hockey even more.

I remember my freshman year meeting Nick Bellinger for the first time. Really met him, not just a 'hi' in passing. We were about five games into the season. I wasn't even really playing with Nick a lot yet. He asked me to stay back after practice when all the guys were going into the locker room. I was racking my brain trying to figure out what the hell I'd done or why he singled me out.

Once everyone was gone Nick said, 'I can improve your game. Skate a little and shoot. Slapshot. Let's go.'

That's literally all he said. I remember laughing at him and saying something like, 'bro are you kidding me.' I hadn't managed to score with a slapshot while playing in college yet. I wasn't about to make a fool of myself in front of this guy who every single player on the team worshiped. But he was persistent. He told me again he thought he could improve my game.

So . . . I shot.

And missed.

I knew I would.

But Nick told me to do it again.

'Dude, no way, I missed.'

I didn't want to embarrass myself further. He just looked at me. You don't say no to Nick Bellinger.

Round two. I missed it again, of course.

Nick came over to me and said he was going to make some tweaks. He told me to loosen my grip, showed me what stance to take, pulled my shoulder back and in or something very specific that I can't describe. I felt so weird. I would never stand or shoot like that.

'Now try,' Nick said.

I laughed and fell out of my position. He just looked at me, as if he was asking me what I was waiting for.

I readjusted the best I could. Nick looked at my position-ing, adjusted my shoulders slightly, then nodded, seem-ingly to confirm that I was exactly how he had adjusted me a minute earlier. His hand was over his mouth, and he looked incredibly serious.

I didn't even skate this time. I just took the shot right where I was standing. It hit the goal post.

Nick smiled and patted me on the back.

'I'm going to be the next Wayne Gretzky. But you, Lucas

Donato, are going to be the next Nick Bellinger. All it takes is one shot, bro. Keep taking that one shot.'

He walked off the ice.

Next game, I scored the winning goal.

Thinking about what Nick said to me that day: that I could be the next Nick Bellinger. No one will measure up to that—his loyalty, his passion and positivity, his potential, his sportsmanship, his desire to help everyone who shared his love of hockey. Nick Bellinger is already one of the greats.

It's my honor to share this story on the day we retire the first jersey in West Michigan history. Wyverns' number 88 will always be for you, Nick Bellinger, the great hockey player, the incredible mentor, and the legend we all aspire to be like everytime we're on this ice."

My eyes follow Nick's jersey as it ascends into the rafters. I whisper to myself, "We miss you, buddy. I really do aspire to be like you more and more each day, Bellinger—on and off the ice. Thank you for giving me one shot, Nick."

As soon as I'm off the rink, a body slams into me and arms are around me. It's Lauren. She has tears streaming down her face.

"Thank you for waiting to tell me that story."

Then in front of the team, her parents, and all of the people who came to watch the game, she kisses me.

"Never thought I would kiss someone wearing a Bellinger 88 jersey." She laughs. She's wearing one too.

"Me either."

After the second period, we are up by one goal. I hear an announcement being made and get all the guys to come out of the locker room five minutes early before the new period starts.

Very few people know about what's going to happen. Bren, Lauren's stepdad, Dominic, and I have kept this a secret for months. I'm shocked no one spilled the beans. Lauren's mom doesn't even know.

"As you know, we do many fundraisers every year to support youth hockey programs and charities across the state," Bren begins.

My heart races with excitement when I spot Laur and her mom standing by Coach.

"Well, you might have noticed we haven't announced the main charity we are going to support yet. I am elated to announce a brand-new charity we will be supporting this year. Dominic Rossi, the founder of the charity, is going to say a few words about it."

I steal a glance at Laur, and she's saying "What's going on" to her mom, who shrugs. They both looked more puzzled than a deer in headlights.

"Thank you, Brenna. As Brenna mentioned, I'm Dominic Rossi. I had the privilege of being Nick Bellinger's stepfather. Today I couldn't be more ecstatic to announce the Nick Bellinger Foundation. In Lucas Donato's amazing speech he gave before the game, he spoke about the type of player and man Nick was, on and off the ice," Dominic nervously clears his throat before continuing. "I know he would be honored to have a foundation in his name to support not only youth hockey but college scholarships for hockey as well. Nick would want to make sure every single person who has a love for hockey gets their one shot, and this is the perfect opportunity to help do just that."

Laur and Annabeth are both crying. Laur makes eye contact with me and mouths "did you know?" I just shrug, and her tears fall faster. Dominic is holding a crying Annabeth next to Lauren.

Chapter Forty-One

Laur

My tears have a mind of their own. I can't control them as they steadily stream down my face. What Lucas, Bren, and Dominic have kept from me is the most heartwarming, unexpected secret.

"That's not all!" Bren chimes in again. "With the proceeds of the limited-edition Wyverns jerseys that we released a few months ago and that the team is all wearing tonight that were created from a drawing by Nick Bellinger himself, we have raised over $30,000 so far this season. Isn't that amazing? Oh! Did I mention that The Nick Bellinger Foundation is matching every dollar, one for one, that we raise this year as well? How amazing is that! Make sure to grab yours at the merch table. Once they are gone, they are gone! Go Wyverns!"

Matching all the money we raised this year? My stepdad is really a great man. I wish Nick could have spent more time with him.

Gratefulness radiates off me like the sun beaming down in the desert. I might burst with the overwhelming joy that fills my heart. I run over to kiss Lucas before he goes back to the locker room.

"It was so hard keeping this a secret from you," Lucas admits with a hushed voice.

"Best secret ever. I can't thank you enough, Captain Boyfriend."

My lips find his again. I force myself to remember my mother is probably watching before I jump his bones right here right now.

"How is this possible?" Mom asks Domnic.

"I told you I made some good investments with Cody Stone's brother," Dominic says.

He kisses Mom, who is still shocked and awed. So am I.

It finally makes sense to me that Dominic has always just wanted to love and support me, Nick, and even Mom, not by trying to fill the hole created by Dad's death, but to fill a different space. Dad passed away when Nick and I were so young, I don't think we really remembered him. I think we just clung tight to what people told us about him from his hockey career. Dominic has always supported us and loved us, but today, he has really gone above and beyond.

"Thank you," I say between tears. "Nick would have loved to have a foundation for kids to learn hockey and for scholarship support hockey named after him. This is the best way anyone can honor him."

Dominic gives me a tight hug. Mom and I are still sobbing when the third period starts. It flies by, and the boys are on fire. The Wyverns' streak continues, and we win the game by three points.

Somehow, it's already March and the conference games are literally around the corner. There is only one team in the conference with a better record than ours, and it's luckily not East. I have minimal schoolwork and with no more articles to submit, I dive in hard on the Wyverns, talking to different press outlets about the amazing donations we have been able to give this year, the new charity in Nick's honor, and helping Dominic interview people to eventually run the charity while he's chairman. I'm keeping myself busy while Lucas is focused on hockey.

We manage to squeeze in some time here and there. Before finals for the conference championships, we go on our first official double date with Liam and Bren. East Michigan is playing an Illinois team later today to see who the Wyverns play in the championship, which we'll watch later tonight with the full team.

"Did that girl just glare at me?" I ask Bren as we sit down at Haee's for dinner. There's a table of four girls, and I swear at least two of them are looking at me like they want to claw my eyes out.

Bren laughs. "Well, your man is one of the most wanted on campus, and you're fresh meat. They already know I bite."

"She's got a bite and a bark," Liam confirms, sitting down next to her.

"Seriously? They are glaring at me because I'm with him?" My face contorts with confusion as I point to Lucas.

"Hey! You once told me I was a hot commodity on girls' walls all over campus!" Lucas retorts, throwing a straw wrapper at me.

"You don't need a bigger ego," I tease, kissing his cheek, which earns me another glare from the table of girls. Great. This will be fun to deal with.

We order our dinner. The girls decide to make a pit stop at our table before leaving, asking Lucas and Liam for an autograph.

"Is that your girlfriend?" one of them daringly asks Lucas.

"Yes, isn't she beautiful?"

My heart skips a beat at Lucas' response. The girl rolls her eyes and walks away with her friends. I look at Lucas and start giggling. These girls are ruthless!

We enjoy our dinner with minimal interruptions until near the end. Liam and Lucas' phones both blow up with texts. Lucas usually ignores his phone when we are out and about together. He says if it's important, someone will call him and then he'll answer. Liam picks up his phone immediately.

"Shit!" Liam exclaims. "Luc, look at your phone."

"Holy hell," Lucas reacts as he reads his text messages.

"Someone fill us in please?" Bren asks, annoyed.

"Nathan Kovek is out with an ankle injury. He won't be playing in East's semifinal game today or the conference finals if they win this game and play against us," Lucas responds.

"That's great!" Bren beams. "Well, shitty for him, but who cares."

Lucas leans in and kisses me. A huge grin stretches across my face from ear to ear.

"Not that I want to celebrate anyone's injury, but I'm more than happy we won't have to deal with him for a while."

East loses the semifinal game that night. We watch with the entire team and coaching staff. Looks like Nathan wouldn't have had to play us anyways, but either way, I'm glad I can put him out of my mind for hopefully the rest of the season. I don't really expect East to make the playoffs.

Chapter Forty-Two

Lucas

We played the conference championship game yesterday. It was oddly one of the easiest games this season. The West Michigan Wyverns are conference champions. It's an honor to win, but we've won in years past. I still have my eyes focused on the prize: making it to the Frozen Four and winning it all. There is no doubt in my mind we will make the playoffs, but I'm still nervous until we hear the official announcement on Selection Sunday.

The team goes out for a drink to celebrate, even Coach Andres and the rest of the coaching staff join us. It might be more to monitor some of the guys and make sure we only have a few drinks since we still have games to play and teams to defeat. But at least we have a little break.

Laur's familiar floral scent fills the air around me as her arms wrap around my neck. She's beaming with pride. "Congrats, Captain of the Conference Champs!"

"Thanks Laur." Appreciation fills my heart as I beam at my gorgeous girlfriend.

"It must be because I'm good luck," she jokes, sticking her tongue out.

"I thought you hated that I called you my good luck charm!"

"I never said that! I just am more than that," she replies.

"Of course you are. You're the girlfriend of the Captain of the NCAA Division I Men's Ice Hockey WCHA Conference Champions."

"Wow, that's a mouthful," she teases. "Are you nervous for the play-off games?"

I shake my head before admitting the truth, but only to her.

"A little bit. So many scouts will be there. I haven't had much facetime with any of the Blackhawks scouts this year."

She told me to wait until I make a final decision and have offers to tell her, but I want to play for the Blackhawks more than anything. Well, almost more than anything. Sure, I like what Nashville and even some of the west coast teams have to offer, but my dream has always been Chicago.

"You're always amazing, Lucas, on and off the ice," Laur declares. "After all, you are the Captain of the NCAA Division I . . ."

"Okay smart-ass." I kiss her before she can keep talking. This girl has made my junior year season more exhilarating than I could have ever imagined.

On Selection Sunday, the Wyverns are announced as one of the sixteen teams to go on to the playoffs. Unfortunately, East Michigan is also selected. They made it by the skin of their teeth. Laur isn't happy about it, neither am I, but that's out of my control. I have to focus on what's in my control and clear my head.

We hit the road for the first regional round of the tournament. I gave Coach Andres Nick's notebook, with Laur's blessing. He has notes on literally every single NCAA men's hockey team. He must have spent hours watching games and jotting down notes. Maybe I should start. He weaves Nick's advice in with his pep talks and throughout practices.

Luckily, we don't start off playing East. If we both win this first round, we will have to face them again. Since no one's had the balls to bring it up to me, I'm guessing Nathan Kovek's probably playing again.

We beat the University of Minnesota: Duluth in the first round by two goals. We all watch East Michigan vs University of Michigan game later that day. University of Michigan is ranked much higher based on their regular season wins. I'd still rather risk playing them than playing East. My eyes sweep across the ice, spotting Kovek. I was right, he's off injury, and no one wanted to be the one to tell me. But I purposely didn't look either.

East barely beats University of Michigan in overtime. Great, now we play East and Fuckface to make it to the Frozen Four.

If we win, I will be doubly happy as I would have been winning against the University of Michigan. If we lose, I'll be ashamed, embarrassed, and emasculated. I know it's stupid but having Kovek win against us when I know what type of person he is would make me feel like less of a man, less of a protector, less of a good boyfriend. Just less.

I haven't had time to see Laur; I know she's here, but these games are back-to-back. I wish I could kiss her just once before I facing East. I might sound like I'm whipped for saying it, but I don't care.

I say she's my good luck charm, but truthfully, she calms me. Plus, I want to check on her and make sure she's okay, knowing we are about to play her abusive ex-boyfriend again. I'm not sure how she carries herself with such grace and understanding. She handled it so amazingly the last time we played East.

I'm leaving the hotel with some of the guys, and I hear my name being yelled. I don't think anything of it because there are a lot of people here. But then I hear something that sounds like "Captain Boyfriend."

I turn to see Laur running towards me.

"Who let you past security?" I joke.

We do have some security at the arena and in certain areas of the hotel. Not as much as there is surrounding the Frozen Four games, but security is still prevalent at the regional rounds too.

"Coach did," she retorts out of breath. "But I woke up late."

Her eyes are barely open, and her hair is wild. She does look a little disheveled.

"I just wanted to say good luck and to show you my new jersey," she says. "I didn't get to show it to you before the last game. I thought it would be better in person than a picture over text."

She turns around to show me "Captain's GF" on the back of her black Wyverns jersey. I laugh and kiss her.

"I love it, and I love you," I declare against her lips. "Thank you for finding me."

I'm being ushered out the door to get on the bus to the arena.

"I love you too!" Laur shrieks, "Good luck! Kick his ass! I mean not literally, just win! Good luck!"

I'm laughing again. I'm glad she doesn't seem to be too distraught with Nathan. Luckily, she has her mom, Dominic, and Bren to keep her company. My family is here somewhere, but I haven't had time to say hi to them let alone introduce Laur.

We're warming up on the ice and I see Kovek. Fuckface feels the need to lock eyes with mine. Does he think I'm threatened by him? After the last game, he should know I'm not afraid of him and I can easily kick his ass.

"Luc, we have to play nice," Liam reminds me.

"I know, I'm not doing anything. The guy is just glaring at me. What am I supposed to do?"

"He's trying to get under your skin. Fuck him. He doesn't matter," Tyler sneers, clapping my back hard as if it will give me a confidence boost.

"This is our game to win," Connor chimes in.

They're all right. We've got this; I've got this, and I need to shake it off.

The first period is rather uneventful. It ends 0-0. Luckily, no one is playing dirty, including Kovek, but we haven't been on the ice together for long. Coach Andres gives us a quick pep talk.

We are back out on the ice with more speed, more heart, and more intention than the first period. We score a goal within the first five minutes. Jubilant cheers erupt through the arena. The team is amped, and we are finally on the board, up 1 to 0. All we have to do is keep it up.

There's five minutes left in the second period. It's been a lot of push and pull across the ice, but nothing we can't handle.

Then suddenly, Kovek sends Tyler into the wall on a dirty hit that the refs call as clean. Rage boils up in me at the ref's call. Tyler gets up off the ice, dropping his gloves and rushing toward Kovek. Out of everyone to get in a fight, I thought it would be Liam, me, or Mitchell and his buddy McAllister—not because of Kovek but because they are hotheads. I didn't expect it to be Tyler.

Kovek knew his hit was dirty and didn't give a flying fuck. I know how much Tyler loves and respects Laur. I won't hold him fighting against him even though it could very well cost us the game. Tyler and Kovek are broken up by the refs. Both get two minutes in the penalty box.

"We don't like that guy, do we?" Mitchell asks me as I get to the bench.

"No, Mitchell, we fucking hate that guy. But play nice; we need this win."

"I know, I know. I can play nice, Captain!" Mitchell salutes me and skates away.

"Fuck," I groan under my breath. He better not mess up our chances of winning this game.

The penalties are almost up. So far, Mitchell hasn't caused any chaos, thank Gretzky. East takes control of the puck as soon as Tyler and Kovek both come out of the penalty boxes. Somehow, they get a breakaway and score.

Fuck. The second period ends with a tie, 1 to 1.

"Luc," Tyler's voice is soft, laced with guilt and embarrassment

"Any one of us would have done the same thing if not worse, Tyler. No one's blaming you for anything," I interrupt him before he can get in another word. He knows just the sight of Kovek makes me want to punch something.

"We've got time," Mitchell says.

My eyes widen in surprise. Mitchell chiming in with positivity? That's a first.

Coach Andres gathers us around intentionally, gearing us up for another pep talk.

"Listen to me, Wyverns. We fly high in the sky. We know that the sun rises in the East and sets in the West, do you know what that means, boys?" Coach bellows in the locker room.

We all look around puzzled. What the hell is he talking about? Has he been flying high while we've been putting blood, sweat, and tears on the ice?

"It means we get the last light; we get the last say; we get the last shot; we get the last goal. It's our one shot to take, not theirs."

Hearing Coach Andres' words sends a sensation through my body, my mind and my heart. A sensation of pride, determination, strength, and perseverance. It's a winning sensation. It has to be.

"Coach is right. We have the record this season. We have the skill. We have the team. Let's show them that," I chime in, hyping up my team and ready to get back on the ice. "One shot on three."

We are back on the ice energized, hungry, and ready. We'll get this win. I feel it in my bones. I try to find Laur's face in the crowd. She usually sits behind the team bench, but I know she won't want to be that close to East's bench. I find her on the opposite side in the third row. She turns around to show me the jersey again. Her mom, Bren, and Dominic are all pointing at the "Captain's GF" on the back. I can't help but laugh and blow Laur a kiss.

The first twelve minutes of the third period are a battle. Both teams are fighting with everything they have for the win to make it to the Frozen Four. It feels like it might drag on forever. Mitchell checks Kovek hard against the glass. It's a clean hit, but a brutal one. Kovek loses his shit over the call that it was a clean hit. He starts to argue with the ref that the hit wasn't clean. He's livid and pushes the ref on the shoulder. Whistles are blowing, and he's in the penalty box. Holy shit.

Kovek is lucky his teammates stepped in to avoid him making a bigger ass of himself with the ref. If he did shove the ref, he could have had major disciplinary action—he still might. What an asshole. I look over to the East team bench to see their coach red in the face with anger. That's a big penalty. He'll get five minutes, and we only have four minutes left of the game.

Mitchell skates to the bench and murmurs, "Told you I can play nice. Didn't even chirp back at him!"

For once, I genuinely appreciate Blaine Mitchell. Kovek will be in the penalty box for the second time, and we'll have a power play for the rest of the game. We can win this.

Two minutes go by, and we are fighting hard. We keep the puck on their side of the ice, but their goalie blocks every shot. I think back to the last game against East, Coach's advice, and Nick's book. East's goalie has a hard time blocking shots high and in the corners of the net. I start muttering this to every player and tell them to keep talking about it subtly. We can win this.

I'm on the ice now. With a switch in our lines, Mitchell is on the ice with me. Mitchell sends a flawless pass up to Tyler to take the puck up the ice. Tyler is swarmed by two East players and passes back to Mitchell. Mitchell must have been practicing on his own, he's improved.

Mitchell skates around the ice, passing back to Tyler every so often to avoid having the puck stolen. He sends the perfect pass for me to take a slapshot off of. I aim for the top left corner of the net.

The shot goes in.

"Insane shot, Donato," Mitchell screams to me as all gather to celebrate the shot on the ice. Tyler practically mauls me in celebration. Every player taps my helmet or claps me ecstatically on the back. We could win this game.

"Nice assist Mitchell," I pat him on the back.

We are up 2-1 with less than a minute left.

A buzzer echoes loudly through the arena, signaling the end of the game.

"Holy shit," I whisper, drawing my hand down my face. "We won. We beat East!"

"Hey, Captain, not only did we beat East. But we are going to the fucking FROZEN FOUR!" Tyler screams in my ear.

"Tyler, you are getting kicked out of our hotel room tonight," I shout back at him. He chuckles responding, "I figured."

The entire team is celebrating, screaming, and jumping on each other. You would think we just won the entire tournament with how damn excited we are for this win.

I can't fucking wait to celebrate with Laur in my hotel room tonight.

Chapter Forty-Three

Laur

The team celebrates the win with an incredible dinner at the hotel. Not our typical beer and shot type of celebration with the Frozen Four game in a week. It was very classy, very demure. Lucas and I celebrated too - let me tell you that was the very opposite of classy.

"Lauren . . ." Lucas pulls his lips from mine as my body presses firmly against his, pinning him to the hotel room door. "As much as I love this, I can't get the key out of my pocket, and someone is going to come down the hallway any minute."

Peeling my body from his, I catch my breath. Eagerly muttering "hurry" while he fumbles with the door.

As soon as the door swings open, Lucas picks me up and my surprised squeal fills the hotel hallway. I wind my legs tightly around his waist while he carries me into the room. My arms wrap possessively around his neck as Lucas presses my back to the wall. He trails luscious kisses up my neck, gripping my ass firmly. My lips tingle with the need to feel his against them. I pull his mouth to meet mine, letting out a low moan feeling his bulge grow against me.

"Bed. Now," I mutter against his decadent lips. My desire for him is too strong to be patient. I want his body against mine. And I want it now.

Lucas carries me to the bed, gently lowering me down. My dress is off as soon as I'm on the bed. My greedy hands are ripping his shirt off within seconds, ready to unbutton his pants.

Lucas lets out a soft chuckle. "Someone is eager."

"Yes," I breathlessly respond, shimming out of my panties and un-hooking my bra, putting my body on full display for him. "Don't be gentle."

"Show me how much you want it, Lauren," Lucas growls, letting out a groan as his hungry eyes scan my naked body.

I move to the edge of the bed, spreading my legs. Without a second thought, I slide my fingers into my waiting pussy. My eyes are on him as he watches my fingers slide slowly in and out of me.

"Do you hear how wet you make me?"

Lucas' eyes widen with desire. He quickly kneels on the ground, wrapping his arms around my legs, pulling me to his mouth. My fingers are met with one of his before his tongue finds my clit, making little pleasurable circles around it. His tongue pauses as he pulls back to watch his fingers moving with mine in and out my dripping heat.

"Please," I beg for Lucas to let me have him before he makes me come undone. A mischievous grin spreads across his face as his eyes meet mine. He thrusts his fingers with mine into me again. Whimpers of pleasure escape me as he finds my sweet spot.

"Lucas. Please," my voice is hushed but laced with consuming desire. "Please," I plead again, squirming under his touch.

Lucas stands, his bulge straining against his boxer briefs before taking them off. A small shriek leaves my mouth as Lucas pulls me to the edge of the bed, stroking his cock.

My body trembles with delight as he slides into me—so easily, so smoothly, so perfectly as if our bodies were made to be intertwined. He instructs me to put my legs on his shoulders. A groan escapes him as he buries his cock deep inside my pussy, grazing the end of me. He pumps into me; my rapid breaths causing his name to slip from my lips.

The sound of me moaning his name seems to do something primal to Lucas, his thrusts become rougher and more demanding. My mus-cles tighten around him as I scream his name, euphoria washing over me. He grunts, his release meeting mine. Quivers skate across my body as Lucas plants a soft kiss on my lips before going to get a towel.

After we clean up, I adjust to lay across the bed. The bed shifts as Lucas lays next to me, pulling my sweaty body to his. Blissful silence fills the room as we rest tangled together.

"I love you, Laur," he whispers, placing a delicate kiss on my temple.

My heart flutters. "I love you too, Lucas."

Neither of us gets much sleep that night and it's not because of the flat hotel pillows. We keep celebrating two more very sinful times, including on the hotel balcony.

When we get back to campus, the team is on a new high. I have never seen a group of guys with smiles so big. I've also never heard the words "Frozen Four bound" more in my life. I can't wait to see them play their hearts out.

I remember seeing all the Frozen Four signs for the first time in person three years ago. It was Nick's freshman year. His sophomore year they made it to the playoffs, but not far enough to go to the Frozen Four. I bet his junior year, they would have made it and won with him as captain.

He was giddy with excitement. He texted me so many photos before Mom, Dominic, and I got there. We got great seats and sat with Bren, but I didn't get to go behind the scenes for that game. I hated not being able to be in the thick of it, but even more I hated not knowing any details. I didn't know if he was being interviewed.

Nick texted me that he had some interviews including one with *USA Hockey Magazine*. It's wild that I wrote an article about Nick for the magazine this year. So many things have come full circle. I wish Nick was here so badly to be a part of this Wyverns team. Lucas wouldn't be captain, Nick would be. Would I even be dating Lucas? Who knows what that would look like. Wherever he is now, I know today he's watching this game, proud of his former teammates.

Somehow, Nick never got to experience a Frozen Four win. I hope Lucas, Liam, Tyler, Connor, and the rest of this team get to experience it this year. Nick would wish that for them too.

Chapter Forty-Four

Lucas

This is it. This is my first time going to the Frozen Four not just as part of a team, but as captain. This is what I've been waiting for. I am a bundle of nerves, but it's nowhere near as anxiety-ridden as I was for the last game against East.

I walk around the press area. Tomorrow is the semifinal games. I just had an interview about our season and have another on my journey to captain later today. Even though it's been surreal with so many professional news outlets, I can honestly say, I much prefer when Laur interviews me. I'm more open and calmer. I wish she was able to be here with me through all of these.

"Lucas Donato?" a voice asks. I turn around to see a sharply dressed man in a suit. I've never seen him before.

"Yes?"

"My name is Blake Deschute, you probably haven't heard of me. I try to be discreet and keep my reputation under the radar," he extends a hand to me, and I shake it firmly.

"Nice to meet you," I reply, waiting for him to further explain himself.

"I know you are quite busy, so I'll keep it brief. I previously scouted for the U.S. Men's Olympic Hockey team."

Shit, that's impressive.

He continues, "A close friend of mine convinced me to change career paths and become a scout for the NHL team he is coaching. I've watched you all season and I must say I am—excuse my language—fucking impressed. You are finishing out your senior year before you're interested in a professional playing career, correct?"

He's watched me all season? I haven't interacted with him at all. He's right; I've never heard of him.

"Thank you. Yes, sir, I will finish my senior year at West."

I've always wanted to finish college before going into the NHL. I might need the business degree if I don't make it or if I get injured, who knows where life could take me.

"That's what I've heard but had to ask. I won't disclose what team I am working with just yet, but from everything I have heard about you through the grapevine, I think you'd be very interested. Keep it up and next season, we will be talking again."

He extends his hand out for me to shake again before he walks away. I'm very interested to find out more. I've never had a scout be so discreet before.

Wandering to find a water bottle, I spot Liam.

"Hey Liam, have you ever heard of a scout named Blake Deschute?"

"Never heard of him," Liam says through mouthfuls of a sandwich.

"Have you ever had a scout not tell you the team they work for?"

I'm curious if this happens to anyone else.

"Maybe once or twice my junior year, but nothing I couldn't really dig up or ask around for. Why?"

I spiked his interest. I want to keep this to myself. I know it's illegal to impersonate a scout, but I don't want to bring up the encounter in more detail. Something in my gut is telling me to keep it to myself.

"Just curious. Heard some guys talking. Ready for tomorrow?"

"As ready as I can be," Liam elaborates. "It's high stress with these scouts here. But I already know I have options making it this far with the team. But it's still a lot to process."

I pat him on the back as he starts telling me about what teams he's thinking about and some insights on slimy scouts to stay away from.

It's semifinals game day. Laur texted me a picture of her wearing her "Captain's GF" Wyverns jersey. Regardless of the result of the game, this will be an unforgettable season, and she is a huge part of that.

As we walk out onto the ice to start warmups, I've never heard a crowd so loud. The cheers spike my adrenaline.

Today, we play the Boston University Terriers. They make it to the playoffs every single year and are known to be one of the top NHL recruiting colleges in the country. I don't regret my decision to play for West, but BU is fast and furious with almost professional level skill. They are going to be a hard team to beat but we've made it this far. I'm as ready as I'll ever be for this game.

A bead of sweat drops off my forehead and onto the ice as the first puck drops and the Terriers get possession. BU captain Jedd Linkman is unstoppable on the ice. I'm in awe every time I see him play. We're two minutes into the first period. One of the defensemen sends the puck up the ice to Linkman, who is wide open. He races to the front of the net with another BU offensive player. Our defense tries to steal the puck, but Linkman keeps possession effortlessly. He shoots. The puck soars to the back of the net. Our goalie had no chance of stopping it.

The crowd roars as BU celebrates the first goal of the game on the ice.

Wyverns are down, 1-0.

We hold our own the rest of the period like a well-oiled machine. No more goals are scored by BU, but we had minimal chances to score.

Tension is high in the locker room during intermission. We review some footage from the first period. The coaching staff makes slight adjustments to our lines to compensate for some areas we could improve from the first period. We're playing well, but BU is just really damn good.

Heading back out to the ice for the second period, I catch a glimpse of Laur beaming at me from close behind the players' bench. She smiles her famous Bellinger smile, and my heart swells. I give her a wink before sitting on the bench. I'm lucky to have such a supportive girlfriend who loves hockey. I would bet money that she loves it just as much as I do, just in a different way.

We are ten minutes into the second period with no goals. We've gotten five more scoring chances this period than we had last period, so it's an improvement. Linkman finds a hole and gets a breakaway for BU. Mitchell crashes with him against the boards, sticks clash, but Linkman keeps possession of the puck and passes it to an eagerly awaiting player just left of the net. BU player number 44 shoots, and the puck flies into the top corner of the net, making it by mere centimeters.

I have to admit, the shot was impressive. James is across the back of his jersey. I'm positive that he is BU's second leading goal scorer behind their captain. I make a mental note to look at his stats again.

We hold our ground on defense, but don't score. It's the end of the second period. Wyverns are trailing, 2-0.

During intermission, I get the details on number 44. He's a freshman named Henry James. I was right, he is the second leading goal scorer for BU. That's remarkable as a freshman. Nick didn't even have that bragging right and neither did I. He was the third leading scorer as a freshman, and I was fifth.

The team watches some video feedback of Linkman's goals. His execution is damn flawless.

"We need to keep the puck away from Linkman if we have any chance at coming back," I bellow. "One shot, Wyverns. Let's fly."

With that, we head back to the ice for the last period of the game.

BU continues to maintain their position and hold steady. Their goalie is outstanding, blocking every shot we manage to take. Our goalie, Keith Hall, has blocked at least twenty-five shots from them the entire game. He's playing phenomenally.

The clock keeps ticking down, and every second feels like an eternity. One of the BU players slashes Tyler, and a penalty is called. The arena is booming with cheers for the Wyverns and boos from BU fans.

Can we make a comeback off this power play or at least get on the board?

The crowd noise doesn't soften as we set up our play. Tyler fakes a shot and passes it to Mitchell. He shoots; the shot's deflected by the goalie. I get the rebound and shoot fast, without thinking to the top of the net. The goalie makes a stunning save but only repels the puck to the ice. A BU player is next to me going for the puck, but I'm faster. I take a shot keeping the puck low on the ice to throw off the goalie from the high shot he just saved.

But my shot slides across the goal line seconds before. Wyverns score! A buzzer sounds, and the whistle blows.

The team rushes to me, patting my helmet, and Liam spanks my ass. Shouts ring out for the Wyverns. We are still down, but we are on the board at 2-1 with five minutes remaining.

The next five minutes, we fight for our lives pushing our bodies to the limits, past the exhaustion and fatigue. Someone passes to Mitchell, and he goes in for a shot. It looks like it goes in, but it doesn't hit the back of the net.

Is the shot good?

I can't tell from the angle I was at.

We celebrate like it went in anyway. Mitchell has been playing well during the playoffs and has been less of a pain in my ass than usual.

A ref's voice booms over the loudspeakers to declare the call for the goal.

"After further review, the puck did not cross the goal line before it was saved. No goal. The score remains Terriers 2, Wyverns 1."

Disagreement can be heard in the irritated shouts of the crowd, and disappointment settles across the faces of the entire team.

"We got time boys, heads up!" I howl.

Tyler chimes in with some more pep talk.

The next three minutes seem to go at an agonizingly slow pace. The Terriers and the Wyverns are both holding steady. Neither team is giving up. There's less than a minute left. Liam and I are both at the front of the BU net ready for a pass to try to tie the game.

The pass doesn't come. The buzzer signals the end of the game. BU won. My team's heads hang low.

"Cheer up, boys, we had a hell of a season!" Tyler yells.

"An unforgettable season, boys. We took our one shot, and we'll keep taking it." I bellow back.

We skate to center ice to congratulate BU on their victory.

"Great game, Donato, maybe I'll see you around the NHL soon," Jedd Linkman says to me as he shakes my hand and slaps my back.

"Amazing game, Captain. Where are you playing?" I ask Jedd.

"It's on the DL, but I'm about to sign with Chicago after this tournament is over, if they'll still have me."

"They'd be stupid not to Linkman," I respond and shake his hand again.

"I saw you talking with Deschute. Hope you'll come down for a game," he responds before skating a way to celebrate the win with his team.

He just clued me in that Deschute is a scout for Chicago. My brain starts to swirl with the possibility of signing with my dream NHL team. I knew today was going to be epic, regardless of the game outcome.

Chapter Forty-Five

Laur

The semifinal game was intense. Despite the loss, the Wyverns were a force to be reckoned with.

We stick around to watch the championship game on Saturday. It can't be easy to watch the finals knowing they just lost, but all the Wyverns are all great sportsmen, even Mitchell. Well, at least for today. Some of the guys, including Lucas, Liam, and Tyler know people playing for one of the final two teams. I shouldn't be surprised. It seemed like Nick had friends on almost every team too.

I notice Lucas taking notes in a little blue notebook. He must be trying to emulate what Nick did. It warms my heart knowing how much of an impact my brother has had on the man I love well before I knew Lucas even existed. It's funny how the universe works.

Chapter Forty-Six

Lucas

We arrive back at our home arena. Not all teams wait to have this moment until they are back on their own stomping grounds, but I've always admired that we do. This ice, this locker room, this arena—it's our home that we bleed in, sweat in, and probably cried in all season. It helped shape us every step of the way. It's tradition for the captain to give a speech on the season and Coach to give a few updates.

All eyes are on me waiting for my speech. I walk over to the locker that we still leave empty in memory of Nick, place my hand on the number 88, and start my short but sweet Captain's speech.

"A hockey legend that we all admire and look up to used to ask this team 'If you had one shot, would you take it?' Boys, we took it. We worked our asses off, and we played hard. We were pushed, tried, and tested, more than just on and off the ice. I am proud of every single one of you. You all took one shot to be a better player, a better teammate, a better man. We had a fucking phenomenal season making it to the Frozen Four. That's something to be proud of. It's going to lead us to great success next season, but we'll save that lecture for when we start practicing over the summer."

Coach makes his usual announcements about our training schedule for next season starting pretty much right away, but we have two weeks off in the middle of summer.

Someone mutters something about a trip to a ranch in Texas. I've never actually taken a vacation with the two weeks we have off. I hate being off the ice for too long. I need to keep honing my skills and impress the scouts even more next season. But I could take a few days off. A ranch doesn't sound like something the guys, or I would be very into for a relaxing summer trip but maybe somewhere by the beach. The thought of seeing Laur in a swimsuit is very, very enticing. I could sacrifice some ice time for that if I make sure to up my workouts and maintain my protein intake.

"Now, I am honored to announce that two of our very own seniors have accepted and signed contracts for the NHL. Boys, would you like to share?"

Liam and Connor deserve it. Pride swells in my chest for them but I'm going to miss having them around. I'm losing two of my best friends, but that's the way the business works. I already know where they are both going. They told me the second they signed the contracts. Hopefully, that will be me next year.

Connor excitedly shares that he signed with the New York Rangers. Liam announces he will be moving to Seattle.

I wonder what Bren is going to do with Liam so far away. I heard her mentioning to Suz she wanted to stay at West this summer to support Laur. She was still holding off saying yes to her job offers. Honestly, I'm not even sure where she applied to, but I know she had several offers.

I leave the locker room with Liam, Connor, and Tyler. Laur is waiting for me, giving me one of her famous Bellinger smiles. God, I am so lucky that I get to witness that all summer, all next season, and if I'm being honest, I'm hoping for the rest of my life.

"It was an amazing season, but I'm ready for a little bit of wild this summer," Laur says.

"Wild? I don't know if I can handle a wild summer after that wild season and a stressful one coming up," I laugh.

"You have one shot next season, Captain. Who knows what could happen? I believe in you."

I take her face into my hands.

"I got my one shot this season, Lauren Chip Bellinger. It was always going to be you. I wouldn't change that for anything."

Excerpt from...

Summer Shot

Wyverns Hockey Book Two

A.C. Wonderland

Chapter 1

Laur

The warm August sun shines bright in Frostburg, Michigan. Somehow the summer flew by. In a few weeks, the West Michigan Wyverns hockey team will start their normal practice schedule. Meanwhile, my palms are perpetually sweating with anxiety as I prepare to lead the Wyverns' Student Marketing and PR program for my senior year. Out of the kindness of her heart, Bren, my cousin and best friend who previously led the program, helped Libby, my new best friend I met at West, and me conduct interviews over the summer prior to her sad departure. Bren bounced with joy when she received the opportunity to work in the PR department for the Red Wings NHL team a few months ago.

Last season was unforgettable. The Wyverns made it all the way to the Frozen Four. Even though they didn't make it to the championship game, the team was H-O-T, hot. Not to toot my own horn, but the marketing and PR team went above and beyond last season. We published articles in *USA Hockey Magazine*, ran contests for signed posters raising an insane amount of money for our new main charity—the Nick Bellinger Foundation—and sold custom jerseys and calendars, both of which SOLD OUT! The hockey team quickly became the most popular crew on campus.

My heart races with excitement. All the new members of my marketing and PR team are finally here. An enormous smile overtakes my face knowing I'll get to introduce some of the new members to the hockey team today!

We selected two new sophomores and one new junior to join the small but mighty team. The new members have a much more diverse background outside of hockey, which I think will work to our advantage. Libby and I both have family ties to the sport—we practically bleed hockey—so I think the diverse background will really work to our advantage with getting even more engagement outside of just the school.

One of the sophomore girls, Raven, doesn't have any big connection to hockey, but has a great social media background with fashion and fundraising. My heart practically leaped out of my chest when I reviewed her application, eager for someone with extensive fundraising experience to join our team. She even transferred from another school to take the opportunity!

The sounds of skates and pucks scraping against the ice fill the air as I lead the girls into the arena while the guys are practicing. The girls trail behind me like precious, innocent little ducklings. Coach spots me and signals to give the team five more minutes. Warmth fills me as I spot Lucas Donato, the captain of the team and my hot-shot sexy boyfriend. No matter how many times I've seen Lucas play hockey, my heart always flutters every time I see him in his element.

After a few drills, Coach blows the whistle for the team to circle up and pauses practice, letting us have our planned interruption. I swoon as Lucas Donato tells the team to listen up at the introductions and instructions from me. He gives me a wink before I start my spiel, but someone else speaks up first.

"Hi, Luc." Raven interrupts with a coy tone. Raven, the ironically-blonde new sophomore, stares bright-eyed at Lucas, a flirtatious smile curling her freshly glossed lips.

"Raven?" Lucas' beautiful golden-brown eyes fill with recognition and confusion. How does he know Raven? She called him Luc. It's clear they know each other well . . .

I try not to let it get to me as I introduce the three girls, including Raven, and give the hockey team a quick rundown of interviews we will be conducting over the next few weeks.

Before I turn to leave with the rest of the girls, Lucas grabs my arm and pulls me to him. Jaw clenched and nostrils flaring, Lucas steams with frustration.

"Lauren, how the hell is my ex-girlfriend part of your PR and Marketing team? And why the hell is she?"

My heart sinks into my stomach. Lucas only has one ex-girlfriend that I'm aware of. I don't know her name or age, but I do know she wanted him to give up hockey . . . they broke up his freshmen year because of it.

How did I not know that Raven Matthews, the new sophomore lead on *my* team, was his ex-girlfriend?

More importantly, how the hell am I going to get through this season with my boyfriend's ex-girlfriend not only working closely with me but being around him 24/7? I just started finally working through my past relationship trauma . . .

Now, I have no hope that this season is going to be less stressful, less traumatic, or less dramatic than last season.

I have a feeling it's going to be the exact opposite. It seems like one of my precious ducklings isn't so innocent.

Acknowledgements

First and foremost, there is someone I need to thank that sparked my everburning love for hockey. The only reason he'll even know about this is because I'll text him a picture as soon as *One Shot* is published BUT without him, I would never have watched hockey in the first place. Kyle—thank you for being the best 8th grade boyfriend a girl could ask for by introducing me to the greatest sport. My obsession and love for hockey wouldn't exist without you.

I couldn't have written this book without the support of my family and close friends. I was amazed that not one person was baffled when I told them I was writing and indie publishing a book. Everyone has been insanely supportive, which has made this crazy six-month process infinitely less stressful.

To my family—I truly appreciate the endless advice and support with all of my dreams and the wild places they have taken me. This by far has been the biggest one and you have never questioned my ability to write a story that others can connect to and fall in love with.

Dad, thank you for being my confidant, for always checking on me, and for all your guidance starting my own business. Also...Thanks in advance for skipping the parts I told you not to read.

Mom, I am beyond thankful that you always believe in me, especially when I struggle to believe in myself. Thank you for telling me to "give the people what they want" when I said spicy books are all the rage.

Thank you to my sisters, Brieann and Jessica, for also believing in me every step of the way and always offering to give your thoughts (even if I don't ask for them... they are always helpful I promise).

If you don't have a best friend soulmate who you describe to anyone who will listen as your platonic life partner, then how are you getting through life? I would not be the person or writer I am without my very best friend, Bekah. Bek— I am eternally grateful that the universe blessed me with you. Thank you for being my biggest cheerleader and hype girl, for always being a shoulder to cry on, and telling me what I need to hear even if I don't want to hear it. Eden Waden has many adventures ahead of her!

Thank you to my amazing editor, Cayla. I've learned an insane amount from you in such a short time. I am grateful that you willingly took on my first book and for your incredible guidance along the way. I truly lucked out with the best editor and now you are stuck with me. (Also thank you for never judging how awful I am at grammar, because I definitely judge myself.)

Tina, my incredible artist! I cannot thank you enough for creating not one, but two dream covers. You literally made every image in my head come to life flawlessly. You're wicked talented and I can't wait for all the amazing art ahead!

I wouldn't have been able to make this book possible without my phenomenal Beta readers. Thank you all for coming on this journey with me. Kaitlyn, you have been my sounding board for all things hockey romance and also just hockey in general. Thank you for always making me laugh, sending me hockey updates, and just being a wonderful human. I am so thankful that I found such an amazing friend through this process! Keri, you were one of my first Bookstagram friends and I am beyond grateful for you! Thank you for the continued support, encouragement, and friendship. You're one of the kindest people I know! Steph, I wish I had your extensive grammar and sentence structure skills. You are a guru and I truly appreciate you taking extra time to rereview a million and five things. Bre and

Nat, you both have the biggest hearts! You are sister-in-law goals and I absolutely love that you both came on this journey with me together. Thank you for always sending me heartfelt feedback that made me cry happy tears!

Super special thanks to all the authors I met and all the author groups I've joined. I never imagined that I would find the incredible support system that I have! To my day one author besties—Dev, Amy, and Shaina—thank you for always being willing to share ideas and for always checking on my sanity. Kara, Leena, and LCB, and everyone else in the girls' writing group—I truly appreciate all of your continued advice, honest and genuine opinions, and the endless encouragement. And for always making me laugh when I'm up late.

The indie author community is the book family I never knew I needed. I truly can't put into words how uplifting and life changing it is to be a part of it. I can't wait to be at a book show or book signing some day, raising a glass to your success! I will always be rooting for you!

Huge thanks for my ARC readers and social media supporters. Thank you for taking the time out of your busy lives to spend some time with Laur and Lucas, for sharing content, and for laughing with me (hopefully not at me, but I wouldn't blame you!) while I attempt to make videos. The support from the Bookstagram and BookTok communities is unlike anything I've ever experienced. I never expected to have a hype squad who loves hockey and romance books as much as I do.

Last, but certainly not least, YOU, dearest reader! Thank you for taking *One Shot* on my debut novel and me by picking up this book. You having it in your hands means more to me than I can even fathom. I hope you love the characters and story as much as I do.

Don't worry, there is plenty more to come.

About the Author

A.C. Wonderland has always loved telling stories for as long as she can remember. When she was eight, she wrote and drew an entire twenty-page book for school... even though the assignment was to write one page.

The reality is life isn't always easy. Sometimes you need an escape from everyday life. A.C. thrives on writing novels that let a reader get lost in a whirlwind romance.

A.C never thought she would be an author. But, in July 2024, her first book came pouring out of her. She created a thirty six chapter outline and wrote the first three chapters of *One Shot*, her debut novel, in less than two hours. It was evident that she had a story that was begging to be shared.

You only have one life to live—A.C is taking her "one shot" to pursue her dreams of becoming an author.

When she's not writing, A.C. loves traveling the country, frequenting country music concerts, and, of course, going to hockey games. She lives in Nashville with her dog, Guinness, but is originally from the suburbs of Chicago.

Catch her on Instagram or TikTok at @acwonderlandwrites or check out her website www.acwonderlandwrites.com.

See what she's reading - www.goodreads.com/acwonderland.

is filled with Easter egg clues
including **TWO EXACT TITLES** of
A.C. Wonderland novels publishing in 2025!
hint: these two books are NOT hockey related

Think you found one? Or both?!
If you guess correctly BEFORE the title is announced
you'll recieve a paperback copy of the book for **FREE**
once the book publishes!

Here's how to win
your FREE book !

1. Draft an email to
   OneShot@acwonderlandwrites.com

2. Make the subjectline **"One Shot Easter Egg"**

3. Add your title guess(es) in body of the **and**
   include your proof of purchase of One Shot

4. Hit send on that bad boy! **good girl ;)**

You'll be contacted within 60 days if you guessed correctly!
GOOD LUCK